SLEEP NO MORE

SEANAN McGUIRE

SLEEP NO MORE

AN OCTOBER DAYE NOVEL

DAW BOOKS
New York

Jacket illustration by Chris McGrath

Jacket design by Adam Auerbach

Interior dingbats by Tara O'Shea

Edited by Navah Wolfe

DAW Book Collectors No. 1946

DAW Books
An imprint of Astra Publishing House
dawbooks.com
DAW Books and its logo are registered trademarks of Astra Publishing House

Printed in the United States of America

Library of Congress Cataloging-in-Publication Data

Names: McGuire, Seanan, author.
Title: Sleep no more / Seanan McGuire.
Description: First edition. | New York : DAW Books, 2023. |
Series: An October Daye novel ; #17
Identifiers: LCCN 2023020152 (print) | LCCN 2023020153 (ebook) |
ISBN 9780756416836 (hardcover) | ISBN 9780756416850 (ebook)
Subjects: LCSH: Daye, October (Fictitious character)--Fiction. |
LCGFT: Fantasy fiction. | Novels.
Classification: LCC PS3607.R36395 S54 2023 (print) |
LCC PS3607.R36395 (ebook) | DDC 813/.6--dc23/eng/20220105
LC record available at https://lccn.loc.gov/2023020152
LC ebook record available at https://lccn.loc.gov/2023020153

First edition: September 2023
10 9 8 7 6 5 4 3 2 1

For Navah.
This one's on you.

ACKNOWLEDGMENTS

Okay, wow. Here we are again. Book seventeen, and the start of a two-part adventure that has been one of the most challenging things, structurally, in the entire series to date. We're still deep in the "from the beginning" events, and watching them unfold on the page has been one of the most exciting things I've ever experienced. I hope it's been just as much fun for you!

I dream for me, and I write for my sanity, but I edit and polish and publish for all of you, because I want to share the chaos that exists inside my head. I am honored that you're all still here with me, and that we're able to continue this journey together. I wouldn't want to go it alone. Like the three books before it, *Sleep No More* was conceived during a near-universal lockdown, although it was completed as restrictions were beginning to loosen. The escape it has offered me has still been without peer.

Ongoing thanks to the people who deal with me in daily life, including my various D&D parties, who continue to be very good about my insistence on only playing Tiefling magic-users, my Magic draft and command pod, the Machete Squad, the team at DAW Books, and my agent, Diana Fox, who has continued to go above and beyond all expectations in making sure that Toby's adventures continue not only to be written, but to make sense to people outside my head. This is not always the easiest of tasks!

My convention support swarm reconvened several times during the past year, including Worldcon in Chicago, where I won the Best Series Hugo after several years of appearing on the ballot, and they are a wonderful group of smart, capable, awesome people who do their chosen jobs with skill and grace; they have my deepest thanks. Further thanks to Manda, for making sure I eat even when everything but salad is just too much trouble; to Wish, for keeping me from climbing the walls and crying out of isolation, and to Terri, for coming on as my new PA and handling the endless waves of email. Thanks to all my gaming companions, and to Kyra, for quickly becoming a delightful partner in crime and bringer of endless chaos. Thanks to Shawn and Jay and Tea, to Phil and Mars and a whole list of people, all of whom I adore utterly.

This book sees the exit of Sheila Gilbert as my editor, and the arrival of Navah Wolfe. Sheila has been amazing for more than twenty books, and I'm looking forward to twenty more with Navah at the helm. Thanks to Joshua Starr for his patient wrangling of my endless administrative needs, and to Kayleigh Webb for being the publicist of my dreams. Diana Fox has discovered the ability to Discord message me at midnight, while I continue to love Chris McGrath's covers beyond all reason. All of my cats are doing well: Elsie, Thomas, Verity, and Megara all thrive on my being home constantly, and finally believe that they're getting as many Rocking Lobster cat treats as they properly deserve. I have added a fifth cat to the clowder: Kelpie, who is a cousin of my lost, lamented Alice, and is gracing my days with kitten antics and with joy. Finally, thank you to my pit crew: Christopher Mangum, Tara O'Shea, and Kate Secor.

My soundtrack while writing *Sleep No More* consisted mostly of the Amazing Devil's full discography, endless live concert recordings of the Counting Crows, and the soundtrack to the Beetlejuice musical. Any errors in this book are entirely my own. The errors that aren't here are the ones all the people listed above helped me fix.

Now come on. There's a mist in the trees, and a fire on the hill beyond, and there's so much to be done before the tale is ended . . .

OCTOBER DAYE PRONUNCIATION GUIDE
THROUGH *SLEEP NO MORE*

All pronunciations are given strictly phonetically. This only covers types of fae explicitly named in the first seventeen books, omitting Undersea fae not appearing or mentioned in the current volume.

Adhene: *aad-heene*. Plural is "Adhene."
Aes Sidhe: *eys shee*. Plural is "Aes Sidhe."
Afanc: *ah-fank*. Plural is "Afanc."
Annwn: *ah-noon*. No plural exists.
Arkan sonney: *are-can saw-ney*. Plural is "arkan sonney."
Bannick: *ban-nick*. Plural is "Bannicks."
Baobhan Sith: *baa-vaan shee*. Plural is "Baobhan Sith," diminutive is "Baobhan."
Barghest: *bar-guest*. Plural is "Barghests."
Blodynbryd: *blow-din-brid*. Plural is "Blodynbryds."
Cait Sidhe: *kay-th shee*. Plural is "Cait Sidhe."
Candela: *can-dee-la*. Plural is "Candela."
Coblynau: *cob-lee-now*. Plural is "Coblynau."
Cu Sidhe: *coo shee*. Plural is "Cu Sidhe."
Daoine Sidhe: *doon-ya shee*. Plural is "Daoine Sidhe," diminutive is "Daoine."
Djinn: *jin*. Plural is "Djinn."
Dóchas Sidhe: doe-sh-as shee. Plural is "Dóchas Sidhe."
Ellyllon: *el-lee-lawn*. Plural is "Ellyllon."
Folletti: *foe-let-tea*. Plural is "Folletti."
Gean-Cannah: *gee-ann can-na*. Plural is "Gean-Cannah."
Glastig: *glass-tig*. Plural is "Glastigs."

Gwragen: *guh-war-a-gen*. Plural is "Gwragen."

Hamadryad: *ha-ma-dry-add*. Plural is "Hamadryads."

Hippocampus: *hip-po-cam-pus*. Plural is "Hippocampi."

Kelpie: *kel-pee*. Plural is "Kelpies."

Kitsune: *kit-soo-nay*. Plural is "Kitsune."

Lamia: *lay-me-a*. Plural is "Lamia."

The Luidaeg: *the lou-sha-k*. No plural exists.

Manticore: *man-tee-core*. Plural is "Manticores."

Naiad: *nigh-add*. Plural is "Naiads."

Nixie: *nix-ee*. Plural is "Nixen."

Peri: *pear-ee*. Plural is "Peri."

Piskie: *piss-key*. Plural is "Piskies.'

Puca: *puh-ca*. Plural is "Pucas."

Roane: *row-n*. Plural is "Roane."

Satyr: *say-tur*. Plural is "Satyrs."

Selkie: *sell-key*. Plural is "Selkies."

Shyi Shuai: *shh-yee shh-why*. Plural is "Shyi Shuai."

Silene: *sigh-lean*. Plural is "Silene."

Tuatha de Dannan: *tooth-a day du-non*. Plural is "Tuatha de Dannan," diminutive is "Tuatha."

Tylwyth Teg: *till-with teeg*. Plural is "Tylwyth Teg," diminutive is "Tylwyth."

Urisk: *you-risk*. Plural is "Urisk."

KINGDOMS OF THE WESTLANDS

Kingdom of
Frozen Winds

Kingdom of
Warm Skies

Kingdom of
Evergreen

Kingdom of
Leucothea

Kingdom of
Silences

Kingdom of
Starfall

Battle of
Silences

Kingdom
of the Mists

Kingdom of
Painted Skies

Kingdom on the
Golden Shore

Kingdom
of Angels

Kingdom
of Copper

Priscilla Spencer

ONE

October 28th, 2015

Methought I heard a voice cry "Sleep no more!"
—William Shakespeare, *Macbeth*.

SAMHAIN AND BELTAINE ARE the hubs around which the rest of Faerie's year turns. The two Moving Days, when the least among us—those ranked even lower than changelings like myself—are free to pack up their lives and move along to their next home. That freedom extends not only to the forgettable. On the Moving Days, courtiers, changelings, and servants can move between demesnes without concern for the possibility that they might offend the Lords and Ladies under whom they serve, for Oberon himself has granted his blessing. The skies go dark with flocks of pixies, Piskies, and leaf-winged sprites, and the roads are thick with traveling petitioners, all of them seeking a new place to belong.

Since I reached my majority, it had become my duty to man the door and watch the gate during the weeks surrounding each Moving Day, providing the levels of hospitality required by Oberon's decree and not a crumb or comment more. It was simple work, beneath the others who dwelt in the household, and yet still I took pride in it. On those fleeting nights, I felt shamefully as if I held some actual station in our house.

A family of Hamadryads were the latest to find their way to Mother's tower, three pureblooded adults and two children, both of whom carried the distinct marks of human heritage. The five of them approached along the road connecting us to Shadowed Hills, and one of the children glanced back over her shoulder with glossy eyes and a quivering lip, making me wonder whether they had first sought sanctuary in my uncle's halls. Fools. Wherever they had been before they started this journey must have been glad to see them go, to have released them early and so very unprepared.

I adjusted the drape of my cloak and moved from the window to the hall between the sitting room and kitchen, where I would be able to hear them knocking at whichever door they chose to approach.

If they came to the kitchen door, cutting through the back garden, I would give them parcels of bread and cheese Father had prepared for this very purpose. The bread was rich with herbs he had grown himself, and I sometimes suspected he enchanted it in some small way, to give petitioners luck on the journey yet ahead of them. These people would need it, clearly. For them to have removed changeling children from the household they were born to serve was not a violation of the rules, but it was unseemly at the very least, and unwise by any measure. Such children's lives would always have been short. Now they would likely be hard and brutal as well, for what liege would ever trust them not to flee a second time?

If they came through the front garden to the main door, I would give them nothing at all. It was not Moving Day proper yet, and even if it had been, Mother's careful avoidance of any title save the one she was born to—Firstborn—meant the laws of hospitality had little claim over her. These travelers could no more demand the comforts of her house than they could shake away the evidence of their transgressions.

What happened next was entirely on them. I stood in the hall, eyes closed and head tipped back, breathing in the comforting scent of smoke and roses. I knew the truth of my parentage. Mother could never have gotten August a handmaid through her bridal bed, and there was nothing of Father's lineage in me. Still, it would have been nice to find something familiar in the attenuated air of my own paltry spellcasting. The copper spoke to Mother's blood, at least in the abstract, but freshly cut grass? What self-respecting daughter of a good family smelled like a *lawn*?

The word was devoid of context in my mind, and I opened my eyes, blinking into the dimness. What was a *lawn*? I knew it as a term for fine linen, but laundry had nothing to do with the smell of my magic. No, I had thought of the word as something to do with grass . . . but why?

A heavy knock disrupted my attempts to puzzle out the meanderings of my own mind. At the *kitchen* door, thank Oberon and his beautiful bride. I started for the kitchen, pulling my hood up to hide my ears and shade my features. Everyone local knew of Amandine's two daughters, the tarnished and the true. They would never doubt my loyalties. Even so, those who traveled with changelings were all too often inclined to take my visible mortality as a sign that I might sympathize with them, that I could be called upon to offer aid beyond what tradition required of me, and those things could not have been less true. There is no shame in standing by the rules of your house.

There is still shame, I feel, in misleading someone, however unintentionally. My blood and magic clearly felt the same, for they had never been inclined to illusions, however hard I struggled to master and call them forth. Nothing in me wished to lie.

The knock came again, not impatient, but harried, as if the knocker were on the verge of panic. I stepped up to the door, unlatched it, and pulled it open, allowing the migrants on the step their first and only glimpse of the interior of my mother's tower.

The kitchen is and has always been Father's domain. Cuts of meat and dried alliums hung from the ceiling, suspended alongside sacks of fresh potatoes, squash, and onions. Wheels of cheese and bottles of oil crowded the shelves, and everything smelled of fresh-baked bread and spices.

I have always felt most comfortable in the kitchen and the kitchen garden. The rest of the tower is like the front garden, meant for Mother and for August. I am better left behind the scenes, protected and anonymous. Father sees that need in me, and has always done his best to nurture it.

From the way the Hamadryads stared past me into the gloom, that simple kitchen must have seemed a paradise. I gave them a few seconds to gape at what they would never touch, then cleared my throat, snapping their attention back to me.

"Greetings," I said, tone formal. "I am October, daughter of this house. What do you seek?"

A question was not an offer of aid, nor did it create the expectation of same. The light that had been growing in the eyes of the man at the front of their group flickered out and died, extinguished in an instant. It was better that way. A blunt dismissal might ache, but it was preferable to leading them on.

"I am Eion," he said, touching his chest with one slim-fingered hand. His skin, like many Hamadryads, was a dusty grayish-brown, the color of ash bark, and his hair was the same but several shades darker, trending toward a flaming autumnal red at the tips. A direct descendant of Melia, then, most likely, only two generations removed from Maeve's dishonor.

That made the presence of changelings in his company all the more appalling. The children of the Firstborn are meant to know better, to *be* better as an example for all of Faerie. Even those who claim descent from Maeve should hold themselves to a higher standard.

All the ritual responses I could give would involve offering him the comfort or the kindness of the house, neither of which I was authorized to give, and so I held my tongue, and waited for him to continue.

"We have come from Wild Strawberries," he said, reading my silence for the refusal that it was. "We departed on the first hour of the Moving Day festivities and have made our way this far entirely on foot. The children are weary. We seek a place to rest for the coming day, to let our roots dip into living soil and feed our tired bodies."

"There is no room for wild planting in my mother's garden," I said, and was relieved to know my words were true, for the children looked around themselves with wide-eyed yearning, drinking in the sight of so many green things growing so very, very well. It would have pained me to lie to them.

I would have done it anyway, of course. I knew my duty almost as well as I knew my place.

Eion frowned. "Surely there must be a scrap of ground, somewhere, suitable for us to stop a while," he argued. "Somewhere out of the way, outside the garden walls."

"And had you come any time but immediately prior to Moving Day, I might have been able to find you something," I said. "If we allow you to root here now, with the year about to turn, you would be able to cry for hospitality, and my lady mother would be left with no proper choice save to grant it. We dwell here, between demesnes, because she has no desire to guide or guard a holding, only to live in peace with her family and be left alone."

"We wouldn't do that," blurted one of the women. She stepped forward, putting herself level with the man, reaching for me, and I managed, barely, not to recoil. Like him, her hair ended in flaming red, as if the seasons had hold of her in body, not only custom.

"I swear, we wouldn't," she continued. "Only it's been such a long walk already, and the children are *so* tired, and we have such a long way left to go."

"Maia, please," said Eion sharply.

"What is your destination?" The question drew me dangerously close to showing them the kind of concern that could be taken as an expression of responsibility, and yet I found I couldn't help it. The children truly did look exhausted. If not for their human heritage, I doubted they would still have been on their feet.

Hamadryads are closely related to the true Dryads, although their weakened ties to the purity of flower magic have left them unable to truly bond with their trees. Instead of spending their lives tied to a true and sacred grove, they flit from vessel to vessel, renewing their roots with dips into the soil, hot-blooded enough to procreate with humans. In our lessons, Mother had taught me they were the best Maeve could do in imitating her better sister, and should be pitied but never trusted.

Most Hamadryads chose gestures and the sound of wind or birdsong for their names. That these spoke their names in a shape my tongue could echo told me they had been among a proper Court for some time before setting out on this ill-advised journey. That, and the quality of the clothes worn by the three adults, made me wonder if they traveled now of their own free will, or at a noble's command.

"Golden Shore," said Maia. "We have heard that such as we can be welcome there."

This time, I was unable to control my face quickly enough to hide my moue of distaste. "Yes," I said, pleased when my voice came out level, if not kind. "They are likely to welcome you."

The Kingdom on the Golden Shore stocked our shelves with the things my father could not grow himself, or that we lacked the room to cultivate; for all that Mother liked a good quiche from time to time, she hated the sound of poultry and wouldn't allow Father to keep chickens. As she also refused to allow any member of her family to shop in mortal lands, we had to purchase our eggs from Golden Shore, where they were laid by good, honest Alectryon fowl as Oberon intended. Meat was likewise acquired from their vendors, and all the other luxuries to which August would have been heir, had not Maeve so cruelly cut us off from the deeper lands of Faerie.

Golden Shore provided these wonders through backbreaking labor, and as few among the true fae would choose that life when offered any alternative, they swelled their workforce with changelings seeking a place that would accept them for what they were.

It seemed a cruel life to condemn a child to, unfair in the extreme. But then, it was the best any changeling born without a promised place could hope for.

"You have as far to go as you have already come, and I am not empowered to offer anything which might be taken for hospitality this close to Moving Day," I said. "Why did you choose to travel now, if you know where you're bound?"

"Our girls," said Maia, miserably. "Ashla and Gable. Gable is to be sixteen at Ostara, and our liege—our *former* liege—had begun to speak of placements."

The children, whom I had taken for younger than the age she claimed for them, glanced over at the sound of their names, then went back to watching the garden with hungry, weary eyes.

"There are households in Wild Strawberries glad to have changeling service," she continued. "They call themselves benevolent, for being willing to be so tarnished. For being so very *generous*. But the children they claim rarely last a handful of seasons. They break. Their employers carry none of the blame, of course, and there's no crime in the death of a changeling, but still, they . . . they break."

Either she had caught enough of the angle of my cheekbones in the shadows of my hood, or she already knew my nature. Still, it was dangerous for her to speak so to a stranger. Not all changelings are sympathetic to our own kind. Not all have had my advantages in life.

The children moved closer to the as-yet-unnamed woman, seeking some sort of comfort, their exhaustion evident in the way they pressed themselves under her arms, baby birds seeking the warmth of the nest. Impulsively, I grabbed for the parcels Father had made, taking two in each hand, and thrust them at Eion.

"My father baked this bread himself, with wheat he grew in the fields between here and Shadowed Hills," I said. "The herbs are of his garden. The cheese is from your destination, and should strengthen you. Take this as well."

I plucked a jar of half-eaten blackberry jam from the counter and held it out, pleading silently for him to catch the implication.

"No one claims the blackberry tangles beyond the swamp, which is unreasonably infested with pixies," I said. "It would be deeply unsafe to venture there, especially in the company of children."

"Who makes the jam?" he asked, warily.

"My father and I," I said. "We gather blackberries from the very edge of the tangle, when the pixies allow it, and then we boil them down in this kitchen."

He feared goblin fruit, then, as was only sensible for someone who traveled in such . . . mixed company. I had heard rumor that Hamadryad changelings were more resistant to the call of the fruit than most, but "resistant" is not the same as "immune." Best to avoid temptation until they could reach Golden Shore, where they would be protected by the Kingdom's customs.

Hesitant, he took the jar from my hand. "No one claims it?" he repeated.

"Not past the verge," I said. "The thorns are too thick, and the ground too soft to anchor a knowe. If any venture there, we do not know them."

"Your kindness is noted, and will be remembered," he said, with a small bow. The women didn't mirror his gesture, but watched me with hope and relief in their faces.

I glanced away, not wanting to see them look at me as if I understood their struggle. I didn't, and I knew that. The lives of changelings were short and brutal, better than humans only because they could see the glories of Faerie, worth less than both humans and fae in every other possible way. They were protected by no Law save the rules of hospitality and fealty: by leaving their liege, these people had left their daughters open to all the threats Faerie had to offer. Who was I, orchestrated, wanted, and beloved, to pretend at understanding what they suffered? I had never lived a day outside this tower, and Oberon willing, I never would.

If Mother tired of me and cast me out before August was ready to establish a household of her own, I had little doubt that I wouldn't survive the year. I have never had a head for survival. Mother has made sure I knew that well and truly.

The man straightened, and hesitated before he spoke again. In that hesitation I read the impropriety he was about to commit, and should have slammed the door in his face, should have shut myself away from him before he could somehow taint me with his words.

"You could come with us, if you liked," he said. "You appear old enough to have reached your majority, and Moving Day approaches; you would commit no crime by declaring yourself free of this household."

I recoiled. "My name is October," I said, as I had at the beginning of this unwanted conversation. "I am the daughter of this house. My mother, Amandine, is daughter to Oberon himself, and my father, Count Torquill, keeps no noble Court because he is sworn alchemist to the Rose of Winter, keeping her household well supplied. I have no desire to be free of this place or these people, and by your suggestion, you shame our house. Leave now. We have offered you no hospitality, nor are we obliged to do so."

"M-my apologies, Lady," he stammered. "I read the situation wrongly. I intended no offense."

"Intention doesn't always match reality," I said. Then I glanced behind him, to the two changeling girls clinging to the trembling woman.

They looked at me as if I were the most terrifying thing they had ever seen, worse, even, than the noble who would have handed them off to a liege known for killing changeling children. I wanted to wither under those eyes. I wanted to protest that no, no, I was not a monster; I was simply a girl who knew her place, who was content where she was, who understood her limitations.

And yet here I was, safe and comfortable and cared for, while the best they could hope for was a clean patch of ground amidst the briars, deep enough for them to sink their roots into for a day before they resumed their quest for a place where they could be sure of their futures.

I would have hardened my heart, had I only known how. I did not, and so I grabbed another parcel, this one of sweetened fruitcake, intended for my own supper, and thrust it at the man. He took it, apparently automatically.

"Open roads and kind fires, and all the winds to guide you," I said, and shut the door before I could be drawn any deeper into looping, confounding conversation. Turning my back to it, I leaned against the wood, and waited.

No further knocking came.

Excellent. More tired than I should have been after such a brief encounter, I wiped my brow with one hand and made for the sitting room. Sure, a moment's rest meant taking my eyes off the road, but I would hear the knocking whether or not I could see who was coming up the path, and so long as I stayed here to greet them, I would be fulfilling my duties.

My name, as I have now stated twice, is October. That is all. I have no right to Father's name, for all that the law deems me his daughter, and my mother never told me the name of the man who sired me, the mortal she entreated to her bed for a night of unspeakable ecstasy. I

am born of two worlds, balanced between them as precisely and perilously as anything has ever been. There is more of the fae in me than
mortality, as if that mattered: each of the Firstborn has something they
can do better than any of the others. My mother's trick is in changing
the balance of someone's blood.

Rumor says there were once devices that could be set to the same
end, but they were too difficult to control; they rendered our social
customs unstable and unsustainable, for any changeling child could get
their hands upon one such and remake themselves in Titania's image
without intervention or consent. Better to keep such power where it
would be used responsibly and correctly. Better to keep it in my
mother's hands.

Mother is forever in demand among the Courts, called upon to
make a changeling child a little less fae, so as to render them able to
better stand the sting of iron, or a little less mortal, to not offend a
sensitive noble's eyes. Her services are but one of the many reasons
changelings are better off within the Court system rather than hiding
in hovels with parents who should have known better than to bear
them without.

Because of what I am, I will never marry, never have a household
or children of my own. But Faerie must have servants to function
smoothly, and so changelings are required. Each noble house and
each among the Firstborn is asked to do their duty, to provide a pair
of hands to press into the service of greater Faerie. Mother put off
that unpleasant necessity for as long as she possibly could, until pressures that were not mine to know compelled her to slip into the mortal world long enough to return with me, a babe in arms, my blood
already adjusted to the levels she required.

October, she called me, in honor of an aunt I never knew, who died
long ago in a human war, but whose daughter, January, still dwelt in
her father's halls in Briarholme. It was a cruel and bitter gift to give
to me, who would never be September Torquill's equal, and a perpetual reminder that my place was behind my sister. As August came
first in the calendar, so would August come first in our lives.

Should my sister choose to start a household of her own, she could
ask me to come with her and stand in service—would, in fact, be expected to do so. A pureblood could no more offer insult to a changeling than a cat could look at a king, but if she left and chose not to
take me, it would be assumed that I had somehow offered insult to
her, and I could be made to pay the price.

There are few shades of punishment where changelings are concerned. We are weak to many things that trouble not the fae, but strong against iron, which would be the preferred means of disciplining an unruly commoner who somehow offended a noble. If August left without me, my death would be the likely outcome.

I slumped into one of the uncomfortable couches Mother insisted were appropriate for the sitting room, allowing my eyes to close. The Hamadryads had not been the first such group of travelers to come along our road this Moving Day; most of the people I'd seen had been in clusters that I took for families, almost all of them sheltering a changeling child or two, and none of the changelings older than sixteen. All running for Golden Shore.

Something was terribly wrong, if Faerie's children were so afraid of their own homes, their own places. I frowned to myself, a private expression. Such thoughts were unbefitting. Nothing was wrong. Nothing *could* be wrong, not in Titania's Faerie.

We lived in a perfect world, watched over by a perfect queen who saw to it that everything was balanced, everything was fair, everything was exactly as it was meant to be. To think anything else was to fail her. To fail her was to fail Faerie.

I have been a failure too many times. I forced my eyes open and rose.

Time to return to my duties.

TWO

OBERON'S MERCY WAS WITH me: although I stood attentive for the rest of the night, listening, no one else came to knock upon our door before the distant crowing of a cock alerted me to the approach of mortal dawn.

As I said before, Mother refuses to keep livestock, and Alectryon are difficult to come by, but there is an unattended portal to the human world somewhere in the depths of the swamplands, and mortal chickens have shown an odd proficiency for slipping through, and surviving once here. They make a convenient clock, even more than the sun, whose rise and set could become questionable when Mother wasn't in the tower. She had been called to the Kingdom of Silences to provide her services to the nobility there, as she was often prevailed upon to do. As the most powerful blood-worker Faerie had ever produced, my mother's gifts allowed her to shift the balance of the blood of any favored—and unfavored—changeling to make them more suited to their station. This, along with her beauty and status as one among the Firstborn, means that all of Faerie reveres her and courts her favor.

What no one outside our family knew, or could ever be allowed to learn, was that her gifts went even further: if she so chose, she could strip the immortality from any fae with even a drop of mortal blood, or turn the weakest changeling fully fae. If anyone suspected her powers extended so far as that, our entire household would be blinded and bound to the Iron Tree to be burned alive. Her magic was allowed, for she was a true daughter of Oberon, and Faerie itself had put the art of blood manipulation into her hands. To transform something mortal into something fae, though . . . that would be a blasphemy such as could never be borne.

That, too, is part of how I know my family will always protect me. When I became old enough to be trusted to hold my tongue, Mother herself told me the truth of what it meant to be Dóchas Sidhe. If she didn't love me, she would never have trusted me to help them keep the secret that could easily destroy us all.

The cock crew and I slumped, weary from the long night of waiting and yet somehow filled with tension, the fierce, buzzing energy born of too much inaction. Father would be back soon. He had spent the night in his workshop, serving his Lady, but he always tried to return during the day, to wash and see us fed if nothing else. Mother's absence meant there was no need for me to prepare tonight's bread; he would do it gladly and with skill, where I would fumble and burn myself, as I always did. I have no talent in the kitchen, never have, and am unlikely to develop any at this late stage.

Father is a wizard with a knife, pruning and plucking the proper herbs with his own hand, then mincing and dicing the leaves to sweet perfection. His bread always rises, and his eggs split as if seamed, never casting specks of shell into the pan. Even August can toast a cheese sandwich without blistering her hands. I, on the other hand, remain all but useless in the art of feeding myself or others, and yet when Mother is in residence, the duty remains my own. Knowing that Father would have matters in hand, I stretched until my back cracked, then started toward the stairs that would take me to my room.

Sleep might be elusive, but I would need to begin my chores by midday if I wanted to keep the tower in a livable state. I needed to at least shut my eyes and think of nothing for an hour or two, if not truly rest.

I was halfway up the stairs when I met my sister coming down. August was dressed in a gown of white velvet. White lace gores ran from her hips down to the hem, keeping the gown modest while reducing the weight of the skirt enough that she could still move. The belled sleeves were matching lace from elbow to wrist. One of Mother's selections. August would have been far more comfortable in the colors of mud and trampled grass, like the stains she collected almost nightly from the garden.

Perhaps her yearning to run wild in wooded places somehow

influenced my magic. I think I could love my cut-grass scent if I knew it had started from my sister.

She spread her arms when she saw me, effectively blocking rest of the stairs. "Where do you think you're going?" she asked.

"Up to my chambers, to sleep," I said. When Mother was about, we were expected to be properly mannerly with one another, she speaking to me however she chose, I casting my eyes down and accepting every barb and insult as my due. When we were alone, we were freer with one another, something which Father had always encouraged. He liked his daughters to get along, and as we were already inclined to enjoy each other's company, it was easier to behave as if we were truly sisters. "Day has dawned, and my night's duties are finished. Eight tappings at the door, and eight parties turned away, for we are no one's place to rest, not near to Moving Day."

"So you know the rules well enough to parrot them at me and make them sound almost natural, instead of like trite poetry," said August. "Nice. Anyway, you're not going to bed."

I lifted my eyebrows. "I'm not?"

"No."

When she didn't immediately explain further, I folded my arms and glared at her. "Then I suppose I'm going down to the kitchen to start the bread?"

"No!"

"Out to the garden, to gather herbs?"

"Now you're just being ridiculous."

"Don't call me ridiculous, you walnut, it's not polite."

"I'm only impolite because you were rotten *first*."

"Criticism accepted," I said. "So tell me, sybil sister of mine, what am I doing?"

August's expression turned instantly wary, and she stepped closer, palms still pressed flat against the walls. "Don't even *joke*, October, you know better."

I did. Shame washed through me like a wave. "I'm sorry, I was just—where am I going?"

Seers are forbidden in Faerie, and have been since the sea witch's cruel children orchestrated Maeve's betrayal and abandonment of the rest of us. They were rounded up and taken to the Iron Tree centuries ago, and mercifully, none has been seen among us since. The Dóchas Sidhe, consisting only of myself and August, are as yet a young descendant line. No one knows what we might eventually become. If there were even the slightest rumor that one of us had had so much as a prophetic dream . . .

It could as easily be the end of us as the truth of Mother's magic. Fair Titania would think nothing of having us snatched away in the middle of the day and taken to the Iron Tree for the crime of our existence, and even Father's patron would raise no hand to stop her. Some things are not to be spoken of.

August glared at me before hoisting her chin and sweeping grandly down the stairs, at least lifting her arms as she passed me, so that I was not knocked back against the wall. She had learned that level of exaggerated grandeur from watching our mother, I was sure. Mother could enter a room as if she were the Queen of all Faerie, and we no longer attended Court functions where Titania was expected to appear, out of the rumor that some unwise courtiers had looked between them and found Mother to be the fairer of the two. Best not to tempt fate. Best not to bait the powerful.

"Out," August declared, glancing back at me over her shoulder. "There was a ball at Shadowed Hills last night. Obviously, we did not attend, for we are good girls, and Mother bade us attend no such events without her to chaperone us. There will, however, be much of the refreshment table left for good girls to scavenge from, and I had no dinner last night. Did you?"

In answer, my stomach grumbled. I pressed a hand against it and frowned at her.

"When she told us to avoid the parties without her as our escort, she didn't mean for us to go picking through the remains like common urchins, Aug, and you know that."

"Do I? Do *you*? Can you read Mother's mind now? Oh, can you read mine?" She smiled, a fierce, manic smile, and while I couldn't read her thoughts, I could read her face like a sonnet addressed to me. There would be no dissuading her. She had been left to her own devices for hours, and this was the price to be paid.

August does poorly with idleness, always has, and I quite suspect she always will. When she has a household of her own, I expect it to be one of those where the skies are awash with light every night, and the halls are never silent. It will be a contrast to the life we live now, no question, but I find myself oddly eager for the change. Not that I'm in any hurry to leave Father, or the tower, behind. He'll be so lonely when we're gone.

I sighed. "August. Please. I don't want to get in trouble."

"You *never* want to get in trouble." She pouted at me. "Please, Toby? Please, please? I just want a slice of cake without Mother standing over me muttering about stains on my clothing—as if they would show if she allowed me a speck of color! I heard Sir Etienne took a new squire. I want to flirt with him and see what colors his cheeks turn! I want—"

"Fine, fine," I said, laughter overflowing my lips and spilling down my chin. If I didn't cut her off, she could keep listing her desires until they formed a pile tall and untidy enough to reach the stars. "I will chaperone your adventure."

"Because you are the *best* sister," she said, and darted forward to kiss my cheeks, first one and then the other. "The best and the kindest of sisters. I could search all of Faerie forever, and never find a sweeter sister than yourself."

"As if I've ever told you no," I grumbled, wiping her kisses away with swipes of my hand and trying not to look as if I enjoyed her attentions. It was a small fiction, but one of the few I was allowed.

"Why would you?" She beamed. "You can't search all of Faerie and find yourself, for you are unique in all the worlds. You'll have to settle for me, the second sweetest. I'll get my cloak."

Then she was away, bounding to the cloakroom with all the vigor and enthusiasm that she brought to everything she actually wanted to do. I had never seen her bound to do the dishes, for example, or to tidy her room, but then, why should she? She had me to do those things. She always would.

I smiled as I trailed after her, more slowly. The idea of adventure was August's, but the benefits would belong to both of us. Food would be pleasant. Company more pleasant still. For all of August's jokes about flirting with the squires, we both knew her attention would be focused on Sir Grianne, who was much more entertaining to make blush than any stripling squire.

Not that I'd be flirting with anyone. I had friends below the stairs who would be perfectly delighted to see me, especially if I offered to chip in on the chores, and my relatively indestructible nature makes me ideally suited for fishing dropped flatware out of scalding wash water. My talents are scant and strange. Might as well take advantage of the ones I have.

August's cloak was all the colors her clothing was never allowed to be, red and gold and orange and green, the month she was named for

stitched into a patchwork of velvet, silk, and hand-dyed cotton. It had
been a gift from Father's patron, or Mother would surely have burnt
it long since. Next to her, I was plain to the point of invisibility, my
cloak a simple brown, my dress a worn and practical heather green.
It was best that way, that I should never draw too much attention.

Even Faerie had seen the sense in that. My hair is a shade of ashen
blonde that looks more like a sun-weathered brown than any fully
definable type of gold, and my eyes are a foggy gray that trends into
white to the point of seeming to have no real color at all. August is a
watercolor sketch of a girl, strawberry-blonde hair and eyes the color
of fireweed honey, water white and flawlessly clear, and I am her
washed-out shadow. And as long as we play to that, as long as people
look at her rather than at me, the too-blunt angles of my cheekbones
and the softened points of my ears are less of a concern.

I can disappear in the presence of my sister, and by disappearing,
I remain safe.

I collected my shoes from their place by the door, stepping into
them, and waited for August. As always when preparing for a trip to
Shadowed Hills, I felt as if I were forgetting something, some small
but essential accessory that was required for me to visit the home of
my uncle and his family.

Then August came to meet me, a smile on her face and a sparkle
in her eyes, and the feeling faded. She hooked her arm through mine
as I opened the front door, the wards letting us through with a tingle
on our skin, like stepping into the cool water of a running stream:
there and gone again in an instant. No one outside the family would
be able to access the tower, even with no one home to bar the doors
or guard the windows. As long as we stayed inside, we would remain
perfectly safe.

The world outside was not so kind. We walked through Mother's
garden to the gate. Flowers bloomed in all directions, a miraculous
profusion of colors, their blossoms open to their fullest extent to
drink in the watery light of a Summerlands dawn. True day is rare in
the Summerlands. It comes more frequently to the land Mother controls, the tower and the acres around it that constitute her claim, for
many of Father's herbs thrive better in true sunlight, and her flowers
appreciate it as well. Still, the sun never shines here as directly as it
does in the mortal world. The previous night's moons were still visible overhead. Six of them, currently, all different sizes, and one with
rings.

I pointed upward, bumping August with my hip. "Look," I said. "A ringed moon. I can't remember the last time I saw one of those."

"Last year, just before Lughnasa," said August, then paled, glancing quickly around to be sure she hadn't been overheard. When no one rose from the bushes to accuse her, she calmed, and we proceeded from the garden side by side.

Titania is the Lady of Flowers, but Maeve was the Lady of Frost, the keeper of the winter nights, and when she betrayed us, the bulk of her festivals were stricken from our collective customs, forbidden and unmade. Were it not for the impossibility of erasing Moving Day from our accounting, Samhain would doubtless have been excised. As that wasn't possible, we lost Lughnasa instead, the festival of harvests, proof that the wheel turns.

Titania denies that Samhain ever had anything to do with harvests or the progression of the year into winter, says it was chosen only to balance Beltaine, and perhaps she speaks truly. But August has accompanied Father to the Library of Stars as his research assistant on the few occasions when he's been able to convince her to sit still for long enough, and she's told me what she read in the older histories.

I sometimes wish she hadn't. I shouldn't dare to think, even for an instant, that our True Queen could be fallible. If ever I were to meet August's laughed-about mind-reader, I would be executed that same day, for the crime of doubting the undoubtable. And I would deserve it. If Titania revises history, she does so for good reason, and with Faerie's best interests at heart.

I had barely finished forming the thought when a bolt of pain shot through my temples and I stopped walking to grimace and grasp my forehead with both hands, making a pained sound. August stopped as well, turning to look at me with wide and anxious eyes.

"October! Are you well?"

"Just a headache," I said, trying to wave away her concern. "Probably from my lack of supper."

"Father left you something to eat, even as he left me," she said, suddenly suspicious. "What happened to your supper, October?"

"Would you believe I just forgot to eat?"

"No, but I'd believe you would tell such a transparent lie." She sighed. "What was it this time?"

"A family," I said. "Hamadryads, traveling from Wild Strawberries to Golden Shore."

"Ah. Changelings in their company, then?"

I nodded, momentarily silent. August had watched enough Moving Days to know what that particular destination meant. These weren't people seeking a softer position or a better term of service; they were running for the lives of their children. She reached over and took my hand, squeezing it in her own. We were both all too exquisitely aware of the delicacy of my situation, and how few rights I had.

There were rumors, whispered in servants' halls and in supposedly private rooms, that some changelings fled Faerie altogether, choosing to live fierce, feral lives in the human world, where they would be forever alien and outside, but where their thin, attenuated powers would make them gods among the mortals. People who passed such rumors along had an unfortunate tendency to disappear, which made them all the more likely to be true.

Even with the dangers presented by my life as I now lived it, I couldn't imagine why anyone would ever choose to leave Faerie. Here, at least, I was understood, even if I would never be an equal to those around me. Here, I was cared for and supported. Why would anyone throw that away to struggle and scavenge under the guise of freedom?

"Where did you send them?" she asked.

"The briars beyond the swamp," I said. "The soil is good enough to grow sweet fruit; they'll be able to rest their roots there, and maybe make it to Golden Shore before the span of the festival is finished."

"Clever," she said, with a nod. "No hospitality offered or assumed, and well off Mother's land, but still far enough from the common path that they may have a chance. You gave them a chance, October."

"A chance and my supper," I said. The words were bitter in my mouth. "It wasn't enough."

"I know."

We walked quietly after that, August allowing me time alone with my thoughts, me trying not to dim her excitement for our small and socially permissible adventure.

The morning air was crisp and cool, late summer trending into fall. It grew colder as we walked, and snow appeared alongside the road: transition into true winter. Our Uncle Sylvester has never been a joyful man, and allows the seasons to run as they will on his land. Somehow, this means early snow and late thaw every year.

Father says it is because our grandparents stopped their dancing when he and Sylvester were young, and then their only sister followed, and by then he had settled with Mother to fill their tower with light, while Uncle Sylvester had only the cold comforts of a ducal coronet to keep him warm.

"Romantic love is not required to live a full and happy life, my seedlings," Father had told us, watching carefully to be sure we took his message to heart, "but if you cannot love one who loves you truly in return, find friends, find companions, find people who will tell you the truths you cannot carry and unveil the lies you cannot see. Most of all, cleave to each other, for you will be the only sure support you have in all this world."

"Why isn't Uncle joyful, then, when he has you?" It had been August who was bold enough to ask, August who had looked up at him with wide, trusting eyes.

Still, Father had offered his answer to both of us. He was always so careful in that regard, to be sure no further walls were built between us than the unbreachable wall of our blood.

"He thought to court your mother once," he'd said, solemn. "He came before her as a hero, and reminded her that her father prized heroes over scholars, that he would be the better match for her affections. And she refused him. Three times he asked, as was his right, and three times she answered no, and then she married his worthless baby brother in his stead. He loves me, but he has never quite forgiven me for winning a greater treasure than all his heroics have done."

In that moment, I had been grateful that my status as a changeling meant I would never be expected to fall in love or marry. If such things could come between sisters, then they were not meant for me.

On we walked, into the snow and the cold, as the sky above us darkened, the sunlight chased aside by our uncle's preference for an endless night. The open fields and briars gave way to trees, close-packed and towering, creating a dense forest that swallowed all light. It wasn't threatening, but it wasn't welcoming, either.

Pixies flitted through the trees, wings chiming in soothing, subdued tones, and I flashed them a grateful smile. I have always been fond of pixies. Like me, they belong to Faerie and are held apart from it at the same time, never quite included, never able to step away. Changelings and pixies are both considered pests in certain circles, ones which I would do well to continue to avoid.

Eventually, the well-loved shape of the great manor came into view ahead of us. It seemed smaller than it actually was, so hemmed-in with trees that the structure scarce had space to breathe. When I dreamt of Shadowed Hills, I always dreamt it surrounded by gardens and carefully cultivated fields, open, green, and growing. Not closed in and oppressed as it was now.

August squeezed my hand and broke into a run, dragging me in her wake, and for a moment, I forgot to be tired or hungry or discontent, preoccupied with the need to keep hold of my sister's hand as we wove between the trees. She didn't care if my human heritage made me slower and clumsier than she was. She only cared that we were sisters, and I was there for her to pull onward, to adventure.

Our running came to an end, as it always must, when we burst out of the trees and were met with a detachment of our uncle's knights, Sir Etienne at their front. He was dressed in full armor for the patrol, sword ready in his hand, and he looked us over with no warmth in his eyes or his expression.

Sir Etienne, like many among the pureblooded, frowned upon the existence of changelings. We were weak and lessened, we brought no brightness into Faerie; our presence was tolerated only because Titania ordered it, and because we could be forced into performing the tasks that true fae would prefer not to perform. August would have been acceptable if she had kept me at arm's length, as was right and proper. Her refusal to do so when we were younger meant she was little better than I was, and worthy of his scorn.

"What do we have here?" he asked.

"We've come to help with the cleanup from the Moving Day party," said August. Injecting a sneer into her voice, she continued, "Or *she* has, anyway. *I've* come to steal leftover cake and sip cordials with my peers as we watch the changelings clean the ballroom."

It had been my idea for August to seem less enamored of my company when in the presence of our uncle's knights. She hated playacting as if their prejudices carried any weight with her, but if it kept them from eyeing us with suspicion, it was worth the slinging of a few sharp words.

"You *know* Uncle Sylvester has given us free passage of his lands," she continued. "You've no more right to turn us aside than you have to order our mother to do your bidding. Will you let us pass?"

Etienne hesitated, his pride clearly stung by her facile dismissal. Then he straightened, and looked to his detachment. "We have better things to do than worry about some ill-mannered maids," he said. "See to it that you make no mischief, for we are very close to Moving Day."

"We'll be good," said August, and grabbed my hand again as he turned and marched the other knights away into the wood.

She kept her word to one degree: she swallowed her giggles until they were out of sight, and that was good enough for me.

"Come on, we'll miss the cake," she said, and squeezed my hand again, and broke back into a run, me running alongside.

THREE

THE REMAINS OF THE previous night's celebration were spread out across the grand balcony like the aftermath of a very cheerful, bloodless battle. Untied pennant strings waved listlessly in the breeze, and garlands of wilted roses slumped down the sides of columns, drooping toward the cobbled ground. Various servants, mostly household fae and changelings, picked through the remains, collecting the specific items they had been tasked to retrieve.

August released my hand as we reached the stairs, charging gleefully ahead on her endless search for leftover cake and other treats. Father fed us well, when he was present, but his work for the Rose all too often kept him away, and Mother had yet to truly internalize the idea that children—even adult ones—needed to eat if they were to live. Of course August had never been taught to cook: Mother insisted it was beneath her and there was no point when one day she'd have a household to see to her comfort in all things, and while I *had* been taught, I had no talent for it.

If August's eventual household consisted only of the two of us, we would both starve. An egg I fried was equally likely to become a piece of charcoaled leather or a puddle of uncooked slime, and while I could knead dough that someone else had made, the less said about my actual baking, the better. As the youngest of three, Father knew how to cook; even when his parents were alive, there had been concern that he wouldn't be able to establish a household without a proper title or estate to bring to the arrangement, and so he had been allowed to learn skills that most purebloods would never even consider.

That knowledge had served him very well, once he married our mother; her sensitivity to the balance and burdens of the blood meant she couldn't stand the company of changelings before I was born, and that she won't be sorry to see me go.

As a Firstborn, she could doubtless have found a pureblood from one of the lesser noble families or farming communities who would be willing to serve as her handmaid, but she had chosen to do her duty and bring me into our world instead. I would have resented her for that—who wants to be born out of obligation, and solely to serve someone else?—but my existence meant August would never have to be alone.

She got night terrors at times, my sister, who was the bolder of us in almost all ways. She clawed at the walls and cried, and only my presence soothed her. How could I wish myself away and leave August in the care of some faceless handmaid? I could no more begrudge my mother for bearing me than I could begrudge the sun for tearing down illusions. Faerie creates only what she needs, and for August's sake, Faerie needed me.

At times, after watching Mother try and fail to feed us or herself when Father was away with the Rose, I had wondered somewhat spitefully if her choosing him over his brother hadn't been based purely on the fact that Father was an alchemist, and alchemy is a kind of cooking. At least by choosing Father, she could ensure herself a life of hot food with or without the servants employed by most noble households.

Then I had pushed the thought aside and punished myself for it for three days, denying myself desserts or walks in the garden. A good daughter wouldn't think such things of her mother. A good daughter would be grateful for the gift of her existence, and would know her place.

Right now, my place was among the household staff gathering the party's debris like they were collecting apples fallen from a tree. I slid myself into their number, finding a broom and beginning to sweep up the remains of what seemed to have been an entire pile of plates before it had been carelessly allowed to shatter on the ground.

The nearest servant, a Hob changeling named Kerry, smiled wearily at me as I started sweeping. "Wasn't sure they'd let you out of the house, being this close to Moving Day and all."

"Why shouldn't they?" I asked.

"There's rumors been going around, about a change in the way the Kingdom trucks with changelings," she said, dropping her voice to keep August from hearing. "Not sure they'd apply to you, given who your mother is, but she's protective enough that I'd expect her to keep you close to heel regardless."

August was on the other side of the balcony with a small, brightly frosted cake, her attention focused on a bronze-haired Daoine Sidhe who scowled at my glance in their direction. He wore the arms of the Duchy on the left side of his jerkin, and I silently cursed my sister as I turned my face away.

She hadn't told me *Quentin* was Sir Etienne's new squire.

The boy had been sent to Shadowed Hills as a blind foster when he was twelve years old, and the seven years he'd spent in local company had done nothing to improve his demeanor, nor his fondness for changelings. Rumor said he was the son of some high-up noble house, perhaps even royalty, but I tried to give as little credence to rumors as I could manage. Gossip only hurt the people who indulged in it.

Regardless of his parentage, it was well known that he hated changelings, no matter how necessary Faerie found us, and that he thought my parents allowed me too much freedom to consort with my betters. He wanted me to know my place.

Oh, I knew it. I knew it better than he would ever dream.

The pile of stoneware shards was large enough that I stopped sweeping and looked to Kerry. "Do you have any gloves?"

"I'm sorry, no," she said, her face falling as she realized what I was actually asking. "We weren't able to obtain any from the groundskeepers. Do you want me to handle the mess?"

"She can do it," said a voice behind me. I turned. Quentin had crossed the balcony to stop only a few feet away, watching me with disdain in his cold blue eyes. "She's a changeling. This is the work she was made for."

"Of course, milord," said Kerry, dipping a curtsey. There would be no further defense from her quarter.

I kept my eyes cast down as I said, "My apologies, milord, but the edges are sharp, and I—"

"You? You're a changeling charmaid doing the work she exists to complete."

Where was August? Slightly frantic, I looked past him to where my sister had been only a few seconds before. She was gone. This was Shadowed Hills, my uncle's demesne, and I was among my own kind; she had every reason to expect me not to be abused.

Shrinking back a little, I mumbled, "My mother forbids me to break my skin."

"Well, then, you'll have to be careful, won't you?" Quentin grabbed a dustpan from a nearby wall and shoved it into my free hand. "Clean up this mess."

There was nothing for it but to follow a direct order from my superior. "At once, milord," I said, and turned back to the pile of shards.

It looked even larger than it had a moment before, its myriad edges wickedly sharp. I bent to begin sweeping with as much care as I could manage.

The first two swipes of my broom were smooth and easy, and I kept my fingers well clear. I was beginning to think I might be able to achieve this without incident when something pressed against the small of my back, shoving me forward. My broom struck the edge of the dustpan, sending shards flying in all directions. I flinched as they struck my hand and arm, but managed not to drop the broom, only stood there, shaking, while I watched to see if I had broken the skin.

No blood rose, but I smelled it anyway. I glanced to Kerry in a panic, and saw my expression mirrored in her eyes.

"Meriel will get that, come now, let's go see Mama in the kitchen," she said, moving to grasp my shoulders and guide me toward the door. I let myself be steered away, only glancing back to see Quentin sneering after us. He didn't try to stop us, which only confirmed that his casual cruelty had managed to draw blood.

The smell of blood was getting stronger, but there was still no pain. Kerry led me into the knowe, away from the bustle and noise outside, toward a hidden door in the wall. She pressed her fingers against a decorative lily on the nearby mantel. With a click, the door swung open, and we were able to pass through it into the servant's hall.

I started to hyperventilate as soon as I knew we were alone, letting all my panic out at once. Kerry grabbed my arms.

"Breathe, Toby, breathe," she said. "You broke no rules. You touched no knives, plucked no roses. The cut was small. It's already healed. Mama will wash your face, and you'll be right as rain."

"I *bled*," I moaned. "I can *smell* it."

"You did," she said, voice soft. "You bled, and Mama will wash it away, dilute it in so much water that even an Undine could have no use of it. There won't be a scar. Your sister didn't see. No one will ever know."

"Mother will know."

"Not if we send you to take a load of laundry to Ilya. He can scrub you so clean that even Amandine won't be able to catch the scent."

Kerry was trying to sound reassuring, but I couldn't let myself believe her. Mother was the greatest blood-worker Faerie had ever known, or ever would know. She could pick up the scent of blood on a knife that hadn't been used in years but had been cleaned and polished a hundred times or more. She would know.

A thread of bitterness worked through my panic. *August* was allowed blood magic. *August* was allowed to learn to comprehend and control the gifts we had both presumably inherited from our mother. But I was not, for all that I was as much Amandine's daughter as she was. I had only illusions, which failed as often as not, and nothing of the blood that I was born to.

Why the rules should bind me so, when most changelings were allowed to freely use their talents, I did not fully understand. But as they were set, so I must obey, and if she smelled blood upon me when she returned home, even a speck, the punishment would be dire.

"Come now," said Kerry, taking my hand to lead me through the tangled maze of the knowe down into the kitchens, where her mother, Melly, stood over a pot of something rich and savory, occasionally calling out orders to the other Hobs who worked all around her. None of them spared us a second glance. Here, entirely among the servants, we were allowed to be invisible.

"That bastard squire of Etienne's shoved Toby while she was sweeping up some busted plates, and she got nicked," said Kerry, presenting me to her mother like a baby bird in need of care. "It's healed up already, of course, but there was blood."

"Oh, poor lamb!" said Melly, turning to me. Her eyes widened as she saw what Kerry was talking about, and she grabbed a hand towel, stepping down from the stool she'd been using to monitor her soup as she moved to wet it in a nearby basin. "She'll have to go to—"

"Ilya, yes," said Kerry. "August's upstairs."

"Whatever could have compelled the boy to assault her? Did she— oh, I hate the asking of this, I hate the sound of it, but did she do anything to provoke him?"

Melly seemed to realize I was shaking, and that I wouldn't be able to speak until it stopped. Cutting myself, even by mistake, was one of my greatest fears. I hadn't been allowed to slice my own bread until I was twenty, and Father often used the excuse of my inability to bleed as a reason that I would never be able to cook for an entire household on my own. Mother didn't know enough about keeping a kitchen to contradict him, and Father smelled comfortingly of blood at all times anyway.

"No," said Kerry, with a scowl. "She was helping us sweep, and he was talking to August. Then August went inside, and he come running over to make our day a misery."

"He's just plain cruel, that boy, and whatever household comes to claim him when his fosterage is finished, I hope they're a small and powerless one," said Melly, wiping my cheek with her warm cloth.

"Helen says she was able to get into the Library of Stars last week, and the librarian told her he's a prince," said Kerry.

"You shouldn't be talking to that girl, she's nothing but trouble, and even if he is a prince of some sort, you know better than to go digging into a blind fosterage," said Melly, voice gone surprisingly stern. She handed me the cloth with my blood on it. "Here. I'll get Ormond to put together a load of washing for you, and Ilya will have you right as rain in no time at all."

"Yes, ma'am," I finally managed to croak, and allowed Kerry to steer me back out of the kitchen.

Helen was an unaffiliated changeling, claimed by no specific household, flitting between them even outside the bounds of Moving Day, doing all the tasks good employers would never assign to someone they cared about. Because she was useful, she was allowed to continue as she was, but we all knew it was on sufferance: one day she'd go too far or stumble over an unseen line in the sand, and then she would be one more feast for the night-haunts, and one more sad story for us to whisper in the kitchens late in the afternoon.

But sometimes I envied her freedom. To be able to go wherever she wished, whenever she wished, with no concern that she would disgrace her family or attract the attention of one among the First. Oh, it must have been terribly hard. In some ways, it must also have been wonderful.

Kerry murmured quiet reassurances as she led me down the hall to a smaller room, where we stopped to wait for her uncle to arrive with the laundry. She guided me to a stool where I could sit. I fought not to start shaking again, the smell of my blood somehow even stronger now that it was coming from the fabric in my hand. "I'll be right back," she said, and hurried for the door. "Don't you move a muscle while I'm gone."

"Won't," I said, voice an unsteady croak, and watched as she slipped away.

Then, as if drawn by a hook in my cheek, I turned back toward the cloth in my hand.

It was such a small smear of blood, reddish-brown against the white cloth, still wet and pliable thanks to the water. It would still be viable. If a blood-worker were to get hold of it, they could do almost anything, they could tease out Mother's secrets, they could—

I froze, only realizing that the cloth was more than halfway to my mouth when I stopped lifting it. My throat was dry, so dry, like I was dying of dehydration, like I had never once been given a drop to drink. The water in the cloth would soothe it, I knew, would take the dryness away and leave me well refreshed.

I tried to force my hand back down. It refused to go. The cloth was so close, the smell of blood so heavy in my nose, like there was nothing else left in the world but that. Every scrap of me felt as if it were yearning toward that little speck of red, that cool expanse of white.

My magic wanted this. It wanted this as it had never wanted anything else. Finally, furiously, I gave in, and raised the cloth to my lips.

My blood tasted like my magic, copper and fresh-cut grass, and also like clean linen, fresh water, and then, with a jolt like touching a hot stove, like memory.

The memory felt almost like it was protected by a sugar shell, the fine layer of char and flavor that clung to the top of a crème brûlée. The blood dragged me down and through it, and the shell cracked, and I saw . . .

I'm in a room I've never seen before, one that's dark with shadows, next to a bed where a man sits, watching me with clear and loving eyes. No one looks at me like that, like I'm the whole world, and nothing else could ever matter more. Father looks at me with love, and August with adoration, but I know, without question, that this man would die for me.

I offer him my hands. After a momentary hesitation, he takes them, and his skin is warm, and this feels so real. I know this never happened. Why is my blood showing me such a beautiful lie?

In a kind, curious voice, he says, "Why am I concerned that whatever it is you're about to say will be in some way distressing?"

"I genuinely hope it's not going to be," I say, in the vision. "I mean, we've talked about it before."

"We've discussed a great many things." He eyes me warily. *"Many of them involve knives, blood, and screaming."*

The vision shattered there, and I snapped back into myself with a gasp, almost dropping the cloth. At the last moment, I managed to clench my fingers around it, and stayed as I was, staring off into the shadows.

What in Oberon's name was *that*?

FOUR

KERRY RETURNED IN SHORT order, carrying an armload of
kitchen washing. She dumped it on me, waiting until she was sure
I had everything, before she said apologetically, "Ma recommended
against a basket. If the blood on the washcloth brushed up against the
wood, it could be contaminated."

The comment caused a bolt of alarm to shoot through me. I sat up
straighter. "The shards from outside, what—"

"You didn't bleed enough for it to make it off your face, and the bit
of plate that cut you has already been fed into the fire," she said, reassuringly. "Meriel collected it as soon as she understood what had
happened. She was careful to keep it clutched tight in her fist and not let
it touch any of her clothing. She'll avoid your mother for the next few
months, should Amandine choose to grace us with her presence."

"I . . . I appreciate it," I said. "You're a good friend. My sister . . . ?"

"Is with Sir Grianne in the courtyard," said Kerry soothingly.
"She's a flirt, your sister, and no mistake of *that*. I'd say you have an
hour or better while she assumes you're preoccupied with the likes of
us, and she's preoccupied with flattering a pretty gray-skinned knight
she has no intention of courting."

"August does enjoy a good flirtation," I agreed, with a small smile.

"Enjoy? She's a scholar of flirtation. Eventually, books will be
written." Kerry beamed encouragingly as she helped me to my feet,
laundry still clutched in my arms. "Come along now. You've had a
shakeup, but nothing so bad as to keep you from chores, and Ma says
she'll have stew and bread for you when it's done."

My stomach gave an answering rumble, her comment reminding my body that food existed. I looked sourly down, then nodded to Kerry.

"All right," I said. "Let's go."

She led the way through the servants' halls to an outside door, and through it to the outbuildings on the grounds behind the manor. It might have made more sense for her to carry the washing, but an unoccupied changeling could be set any task a proper occupant of the Duchy wanted to set. This way, I was occupied with the laundry, and she was occupied with making sure I got where I needed to be. Anyone who wanted to interrupt us would need to have an excellent reason to do so, or we'd be able to take it to the Duke, my uncle, who would not favor someone trying to trouble his niece.

It was a good plan, elegantly enough assembled to fit together until we reached the square, squat building with no real frills or ornamentation that housed the laundry. It was the farthest outbuilding from the manor, far enough away to spare the pureblood residents the need to acknowledge that laundry still needed to be done. They preferred to think magic and Titania's beneficence were enough to fill their tables and sweep their floors, and woe betide the changeling who was too obvious with the domestic tasks that were meant to be ignored.

"Ilya is expecting us," Kerry assured me, leading me to the laundry door. She smiled again, this time reassuringly, before she opened the door and waved me inside.

The air was hot and steamy; we were both instantly soaked to the skin. Bubbling vats of cloth stood on all sides, while a vast fireplace took up an entire wall. And at the middle of it stood a stocky man with dark, messy hair, his shirtsleeves rolled up around his biceps and his eyes half-closed, as if he were asleep on his feet.

Looks can be deceiving. Ilya was a Bannick in a laundry. He could probably feel our heartbeats in the soles of his feet, and tell us what we'd had for breakfast yesterday.

"Last tub on the left," he said, with a vague gesture of one hand.

We wandered over there. The tub he'd indicated was barely more than half-full, bubbling away with a mixture of soap and what looked like sheets. With Kerry's help, I hoisted the load of kitchen washing to the edge and dumped it in, taking a long wooden paddle down from the wall and using it to mix the whole mess together. The blood remaining on the cloth would be diluted to nothingness in no time at all.

"Come on now," said Kerry, taking my elbow and tugging me back to Ilya. "Hey, Ilya."

"Hello, daughter of the hearth," he said politely, turning to regard her before swinging his head around to look at me. "Child of the crossroads."

"Uh, hi, Ilya," I said.

"We've had a little accident, and Ma said to ask you to scrub us down," said Kerry.

Ilya looked back at her. "Is that so?"

Kerry twinkled. "I can bake you tea cakes if you do."

Ilya appeared to think about this for a long while. Finally, expression never changing, he nodded. "It will do," he said. "Hold your breath, please."

I took a breath and screwed my eyes as tightly shut as they would go, holding that position as a wave of hot, soapy water crashed over me. Only a few seconds later, it withdrew, leaving me perfectly dry. Even the sweat from the steam was gone, although it would return if we lingered there.

Kerry clearly knew that. She grabbed my hand again, chirping, "Tea cakes tomorrow night. Bye, Ilya! We appreciate the save!" as she dragged me out of the laundry and into the comparatively cool morning air.

Not that it was morning there. No sign of sunlight had come to Shadowed Hills.

Kerry looked me critically up and down before she smiled. "Better," she said.

"It's not going to fool my mother," I said.

"Ah, but see, it doesn't need to fool anyone," she said. "It happened, it has been washed away, and your mother will never know unless she comes looking. It's not lying to her to hold your tongue; we both know you'd tell the truth if she asked you directly, 'Hey, did Etienne's smug fucker of a squire make you bleed?' We just need her not to think she needs to ask. And I'm pretty sure we've achieved that."

"You're a good friend, Kerry."

"I am, aren't I?" She preened a little, beaming. "Now come on. Let's get you something to eat before your sister comes and drags you off again."

Willingly, I followed her back into the knowe and through the halls to the kitchen, where Melly settled us in a safe nook with bowls of stew and loaves of fresh, steaming bread. Kerry said nothing until she'd seen me take several large bites, and then, voice mild, she asked, "Has Moving Day been very bad this year?"

I swallowed, hard. "Why would you ask that?"

"Because while we're used to seeing you here after it's through, you don't normally look this worn-away before we've even reached the main event. They ask too much of you."

I looked down at my stew. "I do only the duty Faerie asks of me."

"D'you know how many people His Grace has minding the doors during the nights?" When I didn't answer, Kerry huffed and said, "Six! In shifts! So no one has to do it alone, or for more than a few hours! And *we* have the space and staff to say yes once in a while, when they're not running from someone who's likely to take offense to us adopting their misfits."

"You can't take offense at someone leaving on Moving Day," I said, blinking at her. "Oberon himself decreed—"

"Oberon also said purebloods weren't allowed to kill each other, and look how often *that* happens," Kerry countered. "Oberon isn't here, and people pay less attention to his rules than they do to looking like they're following his rules. Your parents do you no favors, sheltering you in that tower, letting you go along thinking the whole world is these two demesnes. The world is a lot crueler to changelings than it seems when you're standing here, nice and safe and tucked away."

"Not *that* safe," I said sourly, thinking of Quentin's hand against the small of my back, the way he'd tried to shove me down.

"Yes, *that* safe," said Kerry. "Everyone here knows that if they hurt you, really *hurt* you, they'd have to answer to your father, and to the Duke. Maybe it's unfashionable, but we're an unfashionable Duchy. The Duke doesn't much care about what's in fashion. Outside the Duchy, it's not like that."

"I've heard some stories."

"And if you think no one ever finds a way to claim offense against someone for running away, you haven't believed near half of them as well as you should. Maybe they don't claim it against the one who left. Maybe they claim it against their new liege. Maybe they claim it against someone who stayed behind. Maybe they go back fifty years and find something no one took offense to at the time it happened, then use that as a lever. Even here, we have to be careful."

I thought of the family of Hamadryads from earlier, and felt sick. "What about Golden Shore?"

"They do things differently there, always have," said Melly, coming over with two more bowls of stew. "People have tried to reclaim changelings who've made it past the borders, but none have succeeded."

"Supposedly they still have *shapeshifters* there," said Kerry, dropping her voice like she was sharing a delicious, dangerous secret.

I stared at her. "They would *never.*"

According to the old histories, many of Maeve's lost children had been so bestial that they could change shapes between something decently presentable and something entirely animal. They couldn't be trusted after their mother betrayed us, of course, and an exception to the Law had been made to allow for the removal of such undesirable elements from our society. Fae who bore animal aspects but cleaved to a single shape were fine, if distasteful; the King and Queen of Golden Shore were Ceryneian Hinds, Daoine Sidhe from the waist up, golden-furred deer from the waist down. They knew their place, and without forgetting it, they had managed to claim a crown. So long as they stayed safely in a single shape, they could be trusted.

Chrysanthe and Theron had built a haven for changelings on the Golden Shore—one that was apparently even more important than I had realized. Surely they wouldn't risk that for the sake of saving a few wild animals who had never truly belonged to Faerie in the first place.

Melly put a hand on Kerry's shoulder, frowning at the younger Hob. "Of course they would never, and decent ladies don't speak of such things," she said, firmly.

"I'm not a decent lady, Mama, I'm a changeling," said Kerry, with a degree of cheek I would never have directed at my own parents, not even Father. "A decent lady would be courting and thinking of a household of her own, not sitting patiently and waiting for the day the Duke decides she has to move along to another knowe or take a changeling husband and do her duty."

"Hush now," said Melly, as she moved away. "His Grace has been better to us than we deserve, and we owe him the recognition of that fact."

"Yes, Mama," said Kerry meekly.

She watched Melly move away, then returned her attention to me. "They ask too much," she said again. "Eventually, you're going to be crushed under the weight of what they ask from you."

"You've never spoken like this before," I said. "Are you all right?"

"You've never seemed this likely to listen," she countered, before sighing. "Yes. No. I don't know. Moving Day has been . . . rough, this year, even with the six of us standing shifts. A lot of people seem to be fleeing Wild Strawberries. It makes me wonder what might have changed up there."

"Maybe Father knows," I said. "His patron would know if anything had changed, and she might have said something. I can ask him."

Kerry blinked. "You think he would answer?"

"Father? Yes. Mother . . ." I hesitated. "Perhaps not."

A murmur swept through the kitchen, sharp and strained and quickly quieted. Melly's ladle clicked as she set it against the rim of her stew pot, metal meeting metal, stepping down from her stool once again. This time, she didn't approach us but moved toward the door.

"How may I be of assistance, lady?" she asked, tone all deference.

"I heard you were sheltering my sister," said August, voice ringing through the quiet kitchen like a royal proclamation. "I appreciate it, but she's my responsibility, and I'd appreciate her return."

"No," said Kerry, before I could rise. Her hand shot out, catching my wrist and keeping me in place. "You need to finish eating."

"Then August will be joining us," I said. Where I found the boldness, I may never know. I twisted in my chair to look toward the kitchen door, where August towered over Melly. Hobs tend to be fairly diminutive people; Kerry was the tallest in the kitchen by almost a full foot, and she stood easily eight inches shorter than I did. Among them, August and I were giants.

"August!" I called. "Over here!"

August's eyes snapped to me in an instant, and her shoulders drooped with obvious relief as she hurried in my direction. "Meriel told me what Quentin did," she said, dropping into the third chair at our little table. "How *dare* that little worm put his hands on you?"

No mention of my having bled. A small knot of tension untied itself within my chest. "I wasn't hurt," I said. "Kerry took me to get the dirt off my dress before our parents could come home and see it. I'm fine, August, truly."

"He should never have touched you."

"It's worked out for the best," said Kerry, and quailed as August shot her a sharp look. ". . . my lady," she added.

I studied that look. Was there a disdain there that wasn't present when my sister looked at me? Did she think of changelings the way everyone around us did, and conceal it only for my sake? The idea was repulsive, but I couldn't stop myself from seeking signs, especially when Kerry looked so afraid.

"Why would you say that?" asked August. "My *sister.* He put his hands on my *sister* while I was distracted. He had no right."

"Faerie says he had every right, Aug," I said. "He's a pureblood, I'm a changeling, I wasn't sweeping fast enough, and he disciplined me. Without you or our parents there to tell him not to, he had every right. Please don't yell at my friends because he did something you didn't like, but broke no rules."

"Maybe they're bad rules," August grumbled. "I still want to know what she meant by saying this was for the best."

"Only that Toby had clearly not eaten in quite some time, and his bad behavior has allowed us to feed her," said Kerry. "*And* it meant I got a break, which I appreciate, even if Meriel likely doesn't. She'll take it out of me tomorrow morning, when the big party begins. Will the two of you be in attendance?"

There was a caution to that question, even if she seemed to have otherwise relaxed. For me to attend the party Uncle Sylvester was hosting, someone would have to be committed to staying with me at all times. Otherwise, this could happen again, or even worse.

August shook her head. "I don't think so this year." She turned to me. "Have you eaten enough?"

My bowl was almost empty, and my bread was long since gone. I paused to focus on my stomach. It no longer rumbled but felt full and content. "I'm good," I said.

"Excellent. Uncle Sylvester wanted to see us both before we returned home."

That could be a very good thing, or a very bad one. Uncle Sylvester's moods were famously unpredictable, calm and reasonable one moment, raging at nothing the next. Still, Kerry released my wrist as August stood, beckoning for me to follow.

"I'll see you soon," I told Kerry, and followed my sister out of the kitchen.

With her, I walked the main halls of the knowe, not the hidden servants' corridors. It would have been unseemly for her to use them, and besides, she would have made the actual servants uncomfortable. Purebloods like the Hobs and the knowe's single Bannick were one thing; they were staff. August, though . . . she might have no title of her own, but everyone knew she was going to inherit the Duchy someday. Uncle Sylvester had no other heirs.

She kept her hand tucked into the bend of my arm as we walked, making sure anyone who saw us knew that I was under her protection.

"I'm sorry, Toby," she said, once she was sure we were alone. "He's never been that bold before."

"He's never been a squire before, either." We walked a bit farther in silence before I asked, "Do you know why Uncle Sylvester wants to see us?"

"No," she said. "I was looking for you when Sir Etienne popped in with a message. He seemed dismayed that we weren't together."

"Maybe he knows his new squire's a jerk."

"You know, you're right. What did he *see* in the little weasel?"

"You were the one going on about flirting with him to watch him blush, remember?"

"Yes, but I'm a sheltered young girl of good breeding and little experience. I'm allowed to be wrong about boys. Etienne, on the other hand, is teaching the weasel how to swing a sword and uphold the rules of etiquette and all that other knight-and-squire nonsense, and he should have better judgment than that. One day, just imagine. Sir Quentin." August shuddered theatrically. "He'll have a family name by then, and with a name and a knighthood, he might be good enough to petition Father for my hand."

"Thinking highly of yourself today, aren't you?"

"Worrying about my sister," August countered. "I'm it for the Dóchas Sidhe. You know I'll be expected to marry long enough to have children, and you know your future depends on me taking you with me when that happens. If they marry me off to the weasel, I can't take you. He'd have you dead inside the year."

I grimaced. "Father would *never.*"

"Depending on his family, once it's revealed, Mother might."

I couldn't really argue with that, much as I might want to; August was right. Titania's edicts said the pursuit of political power was as much the duty of the Firstborn as the creation of descendant lines and the birthing of changelings. If that bastard Quentin turned out to come from a powerful family, Oberon forbid, Mother *might* think he'd make a good match for August, and I could wind up in a household with a man who loathed me when he had power enough to assault me in the open rather than hiding his malice away behind closed doors.

It was a terrifying thought, and thankfully, I didn't have long to dwell on it before we were rounding a bend in the hall and approaching the tall oak doors of Uncle Sylvester's receiving room.

"He's lucid today," said August, touching my arm with her free hand. "I think he's in one of his good patches. I'll bet you a sink of dishes next time Mother's away that he can tell us apart."

"Is that a fair bet, if you've already seen him today?"

She dimpled at me. "Maybe I just want an excuse to do the dishes."

I laughed, and was still laughing when she pressed her palm against the door and it swung smoothly open. It looked as if it should have creaked, like the hinges should have squealed and protested, but looks can be deceiving. Melly would *never* have tolerated such signs of disrepair in her own home, *never*.

I stopped laughing.

August gave my arm a reassuring squeeze and stepped into the receiving room, pulling me with her.

The receiving room had been constructed during a time when Uncle Sylvester thought he would eventually court and marry, building a household filled with laughter and with love. My grandparents had apparently been the loving kind, genuinely devoted to each other, compassionate and caring where their children were concerned, and that was the model both their living sons had looked to live up to. But while Father had been fortunate enough to find a wife who cared less for power and station than she did for warm soup and a loving spouse, Uncle Sylvester's attempts at courting had been thwarted again and again, until he had stopped trying and fallen into a deep depression.

He had been in that deep depression for several hundred years now, and seemed to like it there. He sought no lovers, looked for no one to share his demesne, and as long as his Court operated smoothly, the Queen of the Mists left him alone. Depressed Dukes in backwater Duchies weren't likely to raise armies against her or attempt revolutions, after all, and she had her hands full with the rest of the nobility.

In addition to being large enough to contain an entire Court that never came, the receiving room was dark, the windows shrouded by layer upon layer of gossamer-thin cobweb silk. Each of those curtain panels was worth enough to have bought a commoner like me anything we could possibly have wanted, but they were a compromise here; before installing the curtains, Uncle Sylvester had apparently tried to dim the light through the windows with actual spider webs, sending the household staff into absolute fits. I almost wished I could have seen that. Except not, because an angry Hob is a *terrifying* thing.

The floor was black-and-white checkerboard marble, pristine, even as the light through the curtains turned the white squares a grimy gray. The door slammed shut behind us as August and I started across that floor. Neither of us jumped. We were both well accustomed to Shadowed Hills and its theatrics. Instead, we walked toward the far end of the room, where a dais in deepest shadow held a single central chair.

In that chair sat our Uncle Sylvester, chin resting on his hand, apparently content to be all but invisible to me. I frowned, but said nothing.

August was not so decorous.

"You *know* October's eyes are less suited to the shadows than our own," she said, voice gone peevish, and snapped her fingers. A ball of witch-light rose from her hand, glowing bright as an oil lamp as it drifted to a point just above our heads, illuminating the area. "There now. That's better."

"Is it?" he asked, dryly.

Uncle Sylvester was a tall, fair-skinned man with fox-fur red hair and golden eyes, and would have been identical to our Father in every regard had he looked as if he'd enjoyed a solid meal or a hot bath any time in the last five years. As it was, he was a ragged scarecrow of a man, skin less fair than sallow, hair less bright than greasy and garish, until it seemed he flirted with the edge of unattractiveness . . . or at least as close to same as the Daoine Sidhe can come. His clothing was tattered but clean. Melly would have tolerated nothing less, and while she wasn't officially chatelaine, Etienne had no head for the job. He was often absent when not on duty, and allowed her to manage most of the duties that would have accompanied the position.

"It is, Uncle," I said, with a small curtsey. "I appreciate being allowed to see to whom I am speaking. August said you wanted to speak with us both?"

"My nieces. My dearly beloved, closest family." He sat up, then leaned back in his seat, slumping. "Am I not allowed to desire your presence?"

"You're allowed, but you usually don't," I said. "Or you only want to talk to August, since she's, you know . . ." I fumbled for words before I finished, "The important one."

"Yes, but we're near to Moving Day, which changes the pieces on the board." His eyes were sharp as he looked between us. "Have you ever been to Dreamer's Glass?"

"The Duchy to the south?" I asked, perplexed. "I haven't. There's been no need. August?"

"Only once, a long time ago," she said. "I was much younger at the time. Mother took me to oversee the dismantling of a failed fiefdom. Chained Thunder, or something of the like? We stayed in Dreamer's Glass, for the safety of a politically secure demesne around us while we slept. Has something happened?"

"The Duchess of Dreamer's Glass has requested the presence of a member of the Ducal line, on what she considers to be a matter of grave importance," said Sylvester.

"Li Qin Zhou is in charge of Dreamer's Glass," said August.

"I'm glad to see the hours spent in drilling you on the local nobility have not been wasted," said a dry voice from behind her.

We turned in unison, both of us beaming and already delighted. "Father!"

"Hello, my flowers," said our father, Simon Torquill, who had slipped into the room while we were distracted talking to his brother—older brother by almost an hour, as Uncle Sylvester sometimes took delight in reminding us. "Imagine my surprise when I returned early to the tower and found it standing empty, warded and alone. The kitchen window broken, my flowers fled."

"I'm sorry, Father," I began automatically, prepared to draw the blame for our mutual transgression. I didn't remember a broken window, but that didn't mean there hadn't been one. I could be so careless sometimes. "Only we were hungry and—"

"And I insisted," said August. "We missed the party. I wanted to scavenge for cake. We thought we had hours before anyone would be home, and there was nothing to eat but bread and cheese."

"Nothing sufficient for a pair of growing girls," Father agreed. "Very well, then. If you must make mischief, best it were made in this direction. Your uncle will not see you come to harm, even if he will see fit to speak to you of distant shores without the presence of your parents."

"Both girls have passed their majority, and have the right to make decisions for themselves," said Uncle Sylvester. Father gave him a blank look. "It's true! If they want to travel to Dreamer's Glass, they can choose to do so."

"And why should they choose such?"

"As I was saying when you decided to interrupt us, Duchess Zhou has requested the presence of a member of my immediate bloodline. Meaning one of the two of us, or one of the girls."

I wasn't sure how that could possibly work. Faerie considered me my father's child in every way that mattered, but he hadn't sired me; there was nothing of his bloodline in my veins. August, meanwhile . . . he was her father in truth as well as custom, but all four of us knew Mother had pulled even the echo of the Daoine Sidhe out of her first-born child before August had even exited her womb. He had no current part in the body of either one of us. Unless Uncle Sylvester married or lay with a human, the Torquill bloodline was at an end.

From the complicated look on his face, Father knew that, even as he knew that saying it would be a terrible betrayal of Faerie custom and could endanger us all. Smoothing his expression, he looked coolly at Uncle Sylvester and said, "Then you should go."

"I can't. The Duchy needs me. I may be a figurehead, but I'm *their* figurehead, and my absence this close to Moving Day would raise more questions than my staff would like to answer."

"Then I—"

"Is the Rose of Winter in such a generous mood that she would let her favorite dogsbody leave with so little notice right before a night of parties she intends to grace with her glorious presence? Some of which may feature her liege, the Queen of the Mists, while others may involve her mother?"

Father looked away.

"I thought not. And your wife is not of our bloodline. That leaves your girls. Either would do, although the timing of the request means our options are more open than they would be during most of the year."

I frowned, curious. "What do you mean, Uncle?"

"Only that Moving Day is in two days." He smiled, showing teeth that could use a good scrubbing. "A growing girl must chafe at being sealed in a tower for no crime of her own. I know your father and I chafed when we were boys and our parents were overprotective."

"Don't," cautioned Father.

Uncle Sylvester ignored him. "But right now, with the changelings of the Kingdom free to move about as they will, immune to being claimed by the nobles whose lands they pass through, you could go to Dreamer's Glass. Sir Etienne could take you that far, quite easily so, and you could meet with Duchess Zhou before returning here to tell me what she needed so dearly that she would summon a member of my own family to accomplish it."

"Duchess Zhou is Shyi Shuai," said August. "They manipulate luck."

"Unfashionable, yes, but not Seers," said Uncle Sylvester. "It's very likely that she tried to bend the luck around some project of hers and found it would succeed if she had a Torquill present, but fail without one."

"Descendants of Maeve," said August. "How did they miss the purges?" She glanced to Father. "I would have expected the Summer Queen to have declared their tinkering with fate to be a step too close to prophecy, and had them removed."

"When you can twist luck to your own ends, is it such a stretch to assume you might twist it such that you'd be overlooked when something terrible was happening to people like but not *exactly* like yourself?" asked Uncle Sylvester.

"Surely you didn't mean to imply that a descendant line of the Traitor Queen could be more powerful than the Fair Titania," said Father, his own voice a warning.

"Not at all. Just that they might have been beneath her notice. Left to live because they didn't matter." He shrugged. "Diplomatically, it's a good thing for me to answer when a nearby regent calls for aid, and she's asked for something small enough. She says her request is of the utmost urgency, and so I would like to send someone before Moving Day. Because she's willing to accept *any* member of the family, I'd prefer to send her October. Give the girl an adventure when it's safe to do so, perhaps frighten her into another few decades of good behavior before she grows old enough and *Torquill* enough to get restless and start wondering why the burden of her birth should fall upon her own shoulders."

Father sighed, shoulders sagging. "You know Amy will have my head for this."

"Yes, but she'll grow you a new one, and you said she wasn't expected back from Silences until midway through the month. October will be long gone and back again before Amy is an issue."

"It's October's choice. Even this close to Moving Day, there may be those who want to take advantage of the fact that assaulting a changeling is no violation of the Law." Father looked to me, expression earnest. "Well, my sweet girl? What say you?"

I bit my lip. "August needs my help in the tower, preparing for Moving Day," I said.

"I can send a few members of my household to assist her," said Uncle Sylvester. "She need not be alone in your father's absence."

"I think it might be good for me to handle some of the duties myself.

To see what it's like," said August. "I can't be sheltered from reality forever, Father."

"No, I suppose you can't. But the choice is still your sister's. We'll not force her one way or the other," said Father. "I won't forbid it, however badly I want to keep you both safe. I won't command it, either, because that would be cruel and a father should never be cruel to his children. He should love them, and protect them when he can, and support them when he can't."

"Then this time, I'd like you to support me," I said, slowly. "I think I'd like to go to Dreamer's Glass. To meet with the Duchess, and see why she needs a Torquill so badly that she'd accept the least among us. Mother won't be happy when she hears, but if the choice is mine, I'd like to go."

FIVE

THINGS MOVED QUICKLY AFTER my decision was made. Uncle Sylvester called for Sir Etienne, and for Melly, both of whom arrived with remarkable promptness. Melly brought a traveling pack, implying that she'd been waiting for exactly this call, and Sir Etienne brought a scowl but not his squire, which was the best I could have hoped for under the circumstances. I stood next to August and held her hand as Father and Uncle Sylvester discussed my upcoming trip with the staff in low tones.

She looked at me, clearly worried. "You don't *have* to do this, Toby."

"I do, though. It's only safe for me because it's almost Moving Day. The rest of the year, I stay locked in the tower or I risk being hurt, or worse. If I have a window of safety, I should grab it when I have the chance. Even if—maybe especially if—I'm afraid of what could happen. Courage isn't knowing everything will be fine. It's knowing everything might not be, and doing what needs to be done anyway, because someone has to. Besides, would you rather go?"

August wrinkled her nose. "Not in the least. I didn't care for Dreamer's Glass the last time I was there."

"But at least you've *been* there. I haven't really been *anywhere* but home and here. Mother would take you with her when she travels, if only you were to ask. I, on the other hand, would get a very kind lecture about remembering my place and appreciating how good I have things at home. I don't want to sit home and appreciate things. I want to go out and *see* things. I want to be a part of Faerie." I stood a little straighter. "I want to go."

"Then you must, but you also must come home to me." She seized my other hand. "Please, Toby, promise. Promise you won't take any needless risks, you won't try to be brave because you feel like you ought to be. Promise you'll come home to me."

She looked like she was on the verge of tears. I squeezed her hands and said the only thing I had to say: "I promise."

"Good." She let me go abruptly, stepping away. "Good. I love you. You can go. I'll be here when you get back."

Then she turned and fled the room, leaving me blinking after her. August and I had rarely been apart since my birth, but that still seemed like a fairly extreme reaction. I hadn't been expecting that.

Then again, I hadn't been expecting any of this. I was still blinking when Melly approached, holding out the parcel she'd brought with her.

"Human clothing is more form-fitting, and tends to be machine-stitched unless you're wealthy," she said. "These should fit you. You'll want to change as soon as you have the chance. The less magic you have to spend on your disguises, the better. This is already going to be a strain on your illusions."

I hadn't even thought of that. I cast a half-panicked glance at Father, clutching the parcel to my chest. He stepped away from Uncle Sylvester, moving over to me.

"I can walk you through the first illusion," he said. "Since you haven't had much exposure to humans, it'll be easier this way. Once that's done, you'll know what you need to re-cast every morning. You'll be gone two days at most, and two disguises should be easily within your capability, even if you've never had a talent for illusions. All right?"

"A-all right," I said, growing more uncertain by the moment. It was as if August had taken all my bravery with her when she ran away.

"That's my good brave girl."

"I've packed you a lunch as well, since I've no idea what sort of standards they keep in Dreamer's Glass," said Melly. "And there's one of those human telephone devices in there. Sir Etienne has one as well, and his number is programmed into yours. All you need to do is hit the button with the little book printed on it, and then press the only number that comes up, and it will call him."

"I can't answer if I'm patrolling the grounds or outside the knowe," cautioned Etienne. "It took a Gremlin acquaintance of mine weeks to convince those phones to call into or out of the Summerlands, and we can't rely on them at all times. Try not to have any emergencies if you can help it."

"I don't think emergencies are the sort of thing you decide to have," I said, forcing myself not to ask why he would have gone to all the trouble. Perhaps they were short on staff, and he had finally decided to get a changeling of his own to add to the knowe's service. I couldn't think of much other reason the stiffest of Uncle Sylvester's pureblood knights would have been seeking reliable contact with the human world.

And there wasn't time to worry about that, because Father was sliding his arm around my shoulders and guiding me toward a door at the back of the room, one which led to a small dressing room intended for use during parties, when the lesser nobles showed up unprepared and had to weave themselves an outfit for the evening. I didn't resist.

The room was small but warm and comfortable, with a series of screens set up to block off one wall. He motioned me toward them. "Go change," he said, and so I went, too anxious to do anything but obey a direct order.

The parcel Melly had given me contained a brassiere—a piece of human underclothing I was actually acquainted with, as August had brought a few of them home after her trips with Mother, and found their easy emulation of a corset's support hilarious—and a pair of underpants, which would have been scandalous if not for the fact that August had brought those home at the same time, as well as a plain black top, and trousers of a stiff blue material that hugged my legs too tightly to be considered entirely decent. They fit properly, and I zipped and buttoned them into place, trying to ignore the uncomfortable way they enclosed my rump and genitals. Nothing that felt that intimate should be worn out in public.

There was a knife as well, soft silver with a spell-hardened edge, and a belt to keep it fastened at my hip. My gut lurched when I pulled it out of the parcel, and I stopped, staring at the tool—the weapon—the *tool* I was being handed for my own protection. It felt too easy in my hand. It was a thing intended only for the drawing of blood, and if I carried this, I knew, deep down and with absolute certainty, that I *would* bleed.

A sharp crack of pain followed the thought, rattling my head and stopping me from examining that certainty too deeply. I hurried to do up the belt, reaching back into the parcel, and paused as my fingers touched leather. Frowning in mild confusion, I pulled a black leather jacket out of the cloth wrapping, holding it up against myself to check the size. It was heavy and thick, stopping barely shy of armor, and it jangled with zippers and with buttons.

"Are you all right in there, October?"

"I'm fine, Father," I said, still looking at the jacket. I had never seen this before. I still ached as if I had.

The vision. The image I'd seen in the blood, of the dark room and the strange man who looked at me like I was his entire world. I'd been wearing this jacket in my vision.

We know so little about the Dóchas Sidhe. Both Father and the Rose of Winter insist that August and I share a descendant line, since only Mother's contributions to the making of us carry any real weight. Even among the more settled sorts of fae, like the Daoine Sidhe, siblings may have dissimilar talents, and if our magic was not precisely matched, that didn't mean our blood differed. But we might still prove to be a line of Seers, and then we would go the way of all Seers. August and I—

Nope. I shoved the thought aside and donned the jacket, rolling my shoulders until it hung correctly. The leather carried a faint scent of pennyroyal, which seemed somewhat out of place; maybe they'd been storing it with the herbs for some reason?

Wherever it had been prior to this, it was on me now. Hesitantly, I stepped out from behind the screen and spread my arms for Father to see.

He straightened, blinking suddenly bright eyes. "Oh, my sweet girl," he said, before the silence could become uncomfortable. "My dear, sweet girl. You look ready to take on the world."

"I don't *feel* ready," I said, walking toward him.

He put an arm around my shoulder, guiding me to a mirror. "Oh, don't say that. I have to be ready to let you. Now, for this first illusion, we're going to lean on my magic, and just let yours trace the shape of what I'm doing for you. Do you understand? Don't try to push or put any force into it, only gather your magic and let it wrap around mine."

I nodded, worrying my lip between my teeth.

"Good girl. Now." Father looked to my reflection, and the air around us grew rich with the scent of smoke and mulled cider. "Mortals don't have pointed ears, so we'll need to round those down." As his magic brushed my ears, their reflection grew rounder and rounder, becoming human. "Your cheekbones aren't too sharp to be mortal-born, but they're on the striking side. Most humans your age and build are rounder, facially speaking, and you'll have an easier time if you look unremarkable." His magic moved downward, softening the bones of my face, until I looked like myself but a stranger at the same time, someone I had only ever seen in dreams.

He went on to adjust the color of my hair and eyes, making both of them a bit more saturated, a little less like a faded painting of my mother, and finished with my hands, making the fingers ever so slightly shorter, until at last he stepped away and proclaimed me acceptably human, someone who could pass other humans on the street and never raise an eyebrow.

"Now, poppet, do you think your magic can remember this shape?" he asked. "Be honest with me, now. The illusion won't hold beyond the morning sun, and I can't go with you to re-cast it."

"It itches," I said, rubbing one ear. "But yes, I think I can do it." My magic had risen in response to his, and while I still wouldn't trust it for anything more complicated than this relatively simple series of changes, I was reasonably sure I could replicate what he'd done, as long as I didn't have to do it in a hurry.

"My *brave* girl," he said, kissing my forehead. "See to it that you're back with us before Moving Day. I refuse to lose you because I sent you to do a service to the family."

"I promise," I said, and smiled as he took my hand and led me back into the receiving room.

August gasped when she saw me. It was gratifying. Even if she wasn't gasping at my beauty or my brilliance, I had still surprised my sister.

Melly bustled over to me. "Aren't you a sight?" she asked.

"Melly, where did you find this jacket?"

"In the closet where we keep all the human things people have discarded here over the years," she said, waving the question away. "It looked to be about your size, and so I thought it would serve you well. Does it not fit right? Would you prefer another?"

"No. No, this one is perfect. I was just curious." I forced another smile, heart pounding, as Sir Etienne walked over to us. He bowed. I blinked. Knights weren't supposed to bow to *me*. Melly dug her elbow into my side. I yelped and quickly curtseyed my answer.

He was smiling when I straightened. Interesting.

"We must be going," he said, drawing a wide circle in the air with one hand. The scent of cedar smoke and limes rose, and where he had moved his hand, a circular window into someplace *else* appeared.

It was a large, well-appointed hall, the floors teak, the walls draped with banners showing the arms of Dreamer's Glass. No people moved there. I gaped.

Tuatha de Dannan bend space to suit themselves. There aren't many of them among the Courts, and those who serve do so at the very pinnacle of their households, because their uses are near-infinite. Sir Etienne could have gone anywhere and found himself treated like a lord, and this was a harsh reminder of that fact.

Why did he stay there, in a backwater Duchy with a broken Duke, when he could have had so much more? Why not reach for what Faerie offered him?

Then he took my hand and pulled me with him through the circle, which closed behind us, and we were somewhere else, just the two of us. I had never been alone with him before.

"I had hoped it would be you," he said, releasing my hands so he could grab my shoulders. "August would never have agreed to help me. October. I *know* what your bloodline can do. I *know* how your magic bends. And I need your help. My daughter—"

But that was ridiculous. Sir Etienne was unmarried, and had never agreed to do his duty in the mortal world. I stared at him, utterly perplexed, until he let go of my shoulders and stepped away, his own shoulders drooping.

"I should have known," he said. "She's kept too tight a hand for too long, and—I should have known."

"Should have known what?" I asked, but he was already gone, opening another portal in the air, this one to a sunlit street lined with unfamiliar trees and houses that looked like the ones I'd sometimes seen in a mortal magazine, or in a painted picture. It closed behind him, and I was by myself in a strange place, in this room that smelled like incense and unfamiliar magic, the walls so lush with tapestry that they swallowed the sound of my feet on the hardwood floor.

I turned a slow circle, looking around. Dreamer's Glass. I was in Dreamer's Glass. Miles from Shadowed Hills, from the *tower*. I had never been this far from home, or my family, in my entire life. If I messed up there, I might never be this far again.

Duchess Zhou had requested me, which meant I had the hospitality of her house until well past Moving Day. That was a good thing; it would stop people from deciding they were allowed to harm me just because I was a changeling. But I didn't know the rules there, and I would need to be even more careful than I usually was if I wanted to avoid crossing any lines.

Taking care began with staying calm. I forced myself to breathe slow and steady, until I was breathing at a regular pace and my head felt less like it was going to fall off. I had barely managed to get my equilibrium back when someone behind me began to applaud.

I turned. A petite woman in a long red gown was there, standing in front of an open door, applauding vigorously. Her hair was short and black, perfectly straight, cut across the bottom like she had done it with a sword of some sort, and her skin was a tawny shade of brown that perfectly offset her completely black eyes. She had no irises or sclera, just what looked like an all-consuming pupil filling them from one side to the other. It was unnerving, and gave her the air of watching through dark glasses or some other form of personal concealment.

She smiled at me.

"I was expecting the older daughter, I'll admit, but I meant it when I told your uncle that any of you would do perfectly well. I did somewhat hope it would be you. Everyone's very curious about the hidden Torquill girl, and anything I can learn will be coin and currency the next time I go to the Library."

I frowned. "I don't understand why a Librarian would be curious about me. I'm no one important."

"Ah, because your mother is Firstborn, and your parents have been very careful never to reveal or record more than the barest necessities. Your name, your date of birth, and the holding to which you're bound are the extent of what the Library has on record about you."

I knew changelings belonged to their fae parents in every sense of the phrase, but I still bristled at the word "bound." The stranger, whom I assumed was Duchess Zhou, nodded at that, seeming oddly pleased. Then she bowed.

"My manners have faded in isolation," she said. "I am Li Qin Zhou, Duchess of Dreamer's Glass, and you are welcome in my domain. I extend to you the hospitality of my home; none will raise hand nor word against you in my presence or with my approval so long as you walk my halls, and should you give me cause to regret this, you will have three days to vacate my demesne before you will be held responsible for your presence."

"I'm not going to be here past Moving Day, ma'am," I said, then froze, feeling as if I had already made a massive misstep. "I mean, Your Grace. Your Grace, ma'am. I'm supposed to help with whatever you needed a Torquill for, and then go home before my mother gets back from her assignment in Silences and worries about me."

"They haven't taught you much in the way of subtlety, have they?" she asked, sounding amused, and beckoned for me to follow her through the doorway, deeper into the knowe. "Not that I suppose you'd have much need of it, confined to a tower and all."

"I'm not *confined*," I said, bristling again. "I could leave any time I wanted to."

"It's just that you'd have nowhere to go, I suppose."

The hall on the other side of the door was more of the same, all of it very grand and towering. I was beginning to regret the human disguise Father had woven for me, but because it wasn't my magic, I couldn't dismiss it even if I tried. The itching in my ears was distracting enough that I missed half of what Li Qin was saying, and snapped back into the conversation just in time to catch:

"—odd configuration, so I asked the luck, and the luck seemed to think a member of your family would be the answer. I've got no idea why. The last time I saw your mother and sister, they couldn't get out of here quickly enough. It would have been insulting, if it hadn't been so damned funny. You really do live like it's still medieval times out there in Shadowed Hills, don't you?"

I blinked. "I'm not sure what you mean by that, so I'm afraid to answer one way or another. I don't want to insult my home by accident, and I don't want to refute something that's actually a good thing."

Li Qin laughed. "Oh, you're charming! The unspoilt ones always are, of course."

"Do you have any changelings here that I could speak with? I wouldn't want to step on any toes . . ."

"Some members of the household staff have done their duty, and reduced the workload for their fellows, but they're mostly in the kitchens or the scriptorium."

"You have a scriptorium?"

"Naturally. This is the seat of modern human innovation. Silicon Valley is where the mortals go to dream tomorrow's dreams. Faerie can't be left ignorant of what's going on outside our doors, however much we might want to pretend we can just ignore the humans and they'll eventually go away. So my people watch them, work with them, learn their secrets, and write them out for other noble households to comprehend. We're quite wealthy, really, since we've been able to get in on the ground floor of various human enterprises. Which is why you're here today."

I frowned. "Come again?"

"Sometimes my people stumble across . . . call them 'business opportunities,' and they have a certain amount of freedom when it comes to acting on them," said Li Qin, stopping in front of a plain wood door and producing a key from inside a pocket. She slid it into the keyhole, flashing me a sunny smile as she did. "They bring all *sorts* of weird junk home. One of my better finders is a Coblynau named Siôn who has an incredible gift for finding human collectibles. He bought roughly eight thousand baseball cards a year ago, and I'd be annoyed about that, except that he more than quadrupled our money *and* taught half the Duchy a new game that many of my subjects really quite enjoy. So I find it best to let them do as they like."

She unlocked the door. The room on the other side was . . . startling. The walls were gray stone, unornamented save by racks of metal shelving that I instinctively shied away from, even though they gave no sign of being iron. Some sort of rough gray-brown carpet was used to blunt the floor, which was made of the smoothest stone I had ever seen. I blinked down at it, almost more amazed by the fact that she'd been able to find a granite slab this size than by the unexamined wonders packed onto the shelves.

Boxes, bins, and crates of things I didn't recognize stood everywhere. Many of the boxes were made of some sort of stiff white paper with strange words scrawled on the side in thick black ink.

"They really have kept you sheltered, haven't they?" asked Li Qin, not unkindly. I still flinched, having almost forgotten that she was there.

I turned in her direction, aware that my eyes were bulging in my face but not quite able to make myself stop staring. "What do you mean?"

"A changeling your age should recognize most of the things in this room. Hell, a pureblood your age should recognize them. These are common things. Everyday things. The sort of things children are exposed to. They're not doing you any favors by making it impossible for you to blend in with the world outside that tower."

"I don't think it's your job to judge how much I've experienced," I said stiffly. "You wanted me for something."

"That's true, I did," said Li Qin. "Follow me."

She led me deeper into the room, and the door swung shut behind us. Nothing in there was familiar except for her, a Duchess walking with all the calm, arrogant assurance of her kind, and so I kept my eyes on her, seeking comfort in what I knew.

"Another of my finders is a Gean-Cannah changeling who prefers to keep the two halves of their life entirely distinct."

"I didn't realize Gean-Cannah could *make* changelings," I blurted.

Li Qin glanced back at me, sympathy in her expression. Sympathy for who? "They're not supposed to," she said. "They're technically shapeshifters, but as they always look close enough to Daoine Sidhe to pass if they want to, Fair Titania spared them when she purged the rest. The fully fae among them can transform their bodies at will. The changelings have two entirely distinct entities sharing their bodies, and transform at sunrise and sunset whether they wish it or not. They can share information between their halves, but they don't have to. Terrie and Alexander have chosen to live as individuals who happen to share an apartment and never see one another. Terrie works the night shift at a local computer company, with my consent, and tithes her wages to the Duchy; we do keep the major customs here. Alex prefers to roam a bit, and spends his days hunting for bargains and scrap sales. Human companies form, get a budget, spend it on whatever strikes their fancy, and collapse, leaving people like us to pick through the remains. Other companies frequently don't want what's left behind. Some say it's because it's been used, and they demand the best. Others seem to worry that things which belonged to a company that failed to thrive might be cursed, might carry that company's bad luck with them when they find a new home."

"Do you not worry about curses?"

Li Qin shrugged. "I weave luck. If any of these things were actually cursed, I'd feel it, and could pick it apart before it had a chance to impact us. These things are just that: things. Interesting things, often, things I'm glad to purchase once Alex sniffs them out for me, but things all the same."

"What does this have to do with my being here?"

"Alex's latest find was a storage unit in Fremont that was flagged for sale after its owners stopped paying the upkeep," she said easily.

"I acquired the lot, and expected nothing but a few interesting novelties. What I found, though . . . what I found was a mystery."

We had reached the back of the room. Li Qin motioned me to wait as she opened another door, revealing a smaller, less cluttered room. This one was very cold, frigid air pumping from boxes in all four corners, and there were no shelves. Instead, a black rectangle about two feet tall and almost cubical sat in the middle of the floor. Thick cords snaked out of what I presumed was the back, connecting to small white panels at the base of the two farthest walls. The side toward us was brushed gray metal, ridged with long, thin openings and topped with a circular black button whose outline was glowing faintly red.

"Behold the mystery," said Li Qin.

I frowned at the box. "What's so mysterious about it?" *Besides literally everything about it,* I added, silently.

"I've heard the Dóchas Sidhe are supposed to be blood-workers to rival the Daoine," she said. "You tell me."

Her tone made me bristle, feeling belittled even though she hadn't said a single untrue thing. I shrugged, fighting the urge to glare. "Maybe so, but I've never been trained in blood magic. I don't know the first thing about blood magic."

"Ah." If Li Qin was disappointed, she didn't show it. Instead, shrugging, she began to circle the box. "Close your eyes and reach for the presence of magic. You know it's here. You can find it."

"We're inside your knowe," I protested. "All I'm going to find is a headache."

"They really didn't . . . All right. Humor me." Li Qin stopped circling to look at me. "Try closing your eyes and searching for magic. If you don't find it, or you find a headache, we'll stop. I'll buy you dinner at someplace nice out in the human world, so you can feel like you've really had an adventure, and then we'll call Sir Etienne to come and take you home. But if you *do* find it, the mystery will start to make sense to you. Go ahead. Give it a try."

Great. The Duchess of Dreamer's Glass was a major weirdo, and I was stuck with her until I tried her ridiculous party trick. I closed my eyes and tried to focus on "reaching for the presence of magic," whatever that meant. I smelled the cider and smoke of Father's spell, which soothed my nerves. On top of that was the cedar smoke and lime scent of Etienne's magic, and—

And I paused. How could I tell them apart? No one had ever *told* me that Etienne's magic was cedar smoke, but there was no question now that I was really thinking about it. His magic was cedar and lime, and Father's was waxed whitebeam smoke and mulled cider, with all the complexity that implied. What the hell was a whitebeam? I didn't think I'd ever even heard the word before, and the shock of it was almost enough to make me open my eyes before I caught myself and kept reaching. I still wasn't sure how that was supposed to work. Apparently, "reaching for magic" was a fancy name for sniffing the air.

My own magic was layered under both of theirs, cut grass and copper. I could smell black tea and white hydrangea lingering nearby, vital and fresh enough that I assumed it had to be coming from Li Qin. The constant flow of fresh cold air was pushing all the scents down, muddling them. But under Li Qin's magic, faint and almost static, like it was frozen in time, was something else. Something sweet and sharp at the same time, the scent of the moment before lightning struck during a storm. I turned my face toward the scent and opened my eyes.

I was looking directly at the black box.

"What—?" I asked.

Li Qin smiled. "I don't know. Isn't it fabulous? It's a mystery. I was going through the contents of the storage locker, and when I reached this, I felt magic in the case. It's worked into the whole structure of the server. I tried opening the panel on the back, to see whether there were runes etched inside, and I found *wood*."

"Wood?"

"*Wood*. It's as if someone tried to integrate a computer system with a living structure, something like what the Dryads use. It's nothing I've ever seen before, and it's *fascinating*. So of course I tried to turn it on."

"Of course . . ." I said, somewhat baffled.

"But it wouldn't come on!" She sounded both delighted and personally affronted, like the—the server? Why was she referring to a box as if it were a member of the household staff?—had refused to function just to spite her. "Do you understand how Shyi Shuai work?"

"You're not Seers, I know that."

"That's correct. We don't see the future, but we can nudge it when we want to. Sort of sharpen our luck and prod things along."

I blinked. "So why does anything bad ever happen?"

"So many reasons that I couldn't possibly list them all, but the big one where I'm concerned is that we're *not* Seers. We can't influence an outcome if we don't know the outcome is going to need influencing. You understand?"

"No."

"All right, let's look at it another way: when I want something to go one way and not another, I can start poking luck to show me the best path to getting what I want. Sort of asking very narrow yes-or-no questions, and then using them to dowse the correct result. I want this server to come on. So I prodded luck and asked if that was possible. The answer was affirmative."

"You talk to luck?"

She stopped to look at me flatly. "For a changeling living in an enchanted tower, you sure do want things to make sense according to a narrow set of rules. Luck doesn't *talk*. It's not a person with a language and an opinion. But it can answer you, if you ask correctly and know how to listen. That good enough?"

It wasn't, but I didn't think pushing would get me a better answer. I nodded.

"Great. Anyway, once I knew it was possible to turn the server on, I started trying to figure out what that would require. Was it a thing, a spell, a person . . . ? And no matter how I asked, I kept circling back to 'person.' There was someone who could help me get the server to come on. So I started trying to winnow down where they might be. Are they in Dreamer's Glass? No. Are they in the Kingdom of the Mists? Yes. From there, I ran through the various fiefdoms until I hit Shadowed Hills, and this was a long, arduous, mind-numbing process, so I'm going to skip to the part where I figured out I needed a member of Duke Torquill's immediate family. Not the Duke himself, and not his brother, either. Meaning it was either you or your sister."

"You could have requested one of us specifically."

"Um, not so much." She spread her hands. "Your mother is *epic* protective of you two. Like, I know people who think you don't exist, like your mom's trying for the fae equivalent of tax fraud—and you don't know what that means, so forget I said anything—but if I asked for either of you by name, I'd fail. The server would never come on, sad Duchess, no solving the mystery. I had to wait for a time when your uncle *couldn't* respond to a request for a family member by coming himself, and when your mother wouldn't be around to insert herself into the process."

"Moving Day," I said, the timing suddenly falling into place.

Li Qin nodded. "Duke Sylvester is a slacker who never does more than absolutely required by his position, but he does the bare minimum, reliably and always. If I asked during the leadup to Moving Day, and he didn't have a good reason to refuse me, as his equal, he'd ask you or your sister. And if he did it while your mother was out of town, there was a decent chance I'd get the hidden daughter."

She said that like it was some sort of victory. I blinked. "You wanted me in specific?"

"I told you I wanted to know more about you. And all the questions I asked indicated I had the best shot at success if you were the one pressing the button." She stepped back, gesturing to the server. "So please, October. For me, press the button."

"This is really strange, and I'm not completely comfortable with it."

"Understandable."

"What happens if I don't press the button?"

"The server never comes on, and I am sad."

"Never?"

"Not through any other route I've been able to find."

"And if I *do* press the button . . . ?"

"It comes on, and I find out what the server is for." Li Qin smiled. "I couldn't figure out how to ask a question that would get me a straight answer on whether that's a good thing, but I like satiating my curiosity, so I'm calling it a win either way."

"You are very weird."

"I know. Will you please press the button?"

Cautiously, I approached the server. I wanted to tell her to get stuffed. At the same time, she was a Duchess, and I was a changeling, and every bit of training I'd ever received was telling me to do whatever she said. The button continued to glow a steady red.

I looked at it, taking my time, trying to be careful. There was no iron in the thing, nothing that set my nerves on edge; just that faint, distant edge of impending lightning. Still cautious, I reached over and pressed the button.

Pain lanced though my finger as a needle hidden in the center of the red dot jabbed out and stabbed me. I jerked away, shedding drops of blood as I did, and staggered back. "You didn't tell me *that* would happen!"

"I didn't know. It didn't happen when I tried the button."

"Boobytraps aren't usually that picky about who they hit." I could feel my skin knitting itself together over the small injury. I forced myself not to watch.

The smell of impending lightning grew stronger as the server began to make a grinding sound like someone mashing peppercorns in a pestle. The button blinked off.

"Was that all?" asked Li Qin. "Draw blood, then go to sleep?"

"That was *quite enough*," I said, sourly.

The button blinked back on, brighter this time, so bright it projected a fan of red light outward into the air, becoming almost physical. The smell of impending lightning sharpened to become the smell of ozone, hanging heavy all around us. Then, with another, brighter flash, the grinding stopped, and someone else was standing in the room.

She was young, maybe eleven or twelve, and looked Daoine Sidhe. Her hair was the incongruous yellow of buttercups blooming in a field, drawn into two low pigtails, and her eyes were the same honey-gold as my father's, darker than August's. Torquill eyes. She was wearing mortal clothes and mortal glasses, but her ears were pointed, and something about the shape of her face was achingly familiar.

She exhaled slowly, looking around the room before focusing on me and breaking into a wide, innocent grin. "There you are, October. I hoped you would come to reactivate me. How are you?"

What in Titania's name was I supposed to do with *that*?

SIX

THE GIRL FROWNED WHEN I failed to return her greeting, head swinging around until she was facing Li Qin. "Hello, Mother," she said, in the same stilted tone. It wasn't formal, exactly: it was more like speech being run through some sort of filter that stripped away half the normal inflections a voice would hold. She sounded . . . artificial. Then she blinked, and for a moment, her expression was all bewildered child, with nothing fake about it. "Where is Mama? I expected her to be here."

Li Qin said nothing, only stared at her.

The girl turned back to me. "October, where is she? Where is my mother? She should be here, if you've found the way to turn me back on."

"How do you know my name?"

She stopped, and for a moment, it seemed like her image *rolled*, like she was a reflection cast on still water and someone had just tossed a pebble into the pond. Then she was solid again, and looking at me with clear irritation. "I see. The program is a detailed one, I'll give it that. But no amount of detail accounts for everything, ever. If it did, I wouldn't be here."

"Does someone want to tell me what's going on?" I asked. My finger still stung. The wound had healed, but the body remembers pain. The body remembers a lot of things. Thoughtlessly, I stuck my finger in my mouth, instinctively trying to nurse the stinging away.

Blood memory wrapped around me immediately, even more vivid

and undeniable than the last one. There was no sensation of a sugar shell this time, just an immediate plunge into recall.

I'm in another strange room, even smaller than the one Li Qin led me to, but the same tall machine is here, directly in the center, tethered by black cables to the four walls. It hums to itself, operating as intended. I look around, taking note of everything I see. Pink walls; a border of purple rabbits, stenciled on a white background. A bookshelf packed with computer manuals and children's books against one wall, next to another shelf, this one packed with dozens upon dozens of plush rabbits.

A heart-shaped sign above the rabbit shelf tells me this is "April's Room." There is no bed. There is no dresser. Only the machine, the bookshelves, and the rabbits.

Only me. I take a step toward the machine. There's a picture on the bookshelf, the strange girl and a woman with golden eyes and red-brown hair, both grinning widely for the camera. A baby blanket is wrapped around the base of the machine, pink and blue and minty green.

"You're here," says the girl from before. She's behind me. How is she behind me?

I turn slowly. "Hey, April. How are you?"

"Why are you here?" she counters, all scowls.

"I thought I'd come see how you were."

Her eyes narrow. "I am fine. Why are you *here?"*

August said blood memory could be controlled, to a degree, forced to show you what you want to see. I had none of her training. The blood had me, and I was going to follow it for as long as it wanted me to.

"I have some questions I think you can answer," I say, leaning against the wall. This version of me sounds so calm, so confident. I don't know her. "At least, I hope you can." I reach over, straightening one worn cotton bunny's ear.

"Don't touch that!" April vanishes, only to reappear next to me with a crackle of static and snatch the rabbit away. She glares over the top of its head at me. "This is mine. *My mother gave it to* me."

"I'm sorry. I didn't mean to upset you."

"My mother always buys me rabbits." She looks down at the bunny as she strokes its head. "Every time she goes somewhere I can't follow, she brings me another rabbit. I like rabbits."

"I can tell."

"She'll bring me many rabbits this time, because she didn't tell me she was leaving."

"April . . ." I don't recognize any of this. Blood is supposed to carry memory, but whoever this memory belongs to isn't me. I was never here. And still I ache for the child in front of me, rabbit in her arms and innocence in her eyes. *"April, you understand she's not coming back this time, don't you?"*

The memory started to dissolve around me, and for a moment—just a moment—I was seized by the irrational desire to push the button again, to draw the knife Melly had given me, to do whatever I had to in order to bleed and keep following a moment that had never happened in the first place.

Instead, the plain gray room returned, Li Qin looking at me with mild concern but no real fear, the blonde girl looking back and forth between the two of us.

Oh, well. None of this made sense *anyway*. May as well see how little sense it was going to go on making. "Is your name April?" I asked, and was rewarded by the girl's face relaxing with relief right before she disappeared.

The blood memory still fresh in my mind told me not to flinch when she reappeared next to me with a strange crackling sound, wrapping her arms around my waist. She felt perfectly solid, like any other kid who'd just teleported using a completely unfamiliar kind of magic, and who smelled like a thunderstorm about to crash down on my head.

"I knew you remembered me, I *knew* it!" she crowed, squeezing tightly. I kept my arms raised and blinked at her, trying to figure out what I was supposed to do with this kind of exuberance. "Mother and I have been working on building security failsafes into the network for me, to reduce the risk of power interruptions, and when the power cut off, they activated. I have been waiting for someone to come and let me out. I have watched every episode of *Grey's Anatomy*. Twice. Would you like your appendix removed?"

She looked up at me, golden eyes wide and hopeful. I almost hated to tell her no, even if I wasn't sure what she was talking about.

"I think I'm good, actually," I said. "Okay . . . April. I don't remember you. I'm sorry if that's disappointing, but I have no idea what's going on here. Duchess Zhou invited me to Dreamer's Glass because she needed help solving a mystery, only it seems the mystery just made another mystery. Can you please tell us who you are, and who you think we are?"

"And why you called me 'Mother,'" added Li Qin. "I think I'd know if I had children."

"I'm adopted, if that helps," said April.

"Still think I'd have noticed," said Li Qin.

"Very well." April disappeared again, taking the pressure around my waist with her, and reappeared sitting atop her server, weight resting on her hands as she regarded the two of us owlishly through her glasses. "I will explain myself upon one condition."

"I am the Duchess here, and apparently also your mother, so I hardly think you're in the position to be making conditions," said Li Qin.

"You catch on to this 'mother' thing quickly," I said, voice low.

She shrugged. "I wrangle programmers and household staff. How different can motherhood be?"

"What's your condition?" I asked, returning my attention to April.

"I will explain, but you may not interrupt, even to request clarification, until I grant consent for you to do so," she said. "I have no idea the scope of your reprogramming, only that it is extensive, enough so as to have impacted the local network storage, and I would prefer to reach a natural conclusion before I am bombarded with your inevitable bewilderment. Do you accept?"

"Yes?" I said, too confused to say anything else.

April's speech appeared to make more sense to Li Qin, whose eyes widened before she gave a quick nod and said, "I accept your terms and conditions."

"Always read the terms and conditions," said April, with a flicker of amusement. "Very well. My name is April O'Leary. I was originally a Dryad tied to an oak copse that stood some miles from here, closer to the human city of Fremont. When our trees were razed by mortal developers, I was afraid. I did not wish to die. So I grabbed a large branch from my broken tree, the sap still quick and bright within it, and I ran for the first knowe I could find. The humans did not see me. I was not fully within the Summerlands during my flight, but Dryads are protected as pixies are, when we are in our truest and most unfiltered state."

"So did they see a branch running by itself down the road?" It seemed like a reasonable-enough question.

April still looked at me like it was the most foolish thing she'd ever heard. "No. A Dryad *is* her tree. If the branch died—when the branch died—I would die with it. Until then, it was as invisible as I was. You promised me no interruptions."

"Sorry," I said, chagrined. It felt odd to be chastised by a girl less than a quarter of my age, and perfectly natural at the same time. All Dryads are purebloods. While the Hamadryads can have changeling children, their cousins, the Dryads and the Blodynbryd, cannot.

"Do not interrupt again," said April. Her eyes fixed on Li Qin, she continued. "I arrived in the County of Tamed Lightning and begged the aid of its countess, January O'Leary, who was working late, much to the chagrin of her wife. She disliked how willing Countess O'Leary was to spend time in her lab, when she could have been home in the arms of her loving spouse. They had discussed children, but as neither wished to lie with a man for the purposes of getting them, they were waiting for the appropriate time to adopt. I knew none of this, and when I crashed into her presence, January did not think of children, only saving my life. The first thing she did upon knowing me was look at someone who was by many measures already dead and move to save me. That was the moment she became my mother."

She paused to take a deep breath, voice shaking on the inhale. Calming herself, she continued, "She worked through the day and late into the next night, using the talents of her company alchemist, Yui, to keep the remains of my tree from dying as she sliced off slivers of the wood that was my flesh and integrated them with a server she had been preparing to decommission. She warned me before she turned it on that if it worked, things would be different, and she . . . she called her wife." Still watching Li Qin, she said, "She had married a Shyi Shuai, and she begged her to bend the luck around the moment as thoroughly as she could, even knowing this would bring a backlash down on one or both of them. It was the only means she had of saving me. And she had become determined that I should live. Her wife agreed. January put down the scalpel. She tightened the final screw. She asked if I was ready.

"How can anyone be ready to face their own annihilation? Especially in Faerie. The humans live expecting death, understanding that it already knows their names and waits to claim them when the time arrives. We, though . . . we were made to live forever. A Dryad's tree may look as mortal as any other, but its roots drive deep and time will not fell it. I told her I was afraid. She told me she would take care of

me. I nodded to say what my voice would no longer support, and she
pressed a button and everything was gone, replaced by darkness.

"My thoughts—we are so defined by our forms. I had been a tree,
slow and green and growing, and now I was splinters and silicon,
electricity and the movement of information. It took what felt like
years for me to gather myself and reach out to meet her again, and
when I did, she wept, she clasped me close and told me I was safe
now, safe forever. She agreed to be my parent. Her wife did the same.
They loved me long and well, and with all the compassion they had
to offer. I was strange to them, and they to me, and still we found our
common places, until we were truly a family.

"Mama was working on a new form of immortality, one that would
remove all inequalities within Faerie. She wanted to digitize and upload our world. No more barriers of blood, no more differences of
power, just people, stripped of everything else. It was a ridiculous
idea. I can see that now. But at the time, she was trying her best to
resolve what she saw as unreasonable barriers in the path of the people she loved. She *hated* that we could be killed. Even more, she hated
that changelings in her care didn't need to be killed. Over time, they
would simply . . . die."

She stopped, going silent as she stared off into the distance. Li Qin
and I exchanged a look, each of us wordlessly asking the other if she
was finished and we could speak again. Finally, Li Qin decided to
risk it:

"It didn't work?"

"Not as intended," said April, snapping back into the moment.
"The upload stripped a person's mind and magic from their body,
storing it in a temporary matrix until it could be uploaded to a machine. Once there, the packets of information the people had become
were entirely static, frozen and inert. I could enter the server, but I
could not get them to interact with me. Mama was still attempting to
resolve the problem. I believed in her. I knew she would succeed,
given sufficient time.

"What about the people who'd been uploaded?" asked Li Qin, in
a tone of fascinated horror.

"They died," said April. "My other mother said this had to end.
Said it was the backlash from bending the luck to save me, and that
she was equally responsible. She said there was blood on both their
hands. My mothers fought. They had never done that before. I did not
like it. I asked them to stop. And my mother, my Shyi Shuai mother,

said she couldn't stay and watch as everything fell apart, not when she knew this was partially due to her intervention. She never blamed me, but still, I knew I had been instrumental in creating the circumstances which demanded such an extreme twisting of luck. Mama owned a manor house in the mortal state of Oregon, one which had once been connected to her family's holdings, before the War of Silences. My other mother went there to spend a period of time in contemplation, and to purify her luck. She was gone when Mama died."

Somehow, I had known that was coming, the knowledge imparted by both the inevitability of the child's story and the ghosts of impossible memory I'd plucked out of my blood. It still stung to hear it put so baldly.

"I'm sorry," I said.

April waved my apology away. "She got better. My surviving mother returned and, feeling guilt over her own part in the losses, found an ancient blood ritual which could potentially be used to bring back the dead, in conjunction with the files contained on our server. She contacted the most powerful blood-worker any of us knew, and arranged for their resurrection. Mother's body had been burned after her death. We had no means of recovering her. But I remembered a time when the blood-worker we called had summoned the night-haunts to her aid, and I was able to blackmail them into building Mother a new body. She was restored as well, and we were able to return to a life of mundane existence and peaceful scientific exploration. We were happy. All of us.

"But life doesn't cease because you're happy, and the blood-worker I mentioned was a magnet for complications. She continued to attract them, and while we were rarely present, I had befriended her squire and supplied him with a cellular phone, which he used to keep me apprised of developments. The last series of messages I received from him told me of a huge and terrible battle against Queen Titania, Mother of Illusions, who had been returned from her long exile."

Something about the way she was looking at me made me deeply uncomfortable. I squirmed, and didn't say anything.

"He said his knight had managed to overcome the Summer Queen's magic, and that King Oberon had bound her against doing direct harm to the knight and her family. But the fae definition of 'harm' is very broad at times. Mother was yet concerned that Titania might do something terrible. She had heard the stories, you see."

"Then she heard them wrong," I said. "Maeve was the terrible one.

All that's good and beautiful in Faerie stems from Fair Titania. We owe her our existence."

"No one in this room carries the blood of Titania," said April. "I did once, when I was a true Dryad, but my sap is long since dried up and gone. We owe her nothing."

It was a blasphemy, to speak so of Titania, and had April been anything other than a pureblood, I would have left at once rather than hear further such unforgivable things. As it was, I took a step back and glowered, all but waiting for Titania herself to appear and strike this phantom down.

"Mama asked if I was willing to sleep, for a time, and confined me to my server, after asking my other mother to grant her luck. Not the sort of luck that raises the dead—or creates them to begin with. The sort of luck that brings a mystery to the attention of the right eyes, regardless of what else may be happening. The sort of luck that brings her back to me." April looked at Li Qin and smiled, a small, hopeful smile, agonizing hope in her eyes. "I called you my mother because you have been, ever since I first awoke in the server's light. Mama made me, but you saw to it that I understood as much as I could of Faerie. You loved me. Do you truly not remember?"

"I am sorry, but I don't," said Li Qin, with what sounded like genuine regret. "I've never married. Shyi Shuai are rare in the Mists, and my position leaves me little time to go searching for courtship."

"That was part of why Mama was concerned," said April. "In the tales, Titania was always very concerned with the preservation and purity of descendant lines. Titania believed Faerie would not have rendered us so dissimilar if we had not been intended to hold ourselves apart from one another. We were also not meant to mingle with the humans, in her eyes, but that is more inevitable, even in a version of Faerie where she had somehow seized control."

"A what?" I asked.

"A version of Faerie where she had somehow seized control," repeated April. "I'm sorry, was that unclear? Titania is the source of all flower magic. Illusions and deceptions flow from her like water from a spring. Based on what we know of her from her previous time among her descendants, and the fury my friend the squire indicated she was experiencing, it seemed likely she would try to remake Faerie in her own image. I have checked the email queue while I was talking to the two of you. There are many messages from friends and allies in more-distant locations, asking for information they have not received. All contact with the Mists has been cut off since the middle of June. Some of them are quite alarmed, and a few have sent detachments to inquire. None of those detachments have returned to their places of origin."

"This is not—" I began.

April kept talking, almost as if she wanted to be sure I couldn't argue: "Silences and the Golden Shore are likewise absent from their allies. I hypothesize that Titania, furious as she is, can only sustain a revision of this size and complexity over us and our neighboring kingdoms. The Undersea adjacent to those areas has been completely silent since this began."

"Of course it has," I snapped. "The Undersea was destroyed over a hundred years ago. There's nothing down there now but shipwrecks and smelt."

"That is untrue, and I only wish you knew it as well," said April, almost sadly. "When you activated my server, it should have drawn your blood. Did it not do so?"

". . . it did," I admitted.

"And assuming you are in any way the woman I have known, you would not have been able to resist putting your finger in your mouth. You have always claimed to hate and abhor the sight of blood, but you move toward it as a flower seeks the sun. Your power knows its source."

A chill ran down my spine. I didn't like her reading me that well, not when everything I was insisted that we were meeting for the first time. Still, she was right.

"I did," I admitted.

"Did you see a memory that didn't make sense?" She looked at me politely. "Something that might not have happened in the same way after Titania rewrote the world? She has no skill for blood magic, that one, which makes it all the more fascinating that her favorite child bore the most successful line of blood-workers in all of Faerie. Your line will eclipse hers, given time, assuming Titania allows you to survive. Do bindings made in another version of reality count here?"

I blinked, more slowly than I meant to, before I said, "I saw . . . you. I saw something that never happened."

"But it gave you my name. You knew me when the memory faded."

"Yes."

"Then it was true at least in that regard, if not in any other. We share the calendar, October. You *should* know me."

"Would that be true of everyone's blood?" asked Li Qin.

April nodded. "Yes. Memory should remain, whatever is set atop it. Illusion does not replace reality."

Li Qin pivoted on one foot and marched over to me, holding out one arm in a sharp, almost jerky motion. "That knife you have, I want you to cut me with it."

"What?"

"If what she says is true and all this"—she waved her other hand wildly at the room around us—"is an illusion Titania created because she was pissed at some jerk-ass knight who got in her way, that means I have a wife out there." Li Qin looked at me, expression grim. "I have someone I love, who loves me, and we have a daughter I don't even know. Now, maybe the kid's a liar, sure, but my luck seemed to indicate turning the server on would be a *good* thing, and that only makes sense if I was the one to make it possible for the thing to be found and activated in the first place. Sounds like that wife of mine is pretty damn smart. I'd really like to meet her. I can't see memories in blood—my magic is purely water-based—but *you* can. So, you're going to take a peek inside my veins, and tell me whether this kid is telling the truth or not."

"I . . . I can't." I took a step backward, away from her. "I'm not trained, I don't know how to control it, I could see—I could see *anything*, things you don't want me to see. I could get lost in your memory. I could—"

"Can you get lost if you only take a drop?" she asked. "I'm not asking you to slash my palm open. I have nerves and tendons there that I need. I just want you to prick my finger. I want to *know*. Please." She sounded almost agonized. "I have been so bored, for so long, and so lonely, and now someone says I have a family? I have people who love me? And you could tell me everything about them, but you're *scared*? I'm sorry. I don't care."

My heart was beating so hard, it actually hurt. I stared at Li Qin, unable to find the voice for the objections that crowded my throat. This was wrong. Everything about this was wrong. A child couldn't come out of a machine and force me to use blood magic. Titania would never hurt Faerie. Titania *loved* Faerie. That was why she'd stayed with us when Maeve betrayed us and Oberon retreated to his barrow to sleep. She'd stayed out of love. A mother's love. The kind of love only a Queen could carry without breaking.

Li Qin sighed, heavily. "I hate to do this," she said. "Honestly, I hate the whole system. Changelings happen. Changelings have always happened. But ordering people to have children just so the rest of Faerie will have people they feel like they can safely boss around isn't right. It's immoral, if nothing else. And yet. You grew up with these rules. You grew up 'knowing your place.'" The way she said it turned a phrase that had always been a source of pride and comfort into something bordering on an insult.

Silently, still searching for speech, I nodded.

"Fine, then. I, Li Qin Zhou, Duchess of Dreamer's Glass, pure-blooded daughter of the Shyi Shuai, order you, October Torquill, daughter of Simon and Amandine Torquill, to make me bleed, ride my blood, and tell me what you see contained therein." Her face was a mask of cold authority. "You cannot countermand me."

"You're right," I admitted, voice gone soft, "I can't."

Drawing my knife, I stepped close to her once more. "But I can hate you for it," I added. "Give me your hand."

Li Qin nodded to her outstretched arm, her wrist already turned toward the ceiling. "Don't cut too deep," she cautioned. "I need my hands."

"I'll do my best," I said, and pressed the edge of the knife to the outside of her hand, pushing down until it barely—just barely—broke the skin.

The smell of blood washed over me, heavy with the twinned scents of her magic. They smelled truer this way, purer, almost, like they had only ever been meant to be experienced straight out of the vein. It made my mouth water and my head spin, and I hated the contradiction, even as I wiped the knife against the leg of my trousers, tucked it back into its sheath, and grasped her arm with my free hand, pulling her toward me.

"It works better if it comes from you," I said, reciting a half-remembered fragment of a lesson I had once heard Father giving to August. "Try to think about what you want me to see."

Then I clamped my mouth over the wound I'd created, and the room went away.

As with the first time I had tasted my own blood, there was a shell, almost, above the true memory, something hard and sweet and brittle.

It shattered when I pressed against it, unable to keep me out or withstand the slightest pressure, and I plunged down, down, down into the red well of Li Qin.

Unlike my own memories, I am not myself here in the red. I know that without being able to look at the body I currently occupy, which is seated in some sort of soft, leathery chair, hands folded in its lap. In front of me/them, a person I know stalks back and forth.

January. When April referred to January O'Leary, I didn't realize she meant my cousin January ap Learainth. How they would even have met was a mystery, but in this vision, January is on the verge of panic. She moves with the energy of a trapped animal, yanking at her own hair. She wears human clothing—trousers like mine, a sweatshirt with an illustration of a grinning rabbit on it—and for all her anxiety, she wears it naturally, like this is normal for her.

"Calm down," I say, and when I hear my voice, I understand: in this memory, I am Li Qin. "You don't know that she's going to do anything."

"You weren't in Silences when the false Queen invaded us," January snaps. "You weren't there. Titania's a Queen, too. She's going to do something. She has to. Her authority has been threatened, and it's Toby's fault, so she's going to be at the epicenter. The rest of us . . . we're just going to be collateral damage. Like my mother was."

"Jan, please." I/Li stand and move to wrap my/her arm around the unhappy January, trying to calm her. She shrugs me/her off. "It might not be that bad."

"No." January looks at me/us, and her mouth is set in a hard line of conviction. "It's going to be worse."

So January was real, but that didn't tell me anything else about what April had been saying. Li Qin was still bleeding. I tried to focus on that, on the shape of my own skin, and took another swallow. I needed to see something deeper.

She's sleeping, my January, hair spread across the pillow in red and brown streaks, eyes closed for once. For once. Having her here is still a miracle. I/Li thinks it will always be a miracle. Even Faerie isn't supposed to return the dead. Gone is gone. But she never went to the night-haunts, and somehow they've returned her to me/Li. She's here. She's staying. We get to be a family again. Whatever Toby wants, forever, she can have it.

Maybe too deep. It felt like the lines between us were blurring. I broke contact with a gasp, stepping backward, trying to shake off the red-tinted veil of her memories. Li Qin stared at me, eyes wide, expression hopeful.

With a sharp wash of ozone, April appeared by my side, flickering out of the nothingness. "What did you see?" she asked, tone almost academic. "Boring courtly duties and Titania's perfect Faerie, or a complicated, messy, *real* version of our world?"

"I—I don't know what I saw," I said. "I saw my cousin, January. But her last name isn't O'Leary."

"She changed it to match mortal tradition when she moved to the Mists after the fall of Briarholme," said April. "That is a strange thing, to fixate on a name when you saw her reflection in the blood. Strange and small, almost as if you don't want to have seen what you saw."

"She . . . blamed *me*," I said. "For somehow upsetting Titania, she blamed *me*. She said there had been a war in Silences? And this was my fault? That you would be collateral damage? Why would she blame *me*?"

"Because it was your fault." April somehow managed to make what should have been a brutal accusation into a simple statement of fact. Titania was angry enough to have rewritten Faerie to suit herself, splitting up families, doing Oberon-only-knew what other terrible things in the process, and it was somehow supposed to be *my* fault?

April clearly saw the confusion in my expression. She put a hand on my arm, fingers light and barely solid enough to feel. "It was your squire who told me what happened, October. It was you who saved my mother, who saved my family. You are the most powerful bloodworker I have ever known, and if you have angered Titania, I am relieved, because it means I can believe this will be undone. I can believe that you will save us, as you always have before."

SEVEN

SILENCE FELL AFTER APRIL'S proclamation, hanging in the air until I burst out laughing and shattered it past all repair. She recoiled, taking her hand away from my arm. I switched my focus to Li Qin.

"August put you up to this, didn't she?" I asked. "My sister always says I need to have better self-esteem, and this feels like the sort of joke she'd try to put together. I never thought she'd involve a *duchess*."

Li Qin gave me a look full of hurt. "If this were a conspiracy against you, don't you think you would have seen it in my blood?"

"My sister is a very skilled blood-worker. She might have been able to cover real memory with false—"

"That centered you?" asked April. "That featured people you didn't know in completely unbelievable and hence unrealistic situations? I cannot force you to believe the unbelievable, October. But pause, for just a moment. Think of the things you have seen in your own blood. Think of the things your magic knows to be true. Titania can lie to you. You can lie to yourself. Your magic cannot."

"I don't know that," I said. "Maybe my magic lies to me all the time. I've never used it enough to find out."

Li Qin frowned. "How is that possible?"

"I was . . . I've never been allowed to do blood magic," I said slowly. "Mother said it would be too much for me, and unseemly for a changeling to experiment so, and Father was willing to abide by her will. I think . . . August has tried to share her lessons with me, but Mother's nose for blood is so sensitive that any pinprick would catch her attention.

When my menses started, she banished me to Shadowed Hills for two weeks. The week of the bleeding and the whole week after."

It had been one of the most pleasant experiences of my life. Melly had fussed and clucked over me for the whole of my stay, insisting I stay in bed and allow Kerry to wait on me like I was important enough to take care of, like I was *August*.

"She still sends me away when the time comes for me to bleed. She can't be near me."

"Does she banish August?"

Li Qin's question was mild. I frowned as I nodded.

"Of course. But August is a pureblood. She bleeds only every other year. I bleed every sixth month." Kerry told me that was less than a human would, which was horrifying. The thought of spending half of each month away from my sister was repugnant. But it was necessary for my mother's health, and if that had been my reality, I would have gone.

For her, I would go anywhere.

"How many times have you ridden your own blood, October?" asked Li Qin.

"Twice," I admitted. It seemed odd, when I said it so baldly. Surely I would have tasted blood before this, even if only out of curiosity, if only when I had been too young to work and my primary duty had been serving as August's constant companion? She was enough older than me to have been a woman grown while I was a squealing child, but she had loved me from the start, been kind to me, picked me up when I fell, held me tight while I wept over skinned knees, and wiped away the blood as they scabbed over and healed. Somehow, in all those wild and heedless days of my childhood, I had suffered no injuries which painted my tongue.

My tongue! Surely I had bitten my tongue, or pulled free a loosened tooth, or done *something* to give me a third tasting of the blood to point to, something that wasn't complicated and shelled in sugar. But no. Far back as I reached through my memory, I could find none of those small incidents or accidents.

That, more than anything else, was what made me begin to question whether April's version of our world might not have been a true one. Everyone has trouble remembering their childhood. Everyone forgets the unpleasant pieces, the grinding agony of learning to walk or speak, the stretches of seemingly endless boredom, the injuries. But what I found in my own past was like a paragraph written by an author anxious to get to what they considered the good part of the story: broad strokes only, as detailed as the plot required, and not a single sentence more.

There should have been *something*. And its absence was as glaring as any clue has ever been.

". . . only twice," I said. "Both today."

"What did you see?" asked April.

"The second time, I saw you, in a room painted white and purple, with stuffed rabbits on a shelf. You told me your mother always brought you rabbits when she went away, and that she would have to bring you many rabbits this time, because she didn't warn you before she left. I think . . . I think she was dead?"

"She was," said April, with no inflection on the words. "I was unaware that flesh-and-blood people were not capable of disconnecting from the network and rejoining at a later point without loss of fidelity. You were able to assist me in bringing her back online, later. What did you see the first time?"

Even remembering what I'd seen in the blood felt almost too intimate to share aloud. My cheeks reddened and I looked down at my feet as I said, "There was a man. He had very green eyes. The way he looked at me was . . . No one has ever looked at me like that. Not just like he loved me, but like I was the only reason he was willing to let the world keep existing. I had something important I needed to tell him. Something really, really essential, and I was worried about how he was going to react." I shook my head. "I never got to find out what I was going to say, because that's where the memory fell apart. I've never seen him before."

"Did he have dark hair?" asked April.

I nodded.

"That was Tybalt. I was unable to attend your wedding, due to the constraints placed upon my mobility by my mechanical nature, but I am assured that you had a fantastic time, and I was given several photographs and videos of the cake, affording me the opportunity to enter the data stream and taste the ambient idea of it."

"Magic is fun," said Li Qin, when I looked baffled.

That didn't help with the bafflement. I focused on April. "I'm not married. I would know if I were married."

"I didn't," said Li Qin.

"It was a detailed and complicated production, getting you to the altar," said April. "Had your squire's parents not agreed to host the ceremony, I am not entirely sure it would have occurred. If you think I may be misleading you, you have a knife. You could split your skin and see for yourself."

I stared down at my hands. The temptation was definitely there: if what she said was true, that man, who had looked at me with such adoration, was somewhere in the world for me to find. And what difference would that make? She said Titania had remade Faerie in her own ideal and image. If that was so, believing in the truth of April's reality would mean denying the one in which I lived now, the one where I was happy. It wouldn't restore the world as it had been. It wouldn't give me back that version of myself. Why would I want to know?

How could I resist knowing?

I drew the blade across my fingertip and, when the blood rose, brought my finger to my mouth, catching it before the wound could heal. Once again, in veils of red, the world went away.

There was less of a feeling of resistance now, as if I had started breaking holes with my first glimpse into my own blood, and it was losing integrity every time I went back.

I am stepping into an outdoor courtyard that has clearly been the scene of a battle, a sword in my hand and a white dress covering my body. People are dead on the ground. The smell of blood fills the air. The man I saw before paces back and forth in front of a low platform, a complicated expression on his face.

Dropping my borrowed sword, I run for him, barely keeping my footing. He turns at the sound of my approach, and relief replaces complexity as I throw myself into his arms.

"I love this dress. Can we do this to all my clothes?"

"Sadly, no." He lifts me and twirls me once around, like I'm some sort of princess. "I see you've managed to get blood in your hair."

"You knew what you were marrying before we got here. We are still getting married, aren't we?"

"That seems to be up to you," says the woman on the platform before us. "You chose your path. You stood before me with a willing heart. You came back. So, are you getting married?"

"Assuming my groom's still interested," I say, and the man April called "Tybalt" snarls. He keeps hold of my hand as we both look up at the woman.

This is a memory. This is my memory, even if it feels like it belongs to someone else, and so I can't recoil, can't pull away. I want to.

I know her. I have never seen her before, but I know her. She is my mother's sister. Tall and beautiful, with long, blue-black hair that falls to her hips and eyes as deep as the sea. Her dress is a strip sliced out of the sky, somehow wrapped around her and pinned in place. She smiles at the sight of me, displaying shark-sharp teeth.

The sea witch. Banished daughter of Maeve the Traitor and Oberon the Lost, whose deeds are legend, whose words are cutting and cruel, who destroys lives and family for fun. And she's smiling at me as she says, "Good," and whistles, high and shrill.

The clearing goes quiet. Nothing else would be a wise choice. She could destroy us all with a thought. There are no other Firstborn in attendance—Father is close, seated with a man I do not know, but Mother is not here.

The sea witch waves, as for attention. "Hi," she says. "My name is Antigone of Albany, better known as the sea witch, and as I am the highest-ranking child of Oberon currently awake on this continent, I claim the right to perform this marriage. Does anyone wish to contest me?"

I do. I want to contest her so very, very badly. My aunt Eira, my mother, both stand above a disgraced, exiled creature of the deeps. But no one says anything, and it seems they're all willing to let this continue and this is wrong, this is wrong, everything about this is wrong, I refuse to consider a world where I could be married by a monster—

But Tybalt is looking at me again, aching adoration in his eyes, and I am undone. How could I refuse a marriage, even one conducted by the sea witch, when he looks at me so? I want this. I want this so badly . . .

As if the thought controlled the moment, the scene skipped ahead, moving through no small amount of conversation, and when it stopped, the Luidaeg was smiling at me again, warmer than I would have thought possible, given the stories I knew about her. She began to speak, and I sank back into memory.

"You know, I never thought we'd make it this far. I always expected something to get in the way before we could get here. That some disaster or other would step in—and look around, it tried. The world has thrown every obstacle it could think of in your path, and you've just gone over them all, haven't you? Because here we are, the least likely of families, and I can't say we're giving anything away or gaining anything today, because you both belong here already. Where we are is your home and has been for a long time. Do you understand

how impossible that is? How ridiculous this all is? This can't have happened, and yet it did, and now we get to see what happens next." *She pauses to look around. "Whatever happens next is probably going to require the services of a dry cleaner."*

People laugh. "This is where I'm supposed to talk about how well-suited the couple are to each other, but let's be real here: they're not. This should never have worked. They should never have found enough common ground to be friends, much less fall in love. I wouldn't have been voting for this." She shifts her gaze to me. "If you'd asked me when we met, I wouldn't have placed my bet on today. And that's okay. We live in stories, but we're not stories, and sometimes the best endings are the ones no one sees coming. I've already asked if anyone wants to argue with me being the one to perform this wedding. Does anyone want to argue with these people being wed? If you do, now's the time to say it."

There had to be a reason I was still in this particular memory, one more thing the blood wanted me to know, and so I grasped it as tightly as I could, and waited for this to come to a conclusion.

"That's as long as I'm expected to wait, and I'll be honest, if anyone was going to object, I expected it to be the bride." Again, laughter. "All right. My father, Oberon, and my mother, Maeve, both agreed that their children should have the ability to bind our descendants together, to keep the lines of succession clear. In their name, and in the names of your Firstborn, Malvic, first King among Cats, and Amandine the Liar, I, Antigone of Albany, better known as the Luidaeg, say you are wed in the eyes of all of Faerie. May the rose and the root shelter you; may the thorn and the oak protect you; may the branch and the tree grant you peace. Your bloodlines are joined, now and always, even if you choose to part."

The red haze shattered as I snapped, gasping, back into the shape of my own skin, the cool air of the little room with the server at its center. I dropped the knife as I turned to gape at April. She cocked her head, looking calmly back at me.

"Yes?" she asked.

"*Cait Sidhe*?!" I demanded. "You really expect me to believe I was married by the *sea witch* to a fucking *cat*?!"

April blinked, several times. That was mostly disconcerting because every time she closed her eyes, her whole body vanished for several seconds, leaving the space where she had been standing empty. "Oh, dear," she said. "Mother warned me that Titania would make her own amendments to reality as you knew it, but did not include such pejoratives."

"April, the Cait Sidhe have been extinct for centuries," said Li Qin. "They were killed in the great purging, along with all the other shapeshifters. Titania's Faerie is pure. No beasts walk among us. Even the descendant lines who carry such attributes have been driven from society, pushed to the outskirts and forced to find their livings there."

April stared at her, horrified. "The Cu Sidhe? The Roane?"

"The Roane were of the Undersea, and the Undersea is lost to us," said Li Qin.

April flickered, apparently agitated by this piece of information. "This is . . . this is worse than Mother feared it would be," she said. "This is horrific. And you all *accepted* it? Believed that this was how the world was meant to be?"

"I . . . I grew up here," I said, feeling obscurely like I needed to justify myself to her. "This is the only world I've ever known."

"Your blood knows otherwise. You should have known. Somehow, I don't know how, but somehow . . . you should have *known*." Her voice cracked, sounding for all the world like any child who'd been let down by the adults she trusted to take care of her.

"What can we do?" asked Li Qin, stepping toward her. "How can I help?"

"I need my mother," said April. "I *want* you to be my mother, but you're not, not right now, not with the memories of this world and not our own. I want *my* mother. I need her. Can you make her be here?"

"I might have a way," I said, desperate to make her stop sounding so achingly, heartbreakingly lost. I pulled the phone Melly had given me out of my pocket, pressing the button to light up the screen. There was a single name there: *ETIENNE*. I pressed the button again to select it, and felt obscurely like I'd just solved a difficult riddle as I raised the phone to my ear.

It rang. Again and again it rang, until I was on the verge of giving up. Then there was a click, and Sir Etienne's voice was saying, "Hello? October? Are you already finished in Dreamer's Glass?"

"Not quite," I said. "Would it be entirely inappropriate of me to ask you for a favor?"

". . . yes," he said, after a moment's hesitation. "But it would also be surprising enough that I'll allow it, if only for the sake of finding out what you're up to."

"Does your range of travel extend so far as Briarholme?"

The hesitation this time was much, much longer before he said, "I've made the jump before. It isn't the *easiest* thing to do, or the most pleasant, but it isn't outside my capabilities."

"Excellent. Could you please go and inform the Countess January that Duchess Li Qin Zhou would like to see her and, assuming she consents, bring her back to Dreamer's Glass?"

"And what do I get for performing this complicated and difficult task on your behalf, *changeling*?"

The word, while emphasized, was neither as sharp or as cruel as it could have been. I wondered, for an instant, when I'd started hearing the difference. "You mentioned a daughter before. You seemed to think I could help you with something regarding her. I can't promise I'll be able to help you. If you will do this for me, I can promise to hear you out."

"Tell whomever you have called that I will cover for you as necessary, if help is possible," said Li Qin.

"The Duchess Zhou has offered to cover for me, so if I am able to aid you, we won't need to worry as much about getting caught."

Silence answered me, and for a moment, I was afraid I'd pushed the matter too far, that he'd decided it was too dangerous to listen to me. Then, in a voice gone distant and cold, he said, "I will be there, *with* the Countess, as quickly as I can."

The line went dead.

I lowered the phone to find Li Qin and April both watching me expectantly.

"Who was that?" asked Li Qin.

"Sir Etienne of Shadowed Hills," I said. "He's Tuatha de Dannan. He brought me here, and was enjoined to collect me again when I was finished. The phone was provided to make it possible for me to contact him. Shadowed Hills is a very modern Duchy, really."

Expectancy turned into flat disbelief. I decided to ignore it as I put the phone back in my pocket.

"He's going to travel to Briarholme to see whether he can convince Countess January to come here," I said.

"And his daughter?" asked Li Qin.

"I have no idea. He's never married, and to the best of my understanding he has no children in the mortal world. But he asked me about a daughter before, and it seemed like a reasonable way to convince him to do as I had asked."

"Even traveling as the Tuatha do, it will be some time before he can return," said Li Qin. "April, are you able to move around the knowe?"

"At home, we had installed signal boosters to guarantee I could move at will throughout the knowe and certain areas outside," said April. "Without those, my range is limited, but I can travel perhaps two hundred yards from this point."

"That encompasses the kitchens," said Li Qin. "Do you eat?"

"I can, although it does little to sustain me," said April. Then, almost shyly: "I like carrots."

"Very well, then. I think Avebury made carrot cake last night, and there should still be some remaining." She offered April her hand. April took it, clinging like she'd just found some sort of impossible lifeline, and Li Qin beckoned for me to follow them.

She led April back through the room of junk and salvage, me tagging along behind, and we emerged into the room where I had first arrived. From there, we proceeded along a hallway, passing several closed doors, to an open doorway through which the sounds of kitchen work in progress drifted.

Li Qin flashed me an encouraging smile and stepped into the kitchen. I followed.

It was a smaller room than its equivalent at Shadowed Hills but substantially more modern, with gleaming glass and silver surfaces in place of stone. A Barrow Wight stood by a long silver table, kneading bread dough, while a Gwragen changeling stirred a pot of something rich and aromatic-smelling.

The Barrow Wight looked up at our entrance, grinning a gap-toothed grin at Li Qin. "Duchess!" she said, brightly. "Dinner's not for several hours yet, if you were hungry. It's saag paneer tonight, and I'm about done preparing the dough for naan, but if you wanted feeding, it's sandwiches and last night's scampi for the moment, I'm afraid."

Her speaking so bluntly and familiarly to her liege stopped my tongue. I gaped, astonished by the audacity. Li Qin, however . . .

Li Qin *laughed*. "Oh, I would never dream of trying to get my supper early, and a few hours is more than fine. This mite, however"—she indicated April—"has just shown up on our doorstep, and requires a slice of last night's fine carrot cake, if there's any yet remaining."

"October as well," said April. She lifted her chin, stubbornly. "She rarely eats enough."

"October?" asked the Barrow Wight—Avebury, I assumed—as she looked to me.

"Duke Torquill's niece," affirmed Li Qin.

"A pleasure to host you in our house," said Avebury, leaving the dough as she bustled around the table, pausing only to grab a cloth and wipe the flour from her hands. "Of course there's cake for the having, if there's company to be having it. Would you like tea as well?"

"We would," said Li Qin. "If it wouldn't delay dinner too upsettingly, could you bring it to us in the library?"

"In a twinkling," said Avebury, smiling as she moved to begin gathering plates.

Li Qin led us out of the kitchen again. I must have been looking at her oddly, because she raised an eyebrow and asked, "Is there a problem, Miss Torquill?"

"No. Yes. I don't know," I said. "The way she spoke to you . . ."

"Avebury is as pureblooded as I am, if that's what's concerning you," said Li Qin. "Her sister, Minna, came here from . . ." Her face clouded for a moment. "I don't remember where Minna came from, but she brought Avebury with her, and once Avebury was well settled in my household, Minna returned home. She's never come to visit, either. Isn't that odd?"

"Not if their original place of residence was outside the three Kingdoms I have named," said April.

"Fair enough. I can't think of anyone who's traveled outside those three Kingdoms," said Li Qin. "It's like there's a wall between us and the rest of Faerie."

"Because there is," said April.

"It's . . . the way she spoke to you, yes, as if she had the authority to do so," I said. "Uncle Sylvester tolerates what Mother says is a shameful amount of backtalk from his servants, but none of them would dream to tell him his dinner wasn't ready if he deigned to appear in the kitchens asking for it. It was . . . unseemly."

"Ah," said Li Qin. "I always forget how much closer Shadowed Hills is to the Queen's knowe. They have to follow courtly manners much more rigidly than we do here. I promise you, October, when you're not watching, there's plenty of backtalk and sass in your uncle's halls."

The thought was unsettling. I focused instead on the room Li Qin had led us to, which had a green carpet and walls painted in climbing roses, so it was almost as if we were sitting in a small outdoor garden. A circular table sat at the middle of the room, flanked by comfortable chairs. Li Qin settled in one. I took another. April, apparently loath to be parted from the mother who didn't know her, perched on the arm of Li Qin's chair.

Avebury appeared a moment later with plates, forks, and an uncut carrot cake, all of which she put down in front of us.

Li Qin smiled at her. "Your baking is always excellent."

"Will there be anything else, ma'am?"

"Just the tea."

Then Avebury was gone again, presumably to fetch the tea service, and Li Qin was cutting the cake, serving me first, as if I were somehow her equal, and it all made me want to scream, because none of this was right. I was less than she was. I knew I was less. Even August, much as she adored me, never made any bones of the fact that I was born to be her servant; I was not her peer but her plaything.

But did she think that, or did I? I sank deeper into my chair, frowning, trying to puzzle through the conflicting ideas in my head. Some of them mentally tasted of copper, as if they were concepts or ideas I had stolen from the version of myself who'd never existed outside of impossible blood memory, the one who would offend Titania and allow the sea witch to marry her to an animal. The Cait Sidhe—all the shapeshifters—had been little more than beasts, cursed by their mother, Maeve, to such a degree that they were unfit for any reasonable company, seized by wicked instincts to rend and rip and destroy.

The thought turned my stomach just as Avebury returned with the tea, which was hot and sweet and tasted of peppermint, a flavor that made me think of pennyroyal for some reason. Close on that thought was a wave of rejection and revulsion so strong that it almost made me drop my cup.

I didn't like it there in Dreamer's Glass. I didn't like the things it was causing me to think, or the way it was making me feel. The sooner I could get back to Mother's tower and the safety of my family, the better off I would be.

Li Qin was talking quietly to April. The tiny, flickering Dryad seemed to be giving her more details on the world that wasn't. I, resolutely, didn't listen. None of that was true anymore, and I couldn't really believe it had ever been true to begin with, no matter what the blood said. I had no training, by design. Perhaps if I did, I would have received the lessons on blood lies and how to recognize them. I would know that what they told me wasn't true.

Li Qin finally settled with her own plate of cake. I pulled mine toward me and took a bite. She said Avebury's baking was excellent, but what I tasted was heavy clay, sweetened with some sort of cloying sugar. I swallowed, rather than spitting it out, and set the plate aside.

"I believe she is in shock," said April.

"Based on everything you've told me, it's not unreasonable to think that Titania might have hit her especially hard," said Li Qin.

I wanted to shout at them, to tell them I was right there, listening. I didn't. Even if I'd been able to make my lips obey, raising my voice to a pair of purebloods went against everything I'd ever been taught. I couldn't. I could want to all day long. That didn't make it possible.

Wanting something doesn't make it true.

A circle opened in the air, carrying the scent of evergreen trees and rain. Etienne stepped through, then stopped, turning back, and held out his hand for someone to follow.

Taking his hand in hers, Countess January ap Learainth stepped out of the circle, which closed behind her, and into Dreamer's Glass.

As always, she was tall and lovely, with brown hair streaked in Torquill red and wide, golden eyes. She looked around the room, glancing at and dismissing me, finally landing on April, the child who wore what I now couldn't deny was a younger mirror of January's own face.

"What mischief are you making?" she asked, and her voice was high and formal.

"Mother," said April, disappearing from the arm of the chair to reappear next to January and throw her arms around the woman's waist. January blinked, looking mildly trapped.

"No mere mischief; actual trickery," she said, voice turning hard. "What is this?"

"Toby, please," said April, glancing to me. What did she expect me to do? Explain their wild story of a different world to my innocent cousin? January was the only cousin I had. I wasn't going to pour all that nonsense into her ear.

"If you bleed and reach for magic, not memory, you can see spells," said April, now a little frantic. "You can see the way they're woven. You can break them. Please. Please, find the spell, and give me back my mother."

I stood abruptly. "All right, that's *it*," I said. "Etiquette says I listen and agree to whatever you say, but asking me to assault my cousin is a step too far. I'm leaving. Sir Etienne? I'm ready to go home."

"No," he said, mildly.

"No?" I echoed.

"No. You said you'd help me if I got her for you, so even if we left here, I wouldn't be doing it to take you home, but so I could take you to where I need you," said Etienne. "But all of this ridiculousness makes me curious. I've always been a curious man. You can bleed for them. I swear, upon my honor, not to tell your mother."

The thought that I was only refusing because I was afraid he'd tell my mother was nearly hilarious. I somehow managed not to laugh. "Well, I'm not cutting myself."

"In that case, I apologize," said April, and vanished with a snap of static. I turned, trying to see where she had gone, and was looking in the wrong place as she clicked back into existence next to me, the knife Li Qin had used to cut the cake in her hand. She lashed out, laying open the back of *my* hand, blood welling at once to the surface. I shouted, wordless pain and anger, but she was already gone, popping away and reappearing behind Li Qin.

Eyes hard, she looked at me.

"Bleed for me, and bring back my mother," she said.

EIGHT

A DIRECT ORDER FROM A pureblood, even one I'd already decided not to listen to, was a difficult thing to ignore. My hand was halfway to my mouth before I caught myself and glared at her.

"You *cut* me," I accused.

"It wasn't a stabbing," she said. "Your squire is persistently cross about how many shirts you've ruined by getting stabbed."

"Sir Etienne, this girl assaulted me!" I said.

"I saw no assault," he said. "Only a pureblooded child of high spirits making sport with a contrary changeling."

I gaped at him.

"She gave you an order, October," he said. "I would see it carried out."

The wound in my hand was already almost healed, but the blood remained. Glaring at Etienne, I raised my hand to my lips and took a mouthful of blood, swallowing it.

Red memory rose, threatening to overwhelm me. For just a moment, I allowed it, trying to use my own blood to show me what she claimed I already knew:

Looking at the spell, I see threads of prismatic pink, and I know those are what I have to strip away to free him. My poor love. He's going to be furious, but most of all with himself. The Shadow Roads are dark and cold, and still, I take hold of the threads and pull until they snap, one by one—

If I stayed in the memory any longer, all the blood would be used up, and I would need more. Part of me wanted that. The rest of me had been given an order and was finding it difficult to disobey. I shoved the memory away, closing my eyes and trying to see what that other version of me had seen.

The room around me flashed into light, threads of white tied neatly around threads of gleaming black, glistening like opals, and I knew, on some level, that I was looking at Li Qin's magic, at the spells and effects she had woven into the knowe since she claimed it as her own. Around me stood four figures, each outlined in threads like the ones I'd seen in the blood memory. The three whose locations matched January, Etienne, and Li Qin were wrapped in that same prismatic pink, with more muted colors showing through the gaps between the threads that I presumed matched their innate magic. January's was the flashing white of lightning; Li Qin's was opalescent black. Etienne was a soft and lambent gold, like candlelight. The fourth figure, presumably April, was wrapped in green so bright, it almost hurt my eyes, gleaming and glowing, occasionally flashing with moving specks of white.

"January," I said, without opening my eyes, "there's a spell on you that doesn't match your own magic. May I remove it?"

Pulling it away without asking her could be interpreted as assault. April coming at me with a knife wasn't a crime, but for me to assault a pureblood would mean dishonor at best, death at worst.

"None of this makes any sense," said January. "There aren't any spells on me."

The blood was running out, taking the lines with it. I was going to need to cut myself again. Resigned to the approaching pain, I opened my eyes.

"Please," said Li Qin. "I know you've just met me, but please, let her do this. If you do, my Duchy will owe you a great debt."

"Placing a lot of store on luck and a story, aren't you?" I asked.

"Those are the only things I've ever placed any faith in at all," said Li Qin. She kept her eyes on January, pleading.

January sighed, sweeping her hair out of her face with one hand, and turned to me. "Fine," she said curtly. "If you must do this, do it. But remember that I allow this only out of respect for a fellow noble, and not at the request of a changeling."

"You are very kind."

I drew the knife I'd been given and reopened the back of my hand. It was so well healed that it hadn't left a scar, but my body remembered the pain, and all I had to do was trace the aching line across my skin. Blood welled up, bright and clean and smelling, oddly, of roses.

My own magic has never spoken in roses. There wasn't time to get distracted, though; if I did, I'd just heal again and need to make a third cut. I was getting awfully tired of bleeding.

Hopefully this would be the last time. If not forever, then at least for today.

I closed my eyes and lifted my hand, sucking as much blood out of the healing wound as I could. Then I turned back toward January, pushing the red-veiled memories away as they tried to rise and overwhelm me.

The pink lines were back, brighter than before, sparkling with veins of prismatic crystal. Like the black lines knotted through the knowe, they were almost opaline, and so beautiful that the thought of breaking them made me feel like a criminal. Lines of flashing lightning-white and yarrow-gold ran beneath them, both tamped down and ensnarled by the pink. The white and gold seemed to be natural, January's own, while the pink had been tossed over the top of them, pushing them aside and keeping them from maintaining the pattern they were meant for.

"I have no idea what I'm doing," I said apologetically, and reached out with the part of me that could see the lines, grabbing hold of the nearest strands of pink.

I wasn't touching them with my skin, but I still went cold when I grasped them, like all the warmth was being jerked out of me through some half-approved exchange. *She'll know I did this,* I thought, and the idea was enough to leave me giddy with terror and something that felt almost like excitement. I wasn't disobeying anyone. I had been put into a position where the only way to obey my betters was to unweave this spell, whatever it was and whoever it belonged to, and obedience was a changeling's first duty. If this caught Titania's attention, surely I wouldn't be the one to take the blame.

I grabbed several more pink strands, until it felt like the "hands" of my magic were full, and my physical hands were so cold that it felt like I was burying them wrist-deep in snow. Thus entangled, I yanked as hard as I could.

January screamed.

I couldn't let go, not yet, not with the cold freezing my fingers and locking them into place, and this magic—whatever it was—was too new for me to know the difference between my real fingers and the spell's fingers now that I was losing feeling in both. I managed to yank even harder, pulling until the first of the pink threads snapped.

January screamed again. The rest of the pink threads fell away, unable to hold their integrity without that first one holding them in place. Pain lanced through my head and I sagged. The white and gold threads snapped tight, outlining the shape of her as she collapsed in a heap on the floor. I managed to stagger several feet back, and opened my eyes.

January had pushed herself far enough on the floor to be sitting up, propped by her hands. There were tears in her eyes and a stunned expression on her bloodless face. She didn't move, just stayed exactly as she was, staring into nothingness.

April appeared in front of her, stooping to put them eye-to-eye. "Mother?" she asked, in an anxious tone.

"Oak and *ash*, April, what did you *do*?" asked January, in a tone I'd never heard from her before, and April fell into her arms, laughing and crying as they clung to one another.

Li Qin stayed in her chair, watching them, her own face stricken.

"What did you do?" asked Etienne.

Explaining everything would take too long, and my head was already throbbing from the effort of breaking the pink threads on January. I couldn't let myself think about the threads still clinging to Etienne and Li Qin, which might also be clinging to me. Still, I tried: "Duchess Zhou requested my help with a mysterious box she said could only be activated by a member of my family bloodline. When I pressed the button on the front, that little girl over there came out of it, and began telling a wild story about modified memories and shattered families. She claimed my cousin and the Duchess were her mothers, were married, and had been taken away from each other, while she'd been sealed in the box to keep her safe from the force that was doing all of this. Oh, and apparently, we can add 'breaking complicated spells' to the list of 'things Dóchas Sidhe can do that no one ever thought it was important to tell the changeling about,' because they needed me to unbind Countess ap Learainth's memories."

"It's not 'ap Learainth,' it's 'O'Leary,'" said January. "I didn't want to keep my father's name when I couldn't have my father, and at the time, declaring myself a Torquill seemed to be out of the question. Although I understand the family's improving in recent years; I might want to reconsider."

"I do not wish to change my name," said April, still clinging to January as the older woman unfolded herself from the floor and stood.

January gave a little laugh. "Consideration finished, then. I'm an O'Leary, and my daughter's an O'Leary, and we'll stay O'Learys for as long as we choose." She bent to press a kiss to April's forehead before glancing to Li Qin. "You really don't remember us?"

"I'm sorry, but no," said Li Qin.

"And you got Toby to release me anyway?"

"The luck said I should."

"Oberon keep and bless your luck, most beautiful of wives," said January firmly, before turning to me. "Toby . . ." she began, apologetically.

I didn't want to hear what she was going to say next. What I'd done might have been the right thing, but I still felt sick to my stomach, and the taste of blood was harsh and sticky in the back of my mouth. I hated this. This was . . . this was *wrong*. Titania's Faerie was a paradise, one she had planted and cultivated for all of us, even the least among us, even me.

"I can't do that again," I said. My fingers still ached with the cold, which was unusual; that, and the pounding in my head, might be the longest-lasting injuries I had ever sustained. "I'm sorry, if that's what you want to ask of me, I can't."

"We can get by without my memories for now," said Li Qin. "April will tell us what I need to know."

"I will," said April, suddenly beside her. She was bouncing back and forth between her mothers like a bird in a cage, first here, then there, never ceasing to move.

"Toby, no," said January. "I didn't want to ask you to do more for us than you already had. I wanted to say . . . thank you. Thank you, and I'm sorry."

I couldn't have said which of those phrases hit me harder: the forbidden thanks or the apology. My cousin was not my liege; pureblood or no, it was an insult even to a mere changeling for her to imply that I somehow owed her fealty for doing only what had been asked of me. And yet, her face, her voice, her *eyes* . . . they weren't offering the insult that her words would normally imply. They offered genuine gratitude, admiration, and even *friendship*.

How could she, a pureblood, a noble, be looking at me like that?

I gaped at her.

She shook her head. "I know the things I said to you were unforgivable, but they weren't *me*. I would never—okay, so that version of me would, I guess, and that's a shitty thing that I'm going to have to learn to live with—but this version is the *real* version, and I would *never* act like you were somehow my inferior." April appeared next to her again, sliding her arms around January's shoulders, and January put a hand on her wrist, steadying them both. They already looked like a family. They looked like they had never been apart. Li Qin seemed a little subdued, watching them, this unit that she was currently standing just outside of and couldn't enter without the memories I didn't have the strength to unlock yet.

If I could ever unlock them at all. I'd spilled so much blood, there was no way Mother wasn't going to catch the smell of it somehow. She would lock me in the tower for a decade as punishment for allowing myself to be cajoled into doing blood magic, and while I wanted to think that would be a good thing, I couldn't. Not now.

Because if January's memories were true, mine might be too. And if my memories were true, Li Qin wasn't the only one who'd been compelled to forget a spouse for some reason.

Maybe it wasn't so bad, that I'd seen myself married to a beast. He clearly cared for me, and didn't resent me for the low station of my birth. Who else would be willing to see themselves tethered to a changeling, in defiance of all Titania's laws?

If those laws existed at all. Oh, I didn't like to think about it. It made the pounding in my head even worse. Still, if they were true memories, and that man existed somewhere for me to find, I couldn't allow myself to be locked in the tower. I turned to Sir Etienne, intending to tell him as much, only to find him looking at me with blazing eyes, jaw set in a hard line.

"I still need your help, and you promised you would hear my reasons if I did this for you," he said. "I did as you asked, for all that I should not be required to barter my services with a *changeling* to have what's rightly mine, and now you owe me."

"I do," I agreed. "Only my head hurts really badly right now, and Countess ap . . . O'Leary has just recovered her memories. Must we do this now?"

"She's awake and talking and, if what you say is true, freed from the burden of an unkindly intended spell," said Sir Etienne. He waved my concerns away as if they were nothing at all. "Once I return you to your uncle's halls, I will have no excuse to extract you again. Your mother will return soon, according to your father's understanding of her movements, and while I've promised not to tell her you were doing blood magic, she's not going to let me take you on a field trip. You have to do this now. I've waited long enough. *She's* waited long enough."

Even if he hadn't mentioned his daughter before, the brightness in his eyes would have told me he wasn't talking about any "she" currently in this room.

Reluctantly, and extremely aware of how soon even the scant freedom of movement that Moving Day afforded me would end, I nodded.

"All right, Sir Etienne," I said. "I still don't know if I'll be able to help, but I promised you I would listen. If you truly think it within my power, I will go with you now, and I will do my best." I glanced back to January, who was moving cautiously toward Li Qin, like she was approaching an easily startled animal. "Countess? Duchess? Do you mind if we take our leave of you?"

If Li Qin forbade Etienne to take me, I could stay there long enough to eat a proper meal and sleep off this headache. She outranked him. He'd have no choice but to wait.

Please tell him you mind, I thought, hoping that maybe Shyi Shuai had mind-reading magic I'd never heard of or something. *If you tell him you mind, I'll try to take the spell off you once my head stops pounding.*

"Not at all," said Li Qin, staring at January, who had started cautiously stroking her hair with one hand. "We are very grateful for everything October has been able to do for us today, and hope she'll be up for a return visit sometime soon. I can do without my memory for a time. I might eventually prefer to have it returned to me."

"She will be happy to return and aid a pureblood household," said Sir Etienne, before I could reply. "We appreciate your hospitality. October, come."

He grabbed my wrist with one hand, etching a circle in the air with the other. The portal that opened showed a sunlit mortal street—the one he'd disappeared to before. He snapped his fingers, and a human disguise bloomed around him, blunting his ears, softening his face, and toning down the metallic brightness of his eyes.

Without another word, he dragged me into the portal and we were gone, leaving Dreamer's Glass behind us.

NINE

MY FIRST IMPRESSION OF the place on the other side of the portal was correct: I knew it as soon as Sir Etienne pulled me through, even though I had never been there before. We were in the mortal world. The air smelled like woodsmoke, leaf mold, and something chemical and strange that I neither recognized nor cared for. Metal boxes I recognized as "cars" from the magazines Kerry would sometimes smuggle into the kitchens at Shadowed Hills lined the streets, and the sidewalks were cracked by tree roots and long stretches of disrepair.

Sir Etienne didn't let go of my wrist as he started striding down the street toward one of the low, squarish houses, pulling me in his wake. The house he was aiming for had a small porch and a wide front window masked by gauzy curtains. A light was on inside, but the illumination provided no details through the fabric.

"Where are we?" I asked.

He didn't answer, just kept pulling.

Oh, I was getting tired of this. I dug my heels into the next crack in the sidewalk, bracing myself against one of those intrusive roots. Sir Etienne's grip slipped as my sudden motionlessness dragged him to a halt, and he turned to glare at me.

His glare was less impressive when filtered through a human disguise. I wondered if that was true of everyone. Maybe Father's patron wouldn't be so terrifying if I could just get her to filter herself through humanity before she came to remind me of how inferior I was.

"You *agreed*," he snapped.

"I said I'd help you if I could, not that I'd let you toss me around like a sack of potatoes and drag me unfamiliar places without explanations," I said. "You want me to help you, I said I would try, we're fine there. But you wouldn't be doing it like this if it were something you could tell your liege, which means you can't exactly tattle on me if I don't give it my all. You want the best of me, you need to tell me why I'm here."

His temper flared, eyebrows drawing together as he scowled and snapped, "You will speak to me with civility, you little—" The flash of anger faded as quickly as it had come, replaced by what looked like sincere regret. He finally loosened his grasp on my wrist, allowing me to pull free and hug my arms against my chest, trying to make myself feel marginally better.

Somehow, the regret made me feel worse than the anger. Purebloods weren't supposed to look at me like they'd been in the wrong for raising their tempers, like I was somehow deserving of apologies. After January's impossible thanks, I was even more on edge than my surroundings justified.

"I'm sorry, October," he said, voice dropping and turning raspy with what sounded like sincere regret. "I've just been carrying this for so long, and to have a resolution possibly within my grasp . . . You have no idea how long I've been waiting for the chance to fix this, to finish it. It's going to destroy me, and I'll be glad to go, if it means I've made things right."

This was starting to sound serious, and far more important than anything a mere changeling should be involved with. "Can you tell me exactly what's going on?"

"Not out on the street," said Etienne. "We arrived here because my . . . friend . . . dislikes it when I enter the house through other means. She says it's disrespectful. I've already done enough to ruin her life, I prefer not to upset her further."

"But you're not intending to hurt me, or force me to hurt anyone else?" My head was still pounding. I wasn't sure how much of a fight I'd be able to put up if he tried to make me do something I really didn't want to do.

Hopefully, I wouldn't need to find out.

"Stars, no!" said Etienne, sounding properly horrified. I realized I'd stopped thinking of him by his honorific sometime during this conversation on the street. He was a man like any other, and he should be allowed all the complexities that included. "I expect I'll need to ask for bloodshed, but I don't know that it will be yours, and any request would be consensual."

"I stopped because I wanted to know more, and now I feel like I know less," I complained, as I started moving again, stepping up next to him and gesturing for him to keep going. "But you're right about some things not being safe to discuss out on the street. What is that *smell*?"

"Car exhaust," said Etienne, turning off the sidewalk and onto the short walkway up to the house we'd been moving toward. "At least, I assume you know what a bonfire smells like."

"Ha ha," I said, and then winced, barely able to believe that I'd been sarcastic in the presence of a pureblood who wasn't my sister. August would have thought it was funny, not inappropriate. August would probably have congratulated me for finding the nerve.

To my surprise, Etienne also found it funny—or at least funny enough to chuckle, the sound dry and brisk. "As I said, I assumed you'd know the other scents. Car exhaust is the result of motor vehicles burning a mixture of petrochemicals for internal combustion. The smell can be . . . quite surprising, when you're not expecting it."

I was beginning to think I should stop asking for explanations, if every one of them was just going to add further incomprehensibility to the mix.

Etienne shot me an anxious look, no longer laughing. "What you're about to see is private. You can tell no one. Not even your family. I apologize for asking you to keep secrets, but for reasons of safety, I must."

"I . . . I will do my best not to create a situation where I would be asked directly," I said. If someone commanded me to tell them, I would be unable to stop myself.

Etienne nodded gravely. "That may be the best I can hope for." He pressed a small button next to the door.

A bell rang somewhere inside the house. I tensed, moving to stand partially behind him. Etienne shot me a reassuring look, then turned back to the door, clearly waiting.

Seconds ticked by, and I became more and more uneasy standing on this human street in the late afternoon, sunlight all around us and cars occasionally driving by, adding more "exhaust" to the already-heavy air. I was about to grab Etienne's arm and ask him to take me away from there when the door finally swung open, and I saw the last thing I could have possibly expected standing there.

A human woman.

Sure, this was a human neighborhood, and sure, Etienne wore a human disguise, but somehow I had expected some greater secret than the existence of a human where the other humans lived. She was wearing some sort of loose blue shirt with long sleeves and a neckline that had been stretched all out of shape, blue, with the word CAL written across the front in large yellow letters. She had the same sort of trousers on as I did, and they looked no less indecent on someone else.

Her hair, shaggy and brown, was pinned atop her head in a loose knot, held there with several pencils that had been shoved haphazardly through the tangles. Her skin was a few shades lighter than Etienne's, a few shades darker than mine. And she seemed entirely unsurprised to find him standing on her porch.

"Etienne!" she said, stepping back and holding the door open wider. "Come in, come in. I'll make you a cuppa. Who's your friend?"

There was a wariness I couldn't quite read in her question, but I still followed Etienne as he stepped over the threshold. He placed his hands to either side of her face and kissed her forehead while she tilted her head back and beamed at him, utterly at peace, utterly trusting. It ached, for some reason I couldn't quite define, to see them so.

"This is October," he said, letting her go again and gesturing to me. "She's the younger of the two girls I told you about."

"Ah." She looked at me, expression sharper now. "You've gotten an agreement, then? Or you've abducted the poor child for your own ends?"

"A bit of both," he admitted. "October, this is Bridget. Bess."

He paused then, stepping closer to her and putting an arm around her shoulders. Seeming to catch her cue, the human woman—Bridget—leaned up against him, sending a polite smile in my direction.

"My wife," said Etienne.

I stared.

The creation of changelings is among the most essential duties of the pureblood Courts. Firstborn and titled nobility are required to provide at least one, for the enrichment of Faerie; the fact that Uncle Sylvester has managed to avoid his duty for as long as he has is something of a miracle, and a source for much of the idle gossip about Shadowed Hills that August has brought back with her from her travels with Mother. All of this is true.

But the mortals the changeling children are gotten upon are playthings, intended for a night of company, perhaps several, as even a fertile mortal womb can take time to quicken, and destined to be cast aside as soon as a child is secured. If their fairy lover is of a line that can manipulate memory or cast strong-enough illusions, they may be allowed to live after they've been safely relieved of their offspring; if not, they meet with terrible, unpreventable accidents.

It's not a kind system. It's not a system I would have created. It's the system I was born of, and into, and the one Titania has set for us, which means it must be perfect, for all its cruelty.

And nowhere does it include the possibility of marriage. If I was horrified by the suggestion that I'd been married to a beast in some other version of our world, the thought of Etienne being married to a human was far worse.

My revulsion and confusion must have shown on my face, because Etienne scowled.

"I cannot bring her before my liege or to my home, but we were married in the proper way, outside beneath the ash and oak, in full view of both the wilds and the water," said Etienne. "My life is bound to hers, and my only regret is that there is no means known to magic by which I can stretch her life to keep her by my side."

"This is . . ." I took a step backward, shaking my head. "I'm sorry, Etienne, this is a step too far. I don't know what you think *I* could possibly do here to help you with this . . . with this *abomination*, but I can't do it, and I can't keep this—"

"We have a daughter," blurted Bridget.

I froze.

"Her name is Chelsea. She's nineteen, smart as a whip, just finished high school, and started at the university where I teach this semester. She'll be home in a few hours. She knows what she is. How could she not know, when so many things about her differ from her peers? And she knows she can never be considered an equal in the world her father comes from."

"I'm sorry, I truly am, but what do you think *I* can do about it?" I asked. "If you want me to tell her what life as a changeling in the Courts is like, I can, but honestly, Etienne, you should have brought her to the Duke as soon as she was born. A live changeling is a gift from Titania to Faerie. This is *wrong*."

"I don't want you to indoctrinate her," said Etienne, tone going cold. "The hope chests were destroyed after Maeve betrayed us, but Faerie has returned them to our keeping in the form of the Dóchas Sidhe, even if your mother hides that truth. Your own father was born a changeling, and transformed for the sake of his family's honor. His brother was born the same. Your mother changed them both when they were all children together. I believe that you, and your sister, share that ability. Your magic will let you strip the mortality from my daughter, if you command and she consents."

I stared at him. What he was saying was nonsense . . . wasn't it? But then, this whole day had been nonsense, and Father had always looked quietly ashamed when the subject of changelings and his eventual duty arose. I had assumed he didn't want to dally with a woman other than Mother, but Uncle Sylvester had been able to avoid the same edict, when it shouldn't have been possible. Not unless they had been given some quiet, unremarked exemption.

Father was always kinder to me than he had to be, always encouraging me to think well of myself, never allowing me to tear myself down over the things I could not change. Had he done that out of love, or out of guilt that he had been given a great gift that my own mother had not seen fit to offer me?

If I had been born before August, when Mother was among those in need of an heir, would I have been a changeling at all?

"I knew . . . I knew Mother's skills extended to the balancing of the blood," I said, very carefully. "She adjusts changelings for noble houses, to make us more suited to whatever work we might be required for, but even if she *can* do what you're asking of me now, I don't know if that means *I* can. I've never wished to dwell on that possibility, for reasons I should hope would be obvious."

"Not to me," said Bridget, and I remembered that I was still wearing the human disguise Father had spun for me. The itching was still present, but so constant that it had faded into a small annoyance, especially in comparison to my head. "You look like a lovely young woman, if a somewhat angry one, and I'm truly sorry our first meeting has to be me asking you for something you find so upsetting."

She had a faint accent, something I couldn't entirely place, but her words were otherwise kind, and seemed sincerely meant.

"Even if I *could* do what you would ask of me, I have no idea *how*," I said. "The magic of my line is all but bound in blood, and I've received little-to-no training in such work. I could do more damage than good."

"I'm willing to take the risk," said Bridget. "I won't speak for her, but I believe Chelsea will be as well. She doesn't want to be an outsider forever. If that means eventually going into Faerie and claiming to be her own father's cousin, she's willing to make the adjustment."

"My family can never be together," said Etienne. "I told Bridget so when she informed me she was pregnant, and she chose to marry me anyway, to have a father for her child. I've been here as much as I could be, but the girl is grown now, and her magic grown with her. She yearns to see what she's been denied. Nineteen years of mortality can be enough, if she decides."

"So to save your family, you speak of secrets that could see mine slaughtered?"

"I have kept this secret longer than you've been alive, and do not hold it lightly, but yes. To save my family, I would hold the knife myself." He looked at me, unflinching. "Please."

"I . . ." I stopped, and pressed a hand against my forehead. "My head is killing me, I have no way of leaving on my own, and she's not even here. Is there someplace where I can go lie down for a little bit? Until you need me?"

"Of course," said Bridget. She beckoned me toward her. "I'll show you to the guest room. There's clean sheets on the bed, and you can nap awhile, get your strength back before any final decisions must be made."

"Bess—" began Etienne.

She quelled him with a look. "Can't you see the girl's exhausted?" she asked. "You told me these two were kept like orchids in a hothouse, never stirring farther from home than absolutely necessary, and I'll be asking you quite a few questions on how you came to bring me one of them, even if you did it for our daughter's sake. For right now, she needs her rest, and maybe some nice toast with jam and butter when she wakes up. All right?"

She sounded so fierce and so confident that she would get her way that it wasn't a surprise when Etienne nodded, shoulders slumping, and said, "I'll go start that coffee."

"Good lad." Bridget put an arm around my shoulders. It was the first time I'd ever been touched by a human, and I had to fight not to shy away. "Those Courts of yours hammer secrecy so hard, it's a wonder he ever asks anyone for permission to do anything. Asking permission means showing your hand, after all, and we can't risk people knowing we might want to accomplish something! Heaven forfend!"

She guided me out of the room and into a short hall, where she opened a door and flicked a switch on the wall. Light came on, illuminating a small room with a single window, a dresser, and a large, soft-looking bed that I immediately yearned to topple into.

The fae are nocturnal, after all. The fact that we were doing all of this during the day wasn't making it any easier.

"I've been to the Court, of course."

I shot her a startled look.

"Oh, not the one kept by his liege—there would have been too many questions if he'd appeared there with a lady-friend, even one draped in so many layers of illusion that I couldn't even feel the shape of my own face any longer. He took me to see the Queen."

The Queen of the Mists. A tall, beautiful figure with bone-white hair and a voice that could set the stars to dancing. She had no name, because she didn't need one; even as few chose to refer to Fair Titania by her title, unless it was as "the Summer Queen," or "Queen of All Faerie," the Queen of the Mists was so entirely unique that a name would have been an unnecessary burden placed upon her narrow shoulders.

She already carried so much for our sake—translating Titania's wishes for those of us among the lesser orders, keeping us safe from the threats posed by our neighboring kingdoms, and protecting us from the threat of the mortal world—she didn't need to carry anything more.

Only somehow that protection had failed to extend to detecting a disguised human accompanied by one of her own. I wanted to ask about it. I also didn't want to insult this woman whose home I was about to be sleeping in, and I had no way of knowing what would or would not offend a human. It had never seemed like a necessary thing to know before.

"It was lovely. Very archaic by our standards. I'm sure my life seems shabby and dull in comparison to all the bright colors and magical things, but I don't know that I could trade pillars made of formless mist for pizza delivery, or people who can change your clothes with a snap of their fingers for my refrigerator. All worlds have their own sort of magic, I suppose." Bridget stepped into the room, plumping the pillows on the bed with quick motions of her hands. "If you need to sleep, you can safely sleep here. I won't let Etienne wake you until he absolutely has to."

"Your hospitality is appreciated," I said. Then I hesitated. "I would normally take my shoes off, but . . ."

"But you're not actually wearing the ones I can see," said Bridget. "It's all right. I'll forgive your lapse in etiquette just this once." She walked back to the door. "Do you want the lights on or off?"

"Er . . . off?"

It was a gray and cloudy day, but fae eyes see better in darkness than human eyes do, and I'm fae enough to find shadows a comfort.

Bridget nodded, and paused to click off the light before she left the room, easing the door shut again behind her. For the first time since sunrise, I was alone.

Alone, and unguarded. I could have gone for the window, climbed out and tried to find my own way home, but I had no idea how large Etienne's transport range actually was. I could have been almost anywhere, in almost anyone's demesne. This wasn't Shadowed Hills, that much was for sure; he would never have dared do this so close to the area where we both lived. So all I'd do by running away was break a promise and strand myself in an unfamiliar place while the hours before Moving Day ticked down toward an inevitable conclusion.

Custom would only protect me so far, and only until the clock struck midnight on Samhain night. This room, this place, this bed . . . that was the best I was likely to get.

Head pounding, I staggered to the bed and collapsed atop it, burying my face into the cool, soap-scented pillows. I wasn't going to sleep. I was just going to close my eyes and rest until the pain had a little time to fade. I'd heard of magic-burn before. I'd never experienced it.

But I wasn't going to sleep.

Naturally, I slept.

TEN

MY DREAMS WERE A tangled welter of images drawn from the night before, some veiled ever so lightly in red, as if even in sleep, my mind needed to keep a tally of which moments had been inspired by real things, and which by the blood memory. The family of Hamadryads came to the door, but this time, April was with them, weeping tears of tree sap as she begged me to find her mothers.

Then I was back in Dreamer's Glass, and Li Qin was screaming at me for not being strong enough to free them both at the same time, for leaving her outside the walls of her own little family, the only one who didn't remember or understand the bonds between them.

Then I was in the strange room with the man I was supposed to believe I had voluntarily married, and he was looking at me with grave green eyes full of adoration, and telling me, over and over, that I needed to remember what I'd told him, the last thing I'd told him.

"I don't remember *anything*!" I yelled, sitting bolt upright in the bed and blinking at the watery light shining through the window. It was thin and faded, afternoon trending toward evening, and my head didn't hurt nearly as much as it had before I'd gone to lie down.

I stretched, trying to ignore the smell of blood clinging to my unwashed hands. It didn't matter what happened next, not really, because Mother was going to lock me away for a decade after this was over, unless Etienne was hiding a secret Bannick along with his secret human wife and changeling daughter.

Someone rapped lightly on the bedroom door. I looked toward it, blinking. No one had ever knocked before coming into a room containing only me; there was no need. A changeling couldn't bar a pureblood from entry if we wanted to, and why would we be stopping another member of the staff?

"Are you all right in there?" asked Bridget, voice muffled by the wood.

"I'm fine," I said, and stood, heading for the door. Opening it seemed like right thing to do under the circumstances. I didn't want to worry her in her own home.

Bridget was waiting in the hall just outside the room, a mug of something steaming in one hand.

"Etienne said you don't drink coffee, so I've brought you some hot cocoa," she said, offering me the mug. "It's just the thing after bad dreams. How's your head?"

"Better," I said, taking the mug. It was: the pounding had receded to a dull throb. I could almost ignore the pain if I wasn't actively thinking about it. I still didn't think doing more magic would be a good idea—especially not more blood magic—but I'd probably survive an attempt. Surreptitiously, I glanced at my hand. Father's illusion had shifted my skin tone and shortened my fingers, and his magic still clung to me, meaning this was the afternoon of the day when I'd passed out. Dawn hadn't reached us yet.

"You still look human, if that's what you're checking for." I glanced at Bridget, more startled by the wistful note in her tone than by her words. She shrugged, smiling slightly. "Drink your cocoa. And you can't blame me for wanting to see the Fair Folk when I have the opportunity. My mum was very much of the old way of thinking—'the faeries aren't real, and we want them to stay that way, so we're not going to do a thing that might offend them, ever.' She met Etienne the last time she came to the States, and he and I had a good laugh afterward over how rude she'd been to him. Didn't think he was good enough for her only daughter, the genius folklore professor. If she'd known he was of the fae, she might have died on the spot out of fear."

"You tell stories about us?"

"They really have kept you sheltered, haven't they, child? Oh, it feels odd calling you that—you're well older than my daughter, and despite the way you look, I'd wager good money that you're older than I am to boot. Come on. Etienne and Chelsea are waiting for us."

She beckoned for me to follow her down the hall. I did, taking my first sip of the cocoa as I walked. It was thick, rich, and good, with little marshmallows floating on top. It was also the first thing I'd had to eat or drink since losing all that blood, and it was hard not to start gulping. Only the fact that it was hot enough to scald kept me from doing exactly that, and I was still sipping almost politely when we stepped out of the hall into a small, brightly lit kitchen.

A round table covered in a black cloth patterned with festive pumpkins occupied the middle of the room. Two people were seated there. One, Etienne, I knew quite well, and even better now that he was no longer wearing the disguise that made him look like a human. The other was a teenage girl in a shirt like Bridget's, hair black-brown and cut to cover her ears, glasses covering eyes that I could still tell had an unusual—for mortals—coppery sheen. Chelsea.

It wasn't the first time I'd met another changeling, but it was the first time I'd encountered one in the wild, as it were, and it was difficult not to look away as a wave of sudden shyness overtook me. What would she think of me, when she'd been raised to think she was as good as either of her parents? That she had a right to choose Faerie, and force it to accept her as an equal?

"Um, hi?" said Chelsea, sounding equally shy, and I realized that if she was the first free-range changeling I'd ever met, I might be the first changeling, period, she'd ever been introduced to. "I'm Chelsea? You must be October?"

"Yeah," I said, looking down at my cocoa. "I must be. I mean, I am. I mean, that's what my parents named me. We have a thing for calendar names in my family, and I guess they wanted me to feel included."

"A charitable way of looking on an uncharitable act," said Etienne dryly.

Bridget smacked him on the shoulder as she took the seat next to his. "Hush, you. The girls are sizing each other up, and it's important we give them the chance to do that before you start being shitty for no reason."

"I assure you, I have every reason," said Etienne, voice going stiff.

"Da-ad," said Chelsea. "You said you were going to ask October for her help. Don't embarrass me in front of her."

"My apologies, my heart," said Etienne, and put a hand over his own heart as he smiled at her. Any fear I had left that this was some sort of trick or trap died with that smile, because I recognized it. I knew that look almost painfully well. It was the way my own father looked at me, or at August, when my mother wasn't there to remind him that his sweetest smiles belonged to her above all others.

"I'm not embarrassed," I said. "And I don't feel like you're embarrassing. It's okay. Your ... dad ... says you don't want to be a changeling anymore?"

"I fall asleep during the day," said Chelsea. "Oh, and I'm up *all* night, whether I want to be or not. Morning classes are a form of torture."

"For adults, too," muttered Bridget.

Chelsea ignored her. "I can't date. There's no way I could keep an illusion up all the time around a human partner—and would they really be a partner if I was hiding something that huge about myself? I can't go to the doctor. Dad used to have to pay this weird independent healer under the table when I got sick, so someone could actually make me better without us getting caught. Oh, and there's the part where if anyone ever finds me, Dad gets arrested for treason, Mom gets executed and no one gets in trouble for it, because fae don't think it's murder when you kill a human, and if I'm *lucky*, they kill me, too."

This was a bleaker response than I'd expected. I took another slow swallow of cocoa before asking, hesitantly, "What happens if you're unlucky?"

"They brainwash and break me until I'm one of their happy, grateful little servants, honored to be asked to work for my betters, unable to recognize how much I'm being taken advantage of." Chelsea stopped, eyes widening, as she appeared to realize what she'd just said—and more, who she'd said it to. "I'm sorry, I didn't mean—you're not—I'm going to be quiet now."

"You meant it," I said. "That's all right. I know what I am." I finished my cocoa, looking for a tray to put the mug down on.

Bridget caught the way I was scanning my surroundings, and said, "The sink's dirty, dear."

I stopped, staring at her. Did she want me to clean it?

She paused, apparently reviewing, then tried again: "The sink is currently being used to hold dirty dishes. The sink itself is perfectly clean, and suitable for your mug. Don't worry about rinsing it, we have a very good dishwasher."

"I didn't understand all of that," I complained, and moved toward the sink. Glancing into it showed a few plates and a scattering of silverware, so I set my mug down next to them, feeling very pleased with myself for navigating this small facet of mortal life. It wasn't much. It was still more than I could have done yesterday.

Who knew what I'd be able to do tomorrow?

Crossing to the sink put me behind Chelsea, who twisted in her chair to watch me. "Dad says you're nice."

"I try to be." A biddable changeling is a changeling with few bruises and a reasonably long lifespan.

"I know what we're asking is a lot, but . . . he says your mother can turn people's blood from one kind into another kind?" She frowned a little, sounding baffled. "That violates, like, six dozen laws of biology."

I winced, glaring at Etienne over her head. He had been far too cavalier with Mother's secrets, even knowing what they could mean for August . . . and for me. Perhaps Chelsea had no connections within Faerie now, but if I could do what he asked of me, what was going to stop her tongue afterward?

"It violates no laws, because it's magic," I said. "It's also a secret. You can't tell *anyone* what your father's told you. People have been killed for less."

"'People' meaning 'changelings'?"

"Yes, but not only changelings. My family would be in danger, as well as yours." I took a deep breath, steadying myself. "We talk about the fae like we're all one kind of thing, but we're not. Some of us are plants, some of us are mammals, some of us are made of water or wind that thinks, and I'm pretty sure some of us are technically very active rocks. We're not reliably the same *species*. You and I look similar, and because we're both half-human, we're part of the same family tree, in a way, but your dad and my mom? Not the same species at all. My mother can't teleport. She's descended from Oberon alone, crafted from one of his horns, which he broke off in grief when one of his wives betrayed him. Without Maeve, he said Faerie would be out of balance, and so he took steps to correct it."

Steps that had, eventually, resulted in him retreating into slumber, effectively leaving us forever. But he'd left my mother behind with her foster family and her siblings to care for her, and Faerie had thrived in his absence. Titania chose abstinence; no more Firstborn would come after Mother, who bore the dubious honor and grave responsibility of serving as the last among her siblings, and the most accessible idol for their descendants. We were all expected to look to her to see what we were meant to do and be, and that was just one of the many reasons why my birth had been so essential.

"Oh," said Chelsea. "So Faerie's less like a single-species monoculture and more like a functional isolated biome?"

"I don't know what most of that meant, so I'll say yes, but whatever it means, if I do this, you won't be related to your mother anymore. You'll be the same species as your father, and not human at all. One kind of blood can't actually be transformed into another, but it can be removed. And it can't be undone." I didn't know much about Mother's work, but what I did know was that something so wholly stolen was gone forever. Whatever they had been when they were born, not a drop of mortal blood remained in either my father or my uncle, and you can't balance what isn't there.

Bridget leaned over in her chair to hug Chelsea fiercely. "Don't be afraid of what she says, my darling. We always knew this would be the end for us, and there's nothing to fear in it. I'll still be your mother, as long as there's breath in my body and a life to live upon this Earth."

"Family isn't all about blood and relation," said Chelsea, and I nodded, for it was a fact I knew very well: I wasn't related to my own father, and I wasn't adopted by him either, simply his in every way that could possibly matter.

"All right, then." Chelsea stood, pushing her chair back, and turned to face me before saying, formally, "I am asking you to please change me to entirely fae, with no human in me at all, so I won't be a changeling anymore, and Father can take me into Faerie, and I won't have to hide."

"I'll present her as a cousin from the Golden Shore, to explain her familiarity with human customs and her occasional lapses of acceptable knowledge," said Etienne. "I've been making plans for a while."

I was sure he had been. He was one of the most meticulous people I knew. But the existence of Chelsea made something else make even less sense than it had before. I frowned.

"If you don't hate changelings and think we're beneath you, why did you take Quentin as your squire?" I asked. "I've never met someone so convinced of the importance of being a pureblood."

Etienne grimaced. "It wasn't entirely my own choice," he said. "Your father's keeper asked me to take the boy, as a favor to her, and one does not refuse the Rose of Winter if one wishes to live a comfortable life. The boy belongs to some distaff branch of her descent, off in the frozen wastes. He'll have no power when he's grown. Where he got this attitude, I don't know. I'm doing what I can to leaven it as I teach him how to swing a sword and how to weave an illusionary shield that can take an arrow. Beyond that, he's outside my influence."

"Huh." I turned back to Chelsea. "I can't promise it's going to work, or that it won't hurt." Dimly, I remembered Mother tweaking the balance of my blood when I'd been a child. It had been like fire in my veins, like ants made of acid running through my body and tearing at my heart. I sometimes wondered, if I'd been able to handle more of the agony, would she have made me more fae than I was now? Had my weakness denied me centuries of time by my sister's side?

"I can take a little pain," said Chelsea, sounding almost cocky.

"That's good." I pulled the knife from my belt. Flecks of my own dried blood clung to the blade. Looking at it turned my stomach. Chelsea didn't look much happier, and I hurried to reassure her: "Don't worry, I'm cutting myself, not you."

"That's not as helpful as I think you want it to be," she muttered.

I ignored her, trying to remember the last time I'd seen Mother modify the balance of someone's blood. She'd stopped taking me with her as soon as I was old enough to ask questions and attract notice from the householders; she was Firstborn, but she had told me more than once that someone of sufficient importance could have demanded she give me to them for a pet if I'd caught their fancy, and claiming offense in such a situation, as her position would compel her to do, would hardly be worth the fuss it would cause. It had been easier and safer to confine me to the tower. Out of sight, out of the way, out of danger.

The cutting was a part of it, I knew that; she always cut herself before she changed someone's blood. She never had to cut much, needing only a little blood, but she was Firstborn and not part-human; I expected to bleed substantially more than she did. But that wasn't where she started, was it?

This wasn't alchemy or some marshwater charm built on sympathy and the interaction of raw materials. This was just magic. Everything she needed, she had with her. Even the knife was technically optional, I supposed; she could have raked her arms open with her fingernails, or bitten the insides of her cheeks until she bled. Neither of those things were fun, but neither of them required tools.

So what did she do first? What step was I forgetting?

I looked at Etienne, who was taking a drink from a mug identical to the one my cocoa had been in. He swallowed, then sniffed the remaining liquid before setting the mug aside. With that, I remembered.

Before she changed someone's blood, she weighed it out by breathing it in, which made a certain sense; the smell of a person's blood carried their magic, and Mother had always been sensitive to the scent of magic, more so even than August or myself, and we were more sensitive than anyone else we knew. Even I, the changeling, could identify magic with an unerring precision that used to annoy the other children when we were young. They were purebloods, come to the tower only because their parents sought to cultivate a closer relationship to Mother through August, and through showing kindness to the useless younger daughter. They had always resented that I was better than them at something.

I lowered the knife, stepping closer to Chelsea, and breathed in deeply.

I started coughing almost immediately. Covering my mouth with one hand, I turned away. "She's most definitely yours, Sir Etienne," I said, sounding somewhat choked. "Sycamore smoke is not the same as cedar, but I can still recognize it."

Someone with a less-refined sense for magical signatures could have taken either or both of them for simple woodsmoke or the smoke of a recently extinguished candle. To me, though, they were utterly dissimilar and distinct, as was my father's magic from the both of them.

"Is that what her magic smells like?" asked Bridget.

Etienne nodded.

Bridget turned to Chelsea, eyes narrowing. "And is that why your room smells like candles half the time? Chelsea Grace Ames, have you been experimenting with your magic again? I thought we agreed that it was too dangerous!"

"If you knew you could do something, would you not want to understand it?" demanded Chelsea.

I turned to her again, having caught my breath. "Sorry," I said. "That was stronger than I expected. Let me try again."

Closing my eyes, I inhaled a second time, reaching for her magic, reaching for the balance of her blood, the delicate interplay of paternity and maternity that would have initially created her. What I found was sycamore smoke and calla lilies, and not a drop of mortality at all. She had no human heritage.

That didn't make sense. I opened my eyes, studying her as carefully as I could. She looked boldly back, clearly anxious, no sign of deception in her eyes.

The curves of her face were familiar to me, too soft to be fae, too sharp to be human. Her ears were hidden by her hair, which wouldn't have been possible if they'd been as long or sharply pointed as Etienne's.

Even her eyes, with their coppery sheen, weren't the clean, unburnished metallic I would have expected from a pureblooded Tuatha de Dannan. She was beautiful. She was a changeling. Except that her blood told me she wasn't, which meant this was an illusion I didn't understand.

I turned to Etienne. "If this is a prank, it isn't funny. If it's been an attempt to test my loyalty, I would like you to remember that I was brought here without being told what the 'help' you wanted would entail, and all I agreed to do was try. Technically, you've broken no rules, and neither have I. But whatever you're doing, I'd like you to stop now, please."

Etienne looked startled. "What do you mean?"

"The illusion you've cast on this girl. She's clearly a relative of yours—the magic tells me that—but I don't know if she's your daughter or your sister or what, or why you thought you needed to push me into a position where I'd agree to do *blood magic* for you." I shook my head. "She's not a changeling. She has no human blood in her. What the hell is this?"

Bridget said nothing, looking horrified.

Etienne stood, almost knocking over his chair in the process. "She is my daughter, and this is her mother, and I swear, there is no trick, October. I asked for help because I needed to find a way to save her, before—"

He cut himself off before he could go any further. I frowned. "Before what, Etienne?"

"Nothing. Only rumors in the Court of the Queen. I attend on Duke Torquill's behalf, to represent Shadowed Hills, and some of the courtiers have looser tongues than is good for them." He looked away, no longer facing me. "I assure you, Chelsea is my child, and Bridget is her mother. I was present for her birth. All three of us were. She is as changeling as you are. Help her."

"Why is this so urgent all of a sudden?" I asked. "What did you hear?"

"Nothing!" He still wouldn't look at me. "Your mother is Firstborn, your beloved uncle a Duke, your father the dogsbody of one of the most powerful women in Faerie. I heard nothing that applies to you."

"But you heard something, Etienne," said Bridget. "Please. Tell the woman you've asked for aid. Tell *us*. We've known for some time that Chelsea would need to find a way into Faerie for her to live a proper life, and not spend her days in hiding. It's never been urgent like this before. You've never tried to force the issue."

"Changelings are born when fae and humans meet," said Etienne, very slowly. "Once, they were born mostly out of love, like our girl was. Today, they're born mostly out of duty, nobles trying to follow Titania's edicts and please her, either by creating their own servants or by ordering their lower-ranked subjects to do it."

I wondered, like a brief, bright bolt of light, whether that had been the case with the family of Hamadryads I'd seen earlier. They had clearly loved their girls, but had they borne them because they were ordered to do so? I'd always known that was something that happened, but had done my best not to think about it unless I absolutely had to.

"Titania feels . . . as our Queen, the True Queen, the one who stands above all petty monarchies and regional divisions . . . she understands the need for changelings, and their inevitability, which is why she orders their creation. When Oberon left us, he somehow sealed the doors to deeper Faerie, and even she, perfect in her power as she is, has been unable to crack them open. We're trapped in the Summerlands, adjacent to the mortal world, with no way to remove ourselves from temptation. And like a hungry changeling left alone with a goblin-fruit bush in full fruit, some of us will inevitably cross even the most forbidden lines. It's the nature of the heart."

"Are you saying you're sorry I was born?" asked Chelsea.

"No!" responded Etienne, so quickly and clearly that I had no question of his sincerity. "You are most precious to me, the greatest thing I've accomplished in this world or any other. I love you beyond love itself. But Titania, who ordered the birth of most of Faerie's changelings, begins to feel as if we've become too accepting and accommodating of our changeling children. She fears another uprising, as happened before the breaking of the Three, when she ruled flanked by almost-equals, and not alone. There are whispers in the Court. Whispers of a change to her command, of a Wild Hunt, and a purge to come." He finally looked at me. "They may come to nothing. They may come to everything. Either way, to be a changeling without the protection of a Firstborn parent or a strong noble house is to be a changeling in deep danger. Please, October. I know you're new to blood magic. You're confused. But please, help my child."

I stared at him for a moment, trying to absorb the enormity of what he'd said. There hadn't been a Wild Hunt in centuries, and certainly not one targeted against the most powerless of Faerie's denizens. If he was right about this, my friends, all the staff at Shadowed Hills—so many people were going to be in danger.

And he'd only cared about saving his own child. There was the Sir Etienne I knew. Married to the rules until he needed them broken.

I glanced at Chelsea, on the verge of telling him to figure it out himself, and stopped when I saw the naked pleading in her eyes. She was terrified, as well she ought to be, and like anyone else faced with the possibility of her own death, she didn't want to take the risk. I could walk away to punish him. I couldn't walk away to punish her, or her mother, who deserved so much better.

"I can try," I said, slowly. "Chelsea, stay still." I closed my eyes again and breathed in deep, reaching out at the same time with the not-quite-sense I'd used in Dreamer's Glass when I needed to see the tangled threads around Li Qin and January. It was a hunch. But with everything else getting so strange, playing a hunch didn't feel like such a bad idea.

As I had more than half-expected, the same pink, prismatic weave of tangled-up threads appeared around Chelsea. I glanced to the side. The same web of threads surrounded Etienne, as strong and bright as they had been in Dreamer's Glass. The tangle of threads around Bridget was more of a surprise. Seeing such clear evidence of a spell cast on a human was nearly enough to make me lose my focus.

All fae knew that coexistence with humans was impossible because they lacked the magic to hook any sort of standing enchantment on to: while illicit substances like Faerie ointment could be used to give them the temporary ability to perceive enchantments and hidden things, they never lasted. You couldn't take a human into a knowe, or use them as the anchor for any sort of spell. But Bridget was currently under some sort of enchantment, and it hadn't originated with Etienne; seeing things this way was still new to me, but I could already start to see some of the logic behind it, the ways the smell of magic would translate into its own visual counterpart. Etienne's magic was many things. None of them were prismatic and pink.

"I think I'm the one who needs to bleed here," I said, keeping my motions slow and obvious as I reached for the knife at my hip. "Bridget, you may not want to watch this."

I didn't really know how humans felt about bloodshed, but the last thing I needed right now was to upset the woman and have her rush me while I was trying to work an unfamiliar bit of magic on her daughter.

"I'm staying," said Bridget, ice in her tone.

"That's fine. Please don't interfere." I pulled the knife, a little amazed by how easy and familiar the gesture already seemed. I pressed the edge against the back of my hand, tensing against the anticipation of pain. I couldn't see Chelsea with my eyes closed, and couldn't see the threads if I opened them, so I had to count on her staying calm when I started bleeding everywhere. Because that wasn't stressful or anything.

"Chelsea, I'm going to cut myself, and then I'm going so swallow some of the blood. It's gross, but that's the way blood magic works for my kind of fae. You need to stay as calm as you can, because like Etienne said, I'm still pretty new to this, and I could lose focus if you freak out or distract me, okay?"

"Okay," said Chelsea, voice much more subdued now that this was actually happening. She still sounded determined, and so I decided to keep going, forcing my way forward.

I ran the knife across the back of my hand. It was easier than it had been the first time I'd cut myself, not because it didn't hurt, but because now I was reasonably sure it would heal. The scent of my blood filled the room, overwhelming the signatures of Etienne and Chelsea's magic with my own. It was still organic and vital, but it was cut-grass and copper at the same time.

Eyes firmly closed, I sheathed the knife and raised my hand to my mouth.

This time, I wasn't fast enough to shunt aside the red veil of blood memory before it caught me, even if only momentarily.

I stand in a kitchen I don't know, staring into a tall white box filled with cold food and drinks. The memory supplies the name: 'refrigerator.' There's one in Bridget and Etienne's kitchen, on the wall across from where I left my actual body. I'd dismissed it as some form of wardrobe, and I guess that's what it is, just a wardrobe for food.

I am looking for something to eat, and there are so many things, meats and cheese and leftovers wrapped in shining silver metal. I reach for a carton labeled orange juice, and close the fridge just as a stampede of teenagers bursts into the room.

The first is a boy with deeply tanned skin and russet-red hair, each strand tipped in black, like he's been caught in some sort of ink fight. He's wearing mortal clothes, but his ears are pointed and his pupils are vertical slits against amber-gold eyes. The combination of red and

*gold should have marked him for a Torquill, but it somehow doesn't;
the shades are all wrong, as is everything else about him.*

*Hot on his heels comes . . . Chelsea Ames. Laughing, no disguises,
clearly enjoying the chase.*

"Raj, you give back the remote or I'm going to skin *you!"*

"You can try," *he counters, and they thunder past me as the vision
breaks.*

"October?" The voice was Bridget's. The concern was sincere.
More sincere than I ever would have expected it to be. "Are you all
right?"

"You took a mouthful of blood and then you went still," said Chelsea, clearly trying to help. "Do we need to stop?"

"No," said Etienne.

"No," I said. "I'm all right. I just . . . I lose control sometimes. This
is all still new for me. Hang on." I sliced the back of my hand again,
reopening the healed wound, and took another mouthful of blood.

The red veil tried to descend. I shoved it aside and reached for the
threads with the hands I didn't actually have, feeling the chill spread
through my real fingers almost immediately.

As with January, the pink threads were wound tight, knotted together until it was impossible to pull any single one of them loose
without shifting all the others. As I pulled, the pain in my head returned, even brighter and more urgent than before, and Chelsea
screamed.

It was a high, agonized wail, like she was the one being slashed and
stabbed, even though I wasn't touching her. I heard Bridget yell
something, heard Etienne's voice raised in what could easily have
been panic, and kept pulling. If they were going to try to stop me, I
needed to unravel this as fast as I possibly could.

Because now that I had my hands on the web, it felt utterly essential that I finish what I'd started and rip it cleanly away. As with January, it was wrapped all around and through her, anchored somewhere
behind her breastbone. Even as my hands were freezing, I wondered
whether the fact that the spell was also wrapped around Bridget
meant mortals had some magic after all—something for the spell to
latch onto—or whether it was somehow feeding off the ambient magic
generated by the presence of Chelsea and Etienne.

Then things started happening very fast.

The first thread snapped in my hand, sending a bolt of pain through my head and a jet of icy cold all the way up to my elbow. Chelsea screamed again, louder this time, as the scent of sycamore smoke and calla lilies flared right behind me.

I realized what was about to happen a heartbeat before it did, and tried to react. I really did. If I could have opened my eyes or said something, could have asked her not to, it might have been all right.

But no. It was all too fast, and I was in too much pain from what I'd just done, what I shouldn't have been able to do. Chelsea, pained and possibly panicked by whatever the spell had been hiding from her before I broke it—whatever memories it had obscured, whatever illusions it had anchored—rushed forward and shoved me, and I fell through the portal she had instinctively opened in the kitchen behind me, her magic interpreting my efforts to break the spell as a threat.

Etienne yelled something I couldn't understand, and then I was slamming into cold stone, and everything went black.

ELEVEN

"**W**HAT DO WE HAVE here?"
I didn't recognize the voice, which sounded like two rocks being rubbed together until they somehow produced speech. That part was reassuring, at least; it meant the speaker was probably a Bridge Troll. Uncle Sylvester had a Bridge Troll in his service, a knight named Tavis, who had always been reasonably kind to me and who seemed to see tormenting changelings as beneath him. Compared to Bridge Trolls, essentially everyone in Faerie is soft and breakable, and I guess extending that careful approach to the world to cover the occasional part-human servant is easy enough.

"Looks like someone got rolled," said another unfamiliar voice, this one in a more ordinary register.

"Someone was out after dark when she shouldn't have been," said a third voice. This one was lighter, higher, a little smugger—and, oddly, halfway familiar.

My head was throbbing like it had never throbbed before, just one solid, unending ache, and I was reasonably sure trying to rip away a third set of those weird pink threads would kill me. And at this point, maybe that would be a good thing—this hurt so much, I couldn't imagine doing anything beyond continuing to lie limply on the ground.

Then a hand grabbed me by the hair, yanking me into a sitting position. I yelped. I couldn't help myself.

"Told you she wasn't dead," said the third voice, sounding even smugger. The hand released my hair, and I slammed back into the ground before I could move to catch myself.

Groaning, I rolled onto my side and opened my eyes.

We were in a narrow alleyway. The ground beneath me was the same hard black stone that I'd seen outside Bridget's house, the one the cars had been driving on, but here, there were no cars. Instead, there were looming brick buildings with strange metal scaffoldings clinging to their sides, and square metal containers that stank of filth and rotting trash. Light filtered in from either end of the alley, partially blocked by the buildings, but enough to let me see the people around me.

One loomed over the other two, topping them by easily a foot. That was the only indication that this was probably the Bridge Troll I'd heard before. A good illusion can make a giant look like a mouse, or vice versa, but it won't actually change their sizes. Most Bridge Trolls, when they need to move in the human world, choose illusions that are at least close to their actual height, to avoid any awkward explanations.

The other two were an unfamiliar, twitchy-looking man and a woman who, even with her features softened and her clothing replaced by its mortal equivalents, I thought I recognized.

I groaned, and asked, in a weak, tattered tone, "Dame Altair?"

The woman immediately stiffened, looking around the alley like she was afraid I'd been overheard and now we were all going to be in trouble. "How do you know my name?"

"Sorry," I slurred, closing my eyes again.

"You said it was just a changeling," said the Bridge Troll. "Some stupid little chit we could roll for beer money and leave for dead. If she knows you, El, that means she's a changeling with one of the noble houses, and that changes things. We can't leave her out here knowing who you are."

"She seems pretty drunk already. Maybe we can stick with the original plan, and she won't remember this in the morning," said the other man.

"How was I supposed to know one of my peers had been careless enough to lose track of their staff?" demanded the woman, shrilly, and now I definitely recognized that voice: Dame Eloise Altair, minor local noble. She was Daoine Sidhe, and had come around Shadowed Hills a few times, making broad and unsubtle propositions toward Uncle Sylvester. He shrugged them off, of course, but that didn't stop her from trying again. And again. And again.

And apparently, she liked to attack changelings for no apparent reason beyond them being out and unprotected. That didn't mesh well with the way she simpered and sighed in Court. She'd always been performatively nice to me and to the rest of the staff when we crossed her path. Maybe the key word there was "performance." Maybe I was finally seeing her real and unfiltered, the way she was when she wasn't trying to ensnare my uncle.

I wanted to tell her she'd never be welcome in Shadowed Hills after this, even though it would have meant snapping at a pureblood. Under the circumstances, I wasn't sure that could have gotten me into any additional trouble. My head hurt too much to let me form a coherent sentence.

"It's almost Moving Day, and the vermin have been fleeing down the coast all week," said the Bridge Troll. "What's one more that isn't seen tomorrow?"

"Are you suggesting we—"

"It's just a changeling. They vanish all the damn time. No one's going to think it's strange if one more goes missing."

Rough hands scooped me off the ground, and for a moment, they seemed almost gentle.

"Look: she's already covered in blood. That makes this easier."

"Makes what easier?"

"Kyle? It's your turn."

"Can't you just snap her neck?" asked the second man, almost petulantly.

"That doesn't explain the blood, and you know the night-haunts will copy it over. They don't care whether they make things harder with the local police. Now come on."

There was a soft sliding sound, like steel rubbing against stone, and I realized what it was a bare second before a knife drove into my upper abdomen, right below my sternum, knocking the air out of me. That pain, combined with the pain in my head, was so intense that everything else went away: they almost seemed to cancel each other out.

My eyes snapped open again, my hand going automatically to the knife at my hip. I had managed to shove it back into its sheath before Chelsea pushed me out of the kitchen, and it was still with me. Less than a second later, it was in my hand, and I was bringing it up in a hard, slashing motion that seemed born half out of instinct and half out of some incomprehensible muscle memory.

The man's throat opened like a flower, skin parting in a blossom of red blood and yellow fat. He made a startled choking sound and staggered back, dropping his own knife.

Blood was gushing down my front, already starting to slow down, and for the first time, I had to wonder how quickly I could actually heal. Was I going to run out of blood before my body closed the hole? Did it matter? I'd just killed a man. A pureblood, even, one of my betters in every possible way.

I sagged in the Bridge Troll's grasp, all the fight going out of me, trying to ignore the choking sounds from the dying man and the high, agonized wailing from Dame Altair.

"Fuck this," rumbled the Bridge Troll. He shoved me away from him, so hard I bounced off the edge of one of the metal boxes before hitting the ground again. "Come on, El. We're out of here."

"But Kyle—"

"Come *on!*"

Then they were gone. No more screaming, no more stabbing. Just gone, and everything was quiet in the alley.

In the distance, I heard the sounds of the human city. Cars rolling by, some kind of rubber bladder being honked, like children were having a wild party, loud alarms. None of it slowed or stopped for me, as I bled in the alley, alone with a dead man. I tried to pull myself into a sitting position. I couldn't. I didn't have the focus, or the strength.

Then there was a new sound. The sound of wings. I squeezed my eyes as tightly shut as I could, no longer trying to sit up; instead, I tried to turn my face away. Looking at the night-haunts was forbidden. I didn't know why, only that it was. People who saw them never made it home.

The wings got louder, and louder, until I was surrounded in every possible direction. And a small, puzzled voice said, "Aunt Birdie?"

I didn't move.

"Aunt Birdie, why are you here? You were asked not to summon us again."

The voice was close to my face, and I couldn't help thinking that whoever it was, they were speaking to me. I knew I wasn't allowed to look. I knew it would do me no good in this world.

I still opened my eyes.

A figure about twice the size of a pixie hung in the air in front of my nose, held up by wings like fast-beating skeleton leaves, the delicate veins left when the flesh of a leaf has rotted away. It wasn't glowing, like a pixie would have been; instead, it was pale as a moon-washed beach, faintly silvered and alien enough to be unsettling.

If I focused past that, I could tell it was a child, a little girl approaching her teens, wearing a winding white dress and no shoes. Her hair was brown, straight and uncombed, and her ears were softly pointed, topped in tufts of fur like a lynx's. She didn't look like a shapeshifter. She didn't look like any sort of fae I knew. She was something terrifying and new.

"Oh, Aunt Birdie," she said, deep sadness in her voice. "We knew what she'd done—she can't touch the dead, everyone has their limits—but not the whole of it, and I didn't know what she'd done to you. I'm sorry. I'm so sorry my mother is hurting everyone because you tried to save me. I know you tried to save me. I watched, after I joined the flock. I saw more of everything than I wanted to see, and I know you tried. I'm sorry. I'm sorry, and it shouldn't be like this."

I stared at her.

"Tybalt is looking for you. He's getting closer all the time, and he'll have his way clear to you sooner than you might think, if he keeps up like this. It's going to be okay. I know it's going to be okay."

I swallowed. My throat was so dry it ached, and I still couldn't really move, couldn't even tell if I'd stopped breathing. All I could do was swallow, and stare.

The hovering figure darted closer, setting one tiny hand against my cheek for a moment. Her skin was cool.

"This is her fault, not yours, and I know you'll fix it, because you always fix everything," she said. "That's why Faerie makes heroes. Because sometimes we need someone who can fix things. I'm just sorry for what has to happen next. You can rest now. Just for a little while."

The strange flying girl who seemed to know me and might or might not be a night-haunt said I could rest. That was good enough for me. I closed my eyes and listened to the sound of wings as I tried to melt into the ground.

It became a lot less reassuring as it was joined by the sound of ripping, chewing, and chomping, but the wings were still there, and so I tried to focus on the wings.

The ripping stopped. The wings receded into the distance, becoming nothing but the whistling of the wind, and I knew, absolutely, that I was alone in the alley.

I was also too weak to move. That didn't make my situation any better than it had been a few moments before. Well, there wasn't a knife sticking out of me. That part was an improvement. But I had apparently killed a man, and a pureblood man at that. Moving Day made it safer—not safe, but safer—for me to be outside the familiar confines of my family's wards. It didn't make me immune to the Law. If those people who'd accosted me told anyone . . .

I could be tracked down. Blood magic would lead the Queen's guard right to Mother's door, and even she wouldn't be able to protect me. Maybe her powers were great enough to cleanse me of any traces of the dead man's blood, but that would require me not only getting to her but telling her what I'd done.

No matter how this evening ended, I was going to be in so much trouble. I was already in so much pain that thinking was getting harder and harder, although that may have been more about the blood loss than anything else. I swallowed again. Why was my mouth so *dry*? Did blood magic make you thirsty all the time or something?

Of course it did. Blood was liquid, and by bleeding so much today, I'd been dehydrating myself. It was the sort of obvious answer that made me feel foolish for needing to even ask the question. I tried again to sit up.

I failed again.

A new scent—or rather, a new assortment of scents—wafted into the alley right before footsteps came around the corner. Armor rattled, comfortingly familiar and terrifying at the same time, and I heard the people who were wearing it fall into position around me.

"There's a body over here," said a voice.

"This is the spot," said another. "Think that's the girl?"

"Unless we've got another bloody runaway changeling loose on the streets." Rough hands grabbed me by my upper arms and pulled me to my feet, head lolling as I failed to find the strength to hold it up. "She didn't weave this illusion herself. And I'm not sure this *is* the right one. Our tip said the changeling girl'd been stabbed in the gut. No stab wounds on this one."

Great. So I *had* managed to heal before I could bleed to death. August was going to be very interested to hear that, assuming I ever made it home to her. Which, at the moment, was starting to feel like a very, very big "if."

"Not our problem," said the first voice, brusquely. "Queen said to come here, bring her the changeling. We came here, we found a changeling. If this is the wrong one, Queen can send us out again. We're not here to think, we're here to follow orders and please the Queen."

"For the Queen!" said three more voices.

The smell of magic flared around us, bright and sweet and sour and bitter all at once, and then I was being pulled through yet another transportation circle, and the alley was left behind, along with all the blood I'd lost.

Hey, I thought. *I wasn't done with that yet.*

The man who was holding me gave me a sharp shake, almost as if he'd heard my thoughts, and the pain in my head exploded into radiant agony, and for a little while, consciousness left me as a bad investment.

TWELVE

I CAME TO IN A small stone room with heaps of rotting yarrow pushed against the walls as a foul sort of cushion. It did nothing to blunt the chill, which was incredibly strong despite the lack of windows. There was no door; instead, a barred grate blocked the doorway. I wasn't going to get anywhere near that. Even from my place in the farthest corner, I could feel the iron coming off of it in waves, sickeningly strong. It made my stomach churn and my head spin even worse than it had already been.

Staying away from the door wouldn't protect me for long. That much iron, this close, would get to me eventually, and I'd start to get sick. I didn't know the exact symptoms of iron poisoning—Father had always been very firm on the fact that August and I would never need to know—but my chest was already tight, and the air felt like it was too thick, becoming increasingly difficult to breathe.

The Queen. Not Fair Titania, but the Queen of the Mists, my uncle's liege. Those men had mentioned the Queen, and being told to "fetch the changeling." They hadn't known who I was. I raised a hand to my ear and found it as pointed as always. Either they had pulled down my illusions, or the iron had eroded Father's work while I'd been crumpled in the corner. The first option would mean they knew me, and were probably already negotiating my punishment with my parents and uncle. It would be death, of course; a changeling can't just kill a pureblood and get away with it. But it could be a painless death, a quick death. They could let Mother come in there and yank the fae blood from my veins, so I wouldn't be able to heal, then allow one of their executioners to slit my throat.

It could also be a horrible death. They could bind me to the Iron Tree, gouge out my eyes, and burn me alive, as they did to traitors. I was reasonably sure the prismatic pink webs I'd been destroying belonged to Titania herself, and breaking the True Queen's spells had to count as a form of treason, didn't it?

I touched the place where I'd been stabbed, feeling no tenderness. My shirt was caked with blood, as my hands were covered in it, but I was uninjured, save for the distant pounding in my head and the persistent dryness in my mouth. I looked around the cell again. There was no water bucket, and I wasn't sure I would have been able to trust it if there had been; I was a changeling who'd killed a pureblood now, and there were no circumstances that could excuse that fact. I had committed the greatest of all possible crimes, and I deserved whatever punishment they wanted to inflict on me.

Still, water would have been nice.

I huddled deeper into the corner, which was cold and hard but felt like it might actually provide a tiny sliver of distance and protection from the iron. Who would have thought the Queen of the Mists, guardian over one of Fair Titania's most sacred protectorates, would use iron against her own kind? It was monstrous. It was . . . *beastly*.

That was one of the worst things a pureblood could be called, and I would normally have recoiled from the word, rejecting it as cruel and beneath me. After the day I'd had, and the treatment I'd received, I wasn't sure there was anything else that suited. I'd followed the instructions of my betters until those instructions left me alone in the human world, easy prey for the first pack of predators to come wandering by, and now I was going to die because I'd dared to fight back against them.

It wasn't right. It wasn't fair. But then, as I'd often reminded August when she raised the same complaint about the differences in our station, Faerie had never claimed to be fair. The people on top were there forever, and the people on the bottom were only there until we made a mistake and went away.

Well, it looked like it was my turn to go away. Part of me felt like I should fight, like I should find a streak of resistance buried deep in my bones, but most of me knew there wasn't any point. I was outclassed and outnumbered, and I was going to die.

Idly, I closed my eyes and bit the inside of my cheek, worrying the flesh between my molars until I tasted blood. It had been easier when I had a knife; cutting yourself without a weapon was even less fun than cutting yourself *with* one. Still, it was easy enough to make myself bleed.

Swallowing, I raised my hands and *looked* at them in that impossible way that didn't use my eyes. As I'd expected, the pink lines were there the same way they'd been for the other people I'd looked at like this. Well. Not *quite* the same. They were denser, snarled together until they covered every inch of my skin in the opalescent shine of someone else's magic. How did I, a mere changeling, rate that sort of effort?

And how could I unweave it?

Attempting to get my mental "fingers" under the knots did nothing; they slipped away like mist. The pain in my head got even worse, and I stopped trying. Maybe that was the real limit: I couldn't undo spells if they'd been cast on me directly. Annoying, but if I knew what the rules were, I could start to work around them.

The thought was contrary enough to my long-cultivated obedience and agreeability that I paused, contemplating it. It was mine, absolutely: it didn't feel like someone else had somehow planted it there to lead me astray. And how much more astray could I go than locked in the Queen's dungeons for killing a man? Something which felt like it should have been a lot more upsetting than my imprisonment.

A man was dead because of me, and I was sitting there worrying about my headache and the blood on my clothes and the fact that someone—probably Titania—had cast a spell on me for some reason.

I decided I was in shock. It was better than the alternative, which was that I was the worst person who had ever lived, and my impending execution would be doing Faerie a favor.

The smell of redwood bark and blackberry flower drifted through the room, undercut by a faint whiff of apple cider, completely out of keeping with my surroundings. I turned my face toward the wall. It wasn't a magical signature I recognized; if the Queen's men were coming to drag me to judgement, I wasn't going to fight them, but I wasn't going to make this any easier on them than it had to be. If they wanted me begging for clemency or running to them looking for saviors, they were going to be direly disappointed.

I might be a changeling, but I was my father's daughter, whether or not I had the right to his name, and Torquills do not beg.

"Psst."

The voice was female and not far away. It sounded like the speaker was actually in the room with me, which was impossible. I nestled harder into my corner.

"I think she's ignoring you, dear sister," said a second voice. "Quite rude, really, especially for a convicted criminal. Do you think they'll bother with the pretense of a trial, or go straight to the execution?"

I whimpered and burrowed even harder into the corner.

"There: now you know she hears us." The speaker sounded remarkably smug for someone whose primary accomplishment had been speaking in a place where they couldn't reasonably be.

Then again, maybe that was impressive enough to be proud of. With an iron door on the cell, all attempts to teleport or open portals into the room should have been blocked. And these people, whoever they were, had clearly opened a portal.

"Ow!" said the voice. "What'd you go and do that for?"

"You're being a dick," said the first person—at least I assumed it was the first person. It's hard to recognize someone's voice from a "psst." The thought of dealing with more than two strangers right now was too much for me to handle. "Dicks get swatted."

"At last, we see the reason my sister never dates."

"Ha-ha, you're hilarious. Come on. We need to get her out of there."

"I'm not going through."

"Of course not. You're a coward."

There was a soft scuff, as if someone had stepped to the floor near me, and a hand touched my shoulder. "Excuse me, but are you October? October Torquill?"

The stranger was close enough now for me to tell that the redwood-and-blackberry scent was definitely hers, and more, she was a pureblood. I didn't always get that from a person's magic, and especially not this strongly, but there it was, marking her like a brand.

I couldn't ignore a direct question from a pureblood, even if I wanted to. Slowly, fighting the throbbing pain in my skull, I raised my head and twisted very slightly around, opening my eyes.

A woman was crouched behind me, watching me with obvious concern. She wore a patchwork jacket of some sort over a human-design shirt and pants, making her look like a strange hybrid of the two realities. Her hair was so black it was almost purple, and her eyes were mismatched metal, one pyrite, one mercury. Tuatha de Dannan.

That explained how she could open a teleportation circle in the first place, although not how she could get one into a warded cell.

She smiled as she saw me looking at her. "Hi," she said. "You've probably looked better, and I'm sorry to be bothering you at a time like this, but if you could answer my question, that would be fabulous."

"I'm October," I croaked, dry mouth stealing most of the inflection from the words.

The woman nodded in satisfaction. "Great. Well, my name's Arden Windermere, and I'm your ride out of here."

"How?"

"You mean how am I, and my frustrating but devastatingly handsome brother, able to open a gate into a cell laced with so much iron that my teeth are already starting to itch? Make you a deal." She smiled again, bright as the sun, and offered me her hand. "Come with us, and I'll tell you."

"Or?"

"Or, you know. Stay here and die a painful, inevitable, unnecessary death. I guess the choice is yours." Her smile faded as she looked at me. "I know what I'd go with in your position, but the Queen wouldn't put me in your position, would she? Oh, I mean, she would, but for very different reasons. Her advisors would try to find a way to let me go, and all because I can trace my lineage back to Armorica with no diversions into the human realms. Like who my ancestors fucked or didn't fuck makes me special somehow."

I stared at her.

"Of course, then my parents had to go and die on us, and Nolan and I got to go into hiding, because that's always fun and healthy for a pair of orphan kids. We were a whole human children's book all by ourselves, and that's something else I can tell you about, if you'll just come with me."

A door slammed in the distance, the sound echoing along the hall. Arden tensed.

From the other side of the cell, Nolan said, "Sister dear, I don't mean to rush you, but I think you're about to have company."

I glanced in the direction his voice was coming from. A hole hung in the air, showing a bare-earthed field scattered here and there with the orange domes of pumpkins, and a man who looked very much like Arden standing anxiously at its center.

"I *know*, Nolan," she said, tersely. "I'm trying to get her to move. I don't want to just grab her."

"Well, you may have no choice. This charm won't hold much longer, and we don't want them to find two prisoners when they come to haul off their one."

Charm? Well, that explained the whiff of cider. Father has always been gifted at the art of borrowing magic from other people's blood, and in blending it in ways that shouldn't have been possible. But his own magic almost always worked its way into the mixture.

"Sadly, my brother's right, and we're out of time," said Arden. She grabbed my wrist, dragging me to my feet as she stood. "I hate to abduct you after the night you've had already, but it looks like that's what's about to happen."

"Wait!" I yelped.

She stopped, raising an eyebrow.

"Yes, my name is October, and yes, I'm a little tired of being abducted, but I have a headache and I don't know how you can be in here, and I absolutely killed the man they're going to accuse me of killing. I don't need a ride out of here. I need a fair trial and to face justice for what I did."

"Oh, honey. If you think you're getting a fair trial in this Court, they've done more of a number on you than I was afraid they had."

I crossed my arms. "You don't know me."

"No, but I know some people who do, and I know how the Courts treat changelings," she said. "I know that Nolan and I have been evacuating people all up and down the coast since Moving Day began, and I know it's not going to be enough, but I know we can't stop trying, not while there's a chance we might be able to get one more changeling out of harm's way. And I know I'm coming close to the point where the iron does real damage, which means you might already be there and thus not be thinking very clearly."

"Meaning what?"

"Meaning that much like pushing a drunk out of the bar at closing time, I don't feel like I'm really crossing any lines by throwing the changeling out of the iron-riddled dungeon before the guards arrive."

With that, she grabbed me again, twisting around so that she fell backward through the portal her brother was holding open, allowing her own mass to drag me after her. I tried to twist my wrists free but couldn't quite break her grasp, and when she hit the ground, I landed on top of her, and both of us were somewhere . . . else.

The air was different. That was the first thing I noticed. There was no tang of car exhaust, which meant we weren't back in the human world, and the scent of rotting yarrow barely masking iron was absent as well. Instead, I smelled fresh-turned earth and mulch. Arden pushed at my shoulders until I rolled off of her. Then she pushed herself to her feet, not trying to help me up, and turned to her brother.

"I just took a lot of ferrous fuckery to the teeth, so if you could help me out here, I'd appreciate it."

Wordlessly, Nolan produced a stoppered bottle from inside his jacket—which matched hers, I noted; the two of them were dressed virtually identically. Given their respective heights, I wouldn't have been able to tell them apart at a distance if her hair hadn't been so much longer. Braid it and tuck it down the back of her jacket and even that difference would go away. Interesting.

Arden pulled the stopper and swallowed the bottle's contents in two hard gulps before making a theatrical retching noise and wiping the back of her hand, hard, across her lips.

"Sardines and spoiled tomato jam," she said, in a tone like she was making a report. "How does it keep getting *worse*?"

Nolan produced a canteen this time, offering it to her.

"Best brother," gasped Arden, snatching it away and proceeding to wash her mouth out enthusiastically with its contents.

A drink would have been nice. My mouth still felt like a mile of dry sand. My head was spinning wildly. I tried to push myself up onto my hands, and stopped as Arden's attention swiveled back to me.

"Uh-uh," she said. "You were in there longer than I was, and you're not *as* fae, but we don't know how long you were asleep, either. You could be on the verge of actual death."

"Which is a real thing," said Nolan. "I know sometimes it feels like a story told to keep you in line, but I assure you, death happens."

"She knows that," snapped Arden. "She was going to stay there and let herself get executed. Give me the next bottle."

"Did you take that bad a dose?" Nolan sounded alarmed.

"No, silly, it's for her."

"I know she's been annoying, but has she really earned that sort of punishment?"

"Give it to me." Nolan produced another bottle. Arden took it before crouching next to me again, holding it out. "You're a little scrambled right now, so I'm going to forgive you for being a pain in my ass and trying to get martyred for a cause you can't possibly understand just yet. That said, you were in there for a while, and you'll feel better if you drink this. Eventually, I mean."

"What is it?" I asked, warily.

"The alchemist who made it says it binds to the iron in your body and wraps it in a shell that keeps it from hurting you while it works through your system. But then, this particular alchemist says a lot of things, so maybe he's full of shit. What I can say for sure is that if you drink it, you'll hate me, but then the iron will stop burning and freezing you at the same time, and it won't chew any fun new holes in your liver."

I took the bottle. When I removed the cap, it smelled like chocolate oranges. Frowning, I glanced at Arden.

She smiled encouragingly. "First impressions can be deceiving. For example, I think you're petulant and annoying, and you probably think I'm the worst. Let's try to fix that, shall we?"

Right. Well, she might be irritating, but pulling me out of an unbreachable dungeon in order to poison me in a field seemed a little over the top, even for a pair of bored purebloods. I pressed the bottle to my lips, letting gravity do the bulk of the work as I drank.

That was a good thing, because it meant I couldn't stop drinking when the taste registered. It was also a bad thing, because it meant I couldn't control how fast the stuff filled my mouth. I swallowed frantically, trying not to choke, and when it was gone, I sat up and scowled at Arden.

"What the *hell* was *that*?" Yelling at purebloods seemed to be turning into a bad habit of mine. At least this time I had a good reason for it.

"An interesting question," said Nolan, bouncing into my field of view. "We've been taking notes, trying to find any predictable pattern in the flavor. What was it for you?"

"Oysters and mint chocolate," I said, wishing I had something I could use to rinse the taste away, or at least something I could wipe my tongue on. "Ew."

"Wow, that's the worst one I've heard yet." Arden offered me her canteen. "There's still water in there, and don't worry, it's not poisoned. That would be a mean trick, wouldn't it? Get you out of there and then murder you?"

I took the canteen, trying not to show how closely her thoughts had paralleled my own.

The water was sweet and fresh, and possibly the best thing I had ever tasted. I forced myself to drink slowly, aware of just how much I'd been abusing my body, and how angry it was going to be once it had a moment to get over the shock of going from a dungeon to wherever the hell we were now.

Speaking of which . . . "Where *are* we?" I asked.

"Ah-ha!" Nolan spread his arms in a gesture of what looked like triumph. "At last, a sensible question! Welcome, fair maiden, to the Kingdom on the Golden Shore! Bright protectorate of Chrysanthe and Theron, kindest monarchs in all the Westlands!"

"What—how?" Etienne had one of the farthest teleportation ranges I knew of among the Tuatha, and he could barely manage the jump from Shadowed Hills to Briarholme. Getting January to Dreamer's Glass had almost certainly involved a stop somewhere in the middle. Opening gates requires a firm image of the destination, and the strength to bridge the two points. Going all the way from the Queen's knowe—the dungeons, no less—to Golden Shore should have been impossible.

"All will be made clear when you come before the King and Queen," said Nolan, grandly.

"Meaning we'll explain when we get there," said Arden. "Most important thing you need to know right now is that Golden Shore doesn't have an extradition agreement with our neighbors."

"Meaning . . . ?"

"Meaning unless the frosted bitch who runs the Mists wants to rouse Fair Titania from whatever she's currently doing, they can't just send guards to take you back to stand trial," she said. "Agreements were drawn up ages ago, to keep shitty nobles from crossing the border to snatch back 'their' changelings after they managed to get here. You're safe. And if you wanted a more specific location, we're in the Duchy of Cattails, in the main field of Dame vch Gwenlan's farm. She's out right now, overseeing the next stage of the harvest, but if you feel compelled to make a good showing with the local nobility, we could go and find her."

Normally, I would have demanded the chance to present myself before the local noble and apologize for entering their lands without consent. In the moment, I was hungry, exhausted, still thirsty even after emptying the canteen, and relatively sure that if I tried to talk to any sort of pureblood authority, I would vomit foul-tasting tincture all over their shoes. I wasn't sure it was possible for me to be in any more trouble than I already was. That seemed like a good way to find out.

"Can't you see she's dead on her feet?" asked Nolan. "Emphasis on the 'dead.' I've seen more appealing corpses. We're going to be in trouble if we don't let her sleep some of this off."

"In trouble with the bosses, or with the bosses' guests?"

"Both, probably, and if not both, then with the guests."

"Fine." Arden sighed heavily. "No rest for the wicked and none for us, either, I suppose. Well, October Torquill, stabber of muggers and disrupter of evenings, which would you prefer? Straight to the longest and most annoying meeting of your life, or a nice nap in a room where no one's going to hurt you?"

"Um. That second one?" I said, hesitantly.

"Good choice," said Arden, and grabbed my wrist as she sketched a circle in the air with her other hand. She pulled me along as she stepped through, and Nolan followed close behind, looking entirely nonchalant about the process.

We emerged into a round room almost as large as the base of Mother's tower, dominated by two massive canopied beds whose curtains were currently open. There was a single window, with neither glass nor shutters. Everything smelled of redwood, and not just due to Arden's magic; the smell was all but overwhelming, too strong to be anything but live tree.

Pulling away from her, I moved to the window and looked out. Vertigo gripped me as I realized how ridiculously far we were above the ground, and I swayed. A hand fell on my shoulder, steadying me. I glanced back.

Nolan was behind me, a more sympathetic look on his face than I would have expected. "My sister and I lived in a place called Muir Woods when we were younger; we got used to the smell of the redwoods. They smell like home." He guided me away from the window as he spoke. "So when we needed to find a new place to live, and decided on Golden Shore as the best place to settle, we went looking for a place among the trees."

"This tree grows in the mortal world and the Summerlands; the humans call it 'Hercules,'" said Arden. "One of them cut a room into the base, for the other humans to enjoy. Well, we figured, if the humans can do it, why can't we? Only we did our building on the Summerlands side, using the tree itself as our anchor, and we asked nicely before we did anything that might have hurt it."

"Some of the local Hamadryads helped us," said Nolan.

Dryads and their kin just kept cropping up, didn't they? I nodded as if any of this made any sense to me.

"Anyway, this is our room and no one can get into it but us; there's two beds, so you can rest while one of us keeps watch and the other reports in." Arden smiled at Nolan. "I'll take first watch."

"You are the worst of all possible sisters," grumbled Nolan.

"Believe me, I'm well aware." She walked over to one of the two beds and all but threw herself onto it. "I'm also the sister who needs to be a little indolent for a while, due to all the iron poisoning."

For the first time, Nolan looked concerned. "Are you actually injured?"

"I'll be fine," she said, waving him off. "October needs her rest, and I'll rest with her, and then we'll all be ready for the chaos. Please go let people know that we've returned—and unless you're given a royal order by an authority we both recognize, don't bring *anyone* back here."

"But—"

"Yes, I know you're going to get pressured, but ask yourself: is the pressure as bad as what I, personally, will do to you if you disrupt my napping? Come back in an hour and we'll swap off. You'll get the nice warm bed, I'll get the angry purebloods who want their pound of flesh. We'll let October sleep off the iron hangover."

Nolan still looked unsure. Arden threw a pillow at him.

"Get!" she ordered. "I'll see you when you're back."

"I'm telling Madden," he said, and sketched a circle in the air, stepping through it before she could reply.

Arden laughed, sinking down into the remaining pillows. "He can tell Madden as much as he wants. It's not like Madden's getting in here without help."

"Madden?" I asked, as I sat down on the other bed. It was perfectly soft, and smelled of blackberries. I lay down, settling my head in the pillows.

"Best friend," she said. "Nice guy. You'll probably meet him later, he's sort of inescapable when I'm around and not up a tree somewhere. Been with me since Nolan and I were fleeing the Mists, and at this point, I'm not sure either one of us would know what to do without the other. I hope you'll like him."

"M'sure I will." It was getting progressively harder to keep my eyes open. I yawned, the taste of oysters still clinging to my back molars, and wished idly for something else to drink.

Arden was talking again, explaining some convoluted relationship between her brother and her best friend and several people whose names I didn't quite catch, but I wasn't really listening. I was already half-asleep, and increasingly unable to focus on what she was saying.

Then I realized she was talking pure nonsense, reciting what sounded like a piece of human poetry as she lulled me down into sleep.

And curse her for understanding the exhaustion that comes after iron exposure so ridiculously well, because it worked.

THIRTEEN

I WASN'T SURE HOW MUCH of the last day I'd spent asleep or unconscious, but I was sure it was more than I was happy about. In my defense, it had all been part of an effort to recover from some horrible experience or other, beginning with "losing too much blood" and ending in "iron poisoning," and I never intended to do any of those things again. My eyelids felt like they'd been glued shut with something strong and sticky, and as I struggled to open them, I considered the virtues of just going back to sleep, since it was starting to feel inevitable. No one stabbed me when I was asleep.

They *did* take my knives and throw me into cells full of iron. Iron could cause hallucinations when enough of it built up in the bloodstream, and which was more believable? That I'd somehow been yanked out of the Queen's dungeon by a pair of Tuatha in fool's motley and dropped in a pumpkin field, or that I'd already absorbed so much iron that my brain was spinning any story it could come up with to convince me that things were going to be okay?

Things were not going to be okay. I did, however, need to pee, and going back to sleep wasn't going to fix that. I finally forced my eyes open and sat up, my whole body feeling heavy and slightly disconnected, like my veins had been stuffed with cotton wool. I looked around the circular room.

One of the Tuatha was in the other bed, apparently sound asleep, body turned so I couldn't see how long their hair was and know whether I was looking at Arden or Nolan. Not that it seemed to make all that much of a difference. I stood, wobbly-legged, and began shuffling around the room, looking for something resembling a chamber pot or garderobe. There were no doors, but there were a few pieces of furniture that could have been wardrobes, and sometimes those served a dual purpose.

My search came up empty. I was contemplating the logistics of trying to hang my rear end out the window, and whether I'd even be *able* to pee while I was dangling a hundred feet off the ground with no belt or rope, when a circle opened in the air and Nolan stepped through, answering the question of which Windermere was in the bed.

I squeaked, startled, and he shot me an amused look before stalking toward his sleeping sister, one hand firmly held behind his back. I recognized that stalk. It was the one August used on me when she thought I wasn't looking and was about to do something entirely un-civilized that would never have been allowed if I hadn't been her sister.

Indeed, when he reached Arden's bedside, he pulled his hand out from behind his back, revealing a large green bullfrog. "Sister dear," he said sweetly.

Arden made a grumbling noise.

"Sister dear, the queen wants to see us."

I tensed. The queen? Oh, but we were on the Golden Shore, not in the Mists. He was referring to Queen Chrysanthe, who hadn't thrown me in a dungeon any time recently. I forced myself to relax again, and just watched as Arden failed to respond, even when Nolan put a hand on her shoulder and rolled her onto her back.

Then he dropped the frog on her face.

Arden woke with a shriek that was less horror and more indigna-tion as the frog, frightened and confused, launched itself out of the bed with one massive kick of its hind legs. Nolan was laughing like this was the funniest thing he had ever seen, bending over almost double as he clutched his stomach and howled.

Arden hit him with a pillow. He laughed even harder, shoulders shaking with the force of it.

"You're disgusting," said Arden, and all but thrust herself out of the bed, shoving her brother aside in the process. She stormed toward me, and as she got closer, I saw that at least half her fury was an ex-aggeration for Nolan's benefit. "Sorry you had to see that."

"It's okay," I said, relaxing.

"Been awake long?"

"No. Was just looking for the garderobe."

"The . . . oh, *wow*, you grew up low-tech. We at least reached the fifteen hundreds before we decided to shut down progress. We do indoor plumbing here on the Golden Shore."

"They have flush toilets at Shadowed Hills," I said stiffly. "They also have enough space that using them doesn't wake up everyone else in the tower. Mother couldn't install those if she wanted to, we'd never sleep again."

Arden paused. "That may be the best argument for disgusting, inconvenient archaic technology I've heard. But no, we don't have one of those here. You need the bathroom?"

I nodded vigorously.

"So we don't have one of *those* here, either. We just pop over to the royal knowe when we need to use the facilities, then come back here until we're ready for people. I don't know if they'll be that considerate with you, given the situation—we may be going straight into dealing with everything that's been building up. Are you ready for that?"

"It's that, or I'm peeing on your floor," I said tersely. "*Please* take me to a bathroom."

"Your funeral," said Arden, and sketched a circle in the air, gesturing me through.

The hall on the other side was comfortable and warm, all polished wood and slate flooring. The ceiling was high, with exposed beams supporting dangling chandeliers filled with domes of gleaming witch light. Wait, no—not witch light. There were holes in the domes, and as I watched, a pixie emerged from one of them, leaving it to go dark until another pixie darted inside and lit it up again.

I turned to blink at Arden as she stepped through after me.

"Chrysanthe has an agreement with the local hives," she said. "They don't attack the crops, she gives them housing and all the kitchen scraps they can handle. In exchange, they light the halls and hunt the bugs that might otherwise denude some of our more valuable crops. Means we can slap an 'organic' label on things, and charge the assholes in the Mists twice as much as we charge the non-assholes."

"Oh," I said, bemused by the idea of basing pricing on attitude. If a pureblood did it, it couldn't be wrong, and surely they didn't sell directly to any changelings.

"Here, this way," she said, guiding me to an unlocked door.

On the other side was a large bathroom, complete with large bath and floor-to-ceiling mirror. I stopped dead, getting my first look at myself since Shadowed Hills.

If I'd ever looked worse in my life, I couldn't remember when. My hair was matted with blood and a variety of indistinguishable flavors of filth, several of which I was happy not to know anything about. Completing the effect, a few yarrow twigs jutted out of the snarls at odd angles. Father's illusions were gone, which meant I could see how much my normal pallor had converted to a waxen sallowness, and how deep the dark circles under my eyes were.

A jagged hole in my shirt exposed a wide swath of equally blood-caked skin where I'd been stabbed, and my hands were covered in dried blood. I didn't look like I'd eaten, slept, or bathed in roughly a decade, rather than having been safe at home in my mother's tower less than two days before.

Arden, who had entered the room behind me, paused when she saw me staring at the mirror. "You can probably take the time to wash up—I'll run interference if anyone tries to stop you," she said. "Might be better not to go in front of the Queen when you're looking like that. Assuming you want her to listen to you and not shoo you out to go and tend the cattle."

"Do you ever take anything seriously?"

"I try really hard not to." Arden's reflection shrugged broadly. "Last time Nolan or I took anything seriously, a bunch of people died."

I turned to gape at her. "Windermere. I *knew* I knew that name!"

She grimaced, glancing down. "Yeah, well, Nolan didn't want me to change it, so here we are."

"But you're dead!"

King Gilad and Queen Sebille Windermere had been the rulers of the Kingdom in the Mists in 1906, when a terrible earthquake hit the mortal world hard enough to echo into the Summerlands. That was when we'd lost all contact with the Undersea. Prior to that, relations had been strained, but there had still been ways to pass between the Kingdoms. Then the earthquake had shattered their tenuous connections to the land, and their knowes sank so deep that we'd never been able to reach them again.

Titania had mourned, of course. Most of the denizens of the sea were descendants of Maeve and thus not to be fully trusted, but the Merrow were born of one of Titania's own daughters, and she'd loved them dearly. Their loss had hurt her so badly that the rest of Faerie had moved inland in order to honor her grief, no longer living directly on the coasts. When I was a kid, August used to tell me stories about the abandoned knowes along the shore, falling slowly into disrepair, haunted by the shadows of the people who'd left them behind.

They'd given me bad dreams that kept me awake for days, until Father had ordered her to stop torturing her baby sister, and she'd gone looking for other ways to torment me.

The Undersea wasn't the only thing we lost in the Earthquake. An assassin named Oleander de Merelands had somehow managed to break the wards on the royal knowe, slipping in while everyone was distracted by the shaking of the ground and murdering the king and queen in their beds. As far as I knew, no member of the royal family had escaped alive, not even the children. That was why Titania, in her wisdom, had left the choosing of our next monarch to the Rose of Winter, and why we answered to our current Queen, who was a distant relative of the Windermeres, born of a distaff line but close enough to claim the crown.

"We're not, and since we'd like to *stay* that way, we stick to the Golden Shore unless we have no choice, like tonight, when we heard from one of our informants that a changeling had popped out of nowhere into an alley, been assaulted, and fought back, killing a pureblood in the process." She shrugged, stricken look fading to be replaced by smugness. "So we nipped over and picked you up, and now you get to be alive and take a bath and put on some clean clothes before the Queen I *actually* answer to comes and kicks my ass."

"But why?" I asked.

Arden sobered. "Do you remember what happened to the woman who killed my parents?"

"They found her dead, both arms missing just above the elbow, throat slit," I said.

"The Law applies to purebloods killing each other outside of openly declared times of war, you know, meaning that she was as much a murder victim as my parents were." She shrugged. "I'll go get you something to wear."

She turned and left the room before I could ask if she'd just admitted to killing Oleander, her departure clearly indicating that the conversation was over. A moment later, the door made a soft chiming sound, announcing that wards had been set from the outside.

Okay, so I was locked in. At the moment, that wasn't all that worrisome—after all, I was locked in with the bathtub, which was what I wanted more than anything else. Except for maybe a drink, and something to eat, and those could come along in their own time.

Of all my oddly fitting mortal clothes, my jacket seemed to have weathered the day's adventures the best; it was as filthy as the rest of me, but it was nothing a soft cloth wouldn't be able to fix, and when I'd been stabbed, my assailant hadn't hit the leather. I shrugged out of it, gave it a shake to knock off a layer or two of the least-attached grime, and folded it in half before placing it gently on the counter. I let my fingers linger on the lapel for just a moment. I didn't know why I felt so possessive of the thing, but I did, and right now, I was holding on to that.

Removing everything else was a relief. The trousers, especially, were so caked in blood and filth that they clung to my skin, forcing me to roll them off a few inches at a time. There was no hamper in this room, sadly; I'd have to pick them up to take them to a laundry. Folding them wasn't going to make that experience any more pleasant, so I took a certain bleak pleasure in tossing trousers, shirt, and undergarments onto the floor, then kicking everything into a heap in the corner before I turned my attention to the bathtub.

It had been empty when I stepped into the room, I was sure of it. Now it was filled almost to the top with steaming, apple blossom–scented water, and I wondered idly whether it chose the scents for guests based on some magical read of what would make them comfortable, or whether it was apple blossoms all the time. What would happen if someone whose magic smelled like apple blossoms came to visit? Or someone who had a lifelong feud with someone whose magic smelled like apple blossoms?

I was curious, but not curious enough to stay out of the tub, which was deep enough to require me to take two steps down before sinking fully into the water, letting it cover all but my face. I could almost float, it was so large, and I relaxed that way for a while, the water softening the worst of the muck on my skin until it fell away. I worried, very briefly, about marinating in my own filth, before I realized the water was turning clear again as quickly as it clouded.

Whoever maintained this knowe's hearth magic probably deserved a medal of some sort. I sat up and turned around, unsurprised to find shampoo, conditioner, and a bar of soap waiting for me on the rim of the tub, along with a rough cloth to scrub myself down with. I had been indolent long enough. I set myself properly to the business of getting clean.

In reasonably short order, I felt almost like myself again. I rinsed the last of the conditioner out of my hair, then stood, looking up toward the ceiling.

"Thank you," I said, formally. "I know we can't thank each other, but I asked my father once, and he said we're allowed to thank the knowes. So thank you, for letting me be clean and safe for a little while. It's more than I could have asked from you."

There had been long stretches while I was in the bath where my eyes were closed and couldn't see the bathroom. That meant it was equally unsurprising when I found a towel waiting next to the now spotlessly clean leather jacket. The clothing I'd left on the floor was gone, along with the mess it had made.

"I would have swept that up," I said, half-apologetically, as I touched the jacket with my right hand, clutching the towel to my chest with my left.

The knowe didn't acknowledge my apology. I turned again. The tub was empty, and clean clothes were hanging on the back of the door. Much more suitable, familiar clothes than the ones I'd worn in the mortal world, at that: a white linen chemise, more of those scandalous underthings, and a heather green kirtle with a buckled belt to tie it over my hips. I dressed quickly, putting the incongruous jacket back on over the whole thing, and moved to knock on the door.

"I'm clean," I called. "And clothed. May I come out now?"

"Just thought you might want a minute's privacy to catch your breath," said Arden, opening the door and grinning at me. Her expression turned approving when she saw what I was wearing. "Nice. Very nice. You clean up halfway decently."

"I try not to bring shame upon my household," I said meekly, casting my eyes toward the floor.

"Annnnd when you're clean, you fall back on all that Mists-peddled bigotry bullshit. You don't have to do that here."

I glanced up. Arden wasn't smiling anymore. She was looking at me grimly, disappointment and, oddly, grief in her eyes.

"Look, I'm supposed to take you to the King and Queen now," she said. "They don't mind us bringing home strays—it's what they keep us for, since we know fuck-all about farming, and Nolan kills everything he tries to cultivate. I've seen that man kill *mint*. In the *ground*, even. He's a menace to horticulture. But they like to look the strays over as soon as possible, to be sure we haven't snagged anyone who's meant to be spying for the Mists or Titania."

"Titania doesn't need spies," I said, bewildered. "She's glorious beyond measure, and all good things flow from her like fruits from the vine."

"See, that's propaganda, but it's not espionage, and we need to be sure it stays that way," said Arden. "Come on. This way. There's food, if that's a motivator."

I hurried to follow her. She laughed.

"Thought so," she said. "After the night you've had—and Nolan and I did some retracing of your steps after we got you here, so we know it was *quite* a night—you're probably starving."

"Wait. I thought you weren't going to leave me alone."

"And we didn't. There are two of us. When one of us was awake, that one went and tried to put things together. I went to Dreamer's Glass, and wow, did that answer some questions. Raised a whole bunch more, most of them beginning with 'what' and ending with 'the fuck,' but it was a start. Then Nolan went to see your friend Etienne."

"I don't think Sir Etienne would be very happy hearing you call me his friend," I said.

"Well, after the earful his kid's been giving him, I think he'd be a little more accommodating than he would have been yesterday. Either you have the scariest mind-magic I've ever heard of, or you've proven something about your descendant line that we've been trying to figure out for ages. It's part of why Their Majesties are so excited to meet you." Arden started down the hall, clearly trusting me to keep up.

"But we really *are* going to have to work on that conditioning," Arden continued, almost idly. "It was bad when Dad was in charge, but these days, yeesh. I don't understand why we haven't had an exodus *long* before this. You people should have run ages ago."

"We people?" I asked blankly.

"Changelings." She waved a hand. "You're still *people*, even if you're part human, and humans are pretty cool. You can't run an agrarian society without understanding the land you're working with, and the Summerlands mirrors the human world closely enough that we stay in pretty steady contact with the human locals. Oh, they don't know about Faerie, but they know about planting seasons and the best mix for your chicken feed. You meet your share of assholes, of course, but for the most part, humans don't suck."

"Oh," I said, blankly.

"So it's kinda shitty to act like they just exist to breed shorter-lived versions of ourselves that we can throw away without consequence." Arden paused, a complicated look crossing her face. "I know Oberon's gone, and he's not coming back any time soon, if he ever does, but I can't help thinking this isn't what he wanted for us. The old stories say he used to try to keep the peace between his Queens, and that some of the first changelings were born to them. Those changelings even went on to serve as Firstborn of their own descendant lines. Humanity's in us, all the way back to our roots, and we're not helping by pretending that it's not."

I wasn't sure what to say to that, so I didn't say anything as we turned down another, grander hall. This one had gold filigree around the windows, etched out in patterns of fruit and grains; one was surrounded by corn, another by grapes, all of them gilded and glorious. The windows were stained glass, abstract and artful, and they filled the space with light.

This hall ended at a tall pair of double doors, flanked by two silent Daoine Sidhe wearing the heraldry of the Golden Shore. Arden gestured me forward.

"Through there," she said.

"You're not coming?"

"This is a private party," she said, taking a step back. "Strays and orphans blessedly not invited, although we get to crash the dinner afterward. Have fun!"

Then she was gone, stepping through one of those circles in the air and vanishing. I frowned for a moment at the place where she'd been. She and her brother both seemed to use the ability to move through space as a way to get out of potentially uncomfortable conversations, and while I envied it a little, I couldn't say that I exactly cared for it.

Alone in the hall of an unfamiliar, presumably royal knowe, I turned slowly to look at the Daoine Sidhe flanking the door. Neither of them acknowledged my presence. I started closer. They appeared to have been put in place as a matched set: their hair was the same shade of purple, lilac at the roots and darkening as it grew out, they were the same height, had virtually identical features . . . if not for the fact that one had visible breasts, I wouldn't have been able to tell them apart. It was almost eerie.

"I've been dealing with the Windermeres," I complained aloud. "Does this Kingdom only present people in pairs so it can confuse your guests, or what?"

"We were coincidental," said the Daoine Sidhe on the left. "The Windermere children are not twins; we are."

I perked up. You don't meet a lot of twins in Faerie. Father and Uncle Sylvester were the only ones I knew. "Oh."

"Quite," said the one on the right. "You are?"

"Uh . . ." I wasn't normally called upon to introduce myself. Either I was an accessory of my parents, or I was a changeling at work, and thus beneath notice. "October, daughter of Simon and Amandine Torquill?"

"Was that a question or an appellation?"

"It was . . . my name." I took a breath and stood up straighter, trying to look confident. "That is who I am, and Arden Windermere brought me here because she said the Queen on the Golden Shore was requesting my presence. I request admission." I managed to hold my posture and my composure for several seconds before I sagged and added, more meekly, "If it please you."

"That's better," said one of the twins. "It's okay, kid. Things don't work here the way they do where you're coming from, and it's going to get better. Just keep your chin up, keep breathing, and don't freak out." She leaned over to grasp the handle of her door, and pulled it toward her.

Her twin did the same, and together they revealed the grand court on the Golden Shore.

True to the Kingdom's name, the room was golden. The walls were paneled in polished golden oak, pale and gleaming, panels separated by carved friezes of fruit and grains that mirrored the hall, down to the gold leaf used to pick out the details and emphasize the delicacy of the carving; the floor was gold slate, doubtless mined in the demesne, and the styling continued up into the high rafters, which continued the theme of exposed beams and pixie-lit chandeliers. Windows at least fifteen feet in height occupied much of the two far walls, the top five feet or so of them done in panes of carnival glass, and lush gold velvet curtains hung beside them. It should have been monotone. Instead, somehow, it was glorious.

The room was large enough to have held the receiving room at Shadowed Hills three times over, and all but empty. A dais stood at one end, supporting two large golden thrones, each one occupied by a golden hind. I blinked. Arden hadn't mentioned anything about meeting the King.

But then, were two monarchs really worse than one? I kept moving forward.

Like their guards, Theron and Chrysanthe were virtually a matched set, although I knew their similarities were not due to close relation. Both of them were muscular and tan, with the lower bodies of gold-furred deer and the upper bodies of pointy-eared humanoids. Theron's hair was wheat-gold and cut reasonably short, his crown shaped to account for his small but visible antlers, while Chrysanthe's hair was white-gold and waist-length, and she had no antlers at all. Both of them looked over as the door swung shut behind me.

There was a small crowd gathered by the foot of the dais, and they turned as well, and my manners deserted me, because I momentarily forgot that I was in the presence of a king and queen, instead bursting into tears and bolting across the room toward the group, gathering my kirtle in my hands to keep it from tripping me as I ran.

To my burning relief, the figure I was running for detached herself from the group and ran toward me, the two of us slamming into each other as we wrapped our arms around each other and held on for dearest life. August was shaking. I was already crying. I buried my face against her shoulder and waited to feel like I could safely talk again.

She wasn't saying anything either. Father approached us, the comforting smell of smoke and cider accompanying him as he moved to put his hands on our shoulders, my right, August's left. He didn't say anything, either, and without letting go of August, I managed to move my head to press my forehead against his arm.

"I'm sorry, Father," I whispered.

"No, the apologies are mine to make," he said. "I should have seen that the timing was too convenient, the request too specific; this was an engineered attempt to get you away from us. Duchess Zhou confirmed it when I confronted her."

"She told me, too," I said, finally lifting my head and blinking up at him. He looked stern but not angry, like he was more concerned for my wellbeing than he was upset about my misbehavior. That was something of a relief. I hadn't realized how afraid I was that I had disappointed my father until this very moment. "She . . . she . . ."

And to my shame and chagrin, I started crying again.

August was still clinging to me, and Father wrapped his arms around us both, lowering his head so that even as he lowered his voice, we could hear him clearly.

"She told me everything," he said. "She told me what she asked of you, and what you did for her, and what it cost you. I am angry but not with you. Never with you. Now, wonderful as it is to know that both my girls are hale and whole, we have an audience to attend. October, do you think you can compose yourself?"

I sniffled and pulled away, wiping my eyes with the side of my hand. The one disadvantage of the leather jacket: it wasn't absorbent enough to be a good handkerchief, but at least the sleeves were long enough to keep me from using my chemise. Mother would be pleased. She hated it when I used my sleeves to wipe my face, said that it made me look like no one loved me.

August always glared at her when she said that, but she didn't argue. We all knew better than to argue with Mother, even Father, who would just look quietly disappointed and sneak us off for cake and lemonade as soon as he reasonably could.

August let go of me, then pinched me, hard, on the back of the hand.

"Ow!"

"That's what you *get*," she said, hotly. "Blood magic? Letting yourself be taken somewhere other than Dreamer's Glass? Getting *arrested*?"

I noticed she didn't include "murder" on my list of crimes. Maybe she didn't know. I managed a wavering smile. "Yeah, it was lousy," I said. "Too bad you missed it."

"Never do that again." She looped her arm through mine. "Now come on. There are people who want to talk to you."

"What? Why would anyone want to talk to *me*?" I looked over my shoulder at Father, seeking confirmation, and he nodded, lips pressed into a thin line as he schooled his expression to something neutral.

We proceeded across the room to the dais at a more reasonable pace, August holding on to my arm until we were approaching the thrones. There, she let go and stepped a short distance away from the dais, allowing me to continue without her. Father stayed behind me and slightly to the side, as was appropriate for a pureblood parent when presenting a changeling child to royalty.

Grasping the sides of my kirtle, I curtseyed, and wondered why it felt so odd. My body seemed to want to bow, which would have been entirely inappropriate. I nudged that urge aside and sank deeper into my position, face turned toward the floor.

"May I present my daughter, October Torquill," said Father. Despite the way the phrase was framed, it wasn't a question: he was presenting me, and now the question was what they would do in response.

I almost looked up at him in surprise. I had no right to his last name, and we both knew it. For him to be applying it to me now, in front of royalty, no less . . . it should have been exhilarating.

Instead, it was borderline terrifying.

"Not your child born, I assume, Simon?" asked Theron. His voice was light, and surprisingly pleased.

"To my honorable wife, after a trip to the human world to fulfill her obligation to Fair Titania," he said. "Legally, she's as much my child as August has ever been. If you ask my heart, it will answer you the same. She's mine, and I claim her in all regards."

"So you don't regret your wife's decision to follow Titania's command?" asked Theron.

"I was sorry when Amandine was ordered to lie with someone she didn't love," said Father. "Commanding the creation of children is cruel, commanding the creation of children solely for their service is worse, but it seems to me that commanding a conception out of obligation rather than love is also cruel, if not as strongly so. How could it be anything other than wrong, when every step is couched in cruelty?"

My calves were starting to burn from holding myself in position. Still, I didn't waver. To waver would shame my father, and while this was a longer form of the usual interrogation when a changeling was presented, I had heard Uncle Sylvester ask similar questions. I had never heard an answer skirt so closely to criticizing Titania, however, and I feared for him.

"Let the girl stand," said Chrysanthe, in a faintly chiding tone. "She's still recovering from everything she's been through. You may rise, October."

Grateful and afraid, I straightened, dropping my kirtle as I did, and looked down at the steps of the dais, not wanting to risk giving offense without intending it.

"Mmm, 'girl' is a bit dismissive, I think, upon seeing her better," said Chrysanthe. "Woman, then, but still allowed to stand up straight in our presence. You may look at us, October. We don't demand that you avert your eyes."

I glanced up, too startled not to. Chrysanthe was smiling. Theron looked a bit more dubious, but both of them were settled comfortably in their thrones, showing no signs of displeasure at my presence. That was something of a relief.

Not as big a relief as the presence of my family. "Forgive me, Majesty, but how is it that my father and sister are here?"

"Ah. That *is* a tale, and not theirs alone; they came with companions, who we have ignored for too long already." Chrysanthe gestured to the other people who'd been in the room when we arrived.

I looked at them for the first time.

My first impression, that they were a small group, was accurate; there were four of them, and only two were familiar. Those two were

knights in my Uncle Sylvester's service: Garm and Grianne, a Gwragen and a Candela, respectively. They stood next to two strangers.
The man was staring at me with such intensity that I half-expected
him to claim offense against me for the simple crime of breathing in
his presence; the woman was also watching me, but more wearily,
with a sloping cast to her shoulders that implied she'd been running
hard even longer than I had.

I had never seen either one of them before, I knew I hadn't, but
something about the man made me feel as if I ought to recognize
him. It was an odd feeling, quickly chased away by the look he was giving me. I didn't *want* to recognize someone who looked at me like that.

"October," said Garm, sounding dryly amused by the whole
situation.

Both the strangers clearly belonged to the same unfamiliar descendant line, with narrow, vertically slit pupils sketched down the center
of their vividly colored eyes. Their ears were pointed, but not along
any angle I knew. The man had black stripes in his dark brown hair,
while the woman's hair was white at the roots and deepened into a rich
orange as it grew out. She wore it loose to brush her shoulders, straight
and fine. Both of them were dressed as if they'd raided a court's lost
and found, clothing mismatched and somewhat ill-fitting.

The man began to step forward. The woman's hand on his arm
stopped him, and he stilled, stare never wavering. If looks could kill,
I would have been as dead as the man in that alley.

Not the most soothing thought, perhaps, but as they had been
given implicit permission by the Queen on the Golden Shore, all four
of them were moving toward us now. I took a half-step back, stopping
when my shoulder brushed my father's chest. He would protect me,
if it came to that.

August, meanwhile, was putting herself in front of me, her own
wariness evident.

"We came here with you," she said. "We listened to your wild stories and we let you convince us to come, even though it really, really
sucked. Now you're looking at my sister like you want to hurt her.
You're going to stop that *right now*, or we're leaving."

"How were you intending to do that?" asked the strange man, his
voice low and husky and tightly controlled. "It took both of us to
bring you here. Garm would never have been able to make the journey if not for Grianne. How do you plan to escape our company?"

"Their Majesties have their snatchers," said August, more boldly than I would have expected, even from her. "There have been rumors about them for as long as I can remember, and now we know those rumors are true. I'm sure they would be happy to take us back to Shadowed Hills, in exchange for a pledge of silence. The Golden Shore needs to keep its secrets."

"Charming as it is to sit here and listen to you coordinate a somewhat ill-considered blackmail plan against us, I'm afraid we need to be seeing to the banquet now that our guests of honor have arrived," said Theron. "I'll send one of those 'snatchers,' as you so quaintly put it, to collect you when it's time to eat. Please try not to get any blood on the floor." He and the queen both rose, then, and walked away, their hooves making little ringing taps against the polished oak.

"August," I said.

"We'll leave if we want to leave," said August, not to be dissuaded. "And if you don't stop looking at my sister like that, we *will* want to leave."

"August!" I repeated, more sharply. She turned to look at me, hurt and surprise in her eyes. I forced myself not to look away. It was harder than I'd anticipated. "I can't go back with you."

"But . . . we came here to . . . Of course you can," she protested. "Mother doesn't know what's happened, but she won't be angry. None of it was your fault. It's still Moving Day, and we'd be traveling by Tuatha, so there's no chance we'd be stopped. Of course you can come home. Where else would you go?"

I looked to Father, helpless in the face of the pleading note in her voice. She was my sister. I existed to serve her, to be her friend and companion and plaything and helpmeet and all other things she asked of me. I didn't exist to make her look at me like her heart was breaking.

Thankfully, he understood. "August," he said gently. "What your sister has been accused of is a serious crime."

"But she didn't *do* it!" she said. "She can't have *done* it! She doesn't know how to fight, much less how to kill someone! They're—they're confused, and they're pointing fingers because she was an unclaimed changeling in the wrong place at the right time, and they want it to be her. But she didn't *do* it."

"Stupid girl," growled the strange man. "She disappeared from a sealed holding cell belonging to the Queen of the Mists. You really think it matters whether she committed the crime they've accused her of? They'll have her tied to the Tree in the blinking of an eye. Escaping was disrespectful to their precious pureblood authority."

"Tybalt," said the woman, tone chiding.

He shrugged off her hand and turned to stalk away while I was still gaping after him.

No wonder he'd looked familiar: he was the man from my blood memories, the one who'd looked at me with such open adoration, the one I'd supposedly married in some other version of the world. I hadn't recognized him in part because I hadn't been expecting to see him in the real world, and in part because I still couldn't reconcile the way he'd been looking at me *now* with the way he'd been looking at me *then*. What could I possibly have done to upset him so badly?

"He's not wrong," I said meekly. "I was locked up for a crime, and I fled before I could stand trial. If I set foot back in the Mists, anywhere in the Mists, the Queen will have me arrested for violation of the Law—and even if I were to be found innocent, the fact that I defied her would be enough to see me convicted. It's not a crime to kill a changeling. She might still let me die on the Tree, in recognition of my family's stature, but I'd die. I can never go home."

"Mother would never let them hurt you. As long as you stayed in the tower—"

"I'd be a prisoner, and our family would suffer! I can't do that. You know I can't do that."

"We'll find a way," said August, voice small. "I won't lose you."

"Golden Shore has no extradition treaty with the Mists," I said, unfamiliar words clumsy on my tongue. "I can stay here, safely, and as long as I don't make trouble, I might be left alone." I would still be guilty of breaking the Law, but surely a Queen had bigger problems than one insouciant changeling who vanished into the night when her guards were distracted. Surely she would forget about me. And if she didn't, well. I'd live longer there, and not have to see the shame in my mother's eyes.

"Then I'll stay with you," said August. Father blinked.

"You can't," I said. "Mother would never—"

"They're *not* taking my sister away from me!" she said, very nearly shouting, and wrapped her arms possessively around me, yanking me against her and holding me tight as she glared at the rest of the group. The man who'd stalked away—Tybalt—was in the far corner of the room, leaning against the wall in partial shadow, still watching us. I had no doubt that if I'd been any closer, I would have been able to see him glaring.

"No one wants to take your sister away from you," said the woman with the bicolored hair, raising her hands in a placating gesture. "No one has said that. No one at all."

"If she stays here and I don't, how is that not taking her away from me?" demanded August.

"Well, for one thing, you could eventually choose to leave the tower and relocate to Golden Shore, assuming you could get permission from the local regents," said Father, slowly. "They rely heavily on the cooperation of the local pixie colony for their lighting and some of their more delicate tasks; the colony near us is very fond of you, and I'm sure we could convince them to come with you long enough to talk the local pixies into putting in a good word."

Grianne's Merry Dancers bobbed and wove around her head in an elaborate pattern as she shot him an amused look. "You think someone here can talk to pixies?" she asked.

Father shrugged. "They have Piskies and Cornish Pixies in residence. I'm quite sure they can communicate with their smaller kin. So you see, August, no one is trying to separate the two of you, and I'll do whatever is within my power to keep that from happening, but you have to accept that things won't go back to the way they were just because you raise your voice."

August gave him a helpless look before she finally, reluctantly, let me go. "I hate this," she said.

"I hate it, too," I said, relieved that we appeared to be moving away from the topic of whether I had actually broken the Law. August's insistence on my innocence was a pleasant thing. I didn't want to bring it to an end.

"Those of us who've been trying to deal with it for the past four months hate it even more than you do," said the strange woman.

I frowned, looking at her. I couldn't exactly ask if the blood memories I'd seen of her companion were accurate. I knew his name, and mostly knew his face, although the man I remembered had been less hollow-cheeked and haggard, but there was one thing I had yet to confirm.

"I'm sorry, ma'am," I said. Her gaze snapped around to me. "I know this is a rude question to ask so bluntly, but it seems we're shorter of time than any of us would like to be, so: are you Cait Sidhe?"

"I am," she said, with the ghost of a smile. "And you're the first person to recognize that so quickly since this whole mess started. How do you know my descendant line, if I may answer boldness with boldness?"

"I don't," I said. "I mean, I've never met a Cait Sidhe before. But I saw something, recently, that made me think you might be one."

I wasn't ready to admit to doing blood magic. Not yet. Not in front of my family.

There was a heavy smacking sound from the other side of the room. I looked toward it. Tybalt had just punched the wall.

"We have very sensitive ears as a rule," said the woman. "Don't mind him. My name's Ginevra, and I'm either the Queen Regent to the Court of Dreaming Cats, or I'm a visiting Princess from the Court of Whispering Cats. It's very confusing, and we don't entirely understand it ourselves."

I blinked. "Cats have Courts?"

She nodded. "We do. Oberon set us aside long, long ago, to watch over the Divided Courts and keep them in balance as much as we could. The Cait Sidhe are the only line descended from all of the Three. That grants us special responsibilities and privileges."

"And as with all descendant lines, certain unique aspects to their magic," said Garm.

"Well, yes," said Ginevra. "We determine rulership not by birth but by innate magical strength. A royal cat will not necessarily sire or birth a royal kitten. Magic does as it will. All Cait Sidhe are somewhat resistant to being caught in illusions and magical deceptions. Those of us who are born royal are, well . . ."

She paused to shoot a frustrated glance at Tybalt, who was punching the wall again. Returning her attention to me, she continued:

"We're effectively immune to illusions. We can be caught by spells that change the way we understand the world, but only briefly; they never fully take with us, and given time or reason to resist, we'll see through virtually anything."

"Gwragen are among the best illusionists in Faerie," said Garm. "We can't necessarily see *through* illusions, but we know when they're around us, and for the last four months or so, the whole world's been shrouded in illusion. It hurts my eyes. Hurts my head, too. But because we truck so much in illusion, we knew the Cait Sidhe quite well, when they still existed. So these two fetched up, claiming to be the missing cats, and they didn't flicker or have soft edges. Not like everything else around us. Everything I am tells me that means they're speaking truth."

"Truth about what?" I asked, although I was direly afraid I knew.

Ginevra looked at me sadly. "October, you're smarter than that; you already know," she said. "The truth is, four months ago, Titania wrapped as much of Faerie as she could reach in an illusion so seamless that it's taken us this long to find a way to reach you. We need your help if we're going to put Faerie back the way it's meant to be. We need you so we can save our world."

"Oh," I said faintly. "Is that all?"

FOURTEEN

AUGUST STEPPED IN FRONT of me again, scowling at Ginevra. "What do you think my sister is going to do to save your version of Faerie, and why do you think your version of the world is more important than ours is, anyway?"

"Because ours is the real one," said Ginevra. "Ours is the way things really happened, and *this* is the way Titania thinks they *should* have happened, the way that puts her in charge of everything and eliminates everything she can't control. There are hundreds of Cait Sidhe locked inside the Court of Cats right now. Royal cats are rare, and the other cats can't see through the illusion. They can't get out. We've been running ourselves ragged trying to hunt and steal enough food to keep everyone healthy, and it's not going to work forever. And the Undersea—"

Father made a scoffing noise. Ginevra shot him a hard look.

"Out of everyone here, I'd expect you to be the last person who'd scoff at the idea of the Undersea," she said, voice sharp. "They offered you a home when no one else would have you."

"Now I know you're spinning stories," he said. "My home is with my family, and none of them are waterlogged residents of a lost world."

Rolling her eyes, Ginevra turned back to me. "We spoke to Etienne," she said. "You know you can prove what we're saying is true. You know you have the capability."

"I do," I admitted. I didn't want to. Part of me wanted to see the world she kept talking about, where I could fall in love and get married and not be defined by my limitations. Even more of me wanted her to disappear and leave me alone, taking all her uncomfortable questions and unanswerable contradictions with her. I knew the world. I *understood* the world. Why would I choose a reality where I was married to a man who clearly hated me and people threw my father into the sea?

But I didn't want to live in a world that wasn't real. I wanted things to be real. Slowly, I stepped out from behind my sister and extended one arm toward Ginevra, holding out my hand like I was preparing to touch the point of a spindle.

"I lost my knife in the alley," I said. "You'll have to prick my finger."

"Toby!" said August, shocked. "You can't do *blood magic*!"

"I'm not, not really," I said. "I just need to look for something, and blood makes it easier."

"Let her be, August," said Father, putting a hand on her shoulder to keep her from stepping in front of me again. "I don't like it either, but your sister has passed her majority, and if she wants this, we shouldn't interfere."

I *didn't* want this. I didn't want *any* of this. I wanted to find a way to go back to the tower, to the moment when August had suggested going to Shadowed Hills to search for crumbs. If I'd just insisted I was too tired to go out, that I wasn't hungry, all this might have been avoided. There would have been no question of whether or not the world was real, and I wouldn't be a wanted criminal hiding on the Golden Shore, facing a woman from a descendant line that no longer existed who wanted me to save her version of Faerie. I didn't want this at all.

Ginevra nodded before extending her hand to meet mine, a claw growing from the tip of her index finger. It slid smoothly out of her flesh, following a channel that had been concealed until it opened, and I was fascinated enough by watching it happen that I almost missed the moment when she tapped the tip of her claw to my own index finger. The pain was immediate and sharp, like being pricked with a pin.

"Ow!" I exclaimed involuntarily, and stuck my finger in my mouth, closing my eyes. The taste of blood exploded over my tongue, bright and coppery-sharp. There was a heavy tang to it, the remnants of the iron that still lingered in my system. Swallowing, I *reached*.

Webs of iridescent pink thread sprang into view around Garm and Grianne but not around Ginevra; looking at her, I saw only the delicate lavender pulse of her own magic. I turned my head slowly, not entirely sure what I was hoping to see. The same pink webs gleamed around my father and sister; the ones around Father were the thickest I'd seen so far, completely blocking all traces of his own magic. There was no glimmer of pink from the wall, where Tybalt stood.

So these strangers were telling the truth in at least one sense: whatever spell had been cast on the rest of us wasn't touching the cats. But what did that—

Flesh struck flesh with a meaty thud, and Ginevra yelped before hissing, a horrifyingly bestial sound. The smell of someone else's blood filled my nose, red and coppery and underscored with traces of unfamiliar river lupine and limoncello. I opened my eyes.

Tybalt was no longer on the other side of the room. Instead, he was in front of me, having crossed the distance between us with horrifying speed. He had one hand wrapped tight around Ginevra's throat, and his other knotted in her hair, jerking her head back. She was pulling at the hand on her throat with both of her own hands, frantic to break his grip, and there were thin scratches down the side of her face. Garm and Grianne were staring in horror at the scene, not moving.

"Stop it!" I shouted. I felt, rather than heard, August take a step back and away. I wasn't sure she'd ever heard me raise my voice that way before. I didn't look. I was too busy glowering at Tybalt.

He glanced at me, and for a bare instant, he wasn't glaring like he wanted me to die on the floor. His whole face softened, eyes going wide with surprise, and I realized his pupils had expanded to swallow his irises almost entirely, reducing them to thin rings of green around the black. Then he blinked, and the expression of blazing fury returned.

"She *hurt* you," he said, coldly.

"I asked her to!"

"I did not give her consent to *hurt* you." He gave Ginevra a shake, like he thought she might not have received the message. She scrabbled at his hand one more time, then went limp, submitting to his superior position.

"You don't get to give people consent to hurt me," I said. "No one gets to give people consent to hurt me except for me. Not you, not my family, not the damned Queen of the Mists, not even Fair Titania. *No one.*"

"Yet here you stand, willing to remain wrapped up in an enchantment that denies you your identity, your history, your true family— everything you've worked so hard to build." He gave Ginevra another shake, then dropped her to the floor, where she clutched her throat, gasping. "I knew the spell was tangled tight around you. I still expected you to fight."

"I'm not a fighter," I said. "It's not fair to ask me to be."

"No," he snarled. "I suppose it's not." He shot Ginevra a dismissive look, shifting it to me before he spat, "But I still hoped you would." He turned on his heel and stalked away again, back to the far side of the room. This time, he kept going when he reached the wall, striding into the shadow cast by one of the heavy velvet curtains and disappearing with the faintest whiff of musk and pennyroyal.

I glanced in surprise at the jacket I was wearing. The leather had smelled of pennyroyal when I first put it on. Did that mean it had been his? But how would he have been able to get into Shadowed Hills to leave it for me?

Father stepped forward to offer Ginevra his hand, helping her off the floor. She nodded gratefully, producing a handkerchief from inside her shirt and using it to dab at the scratches on her cheek.

"Please forgive him," she said, to the rest of us. "He's been on edge since this whole thing began. We all have. The Court of Cats is in chaos, and each of us has lost something very dear. He just lost something dearer than most."

The memory of the wedding I'd seen in my blood—*our* wedding—flashed through me. I refused to dwell on it. I didn't know this man. I didn't *love* this man. I wasn't *going* to love him. He was terrifying. He glared at me for the crime of existing in his presence, he attacked people without warning or provocation, and he acted like this was all somehow my fault. How could I possibly love someone like that?

If restoring their world meant I had to be with *him*, I was even more sure I didn't want to help them do it.

I made a noncommittal noise, which Ginevra seemed to take as some sort of agreement, because she relaxed, just a little, before she asked, "What did you see?"

"Pink lines. In the air all around everyone but you and *him*. August, did you know our descendant line could *see* magic when we focused the power we get from blood the right way?"

She blinked, looking utterly baffled. "What?"

"Maybe Mother never taught you either because it's not a power she has, and she didn't realize we did," I said. "But yeah. If I have access to blood, and I close my eyes and focus the way I do when I'm trying to pick up on the scent of someone's magic, I can *see* spells. They look like webs in the air, like someone's knotted them out of moonlight or . . . or wind, intangible but solid at the same time." I wasn't explaining this very well. I wasn't sure it was something that *could* be explained very well. How do you breathe? You don't think about it, you just *do* it. Some functions of magic work the same way. The harder you think about them, the more difficult they become.

"There have been a few times when I bit my lip or something, where I saw a flash of what you're talking about, but it never lasted," she said.

"Maybe because you weren't focusing on it? It doesn't seem to happen unless I focus really hard," I said. "April—the little girl in Dreamer's Glass—told me I could do it, and when she cut me and I tasted the blood, I saw myself doing it in a . . . very bad situation. So I just did what the blood already knew how to do. I looked the right way, and I saw the spell."

"Can you show me the memory?" asked August, sounding genuinely interested and not at all upset for the first time since this conversation had begun.

"I think we're moving away from the point," said Garm.

"I think we lost the point a while ago," said Grianne.

That was more than the normally taciturn Candela sometimes said in an afternoon. I blinked at her. She looked calmly back, her Merry Dancers circling her head like tiny satellite extensions of her self.

"You tasted blood," she said. "You looked at us. What did you *see*?"

"I saw threads wrapped around you like a net, until they almost obscured your own magic," I said. "Pink and iridescent and glistening—the magic's alive, it's responsive, it's still being powered by the caster." I wouldn't speak Titania's name, not aloud. Not yet. If these were her spells I was destroying—and they were, all the denial in the world wouldn't change what I knew deep down to be true—then I was committing treason by even looking at them.

"All of us?" asked Ginevra.

"No," I said, frowning a little at being asked to repeat myself. "I already said there weren't any wrapped around you or Tybalt, and the ones around Garm are frayed, like something's been nibbling at them."

"Arden went to meet April and her mothers in Dreamer's Glass," said Ginevra. "She said you were able to break the threads around January, and doing so restored her memories of the other world. The one that existed before the illusion."

"I did, and it did, but it was *exhausting*, and it gave me a horrible headache," I said. "Then Sir Etienne grabbed me and took me to do it again to his daughter—did you know he had a daughter?" I turned to Father. "He's been hiding her in the mortal world, with a human woman. He says she's his wife. Is that even legal? Can we marry humans?"

"It has always seemed such an impossibility that no prohibitions have been set against it," said Father, brow furrowed in thought. "Assuming he never told his wife of the existence of Faerie, he committed no actual crimes. Begetting a changeling and not immediately surrendering their care is allowed, or families like ours would never happen."

"Okay," I said slowly, feeling my way through the syllables. "He said he'd been hiding her because he couldn't subject her to the way our world treats changelings, and that . . ." I faltered. "He said he knew for a fact that our mother could turn changelings fully fae, and that she had done it before. He *knew*."

"You need to stop your tongue, October," said August sharply. "You speak of family matters."

"These secrets are no secrets to us," said Garm. He shrugged. "Our liege drinks. Everyone knows he drinks. And when he does, his tongue loosens, and he shares things he should perhaps leave mired in silence."

"As should you!" snapped August. "You shame your liege by repeating the lies wine tells him." She glanced to Father. "Tell him to be silent."

"August," said Father softly. "I can't."

She blinked, her rage dying in the face of her confusion.

"I'm no threat to your secrets," said Ginevra. With a note of humor, she added, "This version of Faerie doesn't even want to admit I exist, much less listen to whatever wild stories I want to start spinning about their precious Firstborn."

I focused on Father as I continued. "He said if Mother could do that, he believed August and I could, too. And he said he knew this was true, because you and Uncle Sylvester were born changelings." I was coming dangerously close to admitting what I had sworn never to discuss with anyone outside my immediate family. But I had to know. "Is that true? Were you born mortal?"

"I . . ." He looked away from me, taking a deep breath. "October, you have to understand that I . . ."

That was all I needed to hear. My father had always been one of the most talented liars I'd ever met: he could charm the petals off a rose, or the feathers from a bird's wing. But I'd never known him to lie well when it mattered. When faced with something that could harm him or someone he cared about, he stumbled and stammered and was quickly reduced to incoherence. If he was stumbling over his words, that meant Etienne had been telling the truth.

Which meant *he* had been somehow deserving of Mother's magic, but *I* was not, and never had been. *He* hadn't been born destined for servitude, forbidden to have a home and family of his own. Oh, no. Somehow, he'd managed to catch the eye of the only Firstborn who could open Faerie's doors for him in their entirety, granting him place, prestige, and patronage.

I'd always known what Mother could do. As long as I could remember. But she had never offered to do it for me, and I'd never been certain that anyone had experienced her magic in that way, much less someone I was so close to. To find out what could have been, well . . .

It stung. As much for August as for myself. I could have been a full part of Faerie. I could have *belonged*. And she could have known her sister would never leave her, that my mortality wouldn't eventually, inevitably, pull us apart.

"He asked me to strip the humanity from his daughter," I said, my gaze returning to Ginevra. Somehow, she had become the most neutral person there, the one I could look at without fear of censure or shame. "He wanted her to have all of Faerie as her own, not to be forced to the fringes and left there to starve while he was sat at a feast beyond consuming. He asked, and his human wife asked, and his daughter asked. They said it was within the limits of what I could achieve. And so . . . I tried."

"You turned a changeling fully fae?" asked August.

If I hadn't known her as well as I did, it would have been easy to interpret her tone as disgust. As it was, I could hear the amazement, buried under a layer of confusion so thick it pressed the joy out of everything. She'd always been like that, capable of making the best things in the world sound like the worst.

"No. I couldn't, because somebody else already had. She thought she was a changeling, and she wore an illusion so intricately woven that she *looked* like a changeling, but when I looked at her blood, there was no humanity there. She was already a pureblooded Tuatha de Dannan. There was nothing in her for me to change."

"So what *did* you do?" asked Ginevra.

"I pulled the illusion down." It sounded so simple when I said it like that, as if it hadn't been painful and complicated and ended with me knocked through a hole in the world. I paused. "I know Nolan went to speak with Sir Etienne. Do we know whether Chelsea's okay?"

"I'm sure her father would have arrived to tell us about it by now, if she wasn't."

"So October stopped an illusion from making a pureblood girl look like a changeling?" asked August.

"More than that; if January is anything to go by, October will have unlocked her memories of the *real* Faerie," said Ginevra, watching me closely. "Chelsea should remember the same reality Tybalt and I and the other royal cats do."

"The one April comes from," I said slowly. "The other Faerie."

"Exactly."

August slid herself in front of me again, posture and expression screaming challenge as she got closer to Ginevra than necessary, their noses virtually touching. "Do they also remember this one?"

Ginevra blinked, expression clouding. "What?"

"Do they also remember *this* reality? The one we're living in? The one we're a part of right now?"

"I . . . I don't know," she admitted. "This reality never took root with us, and so I don't know the specific ways it was designed to differ. April didn't get these memories either. And January was too busy being ecstatic about being released to go into detail about what she did or didn't remember."

"And you want my sister—my *sister*—to let you do this to her. To make her join your messed-up fringe reality that may or may not exist. How do we know *you're* not the ones under the spell, while we're the ones who are normal? October isn't trained. She doesn't fully understand her own magic. She could be doing something to scramble these people's minds, thinking she's helping them."

"I—" said Ginevra.

August wasn't finished. "These people you're talking about, they consented, right? That's what you're saying, that they agreed to let this happen?"

"They did," I said, putting a hand on her arm to hold her back before she could get any further up in Ginevra's face. "They asked me."

"There you go, then! My sister *isn't asking.*"

Ginevra glanced at me, almost frantic for me to disagree.

If there were sides to be chosen, I would always take my sister's side. "She's right," I said. "I didn't ask, and it wouldn't matter if I had, because I can't pull the spell off myself *anyway*. I already tried. I couldn't get a grasp on it to start breaking the strands." I held up my hands, flexing them as if to demonstrate how hard it would be to use them to grab something intangible that was wrapped all the way around me. "So whatever this is, I'm not going to get out of it any time soon."

Ginevra looked horrified. No complexities, no subtleties: just outright horror, as if this was a complication she'd never seen coming.

August glared at her as she took my arm and moved to lead me away, away from Uncle Sylvester's knights and the impossible Cait Sidhe and our shamefaced father. She didn't say anything. She didn't need to.

Whatever this other Faerie looked like, it wasn't mine. It wasn't the world I knew. And even if I had to spend the rest of my life there on the Golden Shore, it would be worth it, as long as I didn't have to do it alone.

We were almost to the doors when they opened, the two Daoine Sidhe who had been standing guard stepping into the room.

"Dinner is prepared, and their Majesties request the honor of your presence in the Gull Ballroom," said one of them.

"That isn't actually a request," said the other.

FIFTEEN

THE GULL BALLROOM WAS as large as the throne room, and decorated in much the same color scheme, but with carved birds and salmon in place of the fruits and flowers. Several large round tables had been set up throughout the room, while service stations were set up against two of the walls. A long stage dominated the third wall, supporting the high table. At least that part of the layout was familiar. Theron and Chrysanthe were seated there, with Arden and Nolan Windermere settled to Chrysanthe's left. The presence of the siblings was briefly a surprise, but only briefly; even in exile, they were the rightful heirs to the Mists, and it made sense that they'd be shown some measure of respect.

All the other tables had at least a few open seats, although many were already occupied, by people wearing a variety of styles ranging from court formal to "just came in from the fields." Servers moved through the crowd, and I realized with a start that less than half of them were changelings, while more than half the people seated at the tables *were*. Purebloods and changelings took rolls from the same basket of bread, and drank from cups that had been filled out of the same jug. I struggled not to gawk as our Daoine escorts led us across the floor toward the only obviously open table.

Well. Mostly open. Tybalt was seated there, his seemingly omnipresent scowl firmly on his face. He looked over as we approached, but didn't rise to pull out our chairs, or make any other moves to help us get settled.

Normally, I would have been honored beyond measure to be seated between my father and sister. We were rarely in a position to dine at the same table, even in our tower; Mother insisted I eat in the kitchen when we were all at home together, saying that as a changeling, it was vital for me to remain aware of my place.

Apparently, on the Golden Shore, my place was directly before the royal family.

But with Tybalt glaring from across the table and Father too ashamed to meet my eyes, it was difficult to take pleasure in this rare honor. I unfolded my napkin and placed it across my lap, trying to focus on the minutiae of the moment. August elbowed me lightly. I looked up at her.

"I think that's the food," she said, gesturing toward a Satyr pushing a silver serving cart. A variety of entrees were presented there. He would pause at each table he passed, asking the people sitting there which meal they wanted. Each time a plate was removed, an identical one would appear in its place, meaning no one was ever denied their first choice.

Another server approached our table, a jug of spiced tea in hand. As she filled our glasses, I leaned toward her and asked, "Is it like this every night?"

"Oh, no, miss," she said. "This is a fancy night, as we've fancy people visiting. A King and Queen of another demesne, our Lord and Lady say. So while we're not full formal, we are a bit nicer than we might otherwise be."

I blinked slowly. Changelings seated alongside the regular people was *nicer* than they would normally have been? I didn't know how to process that. I leaned back in my chair, watching the room in baffled silence.

The Satyr with the serving cart reached our table, and people began selecting their entrees. Expression defiant, August took a piece of shepherd's pie dripping in cheese and butter. Mother always told her to watch her diet. Father didn't say a word.

I selected a plate of salmon accompanied by asparagus and some sort of risotto. Of all the dishes, it looked the least overwhelmingly rich, and thus the least likely to upset my stomach or be taken away from me when Theron and Chrysanthe realized how many changelings were seated among the members of their court.

"Your story is an interesting one, and has elements to recommend it," said Father politely, to the Cait Sidhe on the other side of the table. "And I do appreciate the aid you've given us thus far in resolving the current unpleasantness. What were you hoping our October could do to help you?"

"I can't dispel the whole world," I said, keeping my eyes on my plate. "It's exhausting, and it *hurts*."

"It wouldn't be if you had access to stronger blood," said Ginevra. "We didn't come here to ask October to remove the enchantment from every person in Faerie one at a time."

"Good," said August, voice sharp.

"We came here to ask her to help us remove it at the source."

I dropped my fork.

The clattering sound it made seemed impossibly loud in the crowded ballroom, cutting across conversation and the more ordinary clacking of cutlery. I lifted my head and stared at Ginevra.

"According to everyone I've spoken to about it, this spell was probably cast by *Titania*," I hissed. "The Mother of Us All." I couldn't articulate the way the magic itself repeated that message, wordless but understandable, at least to me.

"In name only," said Ginevra, disturbingly serene. "Not every descendant line springs from her. Your own doesn't."

"She's still the Queen of All Faerie!"

"And that gives her the right to remake us in her image? To destroy our lives and change our memories? She excised entire *lines* from Faerie. She exiled the Cait Sidhe to the Court of Cats and the Roane to the Undersea. What happened to the other shifters? What happened to the other fae she deemed 'bestial' and thus unworthy of a place in her Faerie? Where are *they*? The Cu Sidhe, the Swanmays, the Reynardine, they don't have anything like the Court of Cats to protect them, but she must have put them *somewhere*."

I wanted to argue. I couldn't. "I'm just a changeling," I said. "I'm not setting myself against Titania."

Tybalt put down his knife and fork and stood, shoving his chair back from the table. "I can't sit here and listen to this," he snarled. He stalked away again, drawing looks and murmurs from the high table. Chrysanthe leaned over and said something to Arden, who nodded and opened a circle in the air, sliding through it and disappearing.

August was scowling after Tybalt. "Does he not understand how to be civil? I would have thought a King would have manners, even if he was only a King of Cats."

Ginevra's poker face was good. If I hadn't been watching for it, I wouldn't have seen the way her eyes briefly darted to me, measuring my response to Tybalt's departure.

Too bad for her that I'd been trained to be a pureblood's handmaid. Keeping my face from betraying me is a skill I've been cultivating since I was old enough to wash the dishes. I didn't react.

Ginevra sighed. "He knows October wasn't immune to the memory change, but I suppose he'd been hoping, rationally or not, that she'd have managed to shrug off some of the effects of Titania's spell on her own. Or that even if she couldn't, she would want to remember who she was before. To set things right."

"Sucks to be him," said August.

"August," snapped Father.

"What?" she asked, unrepentant. "Am I supposed to be upset that my sister hasn't been replaced by a woman I don't know? Because I'm not."

"Upset, no. Polite, yes."

"Fine." August turned to Ginevra. "I won't apologize for not wanting to lose my sister, but I can try to be polite. I guess the only thing that still doesn't make sense is, even if we were to agree to help you, why do you need October? If she can do this, it should be easier for me. She shouldn't have to be the one who suffers."

"Would you have even listened to us, if we'd come begging for your aid? Or would you have driven us from your door, called your uncle to send his guard and hunt us down like the beasts you'd been taught we were?" Ginevra's voice remained calm, but every word was a challenge, and I could see that it was bothering August. "As to why we sought your sister for the magic, and not merely the confirmation of her safety, in the world we remember, you have never been a particular friend to the Cait Sidhe, while October has very close ties to our Court. More, in that reality, you were missing until quite recently, and have never been seen to apply your magic in quite this manner. The Dóchas Sidhe are a new descendant line. There's no guarantee that any specific application of their natural gifts will carry over from one to the next."

What she was saying made sense. Lines normally settled into predictability by the second or third generation, after the direct children of their Firstborn had time to marry and have children of their own. It also conveniently left out the exact nature of my ties to the Cait Sidhe, and I was grateful for her not just coming out and saying it.

Maybe she thought I didn't know, and was trying to avoid frightening me. Or maybe she could guess how my father would react if she said anything about me and a marriage.

"Missing?" asked Father, sharply.

"Yes," said Ginevra. "Missing. If you want to know what happened, you can ask October to unbind you. She might not be willing to help us, but I'm sure she'd be willing to help you. She seems very fond of you, after all."

"My parents were the sort who felt that children should be raised in love, with the expectation that they will one day surpass their parents," he said. "I have striven to raise my own daughters in the same way."

"But you allowed one of them to be raised in a system that said she was less than her sister because of the circumstances of her birth, and always would be," said Ginevra. "How was that raising her with love?"

Father said nothing, only stared at her. I felt the need to step in before anyone said anything that couldn't be taken back.

"I won't set myself against Titania for you," I said. "I'm sorry you remember a different world, one where I was apparently a different person, but *I* live in *this* world, and in *this* world, I don't antagonize royalty. Everything that's happened since I found out about this 'enchantment' you say Titania has cast on all of Faerie has been bad for me. I've been effectively exiled from my home kingdom, I've bled way more than I ever thought possible, and I've had the worst headache of my life. The last thing I need right now is to upset the Queen of us all."

Ginevra raised an eyebrow. "Why do I feel like I heard a 'but' in there?"

I looked down at my plate, not wanting to face my family as I continued on. "But if this isn't the way Faerie's supposed to be, if people are hurting and you think I can help, I *do* want to help. I just won't set myself against Titania to do it."

"We think we may have figured out a way to make the unbinding easier on you," said Ginevra. "The Court of Cats is a fascinating place. You know we had three Firstborn, in the beginning, one claimed by each of the Three."

"Erda, Malvic, and Jibvel," I said, glancing up again.

"Yes. Daughter of Titania by an unknown father, son of Oberon by Titania, and son of Maeve by an unknown father. They were similar enough in feature and form that they came together as children,

cleaving one unto the other, and their descendant lines combined such
that they were only one manner of fae. Half of Erda's children were
sired by Jibvel, while Malvic roamed wild and came back to us from
time to time with kits to be offered to his sister for the raising. In his
roaming, he found many lost places, many lost things—treasures that
would have fallen out of Faerie forever, had they not been gathered
up. And he went to his father, who was still drawing the lines by
which Faerie would function, and he asked if he could have those
things for his den. Oberon was charmed by his boldness and eager-
ness, and he agreed that Malvic and the other Cait Sidhe could have
them. Malvic called those lost places together, and the true Court of
Cats was born."

I frowned. "Why are we getting a history lesson?"

"Because I need you to understand that anything Faerie loses but
doesn't destroy has a good chance of winding up in the Court of
Cats," she said, and reached into her pocket, producing a key, which
she held out toward me, clearly expecting me to take it.

Hesitantly, and half-fearing a trap, I put down my fork and did as
she expected.

It was remarkably heavy for a key only slightly larger than the
norm. It had been either carved from or poured as a single piece of
silver, inlaid with strips of copper, bronze, and gold, the darker met-
als used to pick out and emphasize the subtler aspects of its design.
Rings of ivy and roses were sculpted across the bow and even along
the sides of the shaft, but they never neared the teeth themselves: for
all that it had been so heavily ornamented that it seemed barely us-
able, that ornamentation wouldn't interfere with the functionality of
the thing. It was, in some concrete but undefinable way, the truest *key*
I had ever seen. There were few doors it couldn't unlock.

I could ignore the fact that it was warm, since it had just come out
of Ginevra's pocket, but I couldn't pretend it wasn't glowing, casting
a pale yet rosy light that tinted my skin like I'd been spending hours
in the sun.

"It's a Summer Roads Key," said Ginevra. "Its most recent known
owner is among the missing, and we need to find her. This key will
get us to the place we think she is. We believe that since you've used
it before, in our version of the world, you'll be able to use it again."

"My lady has been searching for that key for *years*," breathed Father, eyes on my hand. "That is the property of—"

"Don't say her name," said Ginevra quickly. "Just . . . don't. There are a few people in this Faerie who shouldn't be able to be here, for various reasons, and she's one of them, but where I come from, if you say her name, you attract her attention."

Father looked stung. "Why wouldn't I want the attention of one of the most wonderful women who has ever lived?"

Ginevra didn't answer, returning her attention to me. "Tybalt and I already agreed that it wouldn't be a good idea for him to come if I was able to convince you to do this. Honestly, I wanted him to stay in the Court of Cats while I came looking for you, but he insisted. He thinks very highly of you, even if he hasn't been at his best since we arrived."

"I see," I said, again grateful that she was continuing to avoid the details of my connection with Tybalt, and careful not to betray my actual understanding of the situation. "And if I do this, if I agree to use this key to find your missing friend, you'll leave me and my family alone?"

"If that's what you want, yes," said Ginevra, sagging slightly. "But I hope you won't be angry if I say I'm going to hold out hope you'll change your mind."

"I don't think I will," I said, honestly. I was angry at my parents for not telling me my mother had given my father what she hadn't been willing to offer me, but I didn't know what the whole situation had been then. My birth had been a public event, the last of the Firstborn finally doing her duty by Faerie, producing a changeling to serve her household. She couldn't have removed my mortality while I was still in the womb, not without betraying her gifts, and there had been no opportunity to spirit me away and rebalance my bloodlines after I left it; even isolated as we were in our tower, eventually someone would have noticed if a second pureblood daughter appeared in place of a missing changeling. My paternal grandparents had been ordinary nobles, protected by the sheer number of their peers. Father's birth would thus have been quieter, more easily overlooked and concealed. I shouldn't resent them for not doing the impossible. I still did.

And even with that complicated emotional stone weighing me down, I liked my life. I had a good family who loved me, and maybe things weren't perfect, but were things *ever* perfect, for anyone? Why would I want to throw all that away for a world I didn't know, where I was married to a man who clearly hated me? I must have been mistaken about the way he was looking at me in that first memory. There was no way their world could be a better place for me.

"But even if I don't change my mind, I'll help you," I added.

"October, I forbid it," said Father, voice wavering.

I turned to blink at him, feeling something brave and hot and a little bit horrible swell inside my chest as I prepared to do something I'd never done before, not once: as I prepared to defy my father. "Why?" I asked. "Why are you not willing to let me help these people, when you know they *can't* unbind me unless August is both capable of it and agrees to do so, when they want my help so much that they're not going to hurt me, when they *need* my help? Why won't you let me be useful when I actually can be? Why would you tell me no?"

"Your mother will not approve," he said.

"My mother isn't here. My mother isn't going to approve of anything that's happened since she's been away, and since when she gets home she'll find out that I've become a fugitive from the Mists, I think she's going to be so busy being furious at me for making her look bad that she won't have time to get pissed off about me running around helping some Cait Sidhe find their friend." I scowled at him. "I didn't ask for all of this to happen. If you want to blame someone, blame Uncle Sylvester for asking me to go to Dreamer's Glass in the first place."

"Or blame me, for asking October to come to Shadowed Hills so we could pick through the party leftovers," said August.

"But don't punish these people by refusing to let me help them, if they really think I'm the only one who can do it." It was a strange feeling, being needed for something when August was right there. I thought it might be pride. I looked back to Ginevra. "You said Tybalt wouldn't be coming with us if I did this. That implies we'd be going somewhere. Where would we be going?"

"The key unlocks a series of very old roads that can sometimes verge on the edge of deeper Faerie," said Ginevra. "Using it requires opening a door. We expect you'll be able to access the Thorn Road that way, since you've done it before. It's one of the kinder of the old paths. Not very pretty, and you have to be wary of the briars, but if you can get there, it considers the toll already paid."

"I've never heard of this," said Father.

"You wouldn't have," said Ginevra. "It was opened for the use of the children of Maeve, when they needed to flee from their brighter brethren. Part of the history of my Faerie," she added, seeing the baffled looks on our faces. "I'm sure Titania has rewritten events in this world to show her in a better light. But where I come from, the children of Maeve needed to hide sometimes, and the Thorn Road was one of the ways they did it."

"And you think I've been there before?" I asked.

"The October I know has absolutely been there before," she said. "I don't think even Titania can change the memories of an object, since they're more about sympathy and resonance than actual recall." She looked at the key, seeming suddenly concerned. "If she has, maybe this was all for nothing."

"Maybe I can try to do that spell-seeing thing you were talking about, and check?" offered August.

I blinked at her. She shrugged.

"We don't know if I can do the same thing you can. Maybe this is a way to find out."

"If you want to try," I said.

"I do." August reached for the abandoned steak knife at Tybalt's place, shooting Father a quelling look. He didn't say anything or move to stop her.

With a quick, easy grace that clearly came from years of practice, August sliced the tip of her finger and brought it to her mouth. I tensed. If her blood, like mine, showed her memories of this other world, I had no idea what she was going to see.

But her training had been so much more extensive than my own, in that she'd received actual lessons in controlling her blood magic, and she must have shunted the memories away before they could begin, focusing on the key.

"Close your eyes," I suggested. "Just close your eyes and try to see the key anyway."

August closed her eyes. Her eyebrows furrowed, coming together as she tried to focus. Finally, she sighed and opened her eyes again, hand already healed as she lowered it to the table. "I didn't see anything," she said. "Maybe you're right, and this isn't something I can do."

"Maybe it just takes more practice? But I can still try to open this door," I said to Ginevra. "I said I'd try your key, and I will. But *only* if Tybalt doesn't come with us. I don't like the way he looks at me."

"I'll go too," said August.

"No," said Father, more wearily this time. "I'm sorry, but no. I refuse to go home and tell your mother I've misplaced both of our daughters, should something go wrong in this . . . this ridiculous undertaking. I wish I could prevent your sister from joining in the foolishness, but she's correct when she says she didn't set any of this in motion, and she's of age."

"She lives in your household," said August. "Her being of age shouldn't matter."

I wanted to ask her whose side she was on there, but Father looked like he was on the verge of tears; interrupting wasn't going to help.

"She no longer lives in the tower," he said.

August paled. "What? You're throwing her *out* because she isn't doing what you want?"

"He's not," I said, as I stood with my salmon still half-eaten, delicious as it was. "August, we've already been over this. I *can't* go back to the Mists. They'll execute me. If I'm an exile, I don't live in the tower anymore. I live wherever the King and Queen on the Golden Shore decide I do."

She visibly wilted, sinking into her chair with a soft sigh. "Oh," she said. "I hadn't thought about that."

"October, please be safe," said Father, turning back to me. "Garm and Grianne can accompany you. My brother owes me that much, for setting all this in motion."

I had almost forgotten my uncle's knights, they'd been so quiet through this whole messy argument. I turned to see them murmuring between themselves, conspiratorially, Grianne's Merry Dancers circling their heads. The two of them looked back at me, and Grianne slowly rose.

"I'm staying here," said Garm. "We know October can see whatever spell has been cast to entangle us all, and as of this moment, we know the Lady August can't. I can't see it the same way October can, but I can perceive the edges, and that may be an advantage."

"You talk as if we're going to war," said Father sourly.

"I fear we might be," Garm replied.

It was hard not to take comfort from Grianne moving to stand behind me, a familiar presence, if not a close friend. I returned my attention to Ginevra. "Do you need to go and find Tybalt, to tell him we're doing this without him?"

"Sir Garm will do it," she said, airily leaving the responsibility on someone else's shoulders. It was almost impressive. She rose, smooth and easy, and bowed to my father. "I do apologize for the necessary loan of your daughter, and I understand this is difficult for you. Please try to believe me when I tell you this is difficult for us, also, and that we want nothing more than to bring her home unharmed."

I noticed she didn't say "return her to you." Father noticed as well. He frowned, a flash of something like understanding in his eyes.

"You said my daughter had a close relationship to the Court of Cats in your world," he said. "Swear to me that you'll protect her. If she's harmed, I'll set myself against you until my dancing ends, and you'll have no peace ever again."

It wasn't a shock that Father would be willing to defend me. It still chipped away at my resentment, replacing a tiny stretch of it with warmth.

Ginevra looked at him steadily. "She has walked our halls and dined from our stores, and she counts many friends among our number," she said, voice grave. "I'll protect her with my own life."

"Swear."

"On the root and the branch, I will keep her safe."

Father nodded, apparently accepting her words.

Ginevra put a hand on my arm. "We should go."

"I can't just walk away without acknowledging the King and Queen," I said, and turned to the high table, curtseying, although not as deeply as I had when I was presented. Chrysanthe looked amused, elbowing her husband to get him to look over at me. He raised his cup and nodded, granting us leave to go.

"Cats don't stand with that sort of formality," said Ginevra, closing her hand and pulling me along with her as she started for the door. Grianne trailed gamely along behind us, and for the second time in not nearly long enough, I left my family behind.

SIXTEEN

"THIS WILL WORK BETTER if we're outside, and Tybalt will kill me—I mean straight-up murder me—if I try to take you through the Shadow Roads, so we need to figure out how to get out of here," said Ginevra, once we were out of the ballroom and walking down the wide, golden hall.

"Maybe I can help," said Arden. All three of us spun around to face her. She grinned, but she looked more than a little strained around the edges. "Hey, Cat Queen, your buddy told me some fun stories about your version of the world. You want to tell me how much truth he was putting on the table?"

"Did he tell you that you were meant to be Queen in the Mists, not a courier for Golden Shore?"

Arden nodded. "He did. He also told me that in *your* Faerie, Oleander got away."

"I never knew her," said Ginevra. "But the damage she did still echoes through your Kingdom, and may never quite be repaired."

"He was real startled when I told him that in *this* Faerie, Oleander died after she offed my parents." Arden's grin faded, replaced by cold, stony displeasure. "In your Faerie, people still argue about whether or not she did it. They *discuss*, like my parents are just a footnote in an unclear history."

"What happened here?" asked Ginevra.

"My brother and I found Oleander standing over their bodies. Nolan screamed, and when he ran, she ran after him. So I opened a gate so that he could get away, and when she grabbed the back of his shirt, I closed it again, with her arms on the other side." Arden's expression never wavered. "She didn't die from that, of course. She fell down and screamed and bled a lot, but there was an earthquake, everyone was screaming a lot. So I took her knife—the knife she used to kill my parents—and I slit her murdering throat. Then we ran for Golden Shore, because someone had wanted our whole family dead, and I knew they could accuse me of breaking the Law, and it wasn't safe for us to stay in the Mists anymore. Do you really expect me to believe that a Faerie where Oleander lived was the better world?"

"You're free there, not confined to someone else's Kingdom," said Ginevra.

"Freedom's overrated." Arden waved her hand, opening a circle in the air, back to the field where we'd first arrived. "Go ahead and do what you need to do, but be sure you know that you're not breaking any enchantment on me or on my brother without our permission. If you try it, I'll end you myself."

Ginevra glanced at the open window on the outside world, then back at Arden. "If you hurt us in any way, Tybalt will take you apart."

"Oh, he's made that perfectly clear," said Arden. "I'm not going to cut you in half. I only did that once, and I had very good reasons. Go on."

"She saved me from the Queen's dungeon," I said. "I trust her."

Then I stepped through the circle, into the field on the other side.

I might have said I trusted her, but I didn't relax until I was *actually* in the field, with all my limbs still safely attached to my body. I took a few more steps, then turned, looking back through the circle into the hall. Grianne rolled her eyes and said something I didn't hear. Then she did a standing backflip, vanishing into thin air. A few seconds later, she and her Merry Dancers stepped out of nothingness to join me. I looked at her.

"Candela don't need gates," she said, with a small shrug.

Ginevra was still in the hall with Arden. She backed up to get a running start, looking nervous. Then she leapt, and was suddenly a small orange-and-white cat instead of a woman. She soared through the circle, landing neatly in front of me, as Arden snorted with amusement and closed her hand.

The gate snapped shut. The cat looked up at me and meowed imperiously.

"Er, hello," I said.

The cat sat up straighter, and then, with a rush of river lupine and limoncello, Ginevra was standing where the cat had been, pushing her hair out of her eyes with one hand.

"Sorry for the dramatics," she said. "I really didn't want to get parts of me cut off."

"I don't think she'd do that," I said. "Oleander was a special case." I'd have done the same, or worse, to anyone who hurt my parents and threatened my sister. That didn't mean I'd be willing to do it to just anyone who got on my nerves. I pulled the key Ginevra had given me out of my pocket. "Am I supposed to do something special with this?"

"I . . . I don't know," she said. "I just know you've used it before."

"In another version of Faerie, when I was someone else."

"Yes."

"Right." I held out my free hand. "If you don't think it'll get you in trouble with the overprotective brute squad later, I should probably check that memory. And that means I need blood."

Ginevra nodded. She tapped the tip of my finger with her claw, and there was pain, bright and swift, followed by blood, welling up like a promise of more pain to come. I barely flinched, only stuck my finger in my mouth and swallowed. No matter what happened from there, I was going to come away a lot more comfortable with blood magic than I'd ever been, or planned to be, before.

The taste of blood blossomed on my tongue, and the red veil descended.

I am standing in the ballroom at Shadowed Hills, and there is blood everywhere. It smears the walls, it drips down all around me. Tybalt is on the floor in a crumpled heap, being tended by an Ellyllon woman, as I face someone I have never seen before.

She is tall and slender and sharp as a thorn, with hair in a hundred shades of pink and red and eyes the color of rose pollen. She looks at me like she hates me too much to stand, and the memory gives me a name for her: Luna.

She holds the key in one hand. I must have given it to her. "This belonged to my grandmother," she says.

"Which one?" I ask.

Luna's head snaps up, eyes narrowing, as if that were the worst question I could ever have asked. Not telling me what I said wrong, she shoves the key into the air between us. The bottom half vanishes, like it has been placed in a lock I can't see.

"My debts are paid," she says, and turns the key sharply to the left, pulling at the same time.

The memory broke there, but I nodded, clinging to the red veil to force it to continue tinting the world as I took a step forward, holding out the key like I was going to slide it into a lock. Some of the curls and twists in its engravings were sharp, and I rubbed my thumb along them until the skin split and I was rubbing blood onto the key itself, feeding it into the metal. The woman in my memory—Luna—hadn't needed blood, but whatever she'd been, she wasn't Dóchas Sidhe. All I had was in the blood. It always had been.

"My debts are paid," I said, almost liltingly, and shoved the bloody key into the air in front of me.

For a moment, I was afraid it wouldn't work. For a moment, I was afraid all the sympathetic magic in the world wouldn't be enough to let me do what the woman had done, that her opening had been powered by a magic of her own. But that's the way enchanted items are made, sometimes: people push magic through them so many times that it just sort of sticks and flavors them, like infusing honey into your tea. The key hit resistance. I pushed harder.

The bottom half of the key vanished into the air, the key itself feeling as if it had been seated in an invisible keyhole. I twisted it hard to the left, pulling it toward me at the same time.

The key didn't budge from whatever impossible keyhole I had pushed it into, and what felt like the heaviest door in creation slowly shifted toward me, revealing a hole in the world.

Tuatha open gates, temporary portals between places, but they're always very clear, something leading to something. This was something leading to . . . not nothing, but a sort of reality *outside* of our own, a place I didn't have a name for and my eyes didn't want to focus on. It wasn't blackness. Total blackness implies either a void or just an absence of light, and either way, that's *something*. This was more darkness, darkness tinged in the very deepest of greens, as if whatever I had opened was alive and growing and waiting for us to come through.

"Come on," said Ginevra, starting past me.

My stomach sank. "What do you mean, 'come on'?"

"I mean, you said you'd help, and we need you if we're going to come back here."

I should probably have expected her to say that. Somehow, I hadn't. Sighing, I pulled the key loose and tucked it into my jacket pocket, shoving it all the way down to be sure it stayed safe.

Ginevra stepped into the dark.

Grianne and I followed, Grianne's Merry Dancers lighting up the space around us so that I could see my impression of greenness had been a valid one: we were dropping into a tunnel completely lined with briars of a type I'd never seen before, deep green and bristling with hooked thorns the color of bone. I barely had time for the sight to register before I realized I was falling and squeaked, flailing my arms in an effort to find purchase that didn't exist.

We only fell for a few seconds before we landed on soft, spongy ground. My feet promptly went out from under me, trying to drop me onto my ass, and Grianne grabbed my arm before I could roll away into the dark. Her Merry Dancers slowed their bobbing and began to circle the three of us in a slow rotating pattern, casting their pale light over our surroundings.

We were standing in a clearing somewhere inside an overgrown forest. The door had slammed shut and disappeared as soon as we were through, naturally; the only way out was through. All I could see were the trees right around us, and still I knew that this wood was ancient and endless. The trees dripped with moss and unfamiliar vines, and more of those thorny briars wrapped around them in lover's knots, making them unsafe to touch. There were paths between the trees, beaten earth somehow not choked off by the vines, narrow and winding off into the dark.

"Something lives here," said Ginevra, voice soft and almost awed.

The air was hot and humid, making my long sleeves and my leather jacket a misery. Taking either of them off in this place would have meant the risk of losing them forever, and I wasn't sure I could count on things lost there to fall into the Court of Cats. I looked to Ginevra.

"I used your key, I opened your door," I said. "Now what?"

"Now we find the woman who owns the key and see if *she* can figure out how to fix this."

"Right." I looked around the endless, looming forest. "I'm sure that's going to be nice and easy."

"Could be a lot harder," said Ginevra, clearly forcing herself to sound optimistic. "I can't track by scent when I'm on two legs, so I won't be able to talk to you for most of this. Maybe I can catch her trail."

"Worth trying," said Grianne. "Don't want to stay here long."

Ginevra nodded and was gone, replaced by the orange-and-white cat. She began prowling around the borders of the lit area, nose low to the ground, sniffing for a trail. After two circuits, she became bipedal again, turning to us in frustration.

"It's no use," she said. "I've never actually *met* the woman, so I don't know what I'm sniffing for. This would have been a lot easier if Tybalt were here."

"Why's he not?" asked Grianne.

"He can't stand to be around me," I told her. "And I don't want him to be around me, why would I want to spend time around a strange jerk who likes to glare at me because he thinks it's fun?"

"Why is it so hard for you to believe he doesn't hate you?" Ginevra asked, some of her frustration spilling over.

"Because he wants me to be someone I'm not," I snapped.

"Because this *isn't*—" She broke off. "I'm sorry, this isn't helping. It's just . . . you're not the woman he knows, but there's enough of you in her, or her in you, that it's sometimes confusing to look at you, so I can imagine how he feels. Especially with you wearing that jacket."

I looked down at the jacket, plucking at the sleeve as I composed myself. I still didn't want to talk about any of this. Once I was sure I could keep a straight face, I looked up, blinking at her. "What about this jacket? Melly at Shadowed Hills gave it to me when we needed me to be dressed in human clothes. She said she found it in a closet, where they put human things people have left in the knowe after parties and the like. It fits pretty well, and it's thick enough to give me some protection—which I think I need in this place."

"Oh. It's only that you own that jacket in our world, and Tybalt left it in Shadowed Hills for you to find after it wound up in the Court of Cats, hoping it would spark your memory. Do you feel anything when you look at it?"

I shook my head. "I feel a little too warm, right now; this is probably heavier than I should be wearing in some sort of weird skerry that you have to access with a magic key. Who owns this place, anyway?"

"This is the Thorn Road," said Ginevra. "Before Oberon sealed the routes to deeper Faerie, there were quite a few roads that were opened by or for specific groups. The Cait Sidhe had the Shadow Roads, and the fact that they belong to us but are also used by the Candela, who Titania didn't try to erase from existence, meant they remained stable enough in our absence for us to access them after she banished us to our Courts." She smiled thinly. "Her 'perfect' world sure does have a lot of loopholes."

"Faerie is complicated," said Grianne dryly.

"All the old roads belonged to one descendant line or another. The Thorn Road was opened for the children of Maeve to use when they needed to flee from Titania's descendants. You're not Maeve's by blood, but she's shown a liking for you in the past, and I'm from Jibvel's descendant line."

"Maeve claims the Candela," said Grianne.

"While Titania claims the Gwragen," I said. The split between the knights made a little more sense now.

Ginevra nodded. "The Thorn Road is one of the safer old roads, if you can access it at all. You have to avoid the thorns, especially if you have bad intentions toward any of the children of Maeve—they'll know, and they have their ways of stopping people from hunting the ones they're supposed to be protecting."

"Uh-huh. So what I'm hearing is that there's no reason for Titania's magic to be anywhere around here, right?"

"Right," she said, slowly.

I held out my hand in what was starting to become an all-too-familiar gesture. "I need you to cut me again. Deeper, this time, so the blood lasts for more than just a few drops."

"This feels wrong every time I do it," she said, extending her claws.

I flashed her a thin smile. "How do you think I feel? A week ago I would have died before I went against my mother by actively practicing blood magic. Now here I am on a sealed road to deeper Faerie with a woman I don't know and a knight I've barely spoken to before now, asking to be cut open so I can track Titania's magic through the dark and get back to my own life."

"It's never going to be the same after this, you know," said Ginevra, pressing the tip of her claw to the meaty pad at the base of my thumb. I realized what she was going to do just before she flexed her hand, driving the claw in deep. The pain was immediate and electric, and didn't fade, as she kept her claw in the wound to stop it from healing. "Even if we can't disenchant you, you're always going to know the world you're living in and the life you're living is a lie. And that you're hurting people by refusing to let it go."

"But I'd be hurting people if I *did* let it go," I said, voice strained, and tugged my hand back toward me. "You can take your claw out now."

She did. Blood welled up, more blood than I'd ever seen before, and all of it mine. I cupped my hand and angled my thumb to let as much of the blood as possible run into my palm, keeping it from being lost on the forest floor. It was inevitable that some would drip down and feed the hungry soil, but no matter how friendly Ginevra wanted to say Maeve was toward me—and that idea was one more horrifying thing added to a whole parade of them—I wasn't excited about the idea of leaving a piece of myself behind.

I raised my hand to my lips and took a mouthful of blood. The effect was electric. A few drops had been enough to make me feel like I could fight the world; the amount I'd been able to get from the back of my hand when April cut me had set my skin on fire. This much blood, though—I could do anything. I could fight not just the world but Titania, and I could *win*. I knew that was the heady rush of power talking, and not anything real, but it was still a dizzying feeling.

I pushed down the blood memories that threatened to rise and overwhelm me, refusing to let them show me anything else from a world I didn't know and still wasn't sure I wanted to know, closed my eyes, and *looked* into the forest.

It was nothing but darkness, shot through with occasional sparks of brilliant green that sparked blue and red, burning bright as anything. It was like I was looking into an infinite mine of fire opals, their red banked back behind the cool colors of the water, and it was beautiful. The longer I looked, the more of those firefly sparks lit up the blackness. I raised my hand again, sipping the last of the cooling blood out of the hollow of my palm as I slowly turned, trying to take in the entire landscape around me.

There, far in the distance, I caught a spark of pink iridescence. It was so unlike the opal green that it stood out like a beacon, and I took a step toward it before I realized that maybe walking into a dark forest filled with thorns with my eyes closed was a bad idea. I opened my eyes as I dropped my long-healed hand back to my side, wiping the last of the blood onto my kirtle, and pointed with my other hand.

"We go that way," I said. "I'll probably need to bleed again before we get there, but we go that way."

Neither Ginevra nor Grianne questioned me, just fell into step behind me as I started for the nearest trail that seemed to go in the right direction. Grianne's Merry Dancers swirled around and ahead of us, lighting up the landscape and helping me keep my footing. Fae are nocturnal by nature, and purebloods can see in the dark incredibly well. As a changeling, my night vision is considerably less acute. As in, sometimes I walk into walls in the tower, and I've lived there all my life, meaning I at least know the walls are *there*.

The Merry Dancers seemed to realize I needed the extra help, because one of them was almost always directly ahead of me, lighting the way as we moved deeper into the forest.

The path wound and looped back on itself, but kept traveling in something close to a direct line in the distance we needed to go. It was what Father used to call a "desire path" when we went down to the edge of the swamp to see the pixies who nested there; a path that wasn't made because someone decided to put a path there, but because it was such an easy way to go toward something desirable that people and animals walked that way over and over again, until their feet pounded the earth down and made it harder for things to grow there. The force of their wanting cut channels in the world.

He used it both as a way to explain the natural trails and to remind August and me not to get too set in our thinking. If we followed our desire paths too many times, nothing would be able to grow there. He didn't want that for us.

I couldn't see the colors in the darkness anymore, and after we'd gone a good distance deeper into the thorn-choked trees, I turned to Ginevra. "I need more blood," I said.

"I wish there was another way," she replied, even as she extended her claws and reached for my hand.

"So do I," I said, and stuck my bleeding finger into my mouth as I turned back in the direction we'd been traveling.

There, closer but still distant, was the tangle of iridescent pink. I nodded, pointing before I opened my eyes, to be sure I had the angle right, and said, "This way."

We resumed.

The forest around us was quiet but not silent. Things rustled in the dark, little things moving through the brush or high in the branches, bigger things stepping their delicate way through the trees. I didn't get the feeling we were in danger, and I didn't know how we were supposed to get out of there, and so I kept on walking, moving toward our unseen goal.

A thick white fog began rising from the ground, getting denser and denser until it reached our waists and the ground was a distant, unseen dream. It was cool enough to chill my legs, even as my upper body still sweltered in the humid heat. If I could have transformed my leather jacket into leather pants, I would have done it, just to try and balance the two conflicting climates.

Grianne's Merry Dancers continued to light our way, while Ginevra stuck close. It was almost sweet, how dedicated she was to making sure I didn't get hurt, even if I knew it was because of the woman she wanted me to retrieve my memories of being, and not because of anything about me as I was. She was clearly afraid of that Tybalt person, and with good reason, from what I'd seen so far.

Onward we walked, until the path widened out into another clearing, this one dominated by a bier made of briars that had wound themselves together until they formed a structure taller than I was. Grianne's Merry Dancers rose to bob in the air above it, and I saw just the edge of what looked like a glass coffin nestled there. Grianne frowned, a slow, bewildered expression.

"How?" she asked. "I saw her last week. She's not supposed to be here."

Ginevra and I both turned to her. "She who?" asked Ginevra.

"The Rose of Winter," said Grianne, sounding utterly bewildered.

I looked back to the bier, straining for any sign that my father's beloved patron was in the coffin at its peak.

"Oh. *Her.*" Ginevra sounded utterly repulsed. "She's one of the people who's in the world right now when she can't be. Some of them are dead. Some of them are just imprisoned. She's elf-shot and sleeping in a skerry, but I thought it was hers, made for the Daoine Sidhe, not an extension of the Thorn Road. It's not like real estate is fixed here. Something must have moved when Titania rewrote the world. Just don't touch the bier, and don't say her name. Whatever puppet version of her you've been dealing with, you do *not* want to meet the real thing."

"Why not?"

"I know you won't believe me now, Toby, but where I come from, she's just about your least favorite person in the world, and she's been responsible for a good number of the things that have hurt you and the people you care about. The woman you know is a fantasy of Titania's, and is probably an idealized version of the real thing. This is the one our world decided was too dangerous to wake up."

That was a horrible thing to contemplate, as was the idea that the Eira I knew wasn't real. Was she just a solid illusion? If I pulled on the threads around her, would she unravel and disappear? Being asked to break spells I didn't fully understand was a dangerous thing. I didn't want to make anyone vanish.

"We have to keep moving," said Ginevra. "This isn't who we're looking for."

"I think I'm glad," I said. "I don't want to bother any of the Firstborn."

Ginevra didn't say anything, and we made our way across the clearing to where the desire path resumed, winding ever deeper into the wood. Again, we went some distance before I had to ask her to scratch me and draw blood, and again, it showed me a spark of pink shining through the dark, giving us a way to go. We were still heading in the right direction.

The fog began to clear, allowing the forest floor to reappear, and we emerged into another clearing.

This one had no bier. Instead, a towering hawthorn tree grew at the center of the clearing, its branches reaching for the sunless sky, the ground around it empty of brush or thorns. It seemed to be living through every season at the same time, green leaves, white flowers, and red berries weighing its boughs down. The trunk was twisted into the outline of a woman's body, her face pressed up against the bark, her mouth open in a silent scream.

The temperature of the air dropped the moment we entered the clearing, until I was shivering inside my leather jacket, my sweat making me even colder. This place was not very interested in treating visitors well.

"I think this is what we're looking for," said Ginevra, voice hushed. "And good."

"Good?" I asked.

"There was a chance—not a strong chance, but a chance—that Titania would have elf-shot the woman we're looking for, rather than throwing her into the enchantment. We don't have any of the elf-shot cure with us, and the person who invented it in our world hasn't had a reason to do that here."

"The person who . . . Oh, now I *know* you're making stuff up about your version of Faerie to make it sound better than it actually is!" I shot her a quick glare before looking back to the tree. Something about it called the eye, making it difficult to look away for long. "There's no cure for elf-shot. There never will be. The Rose of Winter didn't make it to be unmade that easily."

"In *our* Faerie, a brave and clever alchemist worked with a very chaotic knight, and they found a way to wake the sleepers," said Ginevra. "It can even save changelings, if it's administered quickly enough. Elf-shot doesn't have to be a death sentence anymore. And I'm not saying that to make our Faerie sound better. I'm saying that because it's the truth. It's also academic: she's not elf-shot, she's a tree."

"So now what do we do?" I asked.

"We make her stop being a tree."

She said that like it was so simple, so straightforward. Don't like it that someone's a tree? Make them stop being a tree. Just undo it. Uncast the spell, unwind reality, and move on.

"How do we do that?"

Ginevra turned and looked at me. "It's a spell like any other," she said. "You can break it."

I'd known this was why they wanted me along. So we could find this person, whoever she was, and get access to her stronger blood, which would somehow make it less painful for me to disenchant others when they agreed to be released from the real world and into the fantasy we had apparently replaced. "I am real tired of bleeding," I muttered, approaching the tree.

It was a tree. Like any other, save for the odd configuration of its trunk, which could have happened naturally. If not for the way it sought to catch and hold the eye, I would have said there was nothing unusual about it. I circled three times counterclockwise, then stopped, putting my right hand on what would have been the figure's shoulder, had she been anything more than a shape in the bark.

"I don't have much of a choice here, so let's do this," I said. "Ginevra, I need blood."

Quick as a blink, she was beside me, claws already extended. I pulled my hand away from the tree and shrugged out of my jacket, handing it to her. "Don't lose this."

Ginevra blinked, then pulled the jacket close to her chest and held out her hand again, claws at the ready. I shivered in the chill, feeling oddly exposed. How quickly a single piece of clothing had come to feel like a shield against the world.

"Gonna need more blood for this," I said, and rolled up my sleeve, baring my arm for her. "A *lot* more. This is going to hurt. Distract me. Tell me something about your Faerie."

"I was born a changeling," she said. "Me and both my sisters. And when you came to my father's Court—he's a King of Cats up in Silences— you offered to shift the balance of our blood, to make us immortal, if that was what we wanted. All three of us said yes. As soon as the humanity was out of my system, it turned out I had the power to be considered a royal cat, and when Tybalt needed someone to stand regent for his heir so he could get married, I agreed to come here and do the job." She looked at me coolly. "I would have done anything he asked, because he's the one who brought me to you."

She brought her hand down then, raking it across my forearm with lightning speed, claws laying the skin open and biting deep into the muscle. I yelped and jerked away, instinctively bringing my arm to my chest. Then I realized what I was doing and reversed the motion, flinging blood onto the woman in the tree. It stuck in irregular red blotches, then began to dribble downward, a terrible piece of abstract art.

Bringing my already almost-healed arm to my lips, I took a mouthful of the remaining blood, swallowed, and closed my eyes.

It was getting easier and easier to sidestep the memories, letting them slip back down into the deep well of my magic while I grabbed the power the blood offered me and focused it into the *seeing* that had nothing to do with my eyes.

The magic that led me there immediately blossomed into view, an intricate lattice of pink threads and knots in the shape of a hawthorn tree. There was a denser shape inside the tree, a woman outlined in macrame loops of scintillating pink that almost blocked out the storm-dark oceanic color of her own magic. Two spells, then, one nested inside the other, the first to do . . . something . . . the second to transform the woman inside the first spell into a tree. Well, the second spell was in the way of the first, and so I needed to focus on that before I could do anything else. I bit the inside of my cheek for just that tiny bit more blood, reached out, grabbed the first layer of threads, and pulled as hard as I could.

There was nothing subtle or elegant about the way I approached the spell keeping the woman bound inside the tree. Maybe if I'd been there to see it cast, or if I'd had some understanding of the structure, but no. I was working without any sort of a roadmap, and that meant the only thing I could do was aim to create as much chaos as I possibly could.

Pulling on the threads hurt the same way it had before, intense icy cold shooting through my fingers and up my arms, until I was numb to the elbow. I knew that my actual hands weren't touching the tree, but I felt the cold all the same, the magic fighting back against my assault.

"More blood," I gasped, and Ginevra cut me again, just as deeply. This time all I did was drink, filling my mouth over and over until the healing wounds robbed me of my source. For a moment, the temptation to bite and chew and keep the blood flowing was almost too strong to ignore, but I could feel the increasing weakness in my legs, and I knew I couldn't lose much more blood, not when I was already damaging myself against the wall of this seemingly endless spell.

The next time the blood ran out, I stopped pulling, letting the broken threads fall away, and opened my eyes as I turned to Ginevra. "I need more blood," I informed her. "I can't lose any more of my own. Either you or Grianne is going to have to bleed for me."

"Can you use our blood without riding it?" she asked, already rolling up her own sleeve.

"I don't know. Let's find out."

Ginevra paused. "If you ride my blood, you may see some things you won't be very happy about."

Meaning she was afraid I'd find out Tybalt was supposedly my husband. I looked at her calmly. "Look, my knees are starting to buckle, and I can't feel my fingers," I said. "I think I can tear this thing down, but if I bleed any more, there's going to be consequences. Since none of us brought along a hamper or anything, I can't replenish what I'm losing, and I'd rather not pass out. If Grianne wants to volunteer, I'll take it, but you keep going on about how powerful and special royal cats are. It seems like I might only have to bleed you *once*, where I'd have to bleed her several times, and we don't need to incapacitate our only light source."

Grianne was watching us calmly, Merry Dancers still circling her head. If our discussion of who was going to bleed to fuel my magic bothered her at all, she didn't show it.

"Have to be careful, you go drinking cat blood," she said.

Ginevra blinked, looking stung. "Oh, not you too," she said.

"Not me too, what?" asked Grianne.

"Acting like we're animals. I'm as fae as you are. Titania just doesn't like shapeshifters, and she's always done her best to minimize our role in Faerie. As soon as she saw her chance to change things so we were all gone, she did it. My blood is as good for powering someone else's magic as yours is."

"True enough," allowed Grianne. "Your blood also knows how to change shapes."

"What does that have to do with anything?"

Grianne turned to look at me calmly, waiting for me to catch up.

I frowned, then blinked as her meaning hit home. "Father brews draughts and tinctures using blood brought to him by his patron, so he can borrow or recreate the inherent magic of other descendant lines," I said. "I've seen him do incredible things with borrowed blood."

"How much's he trained, to do that?" asked Grianne.

"I don't know. A lot. I know that he and Uncle Sylvester both had a tutor when they were young, and Father was the more talented with blood magic and alchemy."

"Yeah." Grianne stopped there, clearly expecting me to put the pieces together.

I frowned at her again. "Grianne, they've never given me *any* training in how my magic works, not where blood's concerned. I can cast minor illusions and power a marshwater charm, but if it needs to be fueled by blood, I don't really know what I'm doing. And since it sounds like August can't see spells the way I can, I wouldn't have any training at this part *either*. So please. I know you don't like to use three words when one will do, but right now, be as verbose as the rest of us. *Please*."

Grianne sighed and walked over to join us, her long legs turning the motion into a lope. "You use blood for magic."

"Yes."

"Your blood, you either watch your own memories or you power something up."

"Yes?"

"Someone else's blood, you can watch their memories, or you can power something up, or you can borrow their magic, take it for a spin. Do the things they can do, that normally aren't yours to do." She looked at me solemnly. "Me, you might get a brief access to a really limited form of travel through shadows. Have to drain me dry to call your own Merry Dancers. Might not work even then. Her, you could sneeze and turn into a cat."

The image was amusing and alarming at the same time. Eyes wide, I inched away from Ginevra. "Right, good point. Grianne, are you willing to bleed for me?"

Grianne extended her arm in answer.

"Ginevra, will you cut her? Carefully, she doesn't heal like I do."

"Appreciate the caution," said Grianne, with a flicker of dry amusement. Her expression didn't change as Ginevra reached over and raked her claws down the outside of Grianne's forearm, slicing it open in three deep furrows.

Grianne wordlessly extended her arm toward me. Her blood smelled like California buckwheat and pepperberry, like her magic, and what I was about to do should have been horrifying, and instead, it was the most natural thing in the world. I filled my mouth with her blood, and swallowed, and saw flickers of memory, all distant, all protected by that gleaming shell I'd encountered when I first tasted my own blood. She was still wrapped tight in the enchantment, even though she was helping us.

Then I was past the memory and into the power. It was a cool power, not cold but cool, like water rushing in a shallow forest stream, warmed by the sunlight that had been shining on it all day long. It was sweet and clear and pure, with no traces of mortality, and as I considered it, I could see the ways I'd need to twist it if I wanted to borrow her line's gifts for my own. They were right there, ready to be taken, and it felt almost as if the blood was sorry when I turned those gifts aside. I took another mouthful and let go, leaving Grianne free to bind her wounds as I turned my attention back to the tree.

My own power, exhausted as it was, mingled with Grianne's, all of it bent to the goal of fueling my natural abilities. I reached out again, snarling the fingers of my mind through the remaining threads of the tree, and I pulled, ripping them loose one by one. They tried to tangle around my hands, chilling me to the bone, and still I kept on pulling, fighting against my natural desire to recoil from the pain. I yanked even harder, trying to pull apart knots and sunder connections, and was pulling so hard when the last strand finally snapped that I felt it, physically, as that tether broke. The impact shook me down to the soles of my feet, pain like nothing I'd ever felt before lancing through my head.

With nothing to hold on to, I fell down, of course, the conquering hero landing ignominiously on her ass among the litter on the clearing floor.

SEVENTEEN

AT LEAST I DIDN'T black out, which seemed like a real accomplishment after the day I'd had. I groaned, rubbing my face with my less-bloody hand, and pushed myself back into a sitting position. "Everyone okay?"

No one answered me. That wasn't a good sign. I dropped my hand, opened my eyes, and stood, scrabbling in the slippery leaf-litter until I managed to get my feet under me. Both Grianne and Ginevra were standing where I'd left them, their faces lit by the shifting light from Grianne's Merry Dancers. The tree, however, was gone. They were both staring at the place where it had been.

I moved over to join them, the unsteady light of the Merry Dancers making it difficult for me to tell what they were staring *at*. I blinked, and my eyes adjusted, finally allowing me to see the naked teenage girl crumpled motionless on the ground. Her long black hair was loose and tangled all around her, hiding a considerable amount of her body from view; her ears were round. If someone had asked me, I would have said she was entirely human. But she was there, in a place humans had no reason to be and probably couldn't survive, and that meant whatever she was, it was probably something I didn't want to mess with.

And she looked strangely, disturbingly familiar.

"Who is this?" I asked.

"Her name is Antigone of Albany, and we've been trying to find her for months," said Ginevra.

Grianne, as usual, was more succinct. "Sea witch," she said.

I yelped and danced backward, away from the pair. "Sea witch?" I demanded. "As in—you mean the—the *Luidaeg*?"

Ginevra nodded. "Yes. She was one of the people Titania had to get out of the way in order to establish her own version of Faerie. The Luidaeg isn't powerful enough to fight her stepmother's enchantments forever, but she's too strong for Titania to just rewrite the way she did almost everyone else. So Titania put her away."

"You didn't tell me we were trying to find the"—I dropped my voice, in case my yelling hadn't already been enough to wake her—"the sea witch."

"Would you have agreed to help if I had?"

"I barely agreed to help as it was! I'm only doing this because . . ." I stopped. Why *was* I doing this? I wanted them to leave my family alone, and I wanted these people to be able to go home, but since I also wanted to hold on to the Faerie I knew, where I was happy and loved and understood how things were supposed to work, maybe helping them was a bad idea. It didn't seem like our two versions of Faerie could exist in parallel. All or nothing, that was the way this went.

Was I only doing this because I was mad at my father for telling me I couldn't? The thought was dauntingly accurate. Maybe this was all just me throwing a fit about being denied something I didn't even understand wanting.

"Because you're a hero," said Ginevra.

The words sounded perfectly true and utterly false at the same time. I couldn't be a hero. I wasn't built for it. I was a changeling. I existed to do laundry and wash dishes and serve Faerie, not save it.

The woman on the ground—the Luidaeg—groaned and pushed herself up onto her elbows, head still bowed.

"Anyone get the license-plate number for that truck?" she asked. "That was a rhetorical question. Please don't answer. I know what happened."

"Luidaeg! Are you all right?" asked Ginevra, moving to help her up.

The Luidaeg waved her off. "I'm fine. Sore, pissed, and my mouth tastes like a Macy's perfume counter, but fine." She paused then. "You have Toby's jacket. Why do you have Toby's jacket? What did my fucking stepmother do?!"

"Toby's right here," said Ginevra, gesturing toward me. The Luidaeg turned, following the motion, and I looked directly at the sea witch for the first time.

She still seemed almost dauntingly human, impossibly so, given her setting and surroundings. Little scars dotted her cheeks and chin, the ghosts of acne or pox, and she had freckles across the bridge of her nose. But her eyes were black from side to side, and unlike Li Qin's eyes, they were predatory and sharp. She looked at me like I was on the menu, like *everything* was on the menu, and the only limiting factor was how hungry she was at any given moment.

She took a step toward me. I took a step back. She stopped, an expression of slow bewilderment spreading across her face. Then she turned to Ginevra.

"Short version, *now*," she said. It wasn't a request.

"Titania managed to ensnare the Mists and two of the neighboring Kingdoms in a complicated illusion, creating a revised version of reality where Oberon was the one who vanished after Maeve's Ride was broken, not her," said Ginevra, quickly. "She rewrote history and built herself the illusion of a perfect pureblood paradise, where there aren't any so-called beasts and all the changelings know their place. But she didn't count on the cats."

"You always were our safety valve," said the Luidaeg. "Where's kitty-boy?"

"He can't really handle looking directly at some aspects of this reality, so he's off wrangling our allies and not making things worse," said Ginevra.

The Luidaeg's attention swung back to me. I shied away, forcing myself not to back up any farther. It was a struggle, and I was proud when my feet didn't move.

"I think I can guess which aspects you mean," she said, and fully turned in my direction. "Do you know me?"

"By myth and reputation only," I said, before adding a hasty "milady."

"Oh, Dad's fucking fruitful testicles, this is bullshit I did *not* need today." The Luidaeg scowled. "You don't know me at *all*? You don't remember who we are to each other?"

"I've never seen you before in my life. Please don't hurt me."

"Okay." The Luidaeg turned back to Ginevra. "So this is going to be fun. You haven't convinced her to take the enchantment off herself yet?"

"She says she can't," said Ginevra. "Says she can't get a proper grip on the spell."

"Shit. She's probably right about that. We'll have to go down to the Undersea, get the other one."

"August? She was on the surface when the spell came down. She's here. She doesn't seem to be able to see the threads the way her sister can. She can't unravel Titania's enchantments."

"She *can*, she just doesn't know *how*," said the Luidaeg. She looked around. "We shouldn't linger here. How did you even *get* here?"

"Toby bled on the Summer Roads key and used it to open a door," said Ginevra.

"Oh. Well, I guess that'd do it." The Luidaeg looked at me again. It was all I could do not to cower. "Okay, look. I am not your enemy. I'm not always your friend, either, but that's beside the point. I am literally incapable of lying to you. If we walk away and leave you here, you will die. The forest will eventually claim its own. Most people, I'd be down for that if they annoyed me. You, though, I've put a lot of time and effort into, and I'd rather not start over with your gormless excuse for a sister, so I'm gonna need you to come with us. Get it?"

Arguing with one of the Firstborn is never a good idea. Arguing with a naked daughter of Maeve somehow seemed like an even worse idea than *that*. I forced myself to nod.

The Luidaeg threw her hands up, turning away from me. "There, was that so fucking hard? Now we just need to reset her back to her normal irritating baseline before kitty kills someone, and we'll be fine."

"You're naked," said Grianne.

"Am I? I hadn't noticed. I was too busy spitting out roses and hawthorn tree, which, very funny, ha ha, *Stepmother*. I am not Merlin, nor was meant to be." The Luidaeg snapped her fingers. The dead leaves on the clearing floor rose up and slithered along the length of her body like a great, rustling serpent, becoming a form-fitting dress in shades of decay, black and brown and bruised gray-green. "That better?"

"Yes," said Grianne.

"Great. Glad to meet with your approval. Now come on." The Luidaeg began striding imperiously forward, and the rest of us followed her, since it was that or get left behind.

There were no more desire paths, no more need to watch where we were stepping: oh, no. Where the Luidaeg walked, the ground cleared itself, briars retreating into the wood, tree roots flattening themselves beneath the soil to create a perfectly smooth surface. She never looked back, just kept walking, her chin up and her shoulders back, giving no sign that she cared whether or not the rest of us were there.

After a time, she started to talk.

"We always knew she wanted this version of Faerie," she said. "I mean, I guess that's a very sweeping statement, because in this case, 'we' just means Mom and my oldest siblings, but she and Mom used to fight about it where we could hear. Titania wanted Mom and all her kids to go away, to retreat into deepest Faerie and create our own worlds, and leave the worlds we already had for her and her precious, perfect children. And she wanted Dad, too. That sort of goes without saying. I used to lie awake during the day wishing Mom would say sure, okay, whatever, and gather us all up, and retreat into the distance. I was tired of burying my brothers and sisters, tired of hearing the night-haunts' wings. I wanted to rest.

"Then I found out the reason Titania was so set on *us* being the ones to leave, *us* being the ones who abandoned everything was because the Heart of Faerie was part of what she was asking us to walk away from. We didn't talk about the Heart much, even then. People today don't even seem to remember it exists. Faerie came from Oberon and his wives; they came from the Heart. A place and a power that, for some unknown reason, decided to spit out three effective gods who couldn't get along for more than five fucking minutes. Without a connection to the Heart, we would die. So Titania's grand plan, her awesome idea, was for all the beasts and monsters to leave of our own free will, so we could wither and fade far away from her, where she wouldn't have to watch us die. She wanted us gone so badly that she was willing to see us all dead. We refused to go. Dad found out what she'd been trying to talk Mom into, and told her to cut it out, and I guess back then he made it stick.

"Now . . . if she knocked Dad down before she started this whole thing, and I'm guessing she must have, she doesn't have anyone to balance her. She doesn't have anyone to *stop* her. And we sure as hell aren't going to be enough." She stopped walking, taking a deep breath. "We have to break this spell so completely that she'd have to start over from scratch, and hope she's pumped so much power into it that she can't try again."

"And we need to do it fast," said Ginevra. The Luidaeg glanced at her. She shrugged. "Tomorrow's Moving Day. Everyone says the

Summer Queen is planning something big. She's been preparing her Ride for weeks."

"A Ride . . . If she made a strong-enough sacrifice to the Heart while her version of the world is in place, she might be able to convince it to remake Faerie on a more permanent basis," said the Luidaeg, thoughtful and grim. "The whole thing, not however big a sphere she's got now. All of Faerie, as defined by Titania."

"That sounds . . . bad," I said.

The Luidaeg glanced at me. "Normally, this would be sarcastic, but right now: kiddo, you've got no idea."

"Does that mean you're going to tell us?" asked Ginevra hesitantly.

The Luidaeg sighed. "I can't, because I don't *know*. The Three are to the Firstborn as the Firstborn are to their descendants: a magnitude of power enough greater as to defy measurement. Well, the Heart *made* them. The Heart made all of Faerie, when you get right down to it, and while it shapes Faerie through the Three, it's at the root of everything. It's the root, and they're the branches. So yeah, if Titania thinks she can sell the Heart on her idea of a perfect world, that's probably going to suck for everybody she doesn't care for."

"Has she tried this before?" I asked.

"Far as I know, not even she's ever been reckless or sufficiently consumed by her own hubris to try, and if she wanted to, Mom and Dad were there to stop her," said the Luidaeg. "Well, Mom's still missing, and looks like Titania managed to sucker-punch Dad after he lost sight of her. She must have been planning this for a while, though. She moved *fast*."

"Were you there? When she did this?"

"We all were, Toby," said the Luidaeg wearily. "You, me, and your little cat, too. Everyone. And we all pissed her off, enough that apparently she went running to anchor her little shit bomb into the Heart before we could catch and contain her again. We don't *mess* with the Heart of Faerie. The Rides used to chuck it a sacrifice every seven years or so, to try and heal the wound it suffered when it made the Three, but that's about it. It just sits there, being a massive reality engine, not choosing anyone's side. It doesn't need to choose sides. It's the Heart of Faerie."

The brush was getting thicker and thicker around us, the air growing even cooler. I finally leaned over and took my jacket back from Ginevra, shrugging it on. I felt warmer and more secure almost instantly.

The Luidaeg glanced at me, knowingly. "I guess it makes sense that you'd be mired pretty deep in this bullshit," she said. "Your line is susceptible to transformation, and stubborn as you are—and you *are* stubborn—this is a transformation, of a sort. You've been transformed into someone the real October never had the opportunity to be. I'm not sure why she would have wanted to, but I can see where she would have been able to survive, even as you. It's just that survival isn't all that matters, and she was able to thrive as herself. Now we just need to get her back."

"What if I don't want to be replaced?" I asked boldly.

The Luidaeg's expression was surprisingly soft, and filled with sorrow. "Sorry, sweetheart, you're not going to have a choice. If it's Faerie or your happiness, I choose Faerie. I always choose Faerie. Even when it breaks my heart." She turned to face front then, and I did the same.

We were approaching a massive wall of brambles, so tall it vanished into the darkness beyond the range of Grianne's Merry Dancers. The Luidaeg cracked her neck and then her knuckles, eyes on the wall.

"If we want to stop a Ride, we need at least one of Titania's actual kids to help us get the party started," she said. "And it sounds like stopping the Ride is our first priority here. Takes a thief to catch a thief, takes a child of Titania to ruin Titania's day. This spell you're all under—it can't cover the whole world."

"No," said Ginevra. "Like I said, it's the Mists and the neighboring Kingdoms, no more, no less."

"Can anyone inside it go past its borders?"

"No," said Ginevra again, after a brief but suspicious pause.

"Didn't think so. Okay. I know where two of Titania's kids are, but only one of them's likely to be in a place we can reach without some *big* bullshit that would probably attract too much attention. Toby, be glad you don't remember where we're going. You'd get way pissed at me if you did."

I didn't understand that, and so I didn't say anything, hugging the leather jacket around myself and watching her warily instead.

The Luidaeg cocked her head and raised her hands, eyes on the wall of thorns the whole time. Then, in a voice like scales scything through clear water, low and carrying, she said, "You swore once, when we were children together, that no door of yours would ever be locked against me. You swore, and we were children of Maeve both, we understood how easily promises could be broken, and so we bound the bargain in blood, Mug Ruith, we pledged it to the stones. We've broken a thousand promises to one another since that day, but never this one. Now let. Me. In."

With that last word, she lowered her hands in a sharp, decisive gesture. There was a sound like a sheet of paper being torn, and the briars parted, revealing another forest. It was all trees, same as this one, but the sky was subtly different, the shapes of the branches not quite the same. The air in the opening shimmered like a heat haze, and the Luidaeg was frowning as she looked back at the rest of us.

"This is where we hurry," she said, and so we did, all of us, stepping quickly through the gap to the other side. I was the last one through. The briars slammed closed behind me, so fast that I felt the wind generated by their collision. I glanced back.

There was nothing there. Only the forest, stretching off into the distance. I blinked, facing front again. "Because that's not ominous at *all*," I muttered.

"This is my brother's territory," said the Luidaeg. "Or was, before he died. Ominous was very much his stock-in-trade. And right now, I'm glad you don't remember most of what we've been through together, because I swear, I do not want to hear one little question about why I didn't let you use this shortcut when you needed it. There are rules."

I had no idea what she was talking about, and so I just blinked at her as we continued making our way through the darkness.

Not as deep a darkness as it had been on the other side of the briar wall, however: here, the moon overhead cast almost as much light as Grianne's Merry Dancers, gilding everything in silver and making it easier for me to keep my footing. We continued to work our way through the trees, which were plentiful but not tightly packed, almost like they'd been cultivated that way. The four of us stayed close together, the Luidaeg in the lead, unwilling to risk being separated.

The air was warmer than it had been in the other forest, warmer and sweeter, too, with a faint hint of distant bonfires. People lived there, which was more than I could say for the place where this journey started. I wasn't sure I'd want to meet them.

No sooner had that thought formed than a hunting horn rang out through the woods, loud and sharp and far closer than I liked. I froze, legs refusing to carry me any farther. Grianne dropped into a defensive

posture. Ginevra snarled, showing sharp white teeth. And the Luidaeg smiled.

"I knew it wouldn't take long for my sister-in-law to notice she had
guests," she said. "Hold your ground, everyone. We should have an
escort in a moment."

I did as she asked. I couldn't really have done anything else, not
with that horn freezing me in place. It rang again, and terror washed
over me, cold and bright and bitter, filling my mouth with the metallic
taste of my own adrenaline. I had never heard that horn before, but I
knew it all the same. It had been starring in my nightmares since I
was just a child. That horn was the last thing naughty changelings
ever heard.

Hoofbeats began to make themselves known under the ringing,
loud and getting louder by the second as the horses pounded through
the wood toward us. I had a bare moment to consider how foolish it
was to ride horses in a forest this dense, and then we were surrounded.
A dozen massive horses poured out of the dark to circle us, their
hooves tearing divots out of the earth, their nostrils flaring as they
snorted and tossed their heads. Their riders were built to scale, each
easily twice as large as I was, wearing mismatched armor that bristled with spikes and patches. They didn't look like a cohesive force.
They looked like a nightmare.

Every one of them was armed, swords and spears and weapons I
didn't recognize but could all too easily picture doing serious and
even fatal damage. The Luidaeg was unbowed. She crossed her arms,
looking at the rider in what seemed to be the lead of their formation.

"Took you long enough," she said, dismissively. "All right, you
caught us. Fair game, tag, we're it. Now take us to my brother."

"Take us to Blind Michael."

I didn't hear what she said after that, if anything. I was too busy
fainting.

EIGHTEEN

I CAME TO SPRAWLED ON the ground, which was cold and hard. Someone was kicking me rhythmically in the hip. I opened my eyes and blinked up at the starry sky before pushing myself into a sitting position. For once, I was smart enough to keep my mouth shut as I looked frantically around, trying to take stock of the situation.

Well, I wasn't tied up, or in another cell somewhere, and I didn't seem to have acquired any new bloodstains that I could see. The ground was so hard because it was made of stone, not earth. A layer of straw covered it; not enough to soften the surface, but enough to show that someone had at least tried. The person kicking me was Grianne, who smiled and stooped to offer me her hand when she saw me sit up.

"Hit the ground hard," she said. "Didn't wake up. So we moved you."

"Moved me *where*?"

She shrugged and gestured behind her, to a low stone building that looked like it had seen better days. Hell, it looked like it had seen better *centuries*. The roof was thatch, with holes big enough to climb through—or fall through, if you were reckless enough to try climbing on that rickety mess of sticks. Beyond it I could see the red glow of a bonfire. We appeared to be in a similar building, this one entirely sans roof.

"Gin thought you'd be upset if you woke up in the middle of a party; said I'd watch you," she said.

I took her hand, letting her pull me to my feet. "I appreciate it," I said. "I wouldn't have liked to wake up alone."

She shrugged, reclaiming her hand.

I looked at her thoughtfully. Of my three current companions, Gri-anne was the one who knew me in *this* world, not in whatever strange world they came from. "Can I ask you something?"

She nodded.

"Do *you* think we should save their Faerie?"

"Don't know," she said, with another shrug. "I like me well enough. Like my friends. Like the Duke I serve. Even like you. Might not be me in their Faerie. But the way they talk, there's lots of people missing. All the shifters. The whole Undersea. And there's the change-lings. It's not supposed to be this way for you. Shadow Roads are collapsing. Don't like that. Think we might *need* their Faerie."

"So you think their version of Faerie is better."

"Didn't say that. Said I don't know. Because I don't. I can't. Maybe you can, if you look at enough blood memories. Maybe you can tell me."

I blinked at her. "I don't think I've ever heard you talk that much."

She shrugged for a third time, and didn't say anything more, just started for the light on the far side of the stone building. I took a beat to collect my thoughts, then followed her, trying not to get left behind.

We rounded the building, and beheld the source of the light: a massive bonfire had been erected in what looked a lot like a medieval town square, wood piled high and burning bright. All around it, fig-ures in armor were gathered, some sitting on hay bales, others stand-ing, tankards or joints of roast meat in their hands. They chatted easily, apparently at rest. The ones not wearing helmets were . . . dif-ficult for me to look directly at. Their features were subtly distorted from what I expected to see, as if they had been cobbled together from members of different descendent lines. Horns and fangs and gills where they didn't belong met my eyes from all directions.

For all of that, they weren't entirely monstrous: as with everything in Faerie, there was a strange beauty to their tatterdemalion forms, one echoed in the faces and shapes of the children who ran wild around the bonfire's edges, their limbs bare and their bodies clad in patch-work rags that looked like they'd been harvested from a dozen differ-ent time periods. The stories said Blind Michael's Hunt stole children, and either this was the proof or the refutation: looking at those chil-dren, I could think of no place in Faerie they belonged but there.

Two tall chairs had been set up on a platform to one side of the circle. The first of them held a tall man with skin streaked like the bark of an ash tree, auburn hair, and horns like a young stag's. The outline of his body flickered as I looked at him, now powerfully built as any of the warriors, now thin and almost bony. I couldn't tell which was true. In the moment, it didn't matter.

The woman next to him had skin as yellow as a daffodil, and her hair was a mass of gold and brown roots that writhed and restyled itself constantly, never stilling. A scar ran down one side of her face, from just below to eye to her chin, pulling the side of her mouth up in a permanent sneer. She was still beautiful, and she sat in that simple wooden chair as if it was the grandest throne in all of Faerie.

The Luidaeg stood in front of them, saying something I couldn't hear, her hands moving fast as she gestured to emphasize her point. Ginevra was with her, silently observing.

Grianne bumped her shoulder against mine as she stepped past me into the bonfire's light. It wasn't an accident; when I looked sharply up, she was looking at me, eyes calm.

"Think a lot hangs on what you decide you're going to do next," she said. "Make some decisions."

Then she was gone, joining the crowd of impossible people in their easy gathering. None of them blinked twice at the sight of her; one of them handed her a tankard, and she laughed at something I was too far away to hear.

I stepped farther back into the shadows. I wasn't ready for this. I wasn't ready for *any* of this. I was no stranger to the Firstborn—I was raised by one—but the sea witch was her own level of monster, and Blind Michael was the horror we used to threaten naughty children. Supposedly, he snatched misbehaving changelings out of their beds in the middle of the day, saving their parents the embarrassment of knowing them. The children he took were never seen again. I'd been too old for him to target for years, but the fear was there. The fear had always been there.

I shivered, starting to turn away, and yelped as something slammed into me from the side, moving fast through the darkness. I stumbled, not quite falling over as I realized what had hit me was a girl about my age, tall and gawky, long-limbed and underfed. She clung to me like I was the rescue rope she'd been waiting for since time began, and I stared at her with wide eyes, not sure how I was supposed to deal with this.

Unlike the people around the fire, she wasn't patchwork at all: she was Daoine Sidhe, with freckles across the bridge of her nose and a face rendered ashen and pale by the distant firelight. I couldn't see the color of her hair or eyes, but the shape of her face and the points of her ears were dead indicators for her descendant line. I tried to push her off me, and she started to cry.

That was new. I'd never made a pureblood cry before. I froze, unable to figure out what to do next.

"I knew it I knew it I knew if I just waited long enough you'd come for me I knew it," she said, voice shaking. "I knew it I knew you wouldn't forget about me."

"I'm so sorry," I said. "I'm so, so sorry, but I don't know who you are or why you're hanging onto me right now."

She let me go and stumbled back, staring at me. "What?"

"I'm sorry."

"*What*?!" She shook her head, face twisting with confusion and dismay. "No. No-no-no you do *not* get to stand there and tell me you don't know me either. I *waited* for you!"

"I'm so sorry," I said, trying to calm her down before her shouting attracted the people at the fire. "I really don't—let's start from the beginning, all right? My name's October. You are . . . ?"

"Rayseline. Everyone calls me 'Raysel,'" she said, more slowly. "You really don't know me?"

"I'm sorry, but no, I don't. Why should I know you?"

"My father is your liege," she said. "You—when they woke me up after I was elf-shot, you claimed offense against me so I could get out of Shadowed Hills. I'm supposed to be serving your household for a year. You don't remember *any* of that?"

"No," I said, swallowing the urge to tell her to stop lying. I didn't have a liege, but based on the rest of what she'd said, she was talking about my Uncle Sylvester. Who didn't have any children.

"Four months ago. I was in my new room at your house, and then I was here, and no one knew who I was, and no one knew how I could get *out* of here, and you're supposed to be the hero! You're supposed to save me!" She started crying again, putting her hands over her face this time, and said, voice muffled by her palms, "You were supposed to *save* me."

I just stared at her, not sure how I was supposed to respond to this. I'd never seen this girl before in my life. She was a sobbing stranger in a monster's private playground, and no one could have blamed me if I'd turned and run away.

No one but me, and since I'd go with myself anywhere I went, I was the person I couldn't afford to upset that badly.

Cautious, as if I were approaching a wild animal, I moved toward her. "Hey," I said, keeping my own voice soft and level. "Hey, I'm sorry I don't know who you are, but the people I'm with, they're trying to find a way to fix that. They're trying to figure out how we can put Faerie back the way it was before."

Four months. The same thing Ginevra had said. If my reality had really only existed for four months, that explained why my early memories were so . . . flat, for lack of a better term. They really *were* just outlines, placeholders to support the weight of the world Titania was trying to construct.

Raysel raised her head, sniffling as she looked at me. "Really?"

"Really," I said. I glanced around. Titania must have put her here for a reason. I just couldn't figure out what it was. "Are you . . . Firstborn?"

"What? No!" She recoiled, staring at me again. "I'm Sylvester and Luna Torquill's daughter. Not that *she* knows that."

"She who?"

"My *mother.*" She said the word with absolute disdain, like she couldn't think of anything worse.

I blinked. "Your mother? Is she here?"

"She is. Blind Michael's her father. She spends most of her time in her private rose garden, and I think she's happier there than she ever was at home with her family." Raysel frowned, petulant and angry. "This is a version of her who never ran away from home, and I guess it's easier to be happy when you live in a walled garden your whole life and never realize what you might be missing."

Her words, innocent as they were, still stung, and it was all I could do not to wince. "Okay," I said. "Well, I think the Luidaeg is asking Blind Michael for help getting out of here and back to the Summerlands. Do you want to come with us?"

She nodded, immediate and vigorous.

"Is there anyone else here who's going to want to come with us?"

She stopped nodding and, instead of petulant, looked briefly guilty. "What I said before, how no one knows who I am, that wasn't altogether true," she said. "There's one other person here who knows me. But he and I aren't friends, and it's not like he knows the way out of here any better than I do."

I blinked. "Okay. Where do I find this person?"

"Blind Michael divides his people into Riders and Ridden," she said. "The children become one or the other when he hosts a Wild Hunt, but he doesn't have one of those until tomorrow night, so right now, there's lots of children just running around, and we've been hiding among them. I don't know what's going to happen after his Ride." She shuddered. "The children who sleep in his stables, they . . . they *change*. We haven't changed, because we've been staying away from the stables and gathering our own food. Follow me."

She started to move then, heading quickly off into the dark and leaving me to follow. I did, as quietly as I could. We had managed not to attract any attention from the fire while Raysel had her little meltdown, but I couldn't imagine the Luidaeg would be thrilled to hear that I was running off with strange girls who insisted I was supposed to save them.

Or maybe she'd be delighted, since that sort of behavior seemed to fit with the person she thought I was. A person who married beasts and made friends with little girls of living light, who transformed changelings into pure fae out of some weird sense of justice. A person at least two people had called a hero.

I wasn't sure I could be her, even if I wanted to be. I wasn't sure I could learn *how*.

Raysel climbed over the ruins of a crumbling stone wall. I followed. There was a smaller fire on the other side, and a scattering of people sitting around it. None of them had the same patchworked look as the people at Blind Michael's fire, but they were all blends of at least two types of fae, judging by the looks of them. Some were mortal as well, changelings in more directions than one. All of them looked up as we approached, Raysel raising her hands defensively.

"I'm not here to make trouble," she said. "I just want to talk to him."

I stopped, still some distance back, to see how this was going to play out.

It wasn't a long wait. There was an explosion of motion at one end of the rough circle, as a Daoine Sidhe in torn pants and a stained shirt surged to his feet, stalking toward Raysel. His hands were balled into fists, but even so, I could tell his fingers were webbed to the first knuckle, and one of them was missing. His hair looked black in the firelight, shot through with impossible glints of green, and even with the fire behind him, I could see his scowl.

"Go *away*, Rayseline," he snapped. "I'm not in the mood for you to tell me again how we're never getting out of here."

"That's not why I came," she said, voice quick and anxious. "Dean, I—"

But he wasn't listening to her anymore. Instead, he was looking beyond her to me, scowl melting into a look of profound confusion.

"Toby?" he asked, voice cracking on the second syllable of my nickname.

"Um, hi," I said, raising one hand in a small wave. "I'm October. It's nice to meet—"

He didn't give me time to finish before he was rushing at me, just like Raysel had, and wrapping me in a tight, desperate hug. He clung, shaking, and I patted him awkwardly on the shoulder, trying to figure out how I was supposed to extricate myself from this situation.

"Meet you," I finished.

"Meet me?" He loosened his grip enough to lean back and blink at me, searching my face for the answer to a question I didn't know. He didn't find it, because he let go and took a step back, profound disappointment blossoming in his expression. "You don't know us, do you?"

"I was trying to tell your friend here that I didn't," I said, gesturing to Raysel.

"I believed you," said Raysel wearily.

"Look, I'm here with the Luidaeg, one of my uncle's knights, and a Cait Sidhe, and they're trying to convince Blind Michael he should do . . . something and let us go back to the real world." Which might not actually be all that real, and the fact that I was starting to question that scared me more than a little. "I'm sorry, but I've never seen you in my life."

"But . . . I'm your brother," he said, a little stunned.

"I don't have any brothers."

"Oh, for Pete's sake," said the boy, shaking his head as he turned away. "Raysel, she can't help us if she's as tangled up in this thing as everyone else."

"April and Ginevra say Titania cast a really big illusion and caught everybody up in it," I said. "So why didn't she catch *you*?"

"Because they were impossible," said the Luidaeg, from behind me.

I turned, slowly, to find the sea witch standing there, watching the scene with weary eyes. "What do you mean, 'impossible'?"

"Look. Titania hates a lot of people. She hates me, big time. But I'm pretty sure you're currently at the absolute top of her shit list. She *hates* you with a capital H. So when she set up her brave new world, she couldn't do it in a way that would spare you. She wanted you to suffer." She shrugged. "So she took away everyone she knew you loved, and she shoved you into your mother's tower with a man you used to hate and a sister you barely know, and gave you a head full of memories that told you it was your job to be obedient and dutiful—two things you've famously never been good at. But she's the Summer Queen. She's not good at being loved, or at loving other people without conditions. She didn't consider that you'd adapt and find ways to survive in the position she put you into, or that Simon's greatest failing has always been loving too hard and not knowing how to let go, or that August was a little shit because she was starved for affection. And that's on Titania, and all the more to our benefit. At the same time, she was trying really, really hard to make all the pieces of her pretty little picture make sense. Which meant getting rid of the parts she couldn't easily control, like the cats and the fishes. Dean here is the son of a Merrow and the Daoine Sidhe she loved."

Dean raised one hand in an awkward wave.

"If the Undersea has been sealed for over a hundred years, Dean's existence is literally impossible. But Titania can't actually wipe people from reality—not unless she gets the Heart to intercede on her behalf tomorrow night—and she couldn't risk having him elf-shot. What if someone managed to find him? The impossible boy, sleeping in a tower somewhere? No, she needed to put him, and all the other impossible people, the ones born where the sea met the shore, someplace safe and out of the way. Enter my brother's kingdom." The Luidaeg spread her hands, indicating the forest, the fire, and everything around us. "Normally, a skerry like this one would be out of her reach, since my brother was a child of Maeve, and Titania had no claim over his lands or treasures. Sadly for my peace of mind, he went and married a daughter of Titania, Acacia, known as Mother of the Trees. Acacia's roots run deep through this skerry. She's been here for a long, long time. Through her, Titania had access. And she tossed all her misfit toys through that access, then let it slam shut and walked away."

I blinked. "That wasn't very nice."

"Oh, because brainwashing you into thinking you were some sort of enthusiastic Cinderella figure was all sunshine and lollipops?" The Luidaeg glared at me. "The fact that she needed my brother to serve as her monster if she wanted this little puppet show to work is possibly the least nice thing she's done, and she's got a *lot* of not-very-niceness to answer for at this point."

"But Blind Michael *is* a monster," I objected. "He steals children!"

"He did, and I won't make apologies for that, because it was always wrong, no matter what his motivations," she said. "He hurt a lot of people, and he destroyed a lot of families, and he had his reasons, but that doesn't make them good ones. He wasn't a monster, and then he was, and then he wasn't, because a hero took the Blood Road to his lands and killed him for what he'd done and what he'd tried to do. My brother is *dead*, October. He's nobody's monster anymore. *You* killed him. You took up iron and silver and you killed my brother on his own land because he'd hurt people who belonged to you, and I . . . I helped you do it. So the fact that someone is here, in his land, wearing his face? Is a travesty, and one more reason we're going to kick Titania's teeth so far down her throat she has to chew by burping."

I stared at her for a long moment. Finally, a little overwhelmed and unsure what else to say, I said, "I thought you couldn't lie."

"Fortunately, when that binding was placed on me, it didn't cover dramatic exaggeration or humor, or I'd be a lot less fun to be around," she said.

I rubbed my face with one hand. "Blind Michael is dead."

"Yes."

"You say I killed him."

"Because you did."

"I . . . I've never killed *anyone* before yesterday, and now you're telling me I killed one of the First?"

"I am." For a moment, she looked almost amused. "The first time you told me he was dead, I said there was a time when I'd have ripped your heart out of your chest and eaten it in front of your dying eyes for saying something like that to me."

I flinched.

She sighed, amusement fading. "Seeing you scared of me hurts more than I thought it would, and I've just been talking to someone wearing my brother's face like a mask from a children's pantomime. This is quite possibly the nastiest thing my stepmother has ever done to me, and that woman invented nasty."

I bit my lip, turning my head as I looked at the people around me. Raysel and Dean were watching me with expressions of fragile, uncertain hope, like they expected me to vanish at any moment; all the others around the fire just looked exhausted, like even the potential for hope had been beaten entirely out of them. "Four months? All of you?" I asked.

"That's how long it's been," said Dean. "How long . . . ?"

"This is all I remember," I said. "The world as it is goes all the way back to my birth, and for centuries before that. Four months is *nothing*. It's a blink."

"It's how long she's had you all ensnared," said the Luidaeg.

"And you say Blind Michael is dead?"

She nodded.

"But that doesn't make any sense."

"Now she gets it," said the Luidaeg. "Ginevra and Grianne are still trying to convince him to open a path for us, so we can get out of here, but they're not having a lot of luck. He keeps saying he promised Titania he'd keep the doors shut until she came to choose her horses, and getting him to break his word has never been easy. He likes his rules, and he likes to know that people will follow them. Acacia already agreed to give me the blood I need. Titania couldn't turn her into a totally dutiful daughter and still marry her off to my brother, so she's as defiant of her mother as ever, thank Mom."

"I may . . . I may have an idea about how to convince him," I said, hesitantly. I looked around again, this time scanning the people for weapons. If anyone was armed, they weren't openly so, and I frowned. "I need something sharp. A knife would be best, but a bit of briar would do."

"Planning to bleed?" asked the Luidaeg.

"I think I need to."

"Then here." She reached into the leaf-rot depths of her dress and pulled out a single thorn, as long as my middle finger and wickedly sharp. Holding it carefully by the base, she offered it to me. "Just try not to drive it too deep. It's thirsty."

"Not sure I'm comfortable with something you describe as 'thirsty,'" I said, but took the thorn anyway, holding it as gingerly as she had. I turned to the group around the fire. "Do any of you know how you got here?"

They answered in a ragged chorus of negation, denying any knowledge of how they'd been transported from their homes and beds to Blind Michael's lands. A few of them began to cry. I nodded, turning away.

"I don't think we need to worry about these folks," I said, and started walking back toward the other fire, still holding the thorn carefully away from myself.

The Luidaeg followed. So did Dean and Raysel, who seemed determined not to let me out of their sight.

"Mind telling me what's going on in that ridiculous marble you like to pretend is a brain?" asked the Luidaeg.

"I have an idea, and I'm going to see where it goes." It felt weird, talking back to a pureblood, especially one of the First, but I didn't really see any other option. I could do what she told me, let her control how this story went; I could refuse to do anything, let Titania control it all; or I could start pushing and see how far I could get.

I liked pushing. I liked pushing a lot more than I expected to. It felt sort of like I was a person built for pushing, and had been missing out on my true purpose for my entire life—or just for these last four months, if what everyone was trying to tell me was true. And I was increasingly sure that it probably was, although the Luidaeg's description of my life being designed to make me suffer made me want to throw up. I loved my family. I didn't want that love to be built on someone else's lie.

When we reached the building where I'd met Raysel, I paused, then pricked my finger with the tip of the thorn. Unlike all the other things I'd used to hurt myself since this began, the thorn prick didn't hurt.

No wonder the Luidaeg had been concerned about my cutting too deep. It would be easy, with something that pierced painlessly, to drive it all the way down to the bone.

I pulled the thorn away and put my fingertip in my mouth, closing my eyes. Shunting away the blood memories was easier every time I had to do it, and I reached out, looking for the traces of Titania's magic.

As I'd expected, neither of my new companions lit up pink: whatever else they might say, Raysel and Dean were telling the truth when they said they hadn't been enchanted by Titania. The Luidaeg was still carrying the tightly woven spell I had seen beneath the tree.

I turned sightlessly toward the fire, continuing to look into the empty, unseen space where magic hung in shimmering strands. All the people there had traces of pink dancing over their skins, little revisions to make them a part of Titania's revised reality. None were as dense as the webs I'd removed from January or Chelsea: apparently, the residents of Blind Michael's lands hadn't needed as much revision to accept this world.

All save Blind Michael himself, who was a mass of strands so dense he was almost a solid slice of pink, and the woman next to him, who was only slightly less ensnared. They were so brilliantly bright that I missed Grianne at first, until she moved slightly and I saw there was one more person wrapped in pink threads, although hers were more like the ones I'd seen on everyone else.

I gasped and opened my eyes as the blood ran out. "Blind Michael and his consort are both *very* deep in this enchantment," I said.

"That makes sense," said the Luidaeg.

I frowned at her. "But so are you."

She blinked, eyebrows raising. "I am?"

"When I saw you in the tree, there was the transformation on top of you, and another enchantment deeper down. Same caster, but not the same spell."

For a moment, she looked alarmed. "You didn't touch the second spell, did you?"

I shook my head, and she relaxed. "Good. A long, long time ago, Titania bound me in a bunch of exciting ways I hate but that mean I can't tell all of you to fuck off with your petty little problems, I'm going to take a nap at the bottom of the sea now. Which is something I really, truly want to do. But you're not getting out of this bullshit without me, so no matter what else you do, Toby, you *do not break that spell*. Do you understand?"

I blinked. "I do."

"Now what are we going to do about it?"

"Ginevra said we were looking for you because we needed access to your 'stronger blood.'" I looked at her expectantly. "Can you bleed for me?"

"Lots of fae can borrow magic through blood," she said, leaning over to take the thorn. "That's what I'm planning to do with Acacia's magic. But the Dóchas Sidhe are only ones I've met who can borrow magic's strength and use it as their own, with no need to rely on the gifts of the one who gave them the blood to begin with. It's a strange gift on its own. Taken in concert with the rest of what your line can do, I have to wonder if it's not intended to make things like this more possible."

She cupped her left hand and drove the thorn into the center of her palm without flinching. When she pulled it back out, red-black blood filled her hand, pooling in the hollow she had created. Bowing her head, she took a deep breath and closed her hand.

When she opened it again, the blood was gone. Instead, her palm was filled with a scattering of grape-sized garnets, deep red and gleaming in the distant firelight. She held them out to me.

"Here," she said. "I've pulled as much of the memory out of them as I can, so you shouldn't get any bad backlash, but I don't recommend more than one of these at a time. You've had stronger at this point; you may not remember the first time I bled for you right now, but the concerns I had then don't apply anymore. So when you do remember, please also remember this: I did nothing that would hurt you."

I held my hands under hers. She tipped the garnets into them.

"Good to know," I said. "I've been asking people for permission before I remove this spell, because it hurts, and it changes their minds. It seems . . . wrong to change someone's mind without asking first. But if that's not your brother . . ."

"It's not," said the Luidaeg, expression going cold. "You can ask Acacia, but I will not leave an imposter in my brother's place. You will not ask him."

"I can live with that," I said. I glanced toward the fire. "I can't do it from here."

"Follow me," she said, and began to stride toward Blind Michael, moving fast and steady.

I followed.

She stopped in front of him, next to a disheartened-looking Ginevra, and glared up at him. "You," she said, voice tight, "are not my brother."

"Of course I am, little Annie," said Blind Michael, leaning forward and focusing on her. His eyes were milky white and never quite fixed on her face, darting back and forth even as he gave her the whole of his attention.

"My brother died at the hands of my youngest niece," said the Luidaeg. "Neither I nor she needs ask leave of thee to free you from what's been done. His name and honor are in the balance here."

She glanced back at me, clearly waiting for me to move. I did, stepping forward to join her, and popped the first of the garnets into my mouth at the same time. It dissolved on my tongue, leaving behind the taste of marshwater and the feeling of wind rolling across the moors, something that should have been impossible to define with such easy precision. As when I'd been swallowing my own blood, power swept through me, intoxicating and heady. But if my power had been a river, this was a flood, a natural disaster distilled into a single mouthful, and it threatened to take my breath away.

Flickers of memory teased at the edges of my vision, absent the shell I'd seen around the memories of the enchanted, and I brushed them aside as I seized the magic itself, then reached for the spell wrapped around Michael. It was easier to grab hold of it when I was like this, easier to find an opening that would let me work my way into the weave and start breaking things. Threads snapped as the cold started working its way up and into my hands.

It was easier. It also hurt more. I screamed, and Michael howled, and the Luidaeg and Ginevra were holding me up as they both hissed at Michael's people, who were suddenly very interested in advancing on our position. I kept pulling, harder and harder. This was such a dense enchantment compared to the others, and was so tightly knotted that if I lost my grip, I would never be able to get it back again.

His howl became a roar of absolute fury, and something slammed into my leg, something sharp and piercing. I felt it go straight through the meat of my thigh. My knee threatened to buckle and dump me to the ground, but then Ginevra was there, keeping me from falling as I continued to pull.

"This may hurt," she murmured, and yanked the dagger—or whatever it was—out of my leg, clearing the wound so it could start to knit itself closed.

The smell of bonfire and blood was everywhere, drowning the world, and my arms were cold almost to the elbow, making my fingers clumsy, making the remaining threads harder to hold. Still I kept yanking and snapping and pulling them away, until I suddenly smelled peppermint and basil, and the last of the threads came away in my hands, and I opened my eyes.

NINETEEN

MY HEAD WAS POUNDING like a timekeeper's drum, and my eyes wouldn't quite focus. I looked down at my leg. There was a hole through my kirtle but no corresponding hole in me; it had healed cleanly after Ginevra got the dagger out of me.

A woman's voice I didn't recognize rose and fell not far from me, ululating in a steady wail. I tried to force my aching eyes to look at the source of the sound, and finally saw the yellow woman who'd been seated next to Michael—the one almost as enchanted as he was—draped over something in his chair, clinging to it and sobbing.

Then she shifted, and I saw what she was holding.

It was a lanky teenage boy, not quite old enough to be considered an adult, with shaggy hair that was white until about halfway along the individual strands, where it transitioned to brown, giving it the somewhat disconcerting appearance of brown smoke. He was dressed in clothes from the mortal world, and his eyes were closed; he appeared to be unconscious.

"That," I said, somewhat woozily, "is *not* Blind Michael."

"No," said the Luidaeg, tone grim. "That's Anthony Brown."

The name meant nothing to me. Ginevra made a complicated sound, somewhere between a gasp and a groan, and kept holding me up as the Luidaeg moved toward the wailing woman. Blind Michael's Riders still surrounded us, many of them holding weapons at the ready, but as yet, none had made the move to strike.

"Acacia," she said, once she was close enough to have a prayer of being heard above the wailing. "Acacia, I'm so sorry. But that wasn't your husband, and it wasn't my brother. This boy was placed under an enchantment by your mother, who's trying to take over our world. I know it hurts right now. I know. But nothing has actually been lost. Nothing has ended but a lie."

The woman continued to wail, even as the Luidaeg stepped up onto the low platform beneath the chairs, working her arms around the boy and easing him away from Acacia.

"Toby?" she called. "Little help here?"

My head hurt so much that I was afraid it might pop if I tried to shout back or, worse, to do any more magic. Despite that, I knew better than to ignore her. I slipped another of those hard red stones between my lips and let it dissolve on my tongue, washing fatigue and pain both away in a wave of raw, radiant power.

I straightened, standing on my own, and focused my attention on Acacia as I moved to join the Luidaeg. "I can make this all make sense," I said. "Do you want me to?"

Still wailing, she nodded.

I closed my eyes and *reached*.

As before, it was easier to catch hold of the spell than it had been when I was working without the blood of the sea witch on my tongue, easier to grab and pull and unravel something I should never have dared to so much as touch. The pain, however, was back to the level I'd experienced with January and Chelsea, horrible and agonizing but oddly manageable after seeing how much worse it could be. I pulled until the screaming stopped and the last of the threads came loose, and then I teetered, nearly toppling over.

Ginevra was there to catch me, keeping me from doing more than stumbling. "Hey, none of that," she said. "Good job, Toby. You'll be proud of yourself when this is all over and you understand what you've done."

I opened my eyes. "Can I be proud of myself on the other side of a dose of laudanum?" I asked.

Acacia wasn't crying anymore. Instead, she was recoiling, looking in horror at the boy in the Luidaeg's arms. The Luidaeg, for her part, was strangely tender as she held the motionless stranger close, keeping him from touching the ground.

"All right, you assholes," she said, clearly pitching her voice at the gathered Riders. "We don't have the time to break the spell on every

single one of you individually, but your master's gone, and your mistress
is on our side. Can we trust you to keep your hands and your halberds
to yourselves?"

"She just said that for the alliteration," said Ginevra in a low voice,
clearly trying to make me laugh.

It would have worked, too, if not for my throbbing head. I snorted
with brief amusement anyway, then shot her a quelling look. She
shrugged, unrepentant.

Still carrying the unconscious boy, the Luidaeg climbed down from
the platform and walked back over to us. "This is Anthony," she said,
nodding toward his face. "He's your nephew, sort of. His mother was
a good friend of yours, before she had to go away. Titania hates him
and his siblings in specific, but my father bound her against hurting
them the last time he had the chance to make her listen to his rules,
so I guess this was the worst thing she could do, even while she was
building her perfect little nightmare paradise. But this explains a lot."

"It does?" I asked. "How?"

"Anthony is a descendant of Titania. With him *and* Acacia holding
down the skerry, Titania would have no barriers to using this place
as a dumping ground. I can tell from your eyes that you're hurting,
and I'm sorry about that, but I have to ask—do you think you can
look for any more traces of her magic? Just so we know if there's
anyone else here who shouldn't be?"

"All the people by Dean's fire," I said. "They're not supposed to be
here, but they didn't have any magic on them."

"Hey," said Raysel. The Luidaeg turned to look at her. She didn't
flinch. "My mother's here."

"Luna?" asked the Luidaeg, eyebrows raising.

Raysel nodded. "She doesn't remember ever leaving. Doesn't remember Shadowed Hills, or my father, or me. So I'd say she's probably pretty tangled up in Titania's spell."

"But breaking the spell on the rosebush doesn't get us another ally,
and it runs the risk of damaging Toby, which, I don't *think* Tybalt
could actually kill me, but I'm pretty sure he'd try, and I don't want
to kill him if I don't have to."

I blinked slowly. Unlike Ginevra, the Luidaeg hadn't ever re-
frained from alluding to who Tybalt was to me, even if she hadn't
mentioned it outright, and I could admit to myself that pretending I
didn't know why he was so invested in my well-being was getting old.
I was also very tired and in a lot of pain after unwinding two of Titania's

enchantments. "Please don't inspire Tybalt to kill you," I said. "What are we supposed to do now?"

The Luidaeg hesitated, looking at me as I leaned on Ginevra, then down at Anthony, sleeping in her arms, and finally over her shoulder at the still-weeping Acacia.

"We don't have a lot of time," she said. "But with Titania's false Michael unmasked, and Acacia aware of what's really going on, I'd be willing to bet that we just took a bunch of the horses Titania was counting on out of the equation. She's going to need to regroup, and that might be enough to delay the start of her Ride."

"What *is* a Ride?" I asked. "We throw that word around a lot, but no one ever explains it."

"That's because it doesn't always mean the same thing. When the Queens Ride, it's to carry sacrifices to the Heart of Faerie. They used to go down the oldest and longest roads once every seven years, and come back with their company reduced by one, until fair Titania grew jealous of her sister, and asked her oldest daughter to find a way to break the Ride. So she did, and Maeve was lost to us, and the sacrifices stopped. When my brother Rode, it was intentional mockery of the Queens, to spite Titania for having failed to control her children, to shame our mother for being unwilling to help him. There are other Rides, but in the end, a Ride, a true Ride, is always a sacrifice." She looked at me levelly. "Someone always pays."

"And tomorrow night, Moving Day, Halloween night, Titania Rides," said Ginevra grimly. "We don't know who her sacrifice is going to be. We know some of the people it's not, but that isn't as useful right now."

"How can you know that?" I asked.

"Because my father bound her before she did all this," said the Luidaeg. "She can't directly harm you, or any of the Brown children, or anyone you consider family. She's also forbidden to hurt the children of Maeve."

"But that's not right," protested Dean. I had almost forgotten he was standing there. "I'm her *brother*. That makes me her family, and throwing me here sure as hell hurt me! My mother must be terrified, and Quentin—"

"You're thinking like a young thing," said the Luidaeg. "I know you're only a few decades old—"

"I'm twenty-two," he interjected stiffly.

"—but you need to try to think like a pureblood, one who's been around for centuries. I've seen empires rise and fall. I've seen mountains born. A few months in isolation is *nothing*. By the standards of the older fae, Titania has done you no harm at all. Illusions aren't harm. They're cruel and they're wicked but they aren't considered harm. Father would never have thought to forbid her the use of her own magic. I'm not sure he *could*. As long as she raised no hand and dealt no injuries, she hasn't broken her bindings."

Dean's face screwed up in disgust. "That's just . . . You're just twisting things around until they say what you want them to say!"

"Welcome to Faerie, kid," she said, dryly.

"Hold on," I said. "Dean, you've said twice that you were my brother. What do you mean by that?"

"I mean your father married my parents after he divorced Amandine," said Dean. "You chose him in the divorce, and that makes you my sister, sort of. Which is weird only because I was already dating your squire, and he thinks of you as his mom, but we just don't think about that more than we absolutely have to."

I blinked at him slowly. The idea of Father divorcing my mother was unbelievable, and one more reason not to accept their version of Faerie as the superior one. But increasingly, I was starting to think I didn't really have a choice. There were too many people like Raysel and Dean, people who couldn't exist in Titania's Faerie and had been pushed into the corners to get them out of the way. This wasn't stable.

It wasn't going to last, even if I tried to hold on to it with both hands.

"So we're family," I said, and looked back to the Luidaeg. "We're family, but not by blood, and if there was a marriage, Titania unmade it when she rewrote the world. And right now, I don't remember any of this, which means I don't *think* of him as family. Would your father's binding still protect him if Titania wanted to use him as her sacrifice?"

The Luidaeg frowned, deeply. "I don't know," she said, after a moment to consider. "I want to say yes, but I think that's more me trying to find a bright spot in all this than anything real. 'Maybe' is about the best I can do without treading uncomfortably close to telling a lie."

"Would a member of Toby's family be a powerful-enough sacrifice to achieve what Titania's trying to do?" asked Ginevra.

"Depends on who it is," said the Luidaeg. "I know where most of them are, and they're as safe as they can be, under the circumstances."

Ginevra's eyes abruptly widened, pupils narrowing at the same time, until they were black slashes down the centers of her irises, almost invisible. "Tybalt," she said. "She could go for him."

"She could, but I doubt she's going to want to bribe the Heart with someone she considers a beast," said the Luidaeg. "Toby's dead on her feet, and she needs to eat something that *isn't* blood. If we let her keel over, we may as well give up. None of the rest of us can break my wicked stepmother's spells."

I shoved the remaining garnets into my jacket pocket, abruptly remembering they existed. "So we're going to rest *here*?" I asked, glancing around at our admittedly unsettling surroundings.

"Yes," said Acacia, rising from her chair and moving to join us. Grianne was close behind her, Merry Dancers bobbing by her side. "I have access to my late husband's halls, and while you may not remember it, Sir Daye, you are always welcome here."

The name meant nothing to me, but she looked at me as she spoke it, and so it wasn't hard to guess who she meant. "Cool," I said. I could ask more questions, but more and more, I was coming to understand that the questions would never actually end. "I think I could really use a nap. I think we all could."

The Luidaeg nodded, and for a little while, the time for confusing conversations and questions with answers I didn't understand was over. Acacia waved the Riders back to their firelight celebrations, and they went with surprisingly little reluctance, apparently willing to accept anything as long as one of their lieges told them it was all right. The Luidaeg carried Anthony, and Ginevra half-carried me, while Dean and Raysel followed close behind us, unwilling to let me out of their sight.

Blind Michael's hall was as dismal and dire as his bonfire ring when viewed from the outside, a crumbling stone edifice that seemed held together by creeping vines and cobwebs. The torches lit themselves as Acacia led us through the gate and into the great hall, which was filled with shadows that twisted and flickered when I looked at them. The motion made my head spin, so I stopped looking and leaned on Ginevra as Acacia led us farther onward, into a smaller dining hall.

Twinned fireplaces took up most of one wall, flames already burning high inside, and a long table had been set up, loaded with all the pieces of a proper feast. Roasts, trays of buttered greens, baskets of rolls, and platters of delicate sides warred for space. I turned to blink at Acacia.

She shrugged. "The hall knows what's needed," she said. "You should eat."

My stomach rolled, as if suddenly reminded that all the blood I'd shed had to come from somewhere, and I collapsed into the nearest open chair, beginning to fill a plate even as Dean and Raysel fell on the meal like wild beasts, not bothering with plates or cutlery.

The Luidaeg gave us all an indulgent look, walking over to lay Anthony gently down in front of the fire. She took a moment to straighten his limbs and brush his hair away from his eyes, letting her fingertips linger against his skin.

"Will he be all right?" asked Acacia.

"I don't know," said the Luidaeg. "Everyone else just has the wrong set of memories for their actual self. He had a whole new *self*, and I don't know how deep or detailed that was. I want to think he's just in shock, and I know that because of the binding, she won't have done anything she *knew* would hurt him—but I don't have any experience with a personality revision of this scope. Did he seem like himself, these past few months?"

"A little standoffish, a little kinder than usual—it was almost like he was remembering what it had been like in the days when we courted, before Luna ran away," said Acacia. "Now, I can attribute that in part to the fact that neither of us *remembered* Luna running away, but at the time, it was just my husband. I was still sure I had done something to upset him, somehow."

"Why?"

"Because he wouldn't touch me. Not once in the last four months, not even a kiss. At the time, it hurt my feelings. I thought he was falling out of love. Now, of course, I can only be relieved." Acacia sighed. "I wish I could say I don't believe my own mother would do this to me, but then, she cast me from her care when I fell in love with a son of Maeve, and would not have me back even when that love turned sour and broken between us."

"Excuse me." Raysel pushed between Grianne and Ginevra to face Acacia, half a loaf of bread in one hand. "You're . . . you're Acacia, aren't you? The Mother of the Trees? Blind Michael's wife?"

"Yes," said Acacia, with bewildered politeness.

"You're the Firstborn of the Dryads, and of the Blodynbryd."

"Yes." The bewilderment was deepening toward puzzlement.

"I . . . My name is Rayseline? Rayseline Torquill? Your youngest daughter, Luna . . . she's my mother?" Raysel swallowed, hard. "My parents aren't divorced, even though I chose Daoine Sidhe when Toby offered to rebalance my blood to something that wasn't trying to destroy itself. I think you're my grandmother?"

"I am, child," said Acacia, sudden softness chasing away her confusion. "I've seen you at the fire's edge, these past few months, but I'm afraid that in my bewitchment, I took little notice. How did you come to be here?"

"The spell, same as everyone else," she said.

"You two get acquainted," said the Luidaeg. "I'm going to go and check on Toby."

"Yes. The little hero." Acacia frowned, stealing a glance over at me. "If I'm not much mistaken, she goes as green as grass."

"I think you're right about that, but she doesn't know, so we're not going to make it a thing," said the Luidaeg. "I'll let you know when we're ready to move on." She turned, then, and walked over to join me and Dean at the table, taking a seat next to Grianne.

"This is nice," she said. "Sort of like a picnic in the human conception of Hell. Maybe next we can braid each other's hair or, I don't know, get the hell out of here, figure out who my wicked stepmother is planning to murder, break her nasty-ass spell, and fix the world."

"Am I going to have to do it one person at a time?" I asked. "Because I'm exhausted and my head is killing me after four. I don't think I can keep doing this."

"Wow, a Toby who acknowledges her limitations, Titania really did pull out all the stops on this one," said the Luidaeg. She picked up a roll, buttering it with small, fierce strokes of a knife. "But you're right, you can't keep doing this. Your sister might be able to help, if we can sell her on the idea. She's a stubborn one, so I don't know if we can count on it, but it would be worth trying."

"August's not going to help you," I said.

She looked at me, one eyebrow raised. "No? And why not?"

"Because she believes the people who keep telling us that our lives are a lie," I said.

"Continue."

"August's pretty smart, for someone who's never been encouraged to be smart. She pays attention. She doesn't rush in. And when a bunch of people show up with the same ridiculous story and evidence to support it, she listens. Which is *why* she's not going to help you."

"Explain," said the Luidaeg.

"You're telling me our world has only existed for four months.

That everything before that is a lie Titania told for her own benefit."
I paused, long enough for the Luidaeg to nod. "Yeah, well, we *believed the lie.* Completely. And the last four months? Those weren't a
lie. Those were our life. August is my best friend. I love her. I was
born to be her companion. She loves me. And unmaking this spell
means taking me away from her." I shrugged. "She doesn't particularly want that to happen. To be quite honest, I don't want it to happen either."

Dean looked horrified. "But that means you'd be taken away from
everyone else," he said. "And August wouldn't want that, either. Not
the real August. Not the one who's been living with my parents.
Peter—he's our little brother—talks about her. He says she's really
nice, and she likes him a lot, she's always playing fair and making him
feel welcome and she wouldn't take you away from us. She wouldn't
take you away from your family just because she wants to keep the
family Titania made up to punish us."

I shrugged. "August doesn't know any of that. *I* don't know any of
that, not really. Sure, you say it, but maybe we're enemies and have
always hated each other. How can we be sure we won't hate each
other again if the spell is broken?"

"There's an easy answer for this," said the Luidaeg, and called over
her shoulder to where Acacia and Raysel were standing, heads close
together as they spoke in low voices, "Hey, 'Cayci! What do you remember about the last four months?"

"I was with my husband and our youngest daughter, and everything was fine, except for his strange reluctance to comfort me when
I was cold," she said. "I loved him very much. I remember that. I
know now that I haven't loved him in a long time, that I didn't grieve
him when he died, but for those four months . . . I loved him."

"There." The Luidaeg turned back to me, the expression of triumph on her face almost masking her concern. "Whatever else happens, you'll remember the four months as you lived them. You say
you love her? Then you have to let her be who she actually is. If she
loves you as much as you say she does, she'll do you the same favor."

Dean abruptly paled. "My parents . . ."

"Are fine," said Ginevra. "I had to practically threaten your mother
before she'd agree to stay below. I was *not* trying to babysit her *and*
Tybalt when we didn't know how this was going to go. Strange as it
probably sounds to you, this"—she waved a hand, indicating the gloomy
hall around us—"is the best-case scenario. We've managed to find

Toby *and* the Luidaeg, and while Titania's certainly going to be responsible for some hefty therapy bills going forward, she doesn't appear to have physically harmed anyone. If anything, she set up a logical situation, and then she let people wind up where it made sense for them to be if that was the way the world had worked all along. Cait Sidhe don't exist anymore? Fine, all the Cait Sidhe are in the Court of Cats. The Undersea's been cut off for a hundred years? Okay, anyone who was underwater when the spell came down is cut off, and anyone who couldn't have been born if not for the Undersea gets shunted here, to Blind Michael's skerry, where everyone knows time works differently than it does everywhere else. You could have been here, exactly as you are, for a century. You don't prove anything about the Undersea's continued existence."

"She always was more dedicated to looking clever than she was to doing the work to actually *be* clever," said the Luidaeg. She looked at me again, slow and measuring. "You should sleep while you can. You need it more than you know, and there's not going to be much time for sleep once we get back to the mortal world. Everything's going to happen really fast once it starts happening. And you're going to have to figure out which side you want to be standing on when the dust finishes settling."

"Is that a threat?" I asked, uneasily.

She shook her head. "No. I sort of wish it were, because then it would be something I could make good on, but no. It's just a statement of fact. There are a lot of people out there who love you, and not all of them will be as patient as I am. We still have a little time for you to sort your shit out and get on the right side of this question. Now if you're done eating, get some rest."

I frowned and rose, pushing gingerly back from the table. Acacia and Raysel were still deep in conversation, and neither of them looked up as I approached. I cleared my throat. Acacia finally raised her head, blinking slowly.

"Yes?" she asked.

"Is there a place where I could, you know, lie down for a while?" I asked. "Please? I'm tired, and even the sea witch says I need to sleep."

"Of course," she said, and touched Raysel lightly on the shoulder, saying, "I'll be right back," before she moved to lead me to a small door on the far wall. Opening it, she gestured me through ahead of her.

"It's nice to see you again, even if you don't remember the last time you were here," she said. "You don't visit often enough."

"I'm . . . sorry?" I ventured. "I wish I remembered you. I wish I remembered a lot of things."

"Well, tomorrow is another day, as the mortals say, and perhaps soon you'll smash my mother's mirror into pieces." Her expression was suddenly fierce as she walked across the chamber we had entered, adjusting the pillows on a large bed that was the most beautiful thing I had ever seen simply because it existed.

"Don't you mind, ma'am?" I asked, following her to the bed.

"Mind what?"

"That we're opposing your mother." The question was ill-fitting in my mouth and set up a strange twisting in my gut. Even the thought of opposing my mother's will was an uncomfortable one. I couldn't remember ever having told her no, even when I'd been a child and inclined to a degree of stubbornness ill-befitting a changeling.

Of course, according to everyone around me right now, those memories were all lies made up by the Summer Queen, and I couldn't trust them.

If I hadn't already had a headache, the contradiction would almost certainly have given me one.

"Ah," said Acacia. "I opposed my mother a long, long time ago, when I fell in love with a son of Maeve and allowed him to spirit me away to a kingdom of his own creation. This was a beautiful place once, before my Michael sank too deeply into the poisoned mire of his own heart. We planted a glorious garden together, he and I, when he was not yet a monster. My mother never forgave me for that. She said that until I cast him from my bed and my side, I was no child of hers, and now that he's gone to the ground and the grave, lost to us forever, what does she do? She recreates him in an innocent boy's body, and sets him beside me again, as if he still belonged there. As if she had the right to sculpt my bridal bed. No, I don't care if you tear down everything she's made. A garden planted in poisoned ground will bear only toxic fruit. Burn it all for all I care."

She smiled at me then, before she turned to walk away.

"Pleasant dreams, October," she said, and she was gone, and I was alone.

TWENTY

MY DREAMS WERE STRANGE and tangled things. I ran through mazes of grasping vines, following the sound of my sister's laughter, until it became the sound of weeping. I rounded a corner in the maze, and there was Tybalt, sitting on a bench beside a decorative garden pond, his face in his hands, his elbows on his knees. I stopped running.

"Why are you in my dream?" I asked, challenging.

Lowering his hands, he looked at me. Without anger, without hate, with only sorrow and love in his eyes. "Because, little fish, a man is allowed to weep for the loss of his heart," he said.

Gasping, I sat upright in my bed, one hand clutching my middle and the other at my chest, as if I could keep my hammering heart inside with the force of my denial. It worked, to the degree that my heart stayed inside of my body. It didn't work, in that it kept on aching.

I knew it had been a dream. I *knew* that. But it had been built from memories buried in my blood, and even if they were currently inaccessible to me, they were real. I couldn't deny that. I didn't want the world to change. I didn't want my life to have been a lie.

And sometimes what I want doesn't matter. Sometimes what matters is what's right, and what was right was the world where these people knew and loved me, where they were waiting for me to join them. Where they'd be waiting forever if I didn't stop pushing them all away as hard as I could for the crime of knowing a different version of reality.

Cautiously, I took my hand away from my chest and breathed slowly in, steadying myself. The panic that woke me seemed to have faded, and my head wasn't throbbing anymore. That was swell. If Titania was willing to delay her Ride long enough for me to take a long nap between unbindings, maybe this would work out after all.

"Glad to see you're feeling better," said a voice from the corner of my room. I stiffened again, turning toward it. "I was worried when you sat up like that."

"Luidaeg?" I asked, finally identifying the voice. "What are you doing in here?"

"Cayci and Raysel had a lot of catching up to do, and the people you came with needed to sleep, so I moved in here with Anthony after I bled my sister. He's still out."

Something about the way she said that made me look to the other side of the bed. There, motionless and barely visible in the gloom that filled the chamber, was the sleeping form of Anthony Brown.

"Why this kid?" I asked. He looked innocent, sweet, and very, very young. I'd have been stunned if he was twenty mortal years old.

"Oh, because he's her son," said the Luidaeg easily.

I managed not to recoil. Firstborn? I'd been sleeping next to one of the Firstborn? You'd think being raised by one would make them less impressive, but if anything, it had the opposite effect. I know exactly what my mother is capable of when she gets upset about something. The amount of power she can put into a temper tantrum . . . being defenseless around the Firstborn is a good way to wind up dead, or with a skeleton made entirely of earthworms, or worse. And there's always, always worse.

"In the real version of Faerie, Maeve's Ride broke just like it did here, but Titania wasn't as good about keeping her mouth shut afterward," said the Luidaeg. "She bragged about being responsible for her sister's downfall. *Bragged*, like it was something to be proud of. Oberon heard her, and he realized, finally, that maybe having a Queen who was bound and determined to erase one-third of Faerie from existence was a bad thing. So he bound her. Overwrote her mind with someone entirely new, hooked the spell into her own magic so it would be self-renewing, and sent her out into the rest of Faerie to learn compassion and humility. That spell looked a lot like a smaller version of this one. Hell, maybe it's where she got the idea."

She paused, and I heard footsteps approaching the bed. I forced myself not to shy away. "Regardless, that spell made her live out life after life among her own descendants, pretending at being small and harmless without knowing that she was pretending. And the most recent of those lives was a woman named Stacy Brown, who was your best friend since childhood. You loved that woman, and she loved you, and you were honorary auntie to her children. Until the spell started to break down, and Titania started showing through."

None of this meant anything to me, but the way she spoke, slow and implacable, filled me with a crawling horror.

"She killed one of the children, a little girl named Jessica, and a whole lot of very nasty stuff happened, and in the end, you undid Oberon's spell and let Stacy go, because she'd never really been there, and it was the only way to stop Titania. Oberon bound her again, and in his binding, he forbade her to harm the children of her last incarnation. He'd seen how much they meant to you. He felt . . . sorry, as much as he's capable of that emotion, for having caused you pain by letting them be hurt. So she can't directly harm Anthony, or his siblings, but they also can't exist in the world as she's remade it, and that meant she had to get creative. So she's using them to patch the holes, to fill in the characters she decided were necessary but whose actors have already stopped their dancing. I'd be impressed, if I weren't so busy hating her."

"I don't understand how this isn't causing harm," I said. "I get how she's justifying it to herself, but that doesn't make it true. She's causing harm."

The end of the bed dipped as the Luidaeg sat. I focused on my breathing, not letting it get unsteady or too fast. Not just in a room with two Firstborn. In a bed with two Firstborn.

Oh, I was so going to die.

"You know, the Toby I know spent some time as a fish because my sister wanted her out of the way, and the man she'd sent to do the removing couldn't go through with it," she said, mildly. "Instead of killing her like he was supposed to, he transformed and left her, and that was the most merciful thing he could have done under the circumstances, and she hated him for it for a really long time. How dare he take her away from her family for fourteen years. How dare he change her without her consent. But he was thinking in centuries, and she was thinking in days. Titania doesn't even think in centuries. She thinks in millennia. In her mind, I'm sure, this is a form of mercy. She did no harm."

"I don't agree," I said stiffly.

"If it helps, neither do I. But this isn't what you want to ask me."

"How do you know?"

"I'm good at listening to the questions people aren't actually asking. Go ahead, girl. Ask me what you really want to know."

"You talk about the other me like you . . . like you know her. I mean *really* know her. Can you tell me about her?"

"Ah. That's what I was expecting." The Luidaeg exhaled, chuckling. "I can even give you this one for free, because it hurts as much as it heals, and that means no payment is required. Yeah. I know October. I met her when she was just a kid, when Amy—her mother— was hiding her in the human world, pulling the fae out of her veins one drop at a time. I met her, and I saw what her mother was doing to her, and I told Sylvester Torquill what was happening that same day. Sometimes I've wondered what would have happened if I'd been able to find his brother and put the burden of October's future on his shoulders. Simon was in service to my sister by that point, tangled tight in poisoned thorns and half-lost to himself, but he still loved his wife, and he was October's father in the eyes of Faerie. I might have saved them both if I'd asked him to do his duty by the child. But I didn't, and so that wasn't the life we lived.

"The Changeling's Choice isn't a thing in this Faerie, because it's been made already for all the changeling children, but where I come from, when a changeling is born, and gets old enough that their magic starts to show, their fae parent offers them a choice. Are you human, or are you fae? And if they choose fae, they're whisked away to the Summerlands, never to see their human parents again."

"What if they choose human?" I asked cautiously. Surely that didn't happen. Surely no one would look at the choice between magic and mortality and choose the slow, lumbering, *mortal* way.

"They die," said the Luidaeg bluntly.

I couldn't see her face, and so it didn't do me any good to stare at her. I did it anyway, aghast at her calm reply. "How is *that* a kinder world?" I blurted.

"Did I say our world was kinder? Because I don't think I did," said the Luidaeg. "It's not. It's horrible and it's cruel and it's wrong, and when Amy was born with the power in her hands to make that choice a real one, I thought it would end. I thought we'd be able to have our changeling children and take them home forever, or free them to the world they preferred. It's still a one-way choice, and that's still wrong, but it's better than the grave. And then Amy refused to take up the calling her magic demanded, and August was gone and you had no idea what you were, and the changelings kept dying, and Faerie didn't heal. Our problems go a lot deeper than one bloodline's power to resolve, kiddo. But no, the Changeling's Choice isn't kind. It's just the way we can reconcile love with the need to keep Faerie safe and hidden. Can you tell me how stealing children away from their parents in the night, leaving those parents no way to grieve or move on, and forcing those children to become servants for people more powerful than them is kinder than the way we do things? I think both systems are horrible."

She leaned over then, touching my hand, very lightly. "My October has been trying to make things better, as best as she can. She wants changelings to be able to live their lives according to their own terms, and she wants the Choice to be a *choice*. She's a hero. I know you're scared. I know you're afraid of losing everything you think you have right now, and I won't pretend that you're wrong to feel that way. When you get your memory back, you're going to learn a lot of things that will probably horrify you after spending time in Titania's sanitized wonderland. But my October's a hero. She's saved our world more than once. Hell, she's saved *me*. She's still inside you, whether you remember her or not, and she's going to come out when we need her. I believe in her, and you are her, so I believe in you."

"I'm not a hero," I said. "I'm a lady's maid."

Her laughter was short and bitter. "As if servants have never been heroes? They've turned the tide of more than one war with unlocked doors and well-timed poisons. You can be a hero no matter where you're standing in the fray. There are people who need you, and people who love you, and people who would be, quite sincerely, lost without you."

"Tybalt," I said, the word bitter and half-familiar on my tongue.

"Kitty-boy," agreed the Luidaeg. "You remember more there than you want to let on, don't you? Can't say as I blame you. Gin says Titania dealt with the complication of the cats by making it so they all died out centuries ago. Right now, all you know about the Cait Sidhe is legend and rumor, and now here's one of them looking at you like . . . okay, let me guess. Like he wants to peel your skin off your flesh and use it to make himself a nice new pair of boots."

"Everyone seems to think saying his name should be enough to make me swoon and demand my memory back, but he keeps *glaring* at me. He's so *angry*. I can't understand why I would . . . why would *anyone* want to give up a life where they're happy to be with someone who's so mad at them?"

"He's not mad at you, kid," said the Luidaeg. "If I know the cat— and I do know the cat, better than I honestly want to, and I can thank you for some of that—but if I know the cat, he's panicked and terrified, and so mad at Titania that he can't see straight. He's mad at the *spell*, Toby, not the person under it. If he seems mad at you, it's not on purpose. I'm not trying to push you to accept or feel something you're not ready for yet, but you're very important to him. Possibly the most important person in his world. He waited a long time for someone to come along who could love him back the way he needed to be loved, who wouldn't leave him, and that's supposed to be you. Right now, he's probably afraid it's not, and that's got to be tearing him up inside. Try not to blame him for feeling the way he does. He's got big feelings. They get the best of him sometimes."

"I thought you couldn't lie."

"I can't."

"So how are you telling me how he feels, if you don't *know*?"

"I can't *lie*, which means I can't speak an intentional untruth, but I can say what I think, and as long as I don't know one way or another, it's allowed. I can't promise you this is all going to be okay. I can't say no one's going to get hurt, or that you'll definitely remember the last four months with enough clarity for the emotional ties to remain. But I can tell you Tybalt isn't mad at you, because I know him better than that. If he's mad at anyone besides Titania, it's probably himself, for not somehow realizing this was a risk and whisking you off to the Court of Cats before she could cast her spell."

She stood.

"Anyway, you're awake now, and if Anthony's going to sleep this off, he can do it with Acacia to watch over him while we go and get on with things. Feeling up for it?"

"Does it matter if I say no?"

"At this point, not really." She sounded halfway sympathetic, which helped. Of course, she ruined it immediately afterward, by saying, "I spent years beating you into a properly heroic shape, and I can't say I'm a big fan of this showroom shine you've got going on right now. Let's fix it."

She left the room, leaving the door hanging open as a rectangle of slightly brighter dimness in the dark. I rose, my bloody kirtle falling stiffly around my legs, and followed her out.

Grianne and Ginevra were in the main hall with Dean, Acacia, and Raysel, who looked much more relaxed now than she had before. Dean, on the other hand, was clearly even more anxious. He rushed out to meet me, grabbing for my arm.

"We have to go to Shadowed Hills!" he blurted.

"Not the best idea for me," I said. "I'm sort of wanted for murder in the Mists right now, and I don't think I can count on a second magical rescue from the Queen's dungeons."

"Grianne says Quentin is serving as Etienne's squire!"

"He is," I agreed, trying to pull my arm away. "He a friend of yours?"

Dean stared at me. "He's *your* squire!"

I blinked. A lot of what he'd said before suddenly made a whole different shade of sense when looked at from that as a starting point. "He most assuredly is *not*," I said. "I'm a changeling. Changelings don't take squires."

"You're also a knight, and knights *do*," insisted Dean.

"Changelings don't get knighted!"

"Yet you did," said the Luidaeg, wearily amused. "You were even a Countess for a hot minute, before you managed to shuffle that responsibility down the line to dear Dean here. Quentin's been your squire for years. Somehow he's not dead yet, which means one of you is doing a better job than I expected."

"But . . ." I stopped, shaking my head. "But Quentin hates me. Always has."

"Does he hate you, or does he hate changelings?" asked the Luidaeg. "Because I remember some of the ideas about changelings he had when I first met him, and it sounds to me like Titania would have been leaning pretty hard on those prejudices when she gave him his history. She told him changelings were inferior. That they exist so every pureblood gets to feel superior to someone, which probably helps her keep the court structure stable. And that changelings never deserve anything more than their existence. He knows the rules. He knows how the world works. And then you come along and screw everything up, the way you always do."

I blinked at her. "What do you mean? I followed all the rules, just like everyone else."

The Luidaeg laughed. "I don't know which is funnier—that you believe that, or that you think *I'm* going to believe it. Kid, no matter how you slice the situation, you're Amandine's daughter, and this time you got to have Simon for a dad. He's always been a soft touch, and nothing I've seen implies that Titania actually took the time to rebuild people from the ground up. She just gave them new histories and plunked them down to get on with it. Did he treat you like you mattered? As much as your sister?"

I nodded. "The rules were different for me, but . . . I was always his daughter. He always loved me."

"How about Amy?"

"She was more distant. She made sure I knew my place."

The Luidaeg nodded. "That all matches up with what I'd expect from them. So here's Quentin, who knows changelings have no value, and here's you, who has a sense of self-worth, even if it's a twisted one, and a family that loves her like she actually belongs, instead of treating her like a disposable object. You would have been like waving a red flag in front of a bull. Oh, he's going to be *appalled* when this is over and he realizes how he could have turned out."

"I'm appalled right now," said Dean.

"If you're coming back to the Summerlands with us, you need to remember you don't exist there; you never have," said the Luidaeg. "He won't know you. No one will know you."

"What about Goldengreen?" asked Dean.

"Held by the Rose of Winter, as it has always been," said Grianne. "We shouldn't go there."

"She's asleep on the Thorn Road," said Ginevra. "There's another imposter behind her face."

"Good to know," said the Luidaeg. "If it's one of the Browns, you've still got a Firstborn-sized weapon on the field. Power set won't be the same, but that doesn't make them less dangerous while Titania has them. So yeah, we stay away from Goldengreen. Sorry, Dean."

"We have ways of getting to the Undersea if we need to use them," said Ginevra. "Your parents are fine."

Dean sagged, exhaling. "Okay."

"Now that we're done with that digression, Dean's right," said the Luidaeg. "Whatever Titania's planning, it's going to be geared to hurt. She doesn't have any available Firstborn she's both willing and able to sacrifice to the Heart, and she has a bone to pick with October here. So she's likely to be going for someone close to her."

"Father and August are in Golden Shore," I said.

"You mean they were last time you spoke to them, but also, Dad bound her so she can't harm anyone you genuinely think of as family, and right now, that protects them both. But it doesn't protect Quentin, or May, or Gillian."

Two of those names were unfamiliar to me, but both clearly meant something to Dean, who looked horrified.

"They're still family," he protested. "She can't—"

"The binding was very specific," said the Luidaeg. "It can't be based on blood, not when half of Faerie is her distant cousin. If Toby doesn't think of them as family, they're fair game. It's not arrogance to say that she could have set this whole thing up for just that reason. And it's possible that because the Heart pre-dates even Oberon, feeding someone into it is the one exception to the clause against harm. But we're ready. We can fight her." She dipped a hand into her pocket, pulling out a small jar filled with bright pink jewels. "And the blood of her blood is going to help us do it. Acacia! We're going to need an exit."

"You're not the master here, Annie," said Acacia, moving toward us with Raysel by her side. "But yes, you do. Lovely as it is to have my daughter home, I want her here because she chooses to be, not because someone else chose to put her here. And I want her to know my grandchild."

"Even if I don't really want to talk to her right now, it sucks to have your mom forget who you are," said Raysel.

"Great, so we have our field trip," said the Luidaeg. "We head for Shadowed Hills, we ask Sylvester for help, and if he refuses, we unbind him immediately. He'll help us once he understands what's been done to him."

"Excuse me," I said. She turned to look at me, eyebrows raised.

"Wasn't sure you knew those words," she said. "Yes, Toby?"

"How is Uncle Sylvester going to help us?"

"He was a hero once, just like you are in my reality, and he's going to be *pissed*. But he's still a noble, which means he'll have access to whatever knowe Titania is using as a base for her Ride. And he'll be able to tell us who he remembers that he didn't remember five minutes before, and who he doesn't remember being dead or missing, which should help us find the other Brown kids."

"If there is anyone else," I countered. "Why are you so sure he'll be able to tell us something we don't know?"

"Because I'm hoping he'll know where my mother is, even if he doesn't realize it," said the Luidaeg. "Oberon and Titania were both inside the radius of Titania's spell, along with half a dozen Firstborn and your maternal grandmother, about whom the less said, the better. We've been gathering in the Mists for more than a century, and whatever pulled the rest of us there, it will have pulled her too. Mom was in range. We look for the people who should be there but aren't, and then we figure out where Titania put them, and we'll find my mother."

"What if she doesn't want to be found?"

"Well, then, we better pray we can break Titania's Ride without Maeve's help, the way Janet Carter broke my mom's, because otherwise, we're all a little more fucked than we were yesterday, and maybe her world becomes the real one after all." The Luidaeg looked at me levelly. "No pressure."

Nope. No pressure there.

TWENTY-ONE

THE ACT OF OPENING a road out of Blind Michael's lands was remarkably anticlimactic after everything we'd already been through. Acacia walked us through the hall until she found a yarrow-banded door, the hinges black with candle smoke and time, and pried it forcibly open, revealing the knowe at Shadowed Hills. After that, we simply . . . stepped through, passing into the Summerlands in the blinking of an eye.

The door swung shut behind us, and we were alone in the forest behind the manor, the sky overhead a pale, bruised shade of twilight that made it impossible to guess the actual time, the lights of the knowe glittering through the trees.

The Luidaeg squared her shoulders. "All right," she said. "Sir Grianne, if you would let the household know we're here?"

Grianne nodded, bowed, and did a backward somersault into air, vanishing, her Merry Dancers blinking out with her as she passed onto the Shadow Roads. The rest of us clustered around the Luidaeg, a motley bunch if I'd ever seen one, waiting for her to come back.

Seconds crawled by. A circle opened in the air and Sir Etienne stepped through, Grianne close behind him. "October, you're all right," he said, with visible relief, before sweeping me into an embrace.

I froze, going stiff. Nothing in my experience up to this point had prepared me to be embraced by Sir Etienne, who had always kept me at a more-than-polite distance.

Always, before he took me to meet his daughter.

Awkwardly, I relaxed enough to pat him on the shoulder. "I'm fine," I said. "Is everything okay with you? Is Chelsea . . ." I wasn't sure how to finish that question, and so I didn't. I just trailed off, letting it hang in the air.

"She's very sorry for what she did," he said. "She was in pain, her thoughts were in a jumble, and she reacted instinctively. The spell shattered even as she pushed you away. We've been able to find no traces of enchantment."

"You didn't notice them before."

He looked abashed. "True enough, but—she seems truly to have been released. Now she asks us about people we don't know, and speaks of a world we've never seen, and I don't . . ." He stopped, finally seeming to notice my strange companions, looking at each of them in turn without any sign of recognition. I heard Raysel's sharp intake of breath. The Luidaeg put a hand on her shoulder.

"Don't know what to do?" asked Ginevra. "Yeah, we've all been experiencing that a lot since this all started."

"Can you help us?" I asked, before the Luidaeg could jump in and say something terrible that would make him run away and sound the alarms. Oh, I was pretty sure she wouldn't mean to. She was just so accustomed to everyone knowing who she was and why they needed to be afraid of her that she didn't stop to think before she spoke.

And I would *not* be the one telling her that. People who criticize the Firstborn don't tend to have long and healthy lives. People who criticize *Maeve's* Firstborn, when the ones we remember at all tend to have been immortalized as monsters, well . . . I have to assume that would be even worse.

"After what you did for me, I owe you anything you care to ask for," said Etienne fervently. "Chelsea is safe now, or will be, once she can stop speaking of a world that never was. Whatever you need."

"See, that's part of the problem," I said. "The world you say never was—it existed. Up until four months ago, it existed. And these people are trying to bring it back, before this world becomes the only one there is." I tensed, waiting for the explosion.

To my profound surprise, it didn't come. Instead, Etienne seized my hands, holding them tightly. "Truly?" he asked.

I nodded. "Yeah. That's what they want to do."

"Do you think they can?" He gave them a more careful, measuring look.

"The skinny teen in the dress made of dead leaves is the sea witch, so yeah, I'm going to say they stand a chance," I said. Behind me, the Luidaeg smirked and raised one hand in a short wave.

Etienne paled. "The . . . the sea witch?"

"It's been a long night. We need to see Uncle Sylvester as soon as possible, because we're sort of on a timetable. What day is it?"

Etienne blinked, looking even more confused than he had a moment before. "Moving Day, of course. The sun rose in the mortal world about two hours ago."

So around nine o'clock in the morning on Halloween, then. We were almost out of time.

"Right," I said. "Okay. We need to see Uncle Sylvester. You're his seneschal. Can you get us an audience? Any sort of time with him?"

"Melly and Ormond have been handling the Moving Day duties," said Etienne. "I believe he's available now, but you can't be seen moving through the knowe, especially with a band of strangers. Not everyone is as well inclined toward you as I am, and the Queen's men have been here inquiring as to your whereabouts. Grianne, stay with them. I'll be right back."

He opened another circle in the air, stepped through, and was gone.

"That could have gone better," said the Luidaeg.

"He really didn't know me," said Raysel, sounding bewildered. "And what happened to the knowe? There's supposed to be a garden promenade right here! I helped Mother plant the roses!"

"That's your answer, rosebud," said the Luidaeg, with surprising kindness. "He didn't know you. No one here knows you. The knowe doesn't know you. You never existed in this world. Titania erased you because you were inconvenient, thus proving that she hasn't changed in all the time she had playing happy families among the rabble."

"Oh," said Raysel, sounding crestfallen.

I barely knew her, but I wanted to hug her when she sounded like that, like her heart was breaking under the weight of everything she couldn't carry.

I was still fighting the impulse when the air opened again and Etienne's arm appeared, gesturing frantically for us to come through. He didn't step through himself, which was a little unnerving, but the scent of his magic was distinctive enough that I waved for the others to follow me as I stepped into his portal.

It led to the dim hall behind the receiving room, the one people used when they wanted to leave Uncle Sylvester's presence without being seen. Chelsea was waiting there by her father's side. She squeaked and embraced me when she saw us coming through, holding me as tightly as I had wanted to hold Raysel. And much like I assumed Raysel would have, I blinked at her, too bewildered to pull away.

"Uh, hi?" I said.

"Oh, sorry!" She let go, stepping back, and I realized she was properly dressed now, having traded her mortal clothes for a dark blue linen gown. Not noble attire, but suitable for a junior daughter of the household. I wondered, briefly, how Etienne was explaining her sudden appearance. Grown children don't normally appear out of nowhere, especially not grown pureblood children.

"I forgot this is only the second time you've met me," she said, abashed. "I'm used to you knowing me a lot better than—Dean!" I was forgotten as she saw the boy behind me, and she all but threw herself in his direction, wrapping her arms around him and holding on for dear life.

Dean, for his part, hugged her back just as tightly, nodding when she murmured something in her ear.

"You know each other?" I asked.

"He's one of my best friends," said Chelsea. "Has been for a while now. I was so scared when no one knew who you were, Dean!"

"Yeah, well, apparently the Undersea was too much trouble to include in this draft of reality, so it got sealed off when everything changed, and that made me impossible, so I got chucked into Blind Michael's lands."

"Island of the Misfit Toys much," said Chelsea. She looked past him to Raysel and grimaced, just a little. "Oh, and you found Rayseline."

"I'm sorry, have we met?" asked Raysel.

"We don't have time for the full dance of reunions every time we run into someone new," said the Luidaeg. "Sorry if that makes me a party-pooper, but I'd rather win than be polite. Etienne, we asked you to take us to the Duke. Why are we not with the Duke?"

"The Lady Amandine is meeting with him at the moment," said Etienne. "I needed to get you out of sight, but I felt bringing you into her presence would be unwise."

I glanced to the Luidaeg. "I could disenchant her . . ."

She shook her head. "No, kid. You wouldn't care for the results."

Some of the things people had said about my family and my relationships with them were trying to come together to form a picture I really didn't care for. I scowled at her. "Why not?"

"Because she's never going to forgive you for choosing Simon in the divorce," she said, bluntly. "It's not about the fact that he's not related to you by blood, or the fact that she tried—and failed—to turn you mortal before you could fall into Faerie. It's the fact that Amy never learned to share her toys. You were *hers*. Deciding you didn't want to be hers anymore was an unforgivable crime against her. Right now, she doesn't know that happened. Right now, she probably thinks less fondly of you than you do of her, but she isn't actively angry with you. Take the illusion off, and that goes away."

"Take the illusion off, I definitely lose my family," I concluded dryly.

"Take the illusion off, lose the family Titania made up for you, to torture you—and, to a degree, to torture Simon, even if neither of you really understands it's happening." The Luidaeg's expression was grim. "I've seen you both work way too long and hard to find a way to be happy in the *real* world, I'm not losing you to this one. Also, you can't break the spell on more than a few people in one go, and I'm not letting you incapacitate yourself for *Amy*."

She said my mother's name with such sincere loathing that I blinked, briefly taken aback. I was used to people speaking of Amandine in hushed, awed tones, like she was the greatest gift Oberon had ever given to Faerie. But the Luidaeg talked about her like she was a nuisance, and the Luidaeg couldn't lie. It was . . . disorienting, to say the least.

Etienne sniffed, drawing our attention back to him.

"To make matters worse, our fair Queen of the Mists has sent her guard to find you," he said. "His Grace was able to assure them in all honesty that we were not harboring any fugitives from the Queen's justice within Shadowed Hills, and he managed to avoid promising to notify them if you returned home. They're also quite interested in speaking to your father and sister, but they have gone and disappeared for some reason . . ."

He trailed off, clearly hoping one of us would jump in with their location.

"We left them with our traveling companions," said Ginevra, apologetically. "I doubt Tybalt will have been idle while we were journeying.

They could be virtually anywhere by now. I just hope he had the sense not to take them to the Undersea. I doubt Duchess Lorden would take kindly to seeing members of her family enthralled so, and they have no mechanism for breaking the enchantment in the deeps."

"I'm going to pretend that statement made any sense to me at all," I said, with forced cheer. "We split the party in Golden Shore, Etienne. We had to. I couldn't stand the thought of traveling with the King of Cats, and I wasn't dragging August into danger."

"No, just charging into it headlong," said Etienne. He sighed. "This will be the last time you can come here, you understand. If you're caught . . ."

"If I'm caught, I'm likely to be executed, because I made the horrible mistake of being a changeling alone in the city during the period where custom and etiquette says I should have been safe," I said. Chelsea looked guilty. "No, Chelsea, I don't blame you for lashing out. I blame the culture we've all been complicit in, that I never really stopped to think about too hard, for leaving me unable to defend myself—either practically, since I was never allowed to learn how, or legally. Those men assaulted *me*. Those men harmed *me*. But I killed one of them trying to stay alive, and so I'm the criminal. Yes, he's dead, and yes, I agree that there should be some justice for him, but we have blood-workers! They could watch my memory and know I acted in self-defense! I'm not going to let the Queen's men take me, because self-defense isn't going to matter to them, and it should. I *should* be able to say 'He stabbed me in the stomach, I was just trying to defend myself.'"

"And she finds some of her self-respect where Titania hid it in the couch cushions," said the Luidaeg dryly. "Good for you, Toby."

I glanced at her, then looked back to Etienne. "If my mother sees me, she'll turn us all in."

"Yes," he said, sounding relieved that he didn't have to tell me that. "That's why we're out here."

"Where's Bridget?"

"Back at the house." He glanced at Chelsea. "According to Chelsea, in the world she remembers, we were able to live together as a family here in Shadowed Hills. I'm doing my best to believe the things my daughter tells me, but that seems a step too far."

"For this version of Faerie, maybe," said Chelsea.

Someone knocked on the door, light and quick, in a staccato pattern. Etienne turned.

"Ah," he said. "She's gone. We are called to audience."

He and Grianne moved to open the door, and the rest of us stepped through, emerging behind the dais where my uncle's chair sat, presumably with my uncle currently included. There was no one else in evidence. I turned to blink at Etienne.

He shrugged as he followed us through. "I asked the household staff to alert me when I might have a moment's privacy to speak to His Grace," he said. "They generally know better than to linger when such requests are made."

"Right," I said.

It was easy to fall into the habit of wariness. When everyone could be at least two people—the one I knew and the one from a world I couldn't remember—it was hard to trust what anyone said about this "other Faerie." It would be easier when the world was singular again, even as I started to accept that the world as I knew it wouldn't be the one remaining when this was all over. Or shouldn't be, at least. This world was a lie. A beloved lie, but still a lie, and the real world was waiting.

Maybe Tybalt would glare at me less when I remembered why I loved him. Or maybe I was just the kind of person who thought it was a good idea to marry a man who didn't know how to smile. Either way, I wasn't going to force the rest of Faerie to live a lie just because I had issues with my own idea of a love life.

Together, we walked around to the front of the dais, where Uncle Sylvester was indeed waiting, slouched in his chair like always, a goblet of something in one hand. We were too far away for me to smell the contents, but after the night he'd surely had, and the day he was currently having, I'd have been surprised if they weren't alcoholic.

He turned toward the sound of our footsteps, dull interest on his face, and bowed his head in acknowledgement of our presence.

"Ah, more strange faces, no doubt bringing more talk of other worlds and lives lived differently." He scoffed, then took a deep drink from his goblet. "I want to disbelieve it, but I can't." His gaze shifted to Raysel. "And who are you meant to be? My poor dead sister, returned from the night-haunts to torment me for failing to save her when the sky fell down?"

"I'm . . ." Raysel faltered. "I'm really not sure how to answer that question without making things even worse."

"How did Titania think, even for a minute, that she was making a better version of Faerie? Her version of Faerie is full of people who can't exist and people she's locked in little rooms where she won't have to look at them any longer!" My voice was getting louder, and I knew it. My frustrations were starting to bubble over. "Better for *her*, maybe."

That was when the doors slammed open, and a group of armed and armored figures in the Queen's livery marched into the room, swords and polearms at the ready. The figure at the front of their company was sadly familiar, bronze hair glinting in the torchlight, the arms of Shadowed Hills on his breast and a triumphant expression on his face.

"I told you she'd be here," said Quentin loudly, as the figures advanced on our position.

"You little—" I started to step forward. The Luidaeg's hand on my shoulder stopped me.

"No," she said. "We *need* you. If we lose you, the game's up. Come on, we're getting out of here." She turned to Ginevra and said, "Take her where the Liar locked the door."

She pushed me toward Ginevra, who grabbed my arm. "You're going to hate this," she said, apologetically. "I'm sorry."

Then she fell backward, dragging me with her, and we were plunged into the darkest, coldest place I had ever been in my life. There was no air. I couldn't breathe. I struggled against the hands that held me, trying to break away, and Ginevra responded by yanking on me harder, clearly trying to pull me along.

The only thing worse than being there would be being left there with no one to help me make my escape. I stopped fighting and allowed her to pull me, stumbling, through the dark. It felt like my hair was starting to freeze. It felt like *everything* was starting to freeze. I was going to die in the dark. We were both going to die in the dark. I was going to die in the dark, and I was never going to see my sister again—

And then we were breaking back out into light and air and I took a huge, gasping breath, even as I resumed fighting against her grasp, drumming my fists against Ginevra until she let me go and I dropped to my knees in the back garden of my mother's tower, crushing one of Father's mint plants beneath me. The scent of it filled the air, sharp and herbal-sweet, as I fought to get my breath back.

When I stopped feeling quite so much like I was going to suffocate, I raised my head and glared at Ginevra. "What the *hell* was that?" I demanded.

"The Shadow Roads," she said. "They're how the Cait Sidhe get around. Tybalt told me you'd traveled that way before, he said—"

"He doesn't know *anything* about me." I pushed myself to my feet, turning a slow circle. We were alone. "Great. And now we've lost the others. What are we supposed to—"

A circle opened in the air and Etienne tumbled out, the Luidaeg landing on top of him. She had an arrow jutting out of her arm, and while she didn't look particularly bothered by it, she didn't look happy, either.

The next portal followed a moment later, discharging Chelsea and Dean. "Sorry," said Chelsea. "Overshot, wound up in Dreamer's Glass for a second."

"I said 'the Liar,'" said the Luidaeg, picking herself up from the ground.

"Riordan lied plenty when I knew her," said Chelsea, expression going hard.

The air shimmered just before Grianne stepped out of it, pulling Raysel along. Etienne rushed to her. "The Duke?" he demanded.

"Under arrest for sedition," she said, sounding almost amused as she let Raysel go and brushed herself off with her hands. "Guess someone told Queenie he might be willing to talk to a renegade changeling. One of his knights had been acting erratically." She raised an eyebrow, silently indicating that it couldn't have been her, since she'd been gone all night.

"We have to go back," said Etienne. "We have to rescue him!"

"From the Queen?" asked the Luidaeg wearily. "When you know she's got the backing of the lady who created this whole mess? Please. It's not going to happen. We need to focus on our mission. Titania's going to be too busy trying to organize a Ride without horses to oversee a kangaroo court. Sylvester can wait out as much time as we have left on the clock."

"If I see that little snake, I'm going to knock his smug teeth down his throat," I grumbled.

"No, you won't," said the Luidaeg. "Believe me, once he's himself again, the kid's going to be just as upset as you are right now. Guess a world without you playing your normal merry havoc on everything around you is a world where he got to be the prejudiced little princeling my sister was aiming for when she brought him here in the first place. So at least we know she'd be happy here, if she weren't missing the whole thing. Titania didn't *actually* change history. If she had, I doubt we'd be having this conversation, since I'm not sure even getting rid of her sister justifies the thorn in her side that is you. She just made everyone think things had happened differently, and that means all the same pieces are in play."

"I hate this," moaned Raysel, and sat down on the little bench Father kept for his tools—and his daughters. She put her head in her hands. "I should have stayed asleep."

"Why are we here?" I asked. "This is my mother's tower."

"Exactly," said the Luidaeg. "The wards are set to admit family and people family allow, and no one else. If you let us all in, we're safe."

If I let them all in, I was dead as soon as my mother found out about it. Then again, that was already the case. "Sorry, Mom, decided I didn't like being a lady's maid anymore, so I went and helped the sea witch upset the natural order of things" wasn't exactly the sort of excuse she was going to accept.

"Right," I said.

"Before the Queen's guard figures out where we went, if you don't mind," she added, with a slight edge to her tone.

"Right," I repeated, and moved to open the back door. "As guests of the house, you are welcome in my company," I said.

"Great," said the Luidaeg, and tried to walk past me, only to bounce off the wards and fall down.

I blinked at her. "That wasn't supposed to happen."

"Well, it did!"

"I'll go see what's wrong," I said, and tried to walk through the open door—only to bounce off exactly as she had.

I wasn't on the tower wards.

TWENTY-TWO

I STOOD THERE, LOOKING BAFFLED and betrayed, as the Luidaeg got her feet back under her.

"Motherfucker," she said, with fervor. "I should have thought of this."

"Thought of what?" I asked.

"Have you ever gone anywhere alone that you can remember, or— let me amend that—have you gone anywhere alone in the last four months?"

"Of course," I said. "I mean . . ." I trailed off, realizing I couldn't actually remember a time when I'd left the tower without either August or Father by my side to make sure I got back safely. I paused for several seconds, blinking, then looked up at the Luidaeg. "No. I haven't."

"That's what I thought. Remember, I said this wasn't a real world, just something cast on top of the real world. Which means that really, you're the daughter who chose her other parent in the divorce, and really, you're the one she was more than willing to lose. She took you off the wards." The Luidaeg sighed. "We can't hide here."

"Then where are we supposed to go?" asked Dean. "We can't go to Goldengreen, we'll never make it to Golden Shore with just Chelsea capable of covering that kind of distance, the Queen is looking for us, Toby's wanted for murder, and half of us don't exist!"

"I'm wanted too, now," said Grianne. She didn't sound particularly troubled. Rolling her shoulders in a shrug, she looked at me. "Quentin saw me grab Raysel. He knows I'm on your side."

"This just gets better and better," I said. "Okay. Where else can we go?"

"Unless we want to head for the Undersea, I'm not seeing a lot of choices," said Ginevra. "And there's no way most of you would survive the Shadow Roads long enough to get there. Toby would, normally, but right now, I'm a little loath to try it."

"I don't know this world the way people Titania bothered to enchant do, and that's a good thing, because you don't want me on the other side." The Luidaeg looked to Etienne. "Tell me about Chelsea."

He blinked. "I hardly think this is the time—"

"I don't see where we're going to have a better time. I know her story where I come from, and that's the story she knows now too. Tell me *your* version."

"I . . . My liege was having one of his moods, and I felt uneasy in his halls. I decided to go wandering in the human world for a time, and see what could be seen. I admit, I did think to perhaps dally with a mortal woman and fulfill my duty to Faerie, if I found her comely and she found me an acceptable lover." His cheeks flushed red at the admission. "I remembered the tales I had from my own father, of mortal women when he was young. He made it sound like an endless parade of carnality, like the hint of otherworldliness I carried on my shoulders would be an irresistible attraction and they would fall over themselves to bed me."

"But it wasn't like that, was it," asked the Luidaeg, with poisonous amusement. "Turns out, humans are people, and you can't just crook your finger and make their clothes come flying off."

"Indeed," said Etienne, with some vestigial frustration in his voice. "The stories I'd always been told about the human world were untrue, and I began to sate my curiosity by spending time there, trying to learn the fact behind the fiction. I met Bridget in a coffee shop near the university campus, in Berkeley. She was clever and cutting, and before long, I was smitten. When she welcomed me to her bed, it felt not like I was blessing her house with magic, but like she was giving me a great and wonderous gift of which I might not be found worthy. Through her company, I came to learn still more of humanity— and I was not the only one learning. My Bess is what the humans call a 'professor of folklore.' She studies stories of our kind, and passes them on to human youngsters as they prepare for their adulthoods. By the time she found herself with child, she knew full well what I was, having worked it out some time before."

He took a deep breath. "I still thought to be away with the babe in the night. I loved her mother very well, and had no desire to harm her so, but I knew my duty, and I knew why I had dallied with her in the beginning. Chelsea was an infant. She would never have known. I entered the nursery. I picked up my infant daughter. And the door opened, and Bridget was there, an iron pan in her hand, telling me our affairs were not so easily ended.

"We spoke honestly after that, for perhaps the first time, and while it took some time for trust to be reestablished, we found a new peace between us. I stayed by her side, attending to my duties in Shadowed Hills at night and returning to her during the day. We raised our girl together. I taught them both what I could, to keep Bridget safe and Chelsea concealed, and we prepared to run for Golden Shore on the day when concealment ceased to be possible. But Bridget loved her job, and I loved my liege, and we didn't want to go. I began to watch for opportunities to have away with one of Simon's daughters, in the hopes that they could cut our tangled knot in two."

"Was that your only way out?" asked the Luidaeg. "Had you heard rumors, maybe, of a place where changelings could go without leaving the Mists?"

"Everyone's heard those rumors," said Etienne dismissively.

"Yes, but I'm not a part of the world where you were raising your daughter in secrecy, and I'm not part of 'everyone,'" said the Luidaeg. "Tell me what you heard."

"Supposedly," said Etienne, with slow displeasure, "changelings who find themselves dissatisfied with their place can flee to a man who lives in the underworld of the mortal side of San Francisco, and he will hide them, protect them, and put them to work. The rumors say he has a knowe of his own, or perhaps a shallowing, a space scraped out of the Summerlands and barred to pureblood intervention. They say the changelings who go to him are thieves and worse, and that he never lets them go. To serve him once is to serve him evermore and always."

"His name?" asked the Luidaeg.

"Devin," said Etienne.

"Dead in my world, but okay," said the Luidaeg. "Makes sense, though. Stacy was one of his 'kids,' and Titania was Stacy—she remembers everything Stacy knew, which means Devin would seem like a logical safety valve for the pressure that this kind of system is going to build up. People are still people, even here, and even if some of the rules you're living under are so contradictory that you've all learned to tie your own brains in knots to justify them, as long as she leaves you with free will, some of you are going to rebel. Golden Shore catches the ones who want out of the system but don't want to leave Faerie altogether, and Devin takes care of the rest. That's where we can go. We can't stay here, we can't access the tower, and we can't make it all the way to Golden Shore without exhausting Chelsea and getting us all caught. But we can go Home."

The way she said that, it became a proper noun, meant to be capitalized and noted. I frowned. "How are we supposed to get there?"

"We have a decent number of teleporters, but I'm the only one who knows the way, assuming it's in the same place here that it was in reality," she said, frowning, and looked to Chelsea. "Hey. You're used to living in the human world, right?"

"Right," said Chelsea.

"Can I give you an address?"

"Like a street address? Sure. It'd help if you can give me some landmarks to go with it, but if you know where we're going, I may know the way."

"And can you hold a portal open long enough for us all to get through?"

"I held bigger and farther when we went to Toronto for the wedding," said Chelsea smartly.

The Luidaeg smirked. "Just checking. Okay." She rattled off a string of names and numbers that meant nothing to me, ending with the location of something called a "BART station." Chelsea nodded, apparently understanding every incomprehensible word.

She took a few steps away from the group, taking a deep breath. "Okay. I have a longer range than most Tuatha—and that's not bragging, Dad, you're the one who told me that—but I haven't been doing much beyond popping myself around for the last four months. I need a second to center myself before I do this."

"Take as much time as you need, while remembering that eventually someone's going to think to come looking for us here." The Luidaeg smiled at her, showing serrated teeth. "I'd say 'no pressure,' but I can't lie."

Chelsea glared at her without heat. What kind of world was the "real" Faerie, if kids weren't afraid of the sea witch?

Finally, Chelsea raised both hands, inscribing a wide circle in the air. On the other side, I could see a brick wall, stomach-churningly like the alley I'd landed in when she'd shoved me through a different portal. The air crackled with the smell of her magic.

"Through here," she said, sounding strained. "I opened the door in an alley. You should be able to get through without being seen."

"Don't forget human disguises," said the Luidaeg. "We're stepping into the mortal world." She called no magic, cast no spells, but her features shifted subtly as she moved toward the circle, becoming indefinably mortal in a complex, concrete way.

The air hummed with a dozen conflicting scents as everyone else called their magic and wrapped themselves in the illusions they'd need to pass unseen among the mortals. I grimaced. Father had shown me the way of it, but I'd never actually done it on my own before; the thought of doing it now was daunting. And I didn't have any choice.

The blood garnets in my pocket were a sweet temptation, offering strength beyond what I could manage on my own. Too much strength, really, for such a small task. It would be a waste of the Luidaeg's gift, and a betrayal of my own magic, simple as it was. Instead, I pinned the inside of my cheek between my teeth and bit down until pain lanced through me and blood filled my mouth, coppery and sweet.

This time, I wasn't fast enough to shove the memory away.

I am standing in a large, square room littered with ancient furniture, upholstery torn and stained with unknown fluids. A scavenged generator buzzes in one corner, powering two refrigerators, an antique jukebox, and the overhead lights. Harsh, angry music blares from the jukebox speakers, making my sternum vibrate with the beat. The air smells like smoke, vomit, stale beer, and too many people trying to live in too little space.

Changelings lurk around the edges of the room, more than I've ever seen in one place before, making no effort to hide or downplay themselves. One girl has hedgehog spines for hair; another has feathers, white as snow and standing up in all directions. A boy with tusks like a boar watches me mistrustfully as the man in front of me looks me up and down, a small smile on perfect lips.

His eyes are purple, irises patterned with the outline of flower petals, and he fascinates and terrifies me. He looks at me like he knows exactly what I'm worth on the open market, and he can't wait to offer me there.

"October," he says, in a voice like rum and honey. "So glad you came to join us at last. I always knew you'd see the light eventually. We've been waiting."

The memory shattered there, leaving me confused and a little dizzy, the taste of blood lingering on my tongue. I swallowed and grabbed for the air, gathering ribbons of magic out of the nothingness around me. Weaving them into the image Father had shown me, I cast them over myself and pulled them tight, trying to hide myself behind a veil of borrowed humanity.

It fought me, but in the end, with the blood in my mouth, I was stronger than the spell was stubborn, and the illusion fell into place. I shook the last of the gathered magic from my fingers like I was shaking away cobwebs, stood up a little straighter, and stepped forward into Chelsea's circle and out the other side.

The air in the alley was cool and smelled like decay, as well as the various other unpleasant smells I was coming to associate with the human world—car exhaust and a faint, omnipresent hint of burning. I wondered what it must be like for the mortals, to live in a place that smelled like it was on fire all the time.

Chelsea closed her hands. The circle vanished.

"I kept that open for a while," she said, without heat or blame. "Someone might be able to follow us, if they get to the tower before my magic fully dissipates."

"So we get moving," said the Luidaeg. She looked around at our little group, finally focusing on me, Raysel, and Grianne. "The three of you have the least experience in this kind of city. Stay close, don't talk to anyone, and save your questions until we're safely at our destination. Even things you might think of as innocuous are suspect right now and could attract attention. We don't want to attract attention. Attention is bad. And we're going to get enough of it just from the way Toby and Grianne are dressed."

"Says the woman wearing a dress literally made of dead leaves," muttered Ginevra.

I blinked, looking down at my bloodstained kirtle. "I'm sorry," I said. "I don't know how to disguise clothes."

Grianne, who was wearing a human face and her normal livery, simply shrugged. I realized with a start that I couldn't see her Merry Dancers. Their absence made the always-stoic Candela look virtually emotionless, like she'd been disconnected from her own face. It was unnerving.

Everyone looked weird, really, except Chelsea, who'd seemed human when I met her, and the Luidaeg, who wore humanity like a comfortable chemise. She huffed in annoyance and announced, "It would be inconvenient if you got me caught, which makes this selfish as hell," before waving her hand vaguely in my direction.

There was a rush of cold, like a wave had broken over me while somehow leaving me entirely dry. I looked down.

My kirtle had been replaced by more of those strange blue trousers and a T-shirt advertising some sort of festival in the park in bold yellow letters against a green background. I glanced back up, blinking. Grianne was dressed similarly.

The Luidaeg shrugged. "Come on. We need to get to Devin," she said, and stepped out of the alley, making further conversation impossible.

We followed, a small gaggle of visibly uncomfortable people moving down the street in the mortal world, cars blasting by us only a few feet away, humans walking past in both directions. They didn't swerve as they approached our group, just pushed on through like we weren't even there, and none of them gave us a second look.

It was disorienting and disconcerting and borderline exhilarating. I was used to being ignored because I wasn't worth noticing, by purebloods who made sure I *knew* they weren't acknowledging me, but were always aware of my position. This simple social invisibility was strange enough to appeal. I wasn't sure that would last if it kept happening, but for the moment, it was a nice distraction from how absolutely alien everything around us was.

We turned down a smaller street, this one lined with buildings that looked like they were in the final stages of disrepair before they were pronounced no longer habitable and razed to the ground by whoever was in charge of maintaining human cities.

The Luidaeg led us to the worst of the lot, a squat, filthy rectangle with wood covering the windows and graffiti scrawled all across the front. It was wedged between a building promising rooms for the night and a taller building with a sign in the window promising discretion and skilled massage. A simple brass sign hung above the door. HOME: WHERE YOU STOP.

The sign seemed to pulse with the power of the misdirection spells that had been worked over and into the metal, lending a palpable tint to the air. I sniffed, marking it for Coblynau work, and nodded. It was a clever way of keeping humans away.

The Luidaeg jerked her chin toward the sign. "Deflects anyone with less than a quarter fae blood elsewhere. Also makes it pretty uncomfortable for anyone with no human blood in their veins to get too close. So congrats. You're the only one here who doesn't feel like they have spiders in their shirt right now."

I blinked and glanced over my shoulder at the others. They were squirming, clearly uncomfortable, but not running away.

I was so unaccustomed to things being kinder to changelings than they were to purebloods that I didn't know how to respond to that, just turned and looked back at the Luidaeg, waiting for her to tell us what to do next.

She looked annoyed. "I'm not used to you having no self-determination," she grumbled, and gestured toward the door. "Well? This is where you let us in."

That sounded simple enough. I walked up to the door, hesitating when I saw that it was properly closed, then turned the knob and pushed it open, revealing the room I'd seen in my blood memory. Except for the teens lurking in the corners and the song on the jukebox—a word I had definitely recovered from the flashback to someone else's life— nothing had changed. The kids turned to look at us with dull disinterest as we filed inside, none of them giving any clear reaction to our presence. It was as if they'd been instructed to look as unimpressed as possible.

One, a scrawny Daoine Sidhe changeling seated in a tattered easy chair next to the generator, sniffed the air and then glared. It was remarkable mostly because it was the only reaction our arrival had gotten from any of the residents. "Purebloods," he spat, shoving violently purple hair out of his eyes with one hand. "You have no business here."

"Kid, I have business anywhere I want to go, and she's not a pureblood," said the Luidaeg, indicating me as she spoke. "We're here to see the boss."

The teen stood, still glaring at us. "What if the boss isn't here to see you?"

"Oh, he will be," said the Luidaeg. She smiled, and while her face hadn't changed, there was nothing human about her teeth, not anymore. They were a jagged nightmare of points and edges, combining all the worst aspects of a shark and a viperfish. I was at least supposedly on her side, and that smile made me want to run out of the room.

"See, if he has you on front-room duty, he trusts you to watch out for his interests and his place," she said. "He believes you have the sense to recognize a threat. And that includes recognizing one of the Firstborn when we walk through the door. Get me Devin. Right now."

The kid looked around at the other lurking teens, and shrank into himself as he saw no support there. "Stay here," he mumbled, and made for a door at the back of the room, vanishing deeper into the building.

"That wasn't very nice," chided Ginevra, looking around with interest. "Glad to see some things haven't changed."

"This place sure hasn't," said the Luidaeg.

"Its existence is a change for me," said Ginevra. "This was all before my time. It burned to the ground while I was still living in Portland."

"Arson is a real good way of making sure a closed door stays closed," agreed the Luidaeg, as the door at the back opened again, and the teen stepped back out, followed by the man from my vision.

Like all the kids who apparently worked for him, he was a changeling, easy in his mortal clothes like he had never worn anything else in his life, perfectly suited to and comfortable in his surroundings. His hair was a dark gold without the blood tinting it red, and he was strikingly handsome in a way that made my breath catch.

He said something to the teen, who nodded and returned to his former post, looking far more relaxed now that he wasn't being asked to do things for the purebloods in the room. This done, the man walked calmly toward us. He didn't hurry: we weren't worth that. He also didn't dawdle. We might not have earned his urgency, but he had the sense not to give us his disdain.

The Luidaeg looked at him serenely. "She did an excellent job of recreating you," she said. "If I didn't know . . . Well, that's a matter for later. We come claiming sanctuary."

"Home is a place for the runaways and the castoffs of the Courts," said Devin, voice mild. "But only one of you qualifies for the kind of help we have to give. We'll take her." He indicated me. "The rest of you can take your trouble somewhere else. This isn't the place for it."

"All we need is—"

"A place to hide? Yeah, we hear that about once a season, from someone who's managed to get on the wrong side of the Queen. The streets are buzzing with the news that a changeling from Shadowed Hills broke the Law and disappeared. Seems to me you've got her, and you want us to shelter you all while you wait for the problem to blow over. Well, guess what? It's not going to blow over. Murder is one of those things that tend to linger in the air for a while. Can't just wish it away and hope things will go back to normal. We can hide the changeling. The rest of you should run."

I fingered one of the blood gems in my pocket, wondering how dense the web of pink lines around him was going to be when I finally got the chance to check. And I was pretty sure that was where this was going, from the way he was challenging the Luidaeg. I hoped the real Devin, whoever he'd been, had more common sense than that. Defying the Firstborn is never a path to a long and healthy existence.

The Luidaeg snorted. "I am the sea witch, shadow on the tides and monster at the bottom of the sleeping sea," she said. "I don't *run*. I'm the thing people run *from*."

"Yet here you are, asking me for sanctuary."

"Because you're the only one here to offer it."

Devin crossed his arms. "What can you give me?"

The Luidaeg scowled.

The two of them seemed likely to keep going for a while, and so I drifted away, moving toward the Daoine boy with the purple hair. He eyed me mistrustfully.

"Hello," I said. "I'm October."

"Good for you. Parents couldn't afford a name book, had to use a calendar?"

"I'm named after my aunt."

"How kind of them, to make sure you'd never be able to outrun them. My parents did that, too. Gave me a bullshit name no *real* person would ever use for themselves." He looked briefly disgusted. "I left that behind when I split. You can call me Carl."

"Carl?"

"Yeah. A good honest real-people name that real people use without wincing. You should try it."

"I don't think I'd like to be called 'Carl.'"

"Not *my* name, you doofus. You'd pick a new name for yourself, something modern and mundane, something that helps you blend in with everyone else."

The Luidaeg was waving for me to come back. I nodded politely to Carl.

"Not the goal, but I appreciate the advice," I said, and moved to rejoin the group.

Negotiations did not appear to have gone well. Devin was smiling smugly, while the Luidaeg was glowering at him. "I need you to check for the scope of Titania's spell and remove it," she said, curtly.

"You know I can't just—"

"*Now.*"

Her tone didn't leave a lot of room for argument. I popped one of the blood gems into my mouth and closed my eyes, unsurprised by the dense tangle of pink threads that appeared where Devin was standing. It outlined him completely, just like the one I'd seen around Blind Michael—or around the Luidaeg herself, when she'd been a tree.

She'd been a lot less bossy when she was a tree.

Bracing myself, I slipped another blood gem into my mouth and reached out magically, "grabbing" handfuls of the threads wrapped around Devin. His scream was immediate and blood-chilling. Around the room, more clusters of pink shifted as the watching teens began to move in my direction. If I'd been alone, my goose would have been well and truly cooked. As it was, the people I was traveling with fanned out to surround me, protecting me from the advancing figures. I kept pulling.

It was amazing, how quickly this had become almost routine. A small part of my mind noted, analytically, that "can't lie" wasn't the same as "has to tell us everything." The Luidaeg had known this Devin guy was dead before we came there, and that we'd be dealing with an enchanted imposter taking his place. She'd only made a very loose stab at what I could refer to as "diplomacy," if it had even been that, and then pivoted straight to ordering me to unbind him. Whatever she was playing at there, she clearly had a plan and just as clearly wasn't overly interested in sharing it with the rest of us.

I pulled with freezing fingers, feeling the first tendrils of pain uncoil behind my eyes, like flaming worms beginning to burrow into my brain, and ground my teeth together as I forced myself to keep pulling. Even with the Luidaeg's blood in my mouth, this process wasn't *fun*. Oh, it was easier than it had been in the beginning, but that was such a small change that I couldn't really credit it, not now, with my hands full of threads that didn't exist and the cold creeping steadily toward my elbows.

"I *hate* this," I muttered, and bit my tongue hard enough to draw blood.

That was the little extra bit I needed to rally and sink my fingers all the way into the spell, wrenching it away with an effort that left my head pounding and my jaw aching, and not a trace of pink in front of me. Panting, I unkinked my fingers and opened my eyes, just in time to see a much, much smaller figure crumple to the floor. It was a boy, with untidy, pale blond hair, no more than nine years old.

"Andrew," said the Luidaeg, with weary fondness. She moved to scoop the boy off the floor, holding him as easily as if she handled children every day. He dangled in the gawky, totally limp manner of a sleeping child, showing no signs that he was aware of his surroundings.

I bent forward until my hands were resting on my knees, waiting for the room to stop spinning. The teens were still advancing, although they had yet to push the situation to an actual fight.

"What did you do to the boss?" demanded Carl.

I couldn't answer him. I wasn't sure I could talk if I tried. I shook my head, leaving it for the Luidaeg to answer.

"I know you won't like this answer, but she didn't do anything to 'the boss,' because you've never met Devin," she said. "He died six years ago, and Home burned to the ground shortly after. Everything you remember about this place is a lie, planted in your heart like a seed to blossom and grow into a poisonous flower. This isn't your life. This is a cruel joke played on you by someone with so much power that it never occurred to her that she might be doing harm even if she wasn't hurting people directly. And it's all going to be over soon."

"For one of us," he said, and there was a dangerous note in his voice.

Ginevra growled. It was a low, primal sound, and something about the resonance it set up in my bones made my teeth ache while also, paradoxically, chasing away some of the pounding in my head. I stood up straighter, sneaking another of the blood jewels out of my pocket at the same time. I wouldn't have them forever; I didn't want to get addicted. At the same time, I wouldn't be unweaving Titania's spells forever, and I wouldn't need them anymore.

I slipped the blood jewel into my mouth. It burst on my tongue, and the pain receded further, still present but no longer all-consuming. I lifted my head.

Devin's teen army was in a standoff with my equally mismatched assortment of companions, all of whom were watching them with the air of people who didn't want to deal with this right now. Behind me, the Luidaeg turned and walked away, still carrying Andrew.

Chelsea sketched a quick circle in the air and disappeared. The teens flinched and blinked at the space where she'd been, for all the world as if they'd never seen a Tuatha transit before. Maybe they hadn't. Tuatha aren't terribly common in the Mists, and it was entirely possible that these people had never been at a Court that included one.

Sometimes the things we feel are commonplace are the strangest of them all.

Ginevra kept growling. Grianne cracked her knuckles, utterly blank expression all the more unnerving in the absence of her Merry Dancers.

Chelsea reappeared, popping out of the air behind Carl with a coil of braided yellow and green rope in her hands. She tossed one loop of it over his shoulders, then threw the rest of the coil to Etienne, who laughed as he caught it.

"Really?" he asked.

"Really," she said, and disappeared again.

I took a step backward, instinctively shielding Raysel and Dean with the angle of my body as I put a little distance between us and the fight that I could virtually smell coming. The air was thick with tension, and Carl was scrabbling to get the loop of rope off of his shoulders before it could become something more binding.

Etienne handed the rope to Grianne, who curtsied quickly and did a backflip into the air, vanishing. Carl was jerked forward, his efforts to remove the rope ending as he fought to stay on his feet. The rope didn't break, but remained taut, simply disappearing into thin air until Grianne appeared on the other side of the room and jerked it tight, beginning to tie him up by disappearing and reappearing multiple times, the rope somehow never breaking, even when one end of it was clearly anchored on absolutely nothing.

None of the other teens moved to intervene. Willing to intimidate, they might be. Ready to risk their own necks, they most certainly were not.

There had been five of them in evidence when we arrived, including the unfortunate Carl. Now there were seven, two more having emerged from the shadows as the screaming began. None of them looked like they understood what was going on or how they were supposed to deal with it.

Chelsea appeared again, holding more rope. "Anyone who wants to sit down and be tied up without a fuss is more than welcome to surrender," she said, voice bright and cheery. "I'm more than happy to get you secured, and no one has to get hurt. I was a Girl Scout."

That apparently meant something to at least a few of the teens, who immediately sat down to make themselves easier to restrain, expressions of weary relief on their faces. They just wanted to be told what to do. That was an urge I could easily understand. After a life-time of being told what to do, these last few days of being expected to think and decide for myself had been utterly exhausting.

One of the teens decided to try his luck with actually starting a fight, and swung for Ginevra. She moved faster than I would have thought possible if I hadn't watched it happen, grabbing his hand before it could crash into her and pirouetting to bend his arm up behind his back, sweeping his legs out from underneath him at the same time, so that he went crashing to his knees and his arm twisted painfully. He bellowed, the sound more suited to an angry bull than a humanoid figure, and she twisted harder for a moment before plant-ing a foot in the small of his back and shoving him briskly forward to land face-down on the floor. He started to push himself up onto his hands. She kicked him in the side of the head. He stopped trying.

It had all only taken a few seconds. I turned, finally, to see where the Luidaeg had gone. She was sitting on another of those ancient, tatty couches, Andrew stretched out with his head in her lap. She stroked his forehead with one hand, a sympathetic, almost-maternal expression on her face. I staggered toward her.

"What the hell was *that*?" I demanded, once I was close enough that I didn't have to shout. With my head pounding the way it was, shouting would probably have been enough to crack my skull in two. Not wanting to see my brain on the floor, I was keeping my voice down.

"A calculated risk," she said.

"Calculated, my ass. You *planned* this."

"I did." She looked at me calmly. "Blind Michael is dead. She put someone in my brother's place, because she needed a room where she could lock the ones who logically don't exist in this world. Devin is dead. She replaced him so the changelings who broke under the strain of being dutiful little helpers would have somewhere to run. The odds that she was using another of the Brown kids to do it were good enough that I was always going to want to unmask the person who was pretending to be him."

"You could have warned me."

"Not even getting into the layers upon layers of geasa that make that sort of warning difficult for me to give, but no, I couldn't. You would have tried to argue, or pretended you weren't going to do it, and we wouldn't have a place to hide right now, and Andrew would still be wearing a dead man's face." She looked at me coolly. "Trust me, when you're yourself again, you would have been furious if we let him stay bound for even a second longer than we did."

"Why?"

"He's your godson, or as good as," she said. "I told you, his mother was your best friend since childhood. The two of you were teenage dirtbags in this place when you thought you didn't have anywhere else to go, and when the real Home burned to the ground, the kids who survived spoke of you as the ones who got away. Devin didn't like to release his people before he had to, and when you're talking about petty thieves with the potential to live practically forever, well, he rarely felt like he had to do much of anything. You love this kid. On some level, you probably know it even now. There are four living Brown children. We've found two. I have ideas about where the other two might be, and they're not fun ideas, which means they're probably correct. But no, I couldn't have warned you, and no, I'm not going to tell you what comes next, and you should probably check those refrigerators to see if there's anything here worth eating, because we're going to hunker down for a while."

"I thought we were on a timetable."

"We are. The Ride will go down at midnight. It's two o'clock now. We have some time to kill, and you have a headache. I need you to be in top shape when we go up against my stepmother."

"Are we just giving up on finding your mom?" It would have been nice to have a Maeve-sized stick to beat Titania with. We were outnumbered and outmatched, and it was starting to wear on my nerves.

"That was always a long shot, and we don't have the luxury of long shots anymore." She waved the suggestion away. "I wish we could, because *fuck* I am tired of being the adult in the room, but if she wanted to be found, she'd be here now. She's either good or bad that way, depending on how you want to look at it. I *do* believe she's somewhere in the Bay Area, because that's just the way things work right now. I also believe she's not going to get us out of this. Maybe she wants to. Maybe she's locked outside the spell, stuck in the Undersea or just outside the Kingdom. Or maybe she doesn't care, as long as she's left alone to keep getting up to whatever bullshit she's been getting up to while we tear each other apart in her absence. I don't have all the answers, Toby. I just know there's always a way to break a Ride, and Titania's going to choose someone who'll hurt you, which means we'll have the authority to intercede. Now go eat something. It'll help your head."

I threw up my hands and turned to open the nearest refrigerator. Even if everything went back to what passed for normal right now, the fact that I even knew how to open a refrigerator door proved it was never going to be last week's normal, no matter what. Sure, it was just a handle you pulled on, but before the blood memory in Bridget's kitchen, I'd never seen one of these big white boxes before, much less understood that you kept food in them. Now I found that I had all these little whirling bits of information hanging at the edges of my thoughts, telling me things about refrigerators, like that the light inside would go off when I closed the door. Why did I need to know that? Why did anyone need to know that? Did cheese prefer to sit in the dark?

There wasn't much in the way of what I would recognize as food on the shelves. I picked up a package of something that claimed to be ham and a stack of orange flat squares that said they were cheese and carried them with me as I moved toward an open chair.

The tied-up teens glared at me, but none of them tried to interact. That was a relief. I wasn't sure what I would have said to them if they had. "Sorry we had to get rid of your boss, but it's okay, because he was never really him to begin with" was sort of what the Luidaeg had already said, and I couldn't explain it any better than she had.

Dean followed me as I went to sit, Raysel trailing a bit behind him like a pale, anxious shadow. "I'm glad you're back," he said.

"Oh?" I asked, politely, as I began to unwrap the first orange square.

"Yeah. You always know what to do. I'm not so sure about this . . ." He waved his hands, indicating the length of me. ". . . version of you, but you're still you, and you're going to know what to do."

I blinked. His faith in me was staggering, if probably misplaced. I unwrapped another orange square. They were leathery and faintly moist in an unappealing way. "I hope so," I said. "Right now, I don't feel like I know very much, except that I want to go home and I miss my sister."

"Yeah, May's the best," he said.

I frowned at him. "Who? My sister's name is August."

He blanched. "Oh. Um. August's nice too. Right, right, she's your sister before she's my sister— I'm sorry, I'm just not used to thinking of you and her at the same time. She's always Undersea with Peter and our parents, and you're here in San Francisco with May."

"Who's 'May'?"

"Oh. She's your other sister. She was your Fetch when I first met her, and then she wasn't your Fetch anymore, and she's just your sister now."

I stared at him. "My *Fetch*? You mean the death omen? If I had a Fetch walking around, I should be dead by now, not sitting here and trying to help you figure out how to break Titania's Ride."

"Yeah, it was complicated, and I don't all the way understand it. I'm sure someone will explain it to you—oh, or we can get that spell off you, and then no one will have to explain."

"I can't take it off myself, and we need someone else who can tell us more about what they remember after it's broken before we're going to be able to convince August. Acacia is Firstborn, and August will probably wonder if that's why she might have retained more memories than either of us will. My sister can be stubborn like that when she wants to be. Which is pretty much always." I paused, looking across the room to where Chelsea was engaged in a quiet, but apparently vigorous, argument with her father. "Sir Etienne? May I have your kind leave to borrow Lady Chelsea for a moment?"

"I hope this doesn't last long enough for me to get used to you talking like that," muttered Dean.

Raysel giggled behind her hand.

Etienne, meanwhile, looked up sharply, then nodded. "You may, providing she comes right back over here when you're done with her," he said.

"Ugh. Fine, Dad," said Chelsea, and stomped over to join me. "Appreciate the save, Toby. He's being all protective and parental at me, and I'm not used to it, and I don't like it. What can I do you for?"

I decided not to ask about her weird choice of words: it was a distraction from what actually mattered. "I broke the spell that was making everyone take you for a changeling."

"Yes, and I'm way grateful for that." Her expression turned speculative. "Not sure why setting up a whole illusion to lock me out of Faerie was easier than making Dad think my mother was some Tuatha lady who died or skipped town, but whatever. I like my actual mom, and it would have been double-dose trauma if I'd suddenly had to deal with being someone else's kid."

"Up until the spell was broken, though, you really thought you were a changeling. You totally belonged to Titania's version of the world."

"Ah," said Chelsea, and nodded. "You're working your way around to asking how much I remember, aren't you?"

"I am."

She shrugged. "The last four months are really clear. Everything about them is just like I lived through them, all the classes, the commute, watching Mom argue with Dad when he'd get home from the Court, trying not to get caught out by the fae, feeling like something was wrong with the whole world. Like I was out of step with myself. Everything before that is . . . it's there, but it's hazy, almost, like a story someone else told me once and asked me to believe in. The life I actually *lived* is a lot clearer. What's funny, though? I used to be sort of mad at Dad, for not being there when I was a kid. Here I was, not all the way human and trying to cope with that while Mom pulled her hair out looking for ways to hide me, and he was off dancing with the fairies." Chelsea chuckled. "Only in my version of the world, it was because he didn't know I existed. In *this* version, he was there from the beginning. He watched me grow up, he taught me how to throw a punch when I was ten—and I still know how, even if that never really happened. I think I love him more because I dreamt I lived inside a lie. Is that what you needed to know? The love you already had will come back when the spell comes off. The love you grew inside it will still be with you."

"I . . . Yeah," I said. "That's what I needed to know."

I didn't know my own full history, and I didn't see the point in asking. More and more, it looked like breaking the spell was going to be our only real option. Staying as I was wasn't going to be on the table, and to be completely honest with myself, that ship had already more than sailed. I'd seen too many fragments of the other me's life. I understood too many things I should have known nothing about.

And then there was Tybalt.

I didn't know the man. I'd met him once, and I hadn't enjoyed the experience. I was also married to him, and cared about him enough to dream about him even when I had no idea who he was. It was a contradiction in every way possible, and the longer I stayed snarled in this spell, the longer he was living in a world where *I* didn't know *him* but he knew me well enough to look at me the way he had in my first blood memory. I needed to get back to him.

And if what Chelsea said was true, I could do that, and I would still love my sister. That mattered more than anything else. I finally opened the package of ham as Chelsea walked back over to Etienne, pulling out a cold, limp slice of improbably pink meat. I frowned at it. It wobbled.

Glaring at my lunch wasn't going to do me any good. I wrapped the two orange squares around the ham and took a bite, nearly gagging at the taste. It was nothing like either meat *or* cheese, but was some indescribable third thing that my body nonetheless recognized as food. Even as I found the flavor revolting, my mouth demanded I eat the whole roll, and I found myself making a second before I finished swallowing the first.

"Great," I muttered. "Guess this is something I ate before the world changed."

"Yeah, your diet's never been what I would call astonishingly well balanced," said Dean. "If May didn't cook, I think you'd probably have starved by now."

Raysel looked alarmed. "I can't cook," she said.

"Don't worry," said Dean. "If May doesn't feed you, Quentin understands takeout menus."

I couldn't sit through another discussion of Quentin as if he were someone I should voluntarily spend time around. "Excuse me," I said, and stood, walking back over to the Luidaeg. She was still on the couch, eyes closed, clearly awake, since she was sitting perfectly upright and continuing to stroke Andrew's hair with one hand. "Are we just going to sit around here until the Ride starts?"

"You have a better idea?"

"We could *do* something."

She opened one eye. "Oh, very clever. The solver of problems has solved this problem as well. Tell me, o solver, what should we do?"

"We could . . ." I stalled. "We could find my sister. I can't remove the spell from myself, but I think I can convince her to take it off me at this point, if I can just talk to her about it. Back at the tower, you said Chelsea could make it all the way to Golden Shore. She could take me there to look for them. Even if they aren't there, I bet Arden could tell me where they went, and then I could see August. Won't it be easier to break the Ride if I know what I can actually do?"

"That is, somehow, not the most ridiculous plan you have ever proposed to me." She closed her eye again. "But no, Toby. I will not be sending you off on your own to try and find your historically fairly selfish sister and convince her to do something she doesn't want to do. You're staying where I can keep an eye on you."

"Then we should—"

I didn't get to finish saying what we should do. A strange ringing tore through the room, coming from the pocket of my jacket. I blinked, then fumbled to find the source, pulling out the mobile phone I'd

been given all the way back at the start of this adventure. It was ringing. I hit the button to answer it, then raised it to my ear.

"Hello?"

"Is this October?" asked a familiar voice, poisonously sweet and
more menacing than I had ever heard it sound. "You've caused *ever*
so much trouble today, my dear. It's a good thing you're to be executed at sundown, or I'm not sure you would ever be able to show
your face again. Your mother is very disappointed, and your father—
why, your father is heartbroken."

"Hello, Aunt Eira," I said, warily.

The Luidaeg stiffened, sitting up straight as she opened her eyes
once again and turned to face me.

"Where are you, dear heart? I'll send a detachment of knights to
collect you. You must understand that this behavior only brings shame
upon your house. Your sister's prospects will be damaged for years,
if not decades, by your behavior. You're going to haunt her as she
tries to move out into society, making everything harder than it had
to be. If you can't turn yourself in for your mother's sake, do it for
hers. I know you love your sister." Her voice seemed to sharpen as she
went on, going from knife to razor, ready to slice me open and let
everything I was come pouring out.

"I don't think that would be a good idea," I said, stiffly.

"You know I only have your best interests at heart."

"You just said that me being executed at sundown was a good
thing, so no, I don't feel like you have my best interests at heart," I
countered. "I like not being executed."

"Hang up," said the Luidaeg. It wasn't a request.

"I have to go now, Auntie," I said obediently. "I don't think you
should call me again."

"Don't you dare hang up on me, October. I am trying to *save* you."

"By executing me? Goodbye, Eira. I'm sorry we never knew each
other." I could hear her shouting as I lowered the phone, until I finally cut her off with a press of a button. I looked at the Luidaeg.
"They're looking for me."

"We knew they would be," she said. "If the so-called Queen is
herself—which is a possibility, since last time I looked, the real woman
was imprisoned, not elf-shot or dead—she can hurt you. If she's another of the Browns, she can hurt you. What's more, if Titania doesn't
order her to do it, if she's just acting according to her nature, I think

she can do it without triggering Oberon's injunctions. So yeah, they can execute you."

"Anyone ever tell you that you're not very reassuring?"

"Yes. You, several times." She rose, leaving Andrew sleeping on the couch. "Okay, one good thing about this reality: Ginevra says Titania got rid of all the shapeshifting fae a long time ago. That means they don't have Cu Sidhe, they can't track you by scent. And all the magic you've used has been the sort that dissipates quickly, so that's not going to . . . Fuck. Blood. Have you bled since we've been here at Home?"

"No," I said, blinking at her. "I took a few of those blood gems you made for me."

"Okay. Okay. We still need to figure out a place to move to, but that's not as urgent. If you haven't been bleeding . . ."

I wondered about mentioning that I'd bitten my tongue, and decided against it. She was already worked up enough, and that hadn't been *bleeding*, not really. The blood had never left my mouth. It didn't count. Right?

"Stay where you are, and keep not bleeding," she said, and stalked toward Ginevra, clearly on edge. I blinked after her and didn't move. What was she so worried about? The best blood-worker the Queen had was my mother, and Mom would never help them track me down. She might not approve of what I'd been doing, but I was still her daughter. If the Queen asked her to find me, she'd refuse. She was Firstborn. If she really didn't want to do something, nothing in Faerie short of the Three could force her.

The Luidaeg started back toward me, Ginevra beside her. They were halfway across the room when the front door slammed open and a woman surged through, soaring through the air like a dandelion seed on the wind, feet never touching the floor. Flying is a skill inherent to only a few descendant lines, and most of them are bound to the Air Kingdoms, but this figure was as solid as we were, with hair the color of rotting gorse and fingers like long, emaciated talons. Those talons were extended in my direction as she rushed at me, howling.

I shrieked and turned to run, foot hooking on the edge of a nearby chair and sending me sprawling to the floor only seconds before the Baobhan Sith reached the place where I had been. I tried to scramble away, seized with the sudden, irresistible need to flee, and shrieked again as her hand closed over my ankle.

Ginevra slammed into her from the side, roaring, a sound that rolled up and down the scale in primal arpeggios. The Baobhan Sith turned to face her, hissing, and the battle was joined, two constructs of terrible claws and teeth tearing at each other.

The Luidaeg grabbed my arm, helping me off the floor. "I thought you didn't bleed!" she snapped.

"I didn't!" I protested. "I bit my tongue, but—"

"It still counts! She smelled it on your breath! Chelsea!"

Chelsea was abruptly beside her. The Luidaeg shoved me toward her. "Get her out of here. Take her someplace safe. Goldengreen's not an option, but I'm sure you've been someplace submerged."

"Got it," said Chelsea, and began to inscribe a circle in the air, only to stop dead, face going slack an instant before she collapsed to the floor in a boneless heap, a tiny feathered dart protruding from the side of her neck.

Etienne made a wordless sound of despair and lunged to catch her, only to go down in turn as another dart hit him in the upper arm.

Both darts had come from the same corner of the room. I turned to see two Gwragen in the Queen's colors stepping out of the shadow, where they had presumably cloaked themselves in undetectable illusion before they started elf-shooting the members of my party.

They lowered their dart guns, apparently out of ammunition, and drew short swords as they advanced. The Luidaeg looked across the room to Grianne, mouthing the word "Go." The Candela nodded and stepped into the air, vanishing as the men advanced on the two of us.

Ginevra was still occupied with keeping the Baobhan Sith at bay, the two of them ripping and tearing at one another. Three more guards came through the front door, weapons already drawn, just as the Baobhan Sith sank her teeth into the side of Ginevra's throat and bore her, limply, to the ground.

The Luidaeg stepped in front of me. "If we're ever going to get out of this, we need them to take you alive," she said, voice low and tight. "At this point, I think we let them arrest you."

"Can't you do something terrifying and sea-witchy?" I demanded.

"Too many children of Titania," she said. "My hands are tied."

I stared at her. What was the point of following one of Faerie's greatest monsters if she couldn't even protect me from people who wanted to take me to my own execution?

She shrugged, an expression of profound misery on her face, and we stood there, not resisting, as the Queen's men closed in on us.

I didn't really believe any of this was happening until they snapped the rosewood-and-rowan cuffs around my wrists and jerked me roughly forward. One of them grinned at me, a mean little smile.

"Cheer up, changeling," he said. "It's not every day vermin like you gets to go before the Queen."

Oh, hooray.

TWENTY-THREE

THEY CAPTURED DEAN AND Raysel easily, and pried the Baobhan Sith off Ginevra before they cuffed her as well, slapping a sloppy bandage over the bleeding wound in her throat. Two more guards collected Etienne and Chelsea. They left the teens tied up where we'd put them, and didn't bother with Andrew. I didn't point him out. If I was going to be taken, we might as well try to minimize collateral damage.

Then one of them turned to the other and said, "The Queen wants this place burned."

"Hey!" I protested, digging my heels into the floor to stop him from pulling me any farther. He looked at me, disinterested and disdainful. "You can't do that! There are people inside!"

"Changeling runaways," he said, dismissively. "The Law doesn't say anything about them."

"Changelings are still *people*," I argued. "We still feel pain! They're alive, and even if they're runaways, somebody, somewhere, loves them! Someone wonders what happened to them!"

Trying to use someone else's affection for those kids as a justification for keeping them alive felt dirty in a way I couldn't define and had never felt before. People were people. It shouldn't matter whether someone loved us or not. We had a right to exist, and to not be burned alive for the crime of being born.

"The little boy on the couch isn't a changeling," said the Luidaeg, speaking for the first time since they'd clapped the cuffs on her. "He's Firstborn. A son of Titania."

The men exchanged a worried look. "You're lying," one accused.

"If you're smart enough to use the fact that I can't hurt you against me, you know who I am, and you know I can't lie," she said, wearily. "I was bound by your own highest authority to speak only the truth, and I tell you that child was born of Titania. He won't die if you burn the place—only silver and iron together can kill one of the Firstborn—but he'll suffer and scar, and when he recovers, he'll remember. Do you want to be remembered by one of Titania's sons as the man who ordered him set ablaze? It seems like a bad personal choice to me, but hey, I'm just the sea witch. You're going to do what you want."

They exchanged another look, then pushed us roughly toward the door. The rest of the guards were waiting just outside. The one who had been tasked to carry Ginevra caught hold of my arm with his free hand, dragging me with him as the other two went back to start collecting kids.

For a moment, I was afraid they'd stop with Andrew, but then they began pulling the tied-up teens out of their seats, and I understood that they were actually going to get everyone out of the building before they lit the matches. I stopped resisting, as did the Luidaeg, and the two guards pulled us the rest of the way outside.

There were two unfamiliar Tuatha waiting there, along with several more guards. They really had sent a full force to recover us.

It wouldn't have been enough, if the Luidaeg had been able to fight. I knew that, and from the way she was refusing to meet my eyes, so did she. But they kept pulling us onward, toward a circle that had opened in the air—in broad daylight, where any passing mortal could have seen it—and shoved us through, into a whole new reality.

We were in the middle of a vast, fog-choked ballroom. The stuff covered and obscured the floor, wrapping around the tall filigreed pillars that jutted upward into the darkness, covering me to the knees. The trousers and shirt the Luidaeg had magicked for me were gone, replaced by a charcoal gown too long to walk in easily and too fine for me to wear outside the tower. Thankfully, my leather jacket was still there. The cuffs were gone, apparently no longer considered necessary now that we were in the proverbial lion's den. Somehow that wasn't at all reassuring.

The Luidaeg was beside me in the fog, her own clothes likewise replaced, in her case by a gown that appeared to have been woven out of coastal kelp. The leaves shone translucent green and dripping, wrapped around her to form bodice and skirt. She scowled at the room around us, shifting to stand closer to me.

The guards who'd taken us captive were gone, as was the rest of our company: we were, for all appearances, alone.

"Where are we?" I asked. Then, with more urgency: "Where are Raysel and Dean?"

"Whatever Titania was able to salvage of the false Queen's knowe, and they're probably elsewhere in the same place, I'd wager," she said, voice disdainful. "This whole place collapsed in on itself when Arden retook her throne, and I haven't seen any evidence that Titania's actually been recreating spaces. To make her false Home, all she needed was the sign, which I know didn't burn, and the empty lot where the building used to stand. So we're in the Summerlands equivalent of an empty lot right now. It's creepy and it's predatory and *I don't like it.*"

"No one said you had to like anything, dear *sister*," said the woman who stepped out from behind the nearest pillar, looking at us with a sneer on her perfect face. I shrank down inside my dress, trying to keep her attention from landing on me. To no avail: her eyes raked over the both of us, taking our measure and finding us more than wanting.

Eira Rosynhwyr was a familiar sight, of course; she'd been my father's patron and employer since long before I was born, and her largess was much of how we were able to maintain such a comfortable lifestyle while living isolated in Mother's tower. She was tall and elegant, with skin like ivory and opal black hair that gleamed from within with impossible glints of rainbow color. No one else could compete with her for beauty or for grace, not even Mother, who had often complained about how Father went and swore himself in service to someone even more beautiful than she. It was the kind of beauty that hurt the heart, especially mine, and I had trouble looking at her directly even when she *wasn't* angry with me.

She was wearing a gown as botanical as the Luidaeg's, made of tier upon tier of rose petals, arranged to perfectly outline her flawless curves. The bottom of the dress was hidden by the fog, but I knew without doubt that it was tasteful and perfectly designed.

She walked slowly toward us, scowl shifting into a smile as she approached the Luidaeg. "Hello, *little* sister," she purred.

"I'm older than my sister by the span of years," said the Luidaeg, voice gone stiff. "But as you are not my sister, I will not grant you the courtesy of her name, nor address you as such. You are a pale recreation painted by a woman who never knew her own daughter half so well as she believed, or a quarter so well as she should have, and you have no purpose here."

"Ah, yes. I've been told of your charming belief that this world isn't real, as if reality and Faerie have ever been more than kissing cousins," said Eira, running her fingers along the curve of the Luidaeg's cheek. "Does it matter who decides what's real, as long as we're united in believing it?"

"But we're not," I protested. "We never have been! The Cait Sidhe can see through illusions, and they know—"

"The cats are *dead*," she snapped. "The strays you've found in these past few days are no proof otherwise. They're an aberration, a remnant of an older Faerie that we have moved well beyond. We are better than those days of beasts and bloodshed, and soon enough, we'll be beyond changelings also. The human world has nothing more to offer us."

"Titania's Ride isn't about the Ride at all," said the Luidaeg, sounding suddenly horrified. "It's never been about the Ride. It's about the route."

"The what?" I asked.

Eira smirked. "At last, you understand what the wise already knew. I only wanted to see for myself that you were my so-superior sister in the flesh, and not some pale impersonation. Now that I've had what I require, I'm quite done with you, and you can be put away until you're needed." She stepped back, waggling her fingers in a wave.

The fog that had been swirling around our knees surged upward in a sudden wave, wrapping tight around our bodies and dragging us downward.

When it cleared, we were once again in the Queen's dungeons, the air heavy with the taint of iron and rotting yarrow. Raysel and Dean were on the floor nearby, having apparently been flung unceremoniously into the cell by hostile, animate fog, just like we had. The Luidaeg slumped. I dropped to my knees.

"Toby!"

The sound of my name brought my head back up, in time to see my sister rise from the far corner and race, half-stumbling, across the uneven floor to my side. She knelt in front of me, running her hands over my face and shoulders like she was reassuring herself of my survival. Finally, she pulled back.

I made a choking sound and wrapped my arms around her, holding her as tightly as I could.

"So, you finally got caught," said another familiar voice, this one far less well beloved. "Where is Ginevra?"

"The guards took her; she was injured in our arrest, but they bandaged her wounds, at least."

"If she dies . . ."

"If she dies, you'll still know better than to pick a fight with me, kitty-cat," said the Luidaeg, in a tone that left no room for argument. "Now. How many of us have they taken?"

"It's an 'us' now, is it?" asked Tybalt, with no hint of amusement. "Myself, clearly. Sylvester's knight. The renegade Torquills."

"Father's here?" I asked, sniffling as I pulled away from August enough to see her face.

She nodded, glancing over her shoulder at the corner where she'd been when we arrived. I could dimly make out another shape there, huddled in the gloom. "He is," she said. "He's . . . not well at the moment."

"The amount of iron in here would do that to anyone," I said, moving to stand and go to him.

She closed her hands around my upper arms, dragging me back down. I turned to blink at her. She shook her head. "No, it's not the iron," she said. "He's *not well*."

I blinked again. "Is he hurt?"

"They took us in Muir Woods," said Tybalt, voice rough. "We had gone there to meet with our allies from the Undersea. Your father believed his best friend to have died in the earthquake, not gone below the waves to marry a mermaid and shelter in the deeps. He was overjoyed and, in his joy, embraced the man."

I turned to frown at him. "Why should that render him unwell?"

Raysel and Dean stood and moved off to the side, looking like they didn't know what they were supposed to do or whether they were allowed to speak. Tybalt was looking at me like I was both the best and worst thing he'd ever seen in his life, and he couldn't decide which of those feelings was going to win out.

"Patrick forgot that Simon still labored under the memories of another world, and met an embrace from his husband with a kiss, which Simon was not prepared for," he said. "He reacted with shock and shame, and in the interests of avoiding a diplomatic incident, your sister unbound his memory. It was the only way to quell Dianda's wrath."

"That woman has a lot of wrath to go around," said the Luidaeg.

"Even so," agreed Tybalt gravely. "Your father has handled the revelation of the true world . . . poorly."

"But he knows us?" I asked. "He remembers August, and myself, and who he is? Nothing was lost by restoring his memory?" I had confirmed the persistence of our fictional lives twice, and still wanted to hear it said aloud. Maybe I was belaboring the point. I was just too afraid of what might be lost to care.

"He was a happy man before I did this to him," said August fiercely. "He loved our mother and his patron, and he was content to spend his life in service to our family. Now he's lost. He knows himself, but believes his place is beneath the sea, and weeps for things he did willingly and with joy in service to his ladies! How can you not see this for harm?"

"Because you gave back what was taken from him against his will," I said. This time, I was the one who gripped her arms. "August, you can *do* it. You can see and snap the threads. You can release *my* memory!"

"I won't." She shook her head, then shot a venomous glare at Tybalt. "Threaten all you like, you can't force me. I refuse to risk losing my sister as I fear to have already lost my father, as he swears I will lose my mother before this all comes to an end."

"I'm not on the tower wards," I said.

She stiffened, slowly turning to face me.

"Mother removed me in the other Faerie, after the divorce," I said. "She took me off the wards, and it seems she never added me back on, because I went there when neither you nor Father was in residence, and I couldn't get inside. Whether she remembers it or not, I'm not her family. *You* are my family. You, and Father, and several other people, some in this room, who I don't currently remember the way I should. You don't want to unbind me because it might cause you pain. Well, you're causing *them* pain by leaving me as I am. And I think . . . I think you might be causing *me* pain, too. Please, August. This is something you can do. This is something *only* you can do. We know the last four months were real, even if everything before it was a dream. For four months, I have loved you desperately, with every waking hour. That doesn't go away just because I remember who else I love."

"There's so much iron here . . ." August demurred.

"Here." I dipped a hand into my pocket, coming out with several of the blood gems, offering them to her. "The sea witch made them for me. They make my blood magic stronger. I assume they would do the same for you." I glanced to the Luidaeg, waiting for her to contradict me.

She didn't.

"*Please*, August," I said, and looked up, at Tybalt, the man I didn't know but might, if this went the way I believed it would, love with all my heart in just a few seconds. "If you've ever loved me as I've always loved you, let me remember."

She glanced away from me, tears shining in her eyes, even as she took the blood gems from my hand. "Am I not enough for you?" she asked. "Is my love not sufficient to feed your hungering heart?"

"I don't think anyone should depend on just one person to love them," I said. "From what Dean tells me, I'm not the only person who loves you. You don't need to keep me bound to have my affections, August. Please."

Tybalt began to step forward. The Luidaeg's hand on his arm stopped him.

"Let them," she said, softly. "They're getting where you want them to be, you just need to trust Toby to take it the rest of the way. This is what she does. Every version of her. She convinces people to do the things that don't seem like they should work."

August looked back at me, a single tear escaping to run down her cheek. "Promise me," she said. "Promise me that no matter who we were to each other in that other world, no matter what neither one of us remembers right now, you'll still be my sister, and you'll still love me."

"I'll always be your sister, you walnut. If that were something that could be changed, I would have changed it long before now."

She laughed, the sound thick and half-swallowed, and popped the blood gems into her mouth, closing her eyes. I tensed, waiting for the pain I knew was sure to follow.

I had been on the other end of this several times now. I knew it hurt to pull the spell away, and I knew that all the people I'd disenchanted had screamed through the process, as if it were their bones and not a false reality that I was taking from them. I still wasn't prepared for the feeling when August hooked her magic into the spell surrounding me and started to pull. It wasn't just the strands she was actively interacting with. The whole spell seemed to light up, making its presence known as a web of venom wound around my entire body, lurking just beneath the skin. It *burned*.

It burned like onion juice rubbed into a fresh wound, like bee venom dripping into my eye, and I instinctively tried to recoil, only to find myself stopped by hands on my shoulders. I thrashed against them, my own magic trying to rise and force hers away. I shoved it down as best as I could with my every nerve on fire, making it difficult for me to concentrate. If I fought her—*really* fought her—I knew I'd be able to knock her working aside. It was a knowledge as profound and unlearned as breathing, instinct dictating reality.

I also knew this wouldn't be any easier if I made her stop and start over again. So she pulled and I screamed, and the person behind me held me in place, hands on my shoulders anchoring me.

And then the spell began to shred, threads snapping one by one, and the pain, intense as it was, became less essential than the flashes of memory that were threatening to overwhelm me.

These weren't bathed in red and borrowed from blood. They were bright and vibrant and *mine*, memories that had always belonged to me but had been sealed away against my will. They burst into sight and slipped away just as quickly, but they remained, as much a part of me as they had always been.

I saw myself alone in the tower with Amandine, a cold, almost loveless place, no Simon, no August, no one to shield me from her constant disapproval of the daughter she had borne in the mortal world and expected to abandon there.

I saw myself fleeing the Summerlands, desperate to find a way to prove myself in a Faerie that treated changelings, not as a built-in work force but as an inconsequential nuisance best ignored when possible, saw myself going Home and falling into Devin's machinations, and while I could look back now and see how predatory he'd been, how much he'd been taking advantage, at the time, it had felt like salvation.

I saw my relationship with Cliff, serious and sweet in the way young love can be when it's good, bitter and beautiful, saw myself pregnant with Gillian and winning my freedom from Devin. Saw my knighthood and my service to Shadowed Hills, my time under Etienne's tutelage, begrudging as it had been.

I saw Simon and Oleander, and heard his laughter as he thrust me into the pond. It ached even in memory to see the man I knew as my father doing that to me, although the version of me that Titania had made had an easier time understanding why transformation had been a kindness, not a cruelty. Set against the amount of time he had, that I had even as a changeling, it was a way to escape killing me when he had clearly been expected to do exactly that.

I saw my return from the pond, my binding by the woman I thought of as Evening Winterrose, my defeat and then my victory.

And through it all, I saw Tybalt, my sometimes enemy, sometimes friend, eventual love of my life. I saw him confessing his love for me. I saw our engagement. I saw—I gasped, the sound breaking through the screaming and making the hands on my shoulders tighten, grounding me momentarily in my body, back in the world where August was unwinding Titania's enchantment one clinging strand at a time. I saw the moments right before the spell came crashing down, and what I'd learned there, and part of Tybalt's haggard staring made sudden, horrible sense.

He'd been trying to figure out whether I was still pregnant.

With a final wrenching pull that felt for all the world like some terrible briar was being yanked by the root out of my bones, the spell snapped in August's hands, and the pain stopped, not leaving so much as a ghost of itself behind. It had all been in my magic and my mind, after all, not in my flesh. I still sagged, panting, and the hands behind me caught me and held me up, keeping me from collapsing. I opened my eyes.

August was still on her knees in front of me, hair stuck to her forehead and cheeks streaky with sweat, expression pained and pleading. I knew she remained wrapped in Titania's enchantment; until I unbound her, the false world where we'd grown up together was the only one she knew. She needed to know that I was still her sister, even if I remembered another world now.

"Hey, Aug," I croaked, mouth dry and tongue heavy, unwilling to respond easily to my requests. "You okay?"

She stared at me with wounded eyes. "It hurts," she said.

"Every time," I agreed. "Thank you."

She blinked, confusion clear. "I . . . I don't . . ."

"You can always thank family, August," I said. "Don't be ridiculous, you walnut, it's not polite."

Her expression relaxed, relief washing over her. "I'm only impolite because you were rotten *first*," she said, and all but threw herself at

me, flinging her arms around my shoulders and squeezing me as hard
as she could. "I thought I was going to lose you," she whispered.

"Things are going to be different now," I admitted, patting her
back with one hand, "but you were always my sister. We just never
had the chance to find out what that meant for us as a pair. Now that
we know, not even Titania herself is taking me away from you. I
promise."

She pulled back, sniffling as she let me go. I offered her an encouraging smile. Her insecurities were all well and good, and she needed
the reassurance, but there was someone else I needed to reassure. For
his sake, and my own.

I turned to look behind me, more than half-expecting to find him
on the other end of the hands that were still clasping my shoulders,
refusing to let me fall over. Instead, I found the Luidaeg standing
there, her own expression grim, feet braced as she held me up. She
nodded knowingly when she met my eyes, and jerked her head toward the other side of our cell.

"He couldn't bear to come any closer," she said. "Might want to go
make sure he's okay."

"Right," I said, and pushed myself off the floor as she took her
hands away, glancing back to August as I did. She offered me a watery smile, and didn't try to stop me. She'd already done her part in
this. She'd released me, and when the time came, I would release her,
and we would be able to go back to our lives.

It was an oddly bitter thought. I could see now—really *see*, in a way
I hadn't been able to a moment before, when the system had been all
I'd ever known—just how wrong it was to have children just for the
sake of having servants. Changelings weren't less than their pureblood parents, and we didn't exist just so those parents would never
need to do their own damn dishes. Putting a system in place that
forced changelings to exist and then made them something between
pets and people was horrific. It was wrong in ways I couldn't fully
articulate.

The humans figured this shit out centuries ago, or at least the basics of it. How could we not do the same?

And I had been complicit—more than complicit—in the horrors of
Titania's vision. Maybe only the last four months had actually existed
to be lived through, but I had lived through them. I remembered the
people I'd turned away on my last night in the tower, the "eight tappings

at the door and eight parties turned away" as I'd so casually described it to August, and it turned my stomach.

But the guilt could come later, after we ended this and had time to contend with what we'd done when we were different versions of ourselves. Right here, right now, I had a husband to reassure. I turned.

Tybalt, as promised, was standing in the far corner of the room. Like all of us, he was staying as far from the iron door as the space allowed. He had his arms crossed and his shoulders slightly hunched forward, like he was trying to protect himself from a blow that had yet to fall. I took a step toward him.

"Tybalt?" I said, voice more hesitant than I intended it to be.

He didn't look at me.

"It worked. She broke Titania's illusions. I know who I am now." I paused. "I know who you are. I'm so sorry I wasn't strong enough to break it on my own."

"I couldn't have asked that of you," he said, still not looking in my direction.

"But you're hurt because I didn't somehow do it anyway," I said. "You're not looking at me, and you only do that when you're really upset."

"I know . . . I have no right to be angry that you were captured in a spell cast by one of the founders of all Faerie, especially not one which I knew to be tailored specifically to do you harm," he said, words coming brutally slow. "I know you are not to blame, and in all honesty, I feel a relief so vast that it aches behind my breastbone right now, like an injury in and of itself. But I'm still angry. I'm so angry I could scream and throw myself against the walls of the world raging at the injustice of it all." He finally glanced in my direction. The loss I'd been interpreting as murderous rage was still there, only partially masked by misery. "I don't know what to do with these feelings. I thought I had already experienced every form of anxiety you were able to inspire."

"Pretty sure there's always another form of anxiety." I moved toward him until I was within arm's reach, until all he'd have to do was reach out and he'd have me. "That's what loving someone means."

Sweet Maeve, I hoped he'd reach out.

"It was like you were dead, and someone else was walking around in your body." He finally reached for me, hands shaking, and I let him. "You looked at me, and you didn't see me."

"I see you now," I said.

He closed the remaining distance between us in a single step, sweeping me into his arms, into the safe, familiar scent of pennyroyal and musk. I wrapped my arms around him and held on for dear life, feeling, for the first time since I could remember, like I was home.

When I finally let go and began to pull back, I found him watching me. He wasn't smiling anymore. Instead, his expression was grave, like he was looking at something so fragile that he feared he might break it into a thousand pieces with nothing more than a word. I met his eyes, and waited.

"If you ever do anything like that again . . ."

"You'll have to get in line," I said, and leaned in, and kissed him.

We had been apart for four months, and in that kiss, I could feel every one of those long, awful days and nights from his perspective, watching his wife walk through the world with no idea who he was, or what she was risking when she was careless with herself. And I've always been very good at being careless with myself. It's a gift.

I kissed him back with equal fervor. I might not have been aware of missing him, not consciously, but I'd been alone in so many ways, and I wasn't used to being alone anymore. August and Simon were no replacement for a loving family that I'd chosen and assembled entirely by myself. Not that I'd ever been as isolated as I'd liked to think. My time under Titania's enchantment was probably the longest I'd gone without the people I loved, who also loved me, in my entire life.

When Tybalt at last relaxed his grasp and allowed me to step back, he was smiling, and so was I. "I missed you, little fish," he said.

I shuddered involuntarily as the memory of my bath in Golden Shore struck me. "I wish I could say the same," I said, putting a reassuring hand on the side of his neck. "But fuck, it's good to have you back."

"Yes," he said. Then he hesitated, glancing down at my midsection, and swallowed. "October . . ."

"Yeah. I know." I held out my hand, palm toward the ceiling, index finger extended. "I know one of the things you're worried about, and I'm worried about it too, and if we're going to get out of here, you need to not be worried," I said. "Prick my finger."

He jerked like I'd shocked him, eyes widening for a moment before he narrowed them and glared at me. "I will *not* hurt you."

"I'm not asking you to hurt me, just to draw blood," I said. "I could bite my own cheek, but I don't think that's a good idea right now. I've had other people's blood in my mouth and I haven't brushed my teeth. So please, prick my finger."

Slowly, Tybalt nodded, pupils narrowing to slits as he extended his claws, and tapped the tip of my index finger, very gently, barely hard enough to break the skin. Quick, before it could heal, I stuck my finger into my mouth and swallowed the tiny bead of blood that had formed there.

I wasn't looking for power or specific memories this time. I was looking for a truth Titania had forbidden my body to communicate with me, something baked deep into blood and bone, something hidden but soon to be revealed.

I closed my eyes while I listened to what the blood had to tell me, shutting out everything but this brief communion between my body and myself. It wasn't the sort of familiarity I sought very often, and my body had plenty to say about how much I'd slept—or hadn't—in the last few days, along with some salty comments about hydration, eating properly, and doing too much blood magic without sufficient time to recover.

And then it told me something else.

Opening my eyes, I smiled at Tybalt, hoping my relief would come through in that expression alone. In that moment, I couldn't have spoken if I'd tried.

He swallowed, hard, watching my face. "Truly?" he asked.

I said nothing, only nodded.

Slowly, he raised one hand to rest beneath my chin, nudging it ever so slightly higher before he moved his fingers to my cheek, running them softly down to the curve of my jaw. I shivered.

"It wouldn't have mattered," he said. "I would never have blamed you. But I would have set myself to destroying her."

"Here I thought we were going to do that anyway," I said, and before I could say anything else, he pulled me close again, and kissed me for a second time.

It took us longer to pull apart now that we were no longer reuniting but reunited, and felt like we had the luxury of knowing this kiss wouldn't be our last.

When we finally *did* pull apart, the Luidaeg made a huffing sound. "If you two are finished trying to suck each other's faces off like a pair of hormonal teenagers, there *is* the little matter of being locked in an iron-barred dungeon while Titania is preparing to Ride for the Heart," she said, sharply.

I turned to face her, leaning back until my shoulders hit Tybalt's chest. He responded by putting his hands on my upper arms, holding me there. The Luidaeg was watching us with an expression caught somewhere between amusement and disgust, like she'd never expected our reunion to play out any other way.

I mean, if my father, sister, and brother hadn't all been in the room, there might have been more nudity, but that was beside the point.

"How *are* we getting out of here?" I asked. "The last time I had to escape from an iron-laced dungeon, I had a Tuatha de Dannan's blood to borrow. Or, I guess, technically, the *last* time, a pair of Tuatha came and got me. I'm thinking of the time before that. How did they manage that, anyway?"

"I helped them," said Simon, voice dull and resigned. "We knew you'd been arrested, and had gone to Golden Shore hoping we could claim clemency on your behalf. There is no extradition between the Mists and the Golden Shore. I wanted your freedom more than I wanted my own safety. I was able to brew a draught that helped the Windermeres to overcome their normal issues with distance and break through the dungeon wards. I don't have access to my equipment, or to the Windermeres."

"So that's out," I said dryly. "Tybalt?"

"Much as I would love being your savior in this matter, little fish, I couldn't carry this many people through the shadows, even were I inclined to make the attempt. The roads degrade when unused, and most of my Court has been unable to access them for months. They are unsafe for passage."

"Ginevra took me via the Shadow Roads," I protested.

His expression turned briefly murderous. "And we'll be discussing that, once she has been recovered from wherever she's being held. She should have known better than to risk you so."

I turned to the Luidaeg. "I still have the Summerlands key," I said, a note of desperation in my voice. "Could we take one of the old roads?"

"Accessing them with this much iron nearby would be a complicated trick, and not one that I'm sure would play out the way we want it to," she said. "There are a *lot* of roads under the heading of 'old roads.' We could wind up on the Road of Rust, that was opened for the Gremlins, and die in a place where our bodies would never be found. I have a slightly better idea." She gestured toward the door. "Does that thing look like it contains any silver to you?"

I blinked. "No. Why?"

"Because bound and limited as I am, I remain Firstborn, and I know how the Firstborn die," she said. She held up one hand, fingernails growing long and wickedly pointed, like the talons of some great bird of prey or prehistoric creature of the depths. "We die by iron *and* silver. We don't die by iron alone. Go comfort your father-failure. He thinks he's lost you all over again."

I glanced over my shoulder at Tybalt as she moved toward the door. He nodded, and so I stepped away, heading for Simon, still huddled in the corner.

When I got there, I found that he wasn't alone: Garm was with him, back to the wall, face wan as whey beneath the natural gray pallor of his skin. Gwragen always bore a faint resemblance to human corpses. That resemblance was much more pronounced now. He had his knees drawn up, hugging them to his chest, and looked less like a knight than like a frightened child as he warily watched my approach.

"Hey," I said, and the way he flinched from that easy familiarity told me, clearly, that he hadn't had his real memories unlocked yet: this was still a version of Garm who expected me to be polite and biddable, unable to even consider being informal with a titled pureblood. Well, this was going to be fun for him.

I knelt next to Simon, putting a hand on his shoulder. He tried to cringe away from me and lean in my direction at the same time, which was a heartbreakingly impossible combination, and in the end had to settle for looking at me with sheer misery in his eyes. "Hey," I said again. "Simon? You okay?"

"Not by any definition of the word," he said, voice dull.

"Yeah. It's a shock to the system, that's for sure."

"I allowed you to be treated as . . . as something less than your sister," he said. "I was willing to lie with Amy, whom I have foresworn, in violation of my marriage vows, even if she did not choose to have me. I bowed before the woman I swore never to serve again, and while the tasks she set me in this world were less cruel than the ones she set me in ours, they were still bitter things, and I still did them willingly."

"We were all enchanted," I said. "And anything you think you remember doing more than four months ago didn't actually happen. Thankfully. She didn't change the past, she just . . . changed the way we remember it. So come on. Let's go change it back."

He frowned, slow and deep. "You should hate me," he said.

"Yeah, maybe, but I don't, so I guess that's one more thing I'm not doing," I said, and shrugged. "I really hate doing what I'm told when I don't understand the reasons behind it, y'know?"

"You know, now that I can remember you more properly, I had missed your irreverence," he said. "Manners and civility have never been your strongest suit."

"Titania sure tried to make them my strong suit, but yeah," I agreed, and smiled at him. "So what do you say, Dad? You going to come and help us kick Titania's teeth in?"

Garm winced at the threat of physical violence toward the Summer Queen, but Simon smiled, somewhat cautiously. "I would be honored." He took my hand, letting me pull him to his feet. Then he hesitated. "You still think of me like that?"

"I'm always going to wish my mortal father could have been a part of my life, but he wasn't, even if that wasn't his fault," I said. "I remember a life where you raised me—and you didn't do all that terrible a job, especially not when you consider how much Titania *tried* to convince you to do. She couldn't make a world where you were actively abusive to children you considered your own. You were a pretty good dad. I think I'll keep you."

This time, there was nothing cautious about his smile. This time, it could have outshone the sun. He pulled his hand out of mine and embraced me, quickly, then asked, "Is the baby . . . ?"

Of course. Simon was one of the few people who'd actually known I was pregnant before everything went to hell. I nodded. "Baby's fine," I assured him. "I heal like it's my job, and I guess that extends to keeping bad choices made while under a world-revising enchantment from completely destroying my life. Now let's see what horrible thing the Luidaeg is doing."

The horrible thing the Luidaeg was doing was picking the lock on the iron door with her daggered claws, working them into the keyhole and wiggling back and forth until she either heard a click or smoke started to rise from the lock and she pulled her claw free, showing char marks where it had been pressed against the iron. Eight of her ten claws were already scorched when we approached, and she was scowling as she wiggled her ninth claw in the lock.

August moved to my side, looking a little lost. Raysel was standing nearby, watching intently. I was half-afraid she was going to produce a set of lockpicks and ask if she could have a try. Dean leaned against the wall, eyes shut, four months of waiting having worn him into a resignation of waiting forever.

I looked at the Luidaeg's hands and blinked, alarmed. "Luidaeg, are you—?"

"I'm *fine*," she snapped. "This hurts like a fucking bitch and a half, but it's nothing I can't handle, and if you just shut up and let me—get—this!"

She made a triumphant sound as there was one final click and the door swung open, leaving her shaking her scorched and blistered hands as if she could brush the pain away. The talons didn't transform back into fingers.

"We're out," she said. "Now we storm the castle with . . . no weapons, not enough fighters, and two people who still think this is the way the world is supposed to be. Isn't this going to be fun?"

"No," said Dean bluntly.

"I do some of my best work while dramatically underprepared," I said. "Good job on the door."

She was old enough that I wasn't always sure the rules around saying "thank you" applied to her, and she had thanked me in the past. Even so, I didn't want to push it by thanking her directly.

She looked at me speculatively for a moment before she jerked her chin upward in acknowledgment, made a small, almost-neutral sound, and stepped through the open door.

The rest of us followed. No one wanted to spend any more time in that cell than they absolutely had to. Tybalt stayed close to me, with Simon and August following only a little farther back. Raysel and Dean walked behind them, while Garm brought up the rear. As a group we moved into the hall, which was long and narrow, made of plain gray stone lined with more of those iron doors. This wasn't a show prison, wasn't the place you put people when you wanted to frighten them before you let them out again. This was where you put the people you wanted to forget about if you possibly could.

There were no sounds apart from our footsteps and our occasionally labored breathing. Simon and Raysel seemed to have taken our time in the iron-drenched confines of the cell harder than the rest of us. Simon especially was breathing more heavily than I liked, and moving slowly, like every step pained him. I stopped to frown at him, trying not to look as panicked as I felt.

"Hey," I said. "Are you okay?"

His smile was a dreadful thing. "So much better than I was yesterday, or the day before, or four months ago, when you pressed the blood back into my body and compelled my heart to beat. Truly, October, I'm fine, and will only improve from here. I have never had this much to live for."

The Luidaeg moved to stand next to me, her own face concerned. "The Daoine Sidhe have always been more sensitive to iron," she said. "I never worked out exactly why it should be so, only that it is. It does their First no more damage than it does to the rest of us, but her descendants burn with it. Dean's Merrow heritage will have shielded him, at least a little. Simon will suffer."

"Will they be all right?" I asked. I'd dealt with iron poisoning in myself, in Tybalt, and in Nolan and Dianda, none of whom were Daoine Sidhe.

"They should, if we keep them away from iron long enough for their systems to purge the poison and recover." She held up her own taloned, blistered hands. "All things heal, with time. Right now, we need to find Titania and stop her from Riding."

"If this place is modeled off the false Queen's knowe, there should be a stable."

"Great." She looked at me expectantly. "Where is it?"

"I have no idea. You think she invited me to go hunting with her? She would have been happier having an excuse to turn me into a rabbit and go hunting for *me*."

"Oh, please, Toby. Think more highly of yourself." The Luidaeg scoffed. "She'd have turned you into a coyote at the very least. Something she could call vermin and feel good about killing."

I eyed her. "I can't tell if that was supposed to be a compliment or not."

"Good."

"Excuse me."

I turned toward the sound of Simon's voice. He was half-leaning on Dean at this point, one hand on his side, like he was trying to press away a stitch. "I may be able to help."

TWENTY-FOUR

SIMON HAD BEEN EIRA'S favorite errand boy and general assistant during her Evening Winterrose phase. They had played it quietly enough that his descent into presumed villainy had managed to avoid tainting her in the eyes of the Courts, even though everyone at the ducal level or above had been well aware that he was her man.

Which was why he'd attended quite so many functions at the High Court on her behalf, carrying her wishes and her commands to the ears of the Queen. He'd always been well-mannered and well-spoken, even during the days when he'd been used to carry out despicable acts on her behalf, and had been a beloved fixture at the Court, invited to every party and revel that wasn't restricted to the upper nobility.

Which meant he knew how to reach the stables. He led us through the halls, a quiet, furtive group, all of us braced for signs of trouble, all feeling the effects of our time exposed to the iron. For me, it mostly seemed to take the form of muscle aches and a pounding head, which was something I was almost used to after the last several days of cascading misery. Dean, who was half-Daoine Sidhe, was slowing down more and more, and blinking too much, like his eyes were drying out.

I was honestly worried about all of them. August and I were recovering more quickly than the rest, our enhanced healing knocking the iron out of our bodies like it was no big concern. It was nice, understanding our magic the way I did now. The memories of the life Titania had created for me prior to the four months we actually lived were already fading into misty nothingness, like a movie I'd seen once but hadn't particularly enjoyed; those four months, however, were fresh and bright in my memory, and I didn't think they were going to fade more than any normal memories would have done. They were mine now.

Which was going to make my eventual reunion with Quentin awkward as hell, although not as awkward as my reunion with Gillian. How was I supposed to explain to my semi-estranged daughter that I hadn't been able to remember her at all? Even in the grips of Titania's magic, I should have been able to remember my own *child*.

But then, I hadn't been able to remember the one I was actually carrying, and the entire Undersea had been sealed away from us. She hadn't been in Blind Michael's lands, which hopefully meant that she was with the rest of the Roane in the sea. And I couldn't be unhappy about that. I wanted her to be safe. She was probably going to be angry with me, and I couldn't blame her for that, either. This wasn't the worst thing I'd ever done to her—it wasn't even something I'd technically *done*—but it was one more on top of so many others that it was dizzying to think about it more than I had to.

Quentin, on the other hand . . . given the society Titania had designed, it was no real surprise that he would have no respect or compassion for changelings. When I'd first met him in the real world, he'd thought less of changelings just because they were generally less powerful than purebloods. Slapping that attitude out of him had been the work of several encounters and a few life-threatening adventures. This Quentin had never experienced those things. He'd grown up according to the standards of his society, and while I hated it, I couldn't exactly blame him. We are all vulnerable to the things we hear from the people we trust to take care of us, and he'd been a victim of that vulnerability.

Somehow, I didn't think he was going to see things the same way when this was all over. I was a changeling. His mother had been born a changeling. His boyfriend was a mixed-blood, something else that Titania had tried as hard as possible to eliminate from her perfect world. Hard as I tried, I couldn't remember any notable mixed-bloods in her reality except for January, and she'd thrown Jan as far away as possible while keeping her inside the limits of her spell. There had probably been some reason she needed Jan's existence to keep her reality from crumbling, but I couldn't think of what it might be, not right now.

The halls were more deserted than I would have expected, and sometimes we would turn a corner and find ourselves confronted with an expanse of misty nothing instead of another corridor. When that happened, Simon would pause, make an unhappy noise, and then try another route, leading us through the knowe in an increasingly labyrinthine pattern.

We took a brief detour by one of the knowe's kitchens for him to mix up a primitive iron treatment, and our Daoine Sidhe seemed to perk up after that, especially Simon himself. Being able to help the others was almost as medicinal for him as the treatment itself. Thus reinvigorated, we resumed our trek through the halls.

I leaned closer to the Luidaeg as we walked. "Is this going to work?"

"Titania isn't creating new spaces, which means she's working with whatever collapsed and wasn't somehow reclassified as 'lost,'" she said. "I don't understand how that magic works. I don't think anyone does." She looked speculatively at Tybalt as she said that, clearly waiting for him to contradict her.

Instead, he shrugged. "The magic that takes the lost things to our Court is very old. It may be older than the Cait Sidhe ourselves. I don't even know if Oberon actually put it in place; it may have simply arisen from the void, a necessary part of Faerie maintaining its own structural integrity. Or maybe it's a spell so ancient and complex that we no longer understand it, and so we dismiss it as the way things have always worked. Understanding the difference is beyond me."

"So no one knows," I concluded. "Swell. Is there a reason Titania's not making new spaces?"

"She's always been more about refinement than creation," said the Luidaeg. "Mom did most of the intentional creation, back when it was the going thing. And what Mom didn't make, Dad had a tendency to cobble together, to make sure everything kept working properly."

"If Titania didn't create, what did she add to Faerie?"

"She bore many of the First, and her children were by and large successful, if only because they were so good at killing off the competition," said the Luidaeg bluntly. "And they shaped Faerie in her image. Mom could build a bench. Titania would decorate it, turn it into something people would fight and die to protect. Creation isn't the only worthwhile pursuit, and right now, we should be glad of that, because if she were more inclined to make her own things instead of repurposing what belongs to others, we'd be in even more trouble than we already are."

Simon was ahead of us, reaching for a door that looked simpler than most of those we'd passed, plain, sanded wood with a pattern of briars carved around the edges. He paused with his hand on the knob, looking back over his shoulder.

"If she was able to recover anything of the grounds, they should be here," he said. "If not . . ."

"The grounds were in the Summerlands, and even as the knowe collapsed, they should have been stable enough to remain," said the Luidaeg, in what was probably meant to be a reassuring tone. "Go ahead."

Simon nodded and opened the door.

On the other side was a wide stretch of green, wisps of fog dancing around the edges, but no more than would have been expected on a chilly morning. There was no visible sun, only an endless expanse of watercolor gray, clouds blocking out most of the sky. Light still filtered through, watery and pale, but warmer than moonlight would have been. Simon stepped outside, and the ground held his weight. The rest of us followed close behind him.

Stepping out of the haunted house of the false Queen's knowe was a relief greater than I could possibly have anticipated, like a weight being lifted off my shoulders. I stood straighter, taking in a deep breath of the sweet, loam-scented air.

"This way," said Simon, and gestured for us to keep following as he set out across the green.

"Has this always been here?" I asked, hurrying to keep up.

"For as long as I've known the knowe," he said. "I'm a bit surprised you're not familiar, given the story of how you found this place."

"I found it, I didn't claim it," I said. "And it's not like I was exactly welcome to wander around and explore after I surrendered it to the Queen."

Not that I was sorry to have given it away. I'd received a knighthood for my trouble, and that had saved my bacon more times than I could count. Without it, my life would have been very, very different. More like the life I'd just escaped from than the one I'd actually lived.

Little things really can change everything. I pulled my jacket a bit more tightly around myself, shutting out the chill, and reminded myself how much I liked the little things. Sometimes they're all that matters.

The fog reduced our easy visibility to about twenty feet in all directions, and the low, crumbling form of the Queen's knowe was soon swallowed up by the gray, leaving us walking through a seemingly endless meadow. I watched Simon closely. He didn't look anxious or lost; if anything, he looked like he knew exactly where we were going.

That made one of us. The others were still flagging. The blisters on the Luidaeg's hands stood out livid and angry against her skin, red and engorged. They looked like they would burst under the slightest pressure. Garm was lagging farther and farther behind, while Raysel and Dean had put their animosity aside enough to lean on each other, keeping their legs from giving out. Tybalt kept pace with me, expression grim, and I knew that at the slightest sign of danger, he'd be pulling me onto the Shadow Roads.

August would never forgive him for that. I wasn't sure he cared that much about what my sister thought, but *I* cared.

"Who could she be using as a sacrifice?" I asked.

"Can't be a child of Maeve, which means May's safe," said the Luidaeg. "She's been around long enough that she has some Titania-descendant memories mixed up with everything else in that nightmare she calls a head, but while that gives Titania a claim, it doesn't change who she belongs to. Jazz is protected for the same reason."

"Raj is of Erda's line," said Tybalt. "Are the children of Oberon so protected?"

"No," said the Luidaeg grimly. "He could be a candidate. So could Quentin. She wants this one to hurt you, Toby, and that means she's going to be looking at the people you actually care about."

"So Mom's in the clear." Even with four months of fresh memories clustering my mind, I couldn't work up much affection for the woman who had borne me but never once been able to love me.

"Probably," the Luidaeg agreed. "Taking Amandine wouldn't hurt you enough. Neglectful parenting as a form of self-protection isn't exactly a new one on me, but it's one I could have happily gone another hundred years without seeing again."

"How do we stop her?"

"There are two ways to stop a Ride. If it hasn't started yet, and you can grab her sacrifice and spirit them away, that should do it," she said. "They're supposed to receive seven years of paradise before they go to the Heart. Seven years where they get anything and everything they want handed to them without argument, because they're doomed to die, and that makes them special, at least in the short term. She'd have to tear down her whole illusion and cast it again to give someone new seven years of paradise after she's already tricked someone into remembering things that way."

"Which just puts us right back where we started," objected Dean.

"Yeah, but the sacrifice would be out of immediate danger, and it wouldn't be Halloween anymore; she'd have to keep the spell stable until Beltaine to have another shot at Riding," said the Luidaeg. "And now the cats know what to do, and they can do it a lot faster. She can't remove them from the equation entirely, not with the amount of Dad in them, and they'll always get loose. Even if we have to replay this bullshit, we'd still have a chance."

"You're talking about my wife and child as if losing them would be a small thing," snarled Tybalt.

The Luidaeg turned on him. "I never said that was the only option here, or the best one. But it *is* one way to stop a Ride, and there's the possibility it could weaken Titania just long enough to give us time to try to find my mother or father, or to come up with another way to break the spell."

"And if it doesn't work out that way?" The thought of going back into the deep waters of Titania's enchantment turned my stomach. I'd already missed four months with my family. Four months of understanding and nurturing my pregnancy. My bloodline, which the baby shared at least in part, recovered quickly enough from any sort of damage that I didn't expect the neglect to be an issue, but that wasn't what worried me the most. "Even if we stop the Ride now, Titania controls the spell. She's going to remember everything that's happened. There's nothing to keep her from changing the rules, making it so the cats are seen as a deadly threat instead of a defeated enemy, or putting me somewhere Tybalt won't be able to find me. Like Dean said, we'd be right back where we started."

"Or much worse," Tybalt said. "As soon as you give birth, there's nothing to stop her from taking our child. And by the time the next Ride comes . . ."

He didn't finish, but he didn't need to.

"Then there's no other choice," I said, looking around at the others. No one else spoke. "We have to break the Ride." I turned back to the Luidaeg. "How do we do it?"

I glanced to the side quickly. "If we stop her sacrifice and she recasts the spell before we can stop *her*, it's going to hurt," I said. "But it's the sort of hurt we can recover from, while her pulling this off sounds like the sort of thing we *don't* recover from. We don't give her time to start the Ride. If we *can* intervene early, we do it."

The Luidaeg snorted. "Great, glad we've got that settled, then," she said, clearly ready to be getting on with things "Once the Ride begins, you break it by pulling the rider down and holding them as tightly as you can while she tries to use them against you. I don't know if she'll go the classic transformations route or what—Mom's Ride is the only one that was ever successfully broken. She's more likely to use illusions as a weapon than actual physical change."

"Either way, this is going to suck, and either way, we grab that rider and we end this," I said, grimly.

Tybalt caught my arm. I turned to look at him, blinking.

"There is no 'we,'" he said, voice rough. "Your grandmother was pregnant when she interceded with Maeve's Ride, and she lost the baby for her efforts. You will be staying back, and allowing us to break this ritual."

"She may not be able to stay back," said the Luidaeg. "Remember when I took you to break my brother's Ride? You had to have a connection to the rider in order to be allowed to intercede. Depending on who she has, October's help may be necessary."

"I certainly hope not," said Tybalt sharply.

The vague outline of a building was appearing ahead of us, blurred by the fog but clearly more sound than the knowe itself. We kept walking, and it resolved into a long, low stable complex flanked by a barn and a riding ring.

About two dozen horses milled in the ring, already prepared for their riders. Titania had managed to find replacements, but the Ride had yet to begin.

I looked around at the small group of my injured, overwhelmed allies and nodded, once, before starting toward the ring. If the horses were there, Titania's company would be nearby, preparing for their grand attempt at remaking the world on a permanent basis.

We had been so busy determining who the sacrifice *couldn't* be that I felt as if we'd neglected to properly review who it *could* be, and I was terrified of finding some unbearable surprise when I rounded the ring and looked into the open barn doors.

Instead, what I found was Titania and her guard, dressed to Ride, adjusting their clothing as they finished their preparations. She looked up and smiled, sweet as anything.

"Oh, good," she said. "The guests of honor have arrived."

Tybalt's hand closed on my shoulder, fingers digging in almost painfully. "Don't trust her," he hissed, mouth close to my lips. "Something here is not as it seems."

"What?" I asked.

"I don't *know*," he responded. "It takes a moment to shake off an illusion when skillfully cast. I can't be sure what part of this is false."

"Reality is just a mirror throwing back one way that things might be," said Titania, and stepped to the side, giving me a better view of her company.

I didn't recognize most of the figures behind her. They were fae, all of them, and strange and glorious in their forms and faces, beautiful beyond description, almost painful for me to look at directly. Then the crowd eddied, and I saw one face I knew.

Mother's cheeks flushed red as she turned away to adjust the ties on her silken gown, eyes cast down at the knots so she could avoid facing me. I blinked, and stared.

"Mom?"

She wasn't, not anymore—not since the divorce—but I didn't know what else to call her, and after the last four months, the word came easy to my lips. I couldn't look away, just like she couldn't quite look at me.

"Mother!" August sounded like I felt, confusion and despair in her voice as she flung herself toward the company. "What are you doing here? Don't you know what she's intending to do? We can't be a part of this! Mother, say you understand!"

"I do, sweet girl," said Amandine, finally looking up as the daughter she had actually wanted called out for her. Her cheeks were still red, and she still didn't face me. "I'm helping to guarantee a world where we can both be happy, and together, always. She's promised me you won't remember this when it's all over. No one's going to remember this except for your worthless sister, and she's not going to be able to speak of it, to anyone."

I frowned. Quentin wasn't among the people preparing to Ride. "We're here for your sacrifice, Titania," I called. "It's over."

"Yes, you're here to bring my sacrifice," she said, agreeably. "I appreciate it greatly, because it's not over. It's never over before I say it is."

She smiled, venomous as a snake, and snapped her fingers.

Vines burst from the ground and wrapped around our legs, holding us in place—all of us were suddenly tied down, even August, still reaching for Amandine. Her expression was pure confusion. Amandine sighed and smiled, reaching out to run her fingertips down August's cheek.

"Dear child," she said. "I would destroy Faerie to have you home again. Fortunately, I don't have to. Thanks to the Summer Queen, I can save it, instead."

I frowned, suddenly suspicious. "Are you the sacrifice?" I demanded.

Amandine shot me a sour look. "Child, no," she said. "My lady decided, in her glory and her wisdom, that whoever rode today should do so with nothing they could lose in this world. Someone it would hurt you to lose. I suggested the cat, but she refused; said it might taint the sacrifice."

Tybalt strained against the vines at her implied threat, trying to move closer to me. When he failed, he began to make a low snarling noise deep in the back of his throat, rising and falling in a vicious harmony of promised pain. I reached back to take his hand, holding tightly.

"Nor would I harm my sweetest girl." She touched August's cheek again, not seeming to notice when August tried to shy away, expression turning disgusted. "You were such a good child before you fell in with poor company," she said. "That won't happen again. We're making a perfect world. No more cats. No more cowards. No more changelings."

I stiffened as her meaning finally became clear. "You *can't*," I said.

"But child." Amandine looked at me, eyes wide and guileless. "I already have."

She kept smiling as Titania and her company vanished, leaving Amandine alone.

I turned my head, heart sinking as I realized what I was going to see. The riding ring was empty, horses gone.

So was Simon.

TWENTY-FIVE

OR A MOMENT, I was frozen, shock sweeping over me and knocking the breath out of my body. "Luidaeg," I said, voice barely above a whisper. "You said she couldn't hurt my family. You *promised* me."

"I also said that the Heart might give Titania a loophole where that binding was concerned," she said, genuine regret in her voice. "Now that you're no longer under her spell, can you honestly say you still consider him family?"

My mouth worked silently. I remembered a lifetime of him loving me; I also remembered a lifetime of believing he was the monster waiting in the shadows to catch and destroy me. Finally, I found the answer. "I can. I *can*."

I whirled to face Amandine, barely noticing the way the vines rubbed against my skin. "You give him back! He's my father, and you have no right to touch him!"

"I haven't laid a finger on him, nor will I, but I have every right," she said, voice poisonously sweet. "He was my *husband*. What he isn't—and never has been—is your father. He wasn't your father when this began, and he won't be your father as he dies."

"How *dare* you? He *loved* you!"

"He left me," she said, as if that were the only thing that had ever mattered, or ever could. "No one leaves me."

"I did," I said. "August did."

"And now we all are," said the Luidaeg. She moved one hand through the air in a slashing gesture, and the vines dropped away, withered and dry before they hit the ground. "Toby, the key."

I dug the Summer Roads Key out of my pocket and slapped it into her charred hand. One of her blisters broke, fluid and small, wriggling creatures seeping from the wound. She didn't seem to notice.

"August, quick," I snapped, as the Luidaeg thrust the key into the air, where it hung, trapped by nothingness. My sister looked at Amandine for a moment longer, heartbreak in her eyes, before she turned and ran to me, all but throwing herself into my arms.

I closed them around her, even as Tybalt moved to stand beside me, glaring at Amandine with everything he had. "C'mon, Aug," I said. "Let's go rescue our father. Oh, and Amandine? We made the right call in the divorce. I hope when you stop your dancing, you do it entirely alone and finally able to understand why."

I turned away from her, arms still around August, to where the Luidaeg had pulled open a doorway in the open air.

"You can't stop this," called Amandine. "You can't save him."

"Watch us," I said, and pulled August with me as I stepped through the door into the dark.

We only fell a few feet before we landed on the path. This time, I didn't lose my balance. Tybalt dropped down a few moments later, Dean and Raysel close behind, followed by the Luidaeg and Garm. Once we were all through, the door above us slammed, and the Luidaeg pushed through the rest of us, throwing balls of witch light overhead as she walked. They illuminated more of the tangled, thorn-draped forest than I'd seen on previous visits, making it brutally clear just how much of this space had been designed to be impassable. We would stay on the path or pay the price.

We stayed on the path.

I peeled August's arms away as I moved to follow the Luidaeg, and she whimpered, scrabbling to get a grasp on me. I took a breath to steady myself, trying to remember the life Titania had woven for us to "live" together; the real August had gone on her own quest and failed it, winding up exiled in Annwn for over a century of solitude and struggle. This August thought she was struggling when she ran out of cream for her morning tea, or when she got a streak of mud on her walking gown. She had no idea what it was to live outside of Amandine's walled garden.

I pushed her away but kept my hands on her shoulders, looking her full in the face as I said, "If we want to rescue our father, we have to walk now. We have to follow the Luidaeg, and trust that she knows where we need to go to intercept the Ride. All right?"

"She's trying to do this the right way, which means the traditional way when you're talking about one of the Three, which means she's going to be following the established routes," said the Luidaeg from ahead of us. "It was always about the route, almost as much as the Ride itself. It's why she couldn't just kill the Cait Sidhe. She needed the Shadow Roads to stay stable. We can take the Thorn Road to the Moorland Trail, and cut from there to the route she's riding. She has to go the long way around. Even if her company was mounted and ready to go when we intercepted them, she had to grab Simon and get him onto a horse. That means they can't be too far ahead of us."

"I thought her sacrifices had to have seven years of paradise," said Dean. "Simon didn't get that."

"No, but Titania's illusions told the people she'd entangled that they *had* been living whatever life she scripted for them for however long she needed them to have been living it. The real Simon knows he's making his own paradise now, that he's living a better and more honest life beneath the sea, but a Simon who doesn't remember leaving Amandine? Who doesn't realize he has choices? For him, seven years with his beloved wife and daughters—the one he feels he failed and the one he never got the chance to care for, in the service of the woman who once promised to protect him—that would seem like paradise. Paradise doesn't have to be real. It just has to be believed." The Luidaeg's tone was grim, unforgiving. "That's what Titania has always done best. She makes people believe her. Little miscalculation on her part, though: Simon knows now that what he had wasn't paradise. He doesn't believe her anymore."

"So the Ride will fail?" The idea that it would all fall apart no matter what we did was an appealing one.

Sadly, the Luidaeg shot that possibility down without missing a beat. "She can't have been certain we'd break the spell protecting him from her when we did; she must have had a backup sacrifice. She can change directions in the middle if she has to. It just won't be as convincing, and the Heart may not give her as much power as she wants. So she might only remake half of Faerie in her own image."

"We are *not* letting her sacrifice our father!" said August.

"Glad you're with the program, sis," I said, and walked faster. "Now come on. We need to go kick a Queen of Faerie in the teeth."

"Violence is so rarely the answer, but right now, it feels right," said Tybalt.

I laughed, and we kept walking, through the narrow pathway through the thorns, until the air changed around us, becoming cool and thick with fog, scented with peat and fresh water and the slow vegetable rot of a place that had been decaying since the moment it began. The ground beneath our feet remained firm and stable, but dropped off into murky bog only a few steps away. I glanced at the Luidaeg as she tossed another ball of witch light into the air, illuminating undulating marsh broken with stands of reeds and patches of luminously glowing lilies.

Some things moved among the vegetation. I made the conscious decision not to look too closely.

"The Moorland Trail," she said, sounding pleased.

"This looks more like a bog to me."

"People used to use the word 'moor' to refer to low-lying wetlands as well as remote hillsides," she said. "Language changes. The underpinnings of Faerie don't. My siblings and I used this as a shortcut, and some of them anchored their skerries here. Ismene and Hirsent and others who liked the freedom of the fens. You can't get here unless you're already on one of the older roads and already know the way."

I glanced at Tybalt. "And see, I thought you were all special because you had a secret shortcut through the Summerlands."

He frowned at me. "I'm not sure how I'm meant to respond to that. Are we back to teasing each other, or are we still upset about this whole situation?"

"I can't tell you what to feel, but I was teasing. Being grim right now doesn't get us where we're going any faster." I looked to the Luidaeg. "I still don't see how Titania can take him."

"My father protected people you think of as family, and if she can argue with the magic that he doesn't make the cut, regardless of whether it's in this world or our own, she can at least begin to Ride," she said. "She hasn't touched him. She didn't put him on the horse. If you're being technical—and believe me, she is—she doesn't touch him until she feeds him into the Heart, and that's powerful enough to undo my father's work, if it decides it likes the deal she offers."

I blanched. "Okay, that's awful, for one, and I'm still not sure what happens when we break the Ride, for two."

"A very good question. Luidaeg?"

"Finally getting around to asking what you need to know, eh?" The Luidaeg looked back over her shoulder at us. "Anyone with a vested interest in a sacrifice can try to intervene, and if they succeed, the Ride is broken. But the Heart was primed when Titania led the first steed of her company onto the first leg of the trail. It's going to expect a sacrifice. When Mom's Ride was broken, she was compelled to go in Tam Lin's place, and could no more resist the calling of her own origin than our children can resist us. Even though she had to go, I like to think she would have fought if she hadn't believed that she'd be released in seven years, when the sacrifice came around again."

"Why wasn't she?" I asked.

"Titania didn't Ride for her," said the Luidaeg. "She said her sister had made her own bed, and would be well served by lying in it, and she left her there, and went about making the rest of Faerie miserable, until Oberon banished her for our own good. If we break the Ride, I expect we get at least seven years without Titania, until the Heart gets tired of sucking on her like an everlasting gobstopper and spits her right out."

I snorted. Dean looked briefly amused.

Raysel and August, who lacked a proper grounding in human media, looked bewildered, but didn't say anything. I glanced at them. "I'll explain when we get home."

"You better," muttered August.

"All we have to do is break the Ride and the Heart will do the rest," said the Luidaeg, stepping onto a boardwalk that looked more than half-rotten as it hung above the murky water. "Do *not* try to engage with Titania directly, do you understand me? And I'm sorry, kitty, but as his daughters, October and August will be the ones best positioned to intercede."

"Then October should be spared through the simple fact that she's not his daughter," said Tybalt.

"Not by blood," said the Luidaeg calmly. "But then, neither is August."

August jerked like she'd just been jabbed with a pin, eyes going briefly wide. Then they narrowed again, as she said, "I am furiously angry with my mother right now, and will never forgive her for this, but how dare you imply that she stepped outside the bounds of her marriage bed in the getting of me!"

"I didn't," said the Luidaeg. "Is there any Daoine Sidhe in you, child? Any Daoine Sidhe at all?"

August was quiet.

The Luidaeg sniffed. "Yeah, I thought not. Amandine didn't need to cheat on Simon. He was there at your conception, and then she pulled his blood out of yours while you were sleeping in her womb. I can't say for sure whether she knew she was doing it. I can say she was never sorry. You're his child because parentage is so much more than blood. Parentage is showing up and being present, is love and learning and compassion and care. I was a parent to my siblings when my mother wouldn't—or couldn't—be. October is a parent to her squire. That there's no blood shared there is no measure of a family."

She turned back to Tybalt. "On a technical level, most Firstborn aren't related. The magic that splits us into our own descendant lines sees to that. If, when we reach the Ride, October can tell me honestly that she still doesn't think of the man we're on our way to save as her father, she can stand aside. But if she can't, she has to do this. I know what you're afraid of, kitty. You're not wrong to be scared. And at the same time, your fear doesn't outweigh the needs of all Faerie, even if we both wish that it did. October?"

I froze inside, although my body kept moving automatically forward, following her across the fens. My mouth was dry, and my head was spinning with the pressure of her question. I swallowed, hard. "Simon was my enemy for a long, long time," I said. "He hurt me, badly, and that doesn't go away because he's been trying to make amends. In some ways, it's worse because now I know what kind of man he's capable of being, and what he did anyway. But . . . you can't go on as many wild quests to save someone as I have for Simon and not develop a little bit of love for the person you keep saving. Add that to the last four months, and the things I spent them believing to be true, and—yeah. He's my father. I'm sorry, Tybalt. If I can save him, I have to try."

Tybalt looked at me, utter betrayal in his eyes, and I managed not to cringe away. Then he sighed, and said, "I said I wanted the woman I married back, and it seems I have her. If you must do this, I do it with you. He's the father of my beloved, and that makes him my family as well."

"He's my uncle," said Raysel.

"He's my stepdad," said Dean.

"Then we should have enough hands to break the Ride. After all, Janet did it alone," said the Luidaeg. She stopped walking, looked speculatively at the edge of the boardwalk, and added, "Follow me," before stepping off and plunging into the water below.

When the sea witch tells you to do something, however ridiculous, you do it. One by one, the others followed, until Tybalt and I were alone on the boardwalk. I shook my head, eyes on the murky water. Unlocking my memories of the real world had brought back my transformation and time in the pond, and with it, my fear of being submerged in water. I knew it was irrational—I had just taken a long, glorious bath in Golden Shore, for Maeve's sake!—but the thought of stepping off that edge made my heart race.

And I would have to do it. I turned to Tybalt, grabbed the front of his shirt, and pulled him into a passionate kiss. He didn't fight me, either understanding what I was trying to do or so glad to have the opportunity to kiss me again after so long apart that he didn't care why I was doing it.

I wrapped my arms around him, trying to focus on nothing more than how wonderful it was to be kissing him again. I had missed him, even if I hadn't been capable of knowing it at the time; a feeling like something was missing from the world, under the surface but always there, like an itch I couldn't quite scratch. He kissed me back with unending hunger. Unlike me, he *had* been capable of knowing what was supposed to be there and wasn't, thanks to Titania.

As we kissed, I inched us toward the edge of the boardwalk, and finally tilted hard to the side, dropping us both into the bog.

There was a momentary chill when we broke the surface, and then we were standing on a hillside somewhere in the Summerlands, still wrapped around each other. The sky was clear overhead, spangled with stars like jewels, and the air smelled like autumn. The Luidaeg cleared her throat.

"Whatever gets you into the water, I guess, but it's go time," she said. "Meaning *let go* and focus."

I stepped away from Tybalt, turning to properly see our surroundings for the first time.

The land was wild around us, high grass and verdant forest, and no visible structures, not even in the farthest distance. Four moons shone above us, casting almost as much light as a single sun, and I could hear the approaching hooves of horses. "You have to get him off that horse," she said, voice firm and cold. "I'll handle the recitations, but you *have* to get him off the horse."

Grimacing at the effort, she reached into her pocket and pulled out the jar of pink gems she'd made from Acacia's blood. She tossed it to me. I snatched it out of the air, frowning quizzically.

"Before you pull him down, swallow two," she said. "That should give you the boost you need to break all the way through. Blood of her blood works best. I, on the other hand, just have to invoke my father."

She extended one blistered hand then, running the longest talon of her other hand across the palm. The skin parted, and more of those little white worms came out, accompanied by a gush of cloudy water. There was no blood. She grimaced.

"Fuck," she said. "That's a complication we don't need. Who's down to bleed for me?"

"Titania told me to know my place, and I do," I said. "I bleed when Faerie needs me." I shoved the pink jewels into my pocket as I turned to Tybalt, holding out my hand. "I don't have a knife. Can you?"

He looked pained but extended one claw and split my palm from the heel of my hand to the base of my middle finger. The Luidaeg hurried over to grab me by the wrist, turning my hand so the wound was aimed at the grass as she hauled me in a wide circle. Wide enough to contain us all. When the wound healed, she split it open again with the talon that had failed to draw her own blood, until she finally let me go and I stumbled back, clutching my hand to my chest.

The skin was already knitted back together, the muscle beneath doing the same. The blood was spilt, the circle drawn.

"I forbid you maidens all who wear gold in your hair to come nor go abroad this night: the Faerie Host rides there," chanted the Luidaeg, and stomped her foot dead at the center of the circle she had drawn with my blood. White light blazed up around us as the blood seemed to ignite from within, sending a column of flame into the sky. "And none that fall within their sight but they are lost and gone, sacrificed by moonlight long before the break of dawn."

The hoofbeats were getting louder by the moment, and then Titania's Host came over the rise of a small hill.

There were easily forty of them, on horses of all different colors, their tack polished and perfect, their attire even more so. All of them were too beautiful for me to look upon directly; even trying hurt my eyes.

"First let pass the black steeds, and then let past the brown," chanted the Luidaeg. "Quick run to the milk-white steed and pull the rider down!"

I scanned the horses, looking for traces of white, and when I found them, I froze.

Simon was there, staring straight ahead as if he'd been drugged, not blinking. That was who we were looking for, who we'd come to save.

And seated beside him, on a white horse of his own, was Quentin. Fuck.

TWENTY-SIX

"WHAT DO WE DO, Luidaeg?" I asked, half-frantic. "Can we save them both?"

"We're gonna have to," she said. "But you have to hold on to the one you pull down."

Meaning I could help Simon or I could help Quentin, but I couldn't save them both. I hesitated. Damn me forever, but I hesitated. One way or the other, I was letting someone down.

Then Tybalt touched my shoulder, and said, softly, "The boy will have his lover, and the Luidaeg. Your father needs both of you."

I glanced to the Luidaeg, eyes wide. She was watching Quentin as the horses got closer, and the talons on her hands were finally receding, although the blisters still hadn't healed.

"Go," she hissed, and we ran, August and I keeping pace with each other, me pulling the pink jewels out of my pocket and shaking two out into my hand, then passing two more to her. Whatever gave us the strength to get through this would be worth it.

We swallowed the jewels as we ran, tasting candied roses and fire-charred marshmallows, and I felt a jolt of pure magic run through my veins. It was like a week's sleep and six square meals, all at the same time. I started to think we might actually be able to do this.

Together, we made a straight line for Simon, me grabbing the reins while she pulled him from the horse to the ground. Vaguely, I remembered how this had gone when Blind Michael had tried to Ride with me, and I hurried to help her lift him to his feet, then pulled them both toward the blazing circle. August realized what I was doing and joined in, and together we were able to pull him through the wall of light.

He screamed, and she nearly let go in surprise, only clamping her hands back down at the last second. "No matter what happens now, we can't let go!" I shouted.

She nodded, eyes wide and terrified.

Behind us at the horses, I could see Dean and the Luidaeg repeating our stunt with Quentin, hauling him to the ground and then dragging him to the circle. He woke up from his trance when they were only halfway there, beginning to fight against them. They didn't let go, and then he was screaming as he fell through the light.

I looked down at Simon. His eyes were open, and he was blinking up at us, seeming utterly perplexed.

"Hello, my dears," he said. "Can you tell me where we are?"

"Deep breath," I said. "This is gonna hurt."

"Who comes for them?" demanded Titania.

"Dean Lorden, Count of Goldengreen, beloved companion!" yelled Dean.

"Antigone of Albany, mentor and friend!" added the Luidaeg.

I looked up. "Sir October Christine Daye, Knight of Lost Words, daughter and friend!"

August swallowed. "August Torquill, daughter."

"Both these men are precious to me, and I stand for them," yelled Tybalt.

"That's my uncle!" called Raysel.

Garm said nothing, but he didn't break the circle, and under the circumstances, that was enough.

"Very well, then: suffer," said Titania, sounding almost bored.

"We cast our compass 'round," said the Luidaeg, grimly. "We knew what we were doing."

The world twisted around us, and I had a moment to realize that the Luidaeg was right: Titania wasn't using classic transformation. Then we were standing in the kitchen of the tower, me and August side by side, her already grown, me no more than twelve, hands joined as we watched Simon empty the contents of his herb shelf into a bag.

"You were never enough to hold me here," he said. "A babbling little brat and a mortal bastard? Why would I stay?"

We were standing in front of the door. I shifted a bit to the side, making sure he couldn't brush past us.

"You're worthless, both of you," he said, and he sounded so

reasonable, so convinced, that I could almost have believed him. He started toward us. "Out of the way."

"No," I said.

"No?"

"No."

He kept moving forward, and as he reached for the door, I grabbed hold of his arm, not letting go as he tried to shake me off. August did the same on the other side of him, our hands still connected as we held him down.

The room twisted again, becoming a bedroom, dark and windowless, and all too modern. The furnishings were mortal, chrome and silk, and a picture of Oleander sat beside the bed. Simon was several feet away, adjusting the cuffs of his shirt, hair brushed and oiled into perfection, clothing clearly tailored to fit him. He looked at us with such withering disdain that I almost took a step back, away from him.

"August," he said. "Returned from your little 'adventure,' are you? Of course, I wasn't surprised when you disappeared. You were always too stupid to survive something like that on your own. My lady told me how she convinced you that you could do it, and oh, how we laughed at the thought of your foolishness. We laughed and laughed—and October! I wondered if you would seek me out so I could send you back to the water where you belong. If you must walk among your betters, best you do it in a gown of scales."

He began to move his hands in an intricate pattern, and I all but threw myself across the room to catch him. "First the bird who tries to fly, and then the snake who seeks to strike," I said. "You can spit as much poison as you like, we're not letting you leave this room. We love you, Simon. Patrick and Dianda love you, and I'm sorry, but I'm too afraid of your wife to let a little thing like the Summer Queen put me on her bad side. We're not letting go."

The room twisted again, and he was shirtless and panting, a knife in each hand as he glared at us. Then he lunged, clearly aiming for our throats. I grabbed his arm and pulled it down, forcing him to stab me in the shoulder instead. It hurt, but it wouldn't do any real damage, and as I twisted my body away from him, I took the knife with me. He snarled and slashed at August, who danced back in bewilderment.

"Give it up, Simon," I snapped, pulling the knife out. "You know stabbing us doesn't do anything worth writing home about. Having unbreakable daughters makes physical violence a little pointless."

August caught his second knife in her arm and pirouetted away, pulling it out of his hands. We exchanged a look, nodded, and jumped on top of him, forcing him to the ground and pinning him in place.

We were still there when the room shifted again and we were back on the hillside, white light all around us, on top of Simon. He blinked up at us, face pale, and said, "I don't know why I— I'm so sorry—"

And then he caught fire, blazing up like a brand beneath us. I screamed, tightening my arms against the urge to recoil. August almost let go. I grabbed her arm at the last moment, yanking her down into the inferno.

The last time this had happened in my presence, I'd been the one burning, and it had been easy to overlook how hard it is to hold on to something that's literally trying to melt the flesh from your hands and arms. No wonder Janet lost the baby. She was only mortal, after all. Her body couldn't take the strain.

I held on as tightly as I could, and just as I was reaching the limits of my endurance, the flames blew out and Simon was sprawled in the grass beneath us, once more bipedal, and himself.

And stark-ass naked, which was a little horrifying under the circumstances. August and I both recoiled, finally letting go, and I spared a glance for her. She was charred and broken, skin split to show red, raw flesh beneath, and even as I watched, she was healing, skin smoothing out and knitting back together.

"Simon?" I asked.

"October," he croaked.

I didn't have a cloak to wrap around him, and so I shrugged out of my jacket and eased it around his shoulders, lifting him into a sitting position. He sagged against me. I twisted to look toward the others, craning my neck for a glimpse of Quentin.

Raysel saw me looking and said, swallowing hard, "Quentin's okay. Dean and the Luidaeg, they have him."

I nodded and turned my attention back to Simon. I could feel my own skin knitting back together, like ants running across my body, tissue repairing itself at an incredible rate. August, who looked almost fully recovered, was clinging to Simon and sobbing. The white light blazed all around us.

And on the other side of it, someone was screaming.

I let go of Simon when I realized that, standing slowly and turning to face the sound. Titania was still mounted on her horse, hands wrapped around the pommel as she bent forward and howled in fruitless fury. She wasn't saying anything, just shrieking.

Finally, she sat upright and pointed at the circle with one shaking finger.

"You have made an enemy of me on this day, and you *will* live to regret it," she said.

The sky above her company was lighting up in cascading rainbows, like the Summerlands had looked at the aurora borealis and decided to show those mortal light shows what *real* dramatics looked like. Slowly, Titania took the reins of her horse in her hands and turned its head to the west, then resumed her ride. The others rode after her. The lights got brighter and brighter, until they were almost blinding, then flared with silent iridescence and disappeared, leaving only darkness and stars behind.

"She'll be back," said the Luidaeg wearily, stepping up behind me. "She always comes back. But we'll have time."

That was all she had time for before August and Garm wailed and collapsed. A moment later, Dean shouted, "Luidaeg? Luidaeg?! Quentin fainted!"

The Luidaeg smiled. "We win," she said, and crumpled, motionless, to the ground.

TWENTY-SEVEN

"I'M PREGNANT, NOT INJURED," I complained, as Tybalt swept me off my feet and held me against his chest. At least he'd let me drive the car to Muir Woods. Jin, who had been keeping a very close eye on me for the past three months, had finally managed to convince him that driving was safer for me than taking the Shadow Roads: they might be back down to their normal degree of hostility, but they still didn't care for my presence, and that much cold and asphyxiation wasn't good for the baby.

Tybalt, who would have been happier if I'd agreed to spend the remainder of my pregnancy locked in the house and not going anywhere more dangerous than the grocery store, had been reluctant to believe that strapping myself into a human construction powered by internal combustion could be safer than his magic, but in the end, Jin had managed to wear him down. "October's a remarkably safe driver for someone who's destroyed as many cars as she has," she had said. "She had a good reason every time. Just keep her from having good reasons, and you'll be fine."

Because giving him permission to monitor me at all times was definitely better for my nerves.

"No, and I won't *allow* you to become injured tonight," he replied sharply, starting toward the entrance to the redwoods. "Arden wishes to see you, and you cannot refuse. But I *can* insist that you be escorted at all times."

"I love you, you nerd," I said, and let my head rest against his shoulder.

It was nice to be carried, after all. My feet ached when I stood for too long, and the thought of climbing all the way into the knowe under my own power wasn't a very pleasant one. Oh, I would have done it, if Arden had required it of me: it had been three months since what most people now referred to as "the incident," when they admitted it had happened at all, and this was the first time she'd called a full court and expected me to attend.

As a Hero of the Realm, I wasn't exactly allowed to turn her down. Even though winter in Muir Woods wasn't my idea of a good time, and I would have been happier in my living room, watching BBC Shakespeare recordings with Tybalt and listening to May puttering around the kitchen. Three months hadn't been nearly enough time to fully reacclimate to normal. I wasn't done yet.

Titania's Ride had well and truly broken, and when she had answered the call of the Heart, her spell had shattered. The screaming and fainting inside our circle in the immediate aftermath had been the spell rebounding on the people it still affected. It had cascaded through the Kingdom, and through the afflicted neighboring Kingdoms, knocking everyone unconscious in the backlash.

Lots of people had learned a lot of things about themselves in the aftermath of that spell. Not all of those things were good ones. Etienne, for example, had learned that he would have tried to be there for Chelsea if he'd been aware of her existence earlier. But Quentin had learned that without early exposure to better ways of looking at the world, he would have been susceptible to some very toxic strains of pureblood ideology. He was seeing Helen's therapist now, trying to work on the damage that understanding had done. He woke up screaming less often than he had in the beginning. That was better than nothing.

Sylvester had been forcibly reminded that when he was cut off from his family, he sank into depression and despair, but that some people would stand by him all the same. And Arden had learned that, had things gone ever so slightly differently during the 1906 earthquake, she could have been a happy exile, living for the moment because she didn't quite believe in tomorrow.

I'd learned that I was easy to placate with the promise of a place and people who would at least pretend to love me. But then, I'd always known that about myself, on some level.

The Luidaeg's collapse had been related to the amount of iron in her body and the amount of magic she'd forced into her circle, not to the ending of Titania's spell. Carrying her out of the Summerlands had been one of the most terrifying parts of the whole ordeal, although we'd finally been able to find the back door to her apartment in the swamp behind Amandine's tower, and when we'd knocked, Poppy had been there to let us in, one of the missing, now restored. Seeing her earnest orange face had been one of the first real indicators that this was almost over.

Oberon had spent the entire spell locked in with Poppy, and now flinched when people mentioned mortal television in his presence. Served him right.

August and Simon had returned to the Undersea as soon as we were sure the Luidaeg was going to be okay, diving back into the embrace of the Lorden family. Simon hadn't been back to the surface since, and I wasn't entirely sure he would ever come back again. August, on the other hand, had started showing up every other weekend, learning how to bake scones from May and spending time with Raysel, who was struggling to set aside enough of her fear of Simon to allow him to visit us at the house after his grandchild was born.

I was honestly proud of both of them. They were trying to fit into a world that had changed completely while they weren't looking, and while it wasn't easy, they at least knew what they needed to do.

All the Brown children had woken up after the spell dissolved. Unlike most of the people Titania had enchanted, they had no memory of the parts they'd played in her fantasy world, and none of us were in a real hurry to fill in the blanks. They'd each been given a role to play. They'd all suffered from trying to do it correctly. They'd hurt other people in the process, and it hadn't been their fault. If we could spare them from that guilt, we would do precisely that.

The part of the false Queen had been played, not by an enchanted Brown, but by the actual Queen. She was now back in custody, and Arden was giving serious thought to elf-shooting her, just to keep her from turning up *again*, like the bad penny she was.

Tybalt carried me through the national park and up the path on the hillside, until the air changed around us and we emerged in the Summerlands, in sight of the gates to Arden's knowe. I finally pushed against him then, struggling to sit up.

"Put me down," I instructed, and he did, setting me gingerly on my feet.

I leaned up to press a kiss against his cheek. "Let's go visit the queen."

"As long as it's only this one," he said, sourly, but he smiled as he looked at me, and his touch was gentle as he reached up to brush the hair away from my eyes. "No more Summer Queens for us."

"No," I agreed. "I quite like the one we have. Come on."

He took my hand in his, and side by side, we walked into the knowe, neither of us looking back, neither of us letting go. Safe, in a world once more restored to the way the world was meant to be, and close enough to home that we could feel it in the air.

Titania had tried to create perfection, but she could never have succeeded, because this was perfection, flaws and all. Anything else would have been a lie.

Read on for
a brand-new novella
by Seanan McGuire:

CANDLES AND STARLIGHT

Pinch him, fairies, mutually;
Pinch him for his villainy;
Pinch him, and burn him, and turn him about,
Till candles and starlight and moonshine be out.
—William Shakespeare, *The Merry Wives of Windsor*

ONE

June 13th, 2015

THEY ACTUALLY PREPARED A room for me.

May had told me so during the drive from Muir Woods to the house where I was going to spend the next year of my life. In the mortal world, not the Summerlands; October had never been willing to move back there after leaving her mother's tower, and so my father had given her one of his investment properties as a home to call her own. It was one of the older homes in the City, built shortly after the earthquake, and he had purchased it when it was new, preserving it from the subdivision and reconstruction that had befallen many of its neighbors. In a sea of what May referred to as "condos" and "duplexes," it remained a single-family home.

All this information was imparted to me in the back seat of a Bridge Troll's hired conveyance, the man behind the wheel pretending not to listen as May did her best to reassure me that I was expected, I was wanted, I had been planned and prepared for. After everything I'd done or tried to do to this family, they had still gone out of their way to ensure my comfort once I was allowed to wake.

I hadn't been sure how to feel about that. I still wasn't. But she'd spoken kindly and earnestly and with all apparent sincerity, and I hadn't been able to decide how I was supposed to respond to that before we'd been pulling up in front of the house and she'd been coaxing me out of the vehicle with little gestures of her hands.

May seemed to think I would find her unnerving. And in some ways, she *was* unnerving, and always would be: Fetches are meant to be temporary things, here and gone in a matter of days as they predict the deaths of the people they're connected to. Well, she'd been incarnate for four years now, and showed no signs of disappearing any time soon.

At the same time, she had the face October had worn when I was a child, before my abduction, before—well, everything. She looked like the woman I remembered as my friend and the mother of my playmate, and not like the increasingly fae stranger October had become since we'd both returned from exile. May looked like an October I had never done material harm to, and that was soothing. Looking at her was like looking at a portal to the past, like a second chance I'd never deserved to have. So maybe she was unnerving, but she was also an offer to let me try again.

The car had driven off, May waving, and then she'd turned to walk me to the door, one hand on my shoulder, guiding me along, keeping me from running away. Not that I wanted to: this *was* my escape, the place I was running away *to*, not *from*. I'd stay here for as long as I could. It wasn't going to be easy. I knew that. Perhaps ironically for one of the fae, I had no illusions. But after everything I'd done, I deserved a little difficulty. Asking for a chance at safety and healing wasn't unfair of me. Asking for absolution would have been.

"Toby sets the house wards, and while we're all allowed to bring visitors, she's going to need to be the one who adjusts them to see you as a resident so you can come and go without someone accompanying you," she'd said, as she unlocked the door and tapped the doorframe six times, in what I assumed was the pattern that told the house she had a guest. Then she'd gestured me inside, into a place like none I'd ever seen before.

Shadowed Hills was a place of constant tidiness, where the small army of domestic staff swept through on an almost-hourly basis to ensure that my parents wouldn't be embarrassed by any sign that people actually lived there. This was very much the opposite. The front door opened on a small vestibule containing racks for both coats and shoes, with a honeycomb-gridded mat on the floor designed to catch any mud that people happened to track inside. May had paused to shrug out of her coat and hang it up before turning to me, hand outstretched, and catching herself.

"We'll have to take you shopping, but I have some sweaters that should fit you until then," she'd said, sounding pleased by the notion. No one had ever taken me shopping before. During my confinement, there'd been no need for new clothes, and after my return, my needs had been seen to by the ducal tailors. From the sparkle in her eyes, it seemed shopping was something I might enjoy, and I decided to be accommodating about it.

Forcing a smile, I'd nodded, and turned to study the rest of what I could see of my surroundings.

Beyond the vestibule, a stairway ascended to the second floor, while a hall snaked deeper into the house, open doorways leading to other rooms that were mostly blocked from view by the architecture. What little I could see was cluttered, filled with things, as if the house were somehow desperate to prove its occupancy.

A rattling sound to my left caught my attention at that point, and I turned to see a rose goblin with pink and gray thorns peering into the room. It was among the largest I had ever seen, yellow eyes bright with obvious health and with curiosity.

"Um," I said. "Hello."

"Oh, that's just Spike." May waved a hand, dismissing the rose goblin's presence as unremarkable and understandable. "It stays downstairs most of the time, where the kitchen and the gardens are, but it might come up sometimes, so try not to be startled."

"I'm familiar with rose goblins." Before my enchanted sleep, I'd even been able to understand them, thanks to the magic I'd inherited from my mother. That magic was gone now, along with any hope of understanding. Still, I remembered enough of their body language to feel safe crouching a bit and extending my hand for the beast to sniff, which it did, with exquisite delicacy, before rubbing its cheek against my fingers.

It was careful to rub with the grain of its thorns, not against, and I was unharmed as I straightened and smiled at it,

"This one's quite well socialized," I said. May laughed, bright and merry.

"I should hope so, with as much time as we've all spent spoiling it," she said. "There are two mortal cats as well, Cagney and Lacey, but they're quite old and spend most of their time in Toby's room upstairs, so you're not likely to see them much. I'll point them out if we see them. Are you hungry?"

I shook my head, feeling suddenly awkward and out of place. I never felt much like I belonged anywhere, but I was accustomed to being met either with fawning flattery or with dislike. This plain, practical welcome was enough outside my experience to be confusing.

"Well, if that changes, I can make you a sandwich," said May, warmly. "It's too bad you don't have any luggage, I can't offer to help you with your bags. Come along, this way." And she moved past me, starting for the stairs.

I followed. Refusing would have been both rude and foolish, as it would have left me alone in this unfamiliar place, with no idea what I was going to do next. She took the stairs two at a time, as if moving any more slowly would have been unbearable. I followed more carefully, step by step, looking around as I went.

The walls were painted a plain, unremarkable shade of cream, dotted with framed pictures. It took me a moment to recognize the people in them as October, Tybalt, and their respective teenage wards, all of them draped in the simple veils of their human disguises. There were also pictures of a woman I assumed was May with a dark-haired, brown-skinned woman I didn't recognize at all.

May followed my gaze and smiled. "That's my girlfriend slash fiancée, Jasmine. Jazz. She's probably up in our room right now, sleeping. She's a Raven-maid, so she's basically diurnal. That's one of the things you'll have to get used to, living here. Someone's always awake."

Meaning I would never be entirely alone, even if I got up in the middle of the day. The thought should have been smothering—was I going to be constantly supervised? Instead, it was comforting. No one would steal me away, not from here. No one would seize me and hurl me back down into the dark. October had promised to give me a safe place to heal, and despite the chaos that attended on her at all times, I believed her. If peace was possible, she would provide it.

I didn't say any of this to May, only nodded and let her lead me down the upstairs hall to the very last door on the left. It was closed, as were most of the doors, and a window filled the wall between it and the door on the right, letting the moonlight in. She stopped there, smiling at me, and tapped the doorknob. "This is yours," she said, and opened the door.

At Shadowed Hills, I had a chamber fit for the princess my mother seemed to believe I was, huge and intimidating. I sometimes feared I might get lost in there. This room . . . wasn't that.

It wasn't so small as to be oppressive. If I stood in the center of the room and stretched my arms out as wide as they would go, I wouldn't be able to touch the walls. At the same time, I would be able to *see* them. Losing things in there would be difficult. There was a twin bed, already made and covered by a patchwork quilt in pinks and yellows; a dresser, a desk, and a bookshelf, on which several tattered paperbacks had been placed. Gray curtains covered the window, blocking my view of the outside world, and the closet door was open, showing the small space inside. It was plain, and bare, and beautiful.

I was staring. May stepped out of the way, wincing.

"We didn't want to go too deeply into decorating," she said. "There seemed to be too much of a chance you wouldn't like what we chose, or you'd want something different, and we didn't want you to be uncomfortable while you were still getting adjusted. I know all the best thrift stores in this part of the city, and Jazz owns an antique store over in Berkeley. We can go shopping tomorrow if you'd like, start getting you things you'll actually like . . ."

She was starting to sound genuinely distressed. I realized that if I didn't reassure her, this was going to spiral into something unpleasant.

"No," I said quickly, cutting her off. "I mean, yes, I'd love to go shopping with you, it sounds really nice, but no, there's nothing wrong with the room. This is perfect. I'm going to be happy here."

May blinked at me. Then she smiled, slow and wide, and said, "Oh. Good. Toby'll be glad to hear that too. I'll just let you get settled in then, shall I? I'll be right downstairs if you need me for anything. And don't worry about Toby. She'll be fine. They all will."

On that somewhat vague reassurance, she backed out of the room, and I was alone.

I waited until she was gone before I shut the door, relishing the click it made. I was *alone*. Awake, and alone. I had privacy. It was an intoxicating, dizzying feeling that I didn't fully know what to do with. I spun in the middle of the room, arms stretched out wide, and then stopped before I could make myself dizzy. The bed looked soft and inviting. I walked over and stretched out, closing my eyes.

I didn't intend to sleep.

I slept anyway.

The air around me was cold and heavy, thick with mist and smoke. It wasn't the acrid smoke of a fire trapped inside, but the rich, diffuse smoke of a bonfire, tangled tight with the waxen smoke of a candle—or a hundred candles, all of them lit and burning down somewhere nearby. I mumbled and rubbed at my nose, trying to chase the smell away. Nothing changed.

Maybe the window was open behind the sheltering fabric wall of the curtains. I sat up, not opening my eyes, and moved to get out of the bed, intending to close the window and block the cold from coming further into the room.

The floor wasn't there. Instead, I tumbled to the ground, landing on hard-packed earth strewn with dead, rot-scented leaves and rocks. The shock of the impact snapped my eyes open, and I stared at my surroundings, trying to orient myself.

Vision didn't help. I seemed to be somewhere in the middle of a vast forest, the trees spaced widely, their trunks and branches twisted into elaborate shapes that were unnervingly evocative of the fae form. Some of them looked almost like people that had been wrapped in bark and frozen in the act of fleeing from some unseen threat.

This was not the bedroom May had shown me to. Nor was it the dreamscape I had been pulled into when October and I spoke during my enchanted sleep. This was someplace new, and—from the bruised sensation in my behind—someplace distressingly real.

I stood, grateful to be alone as I tried to rub the sting out of my rump with one hand. My manners might not be as polished as most people would expect from a Duke's daughter, after my period of confinement in the dark, but I'd been old enough when we were taken to know the basics, and "don't caress your own ass in front of people" was one of the things they'd managed to drum into my head when I was still a little girl.

Keeping one hand on the tree I'd fallen out of as the only land-mark I was absolutely sure existed, I began to turn a slow circle, try-ing to figure out where I was and where I was supposed to go from here. The smell of smoke seemed to be strongest to the east, and so, once my bottom no longer ached so much that I wasn't sure I could walk, I took my hand off the tree and started wandering slowly in that direction.

The smell of smoke grew even stronger as I walked, until it stung my nose and made my eyes water. It was acrid and unpleasant, and unsurprising when I finally stepped out of the edge of the trees and into a clearing that had formed around a small collection of stone ruins. The buildings were broken and crumbling: only the largest of them still had anything resembling a roof. The trees nearest the ruins had branches covered in row upon row of tall white candles, some of them apparently freshly-placed, while others had burned down to stubs. Trails of wax dribbled down from them to form long ribbons, some stretching all the way to the ground.

A bonfire burned at the center of the space, with haybales pulled up around it in a rough circle. Some of them were occupied by figures I couldn't quite focus on, their bodies oddly shaped and almost dis-torted in ways my eyes refused to catalog. For all that they had shaped a circle, it had a head, of sorts, defined by a raised platform contain-ing two tall, high-backed chairs. I would have called them thrones in another setting, their arms and legs dark with soot that almost en-tirely obscured the gilded patterning on the wood. One of them was occupied, by a tall, thin figure with skin the color of birch bark and antlers similar to those Oberon was said to have adorning his brow. His eyes were marble white from side to side, and even as he turned his head to look around the clearing, they didn't seem to fully track.

The other chair was empty.

Father isn't royal, but a ducal rank is no small thing among the nobility, and as his child, I would be considered a Lady until I mar-ried into or acquired a title of my own. I had always been taught to seek the aid of nobles when necessary, and so I stood as straight as I could find the courage for, and held my head high as I started toward the man in the high chair.

A raven croaked in the tree behind me. I flinched, barely stopping myself from looking back. More ravens called from nearby branches, their harsh voices spilling through the air. The man in the chair slowly turned his face in my direction.

I couldn't honestly say that he looked at me. It didn't seem like he was looking at anything at all, and even with him focusing directly on me, I wasn't certain he could *see* me in any meaningful way.

"Who are you?" he asked, in a voice like stones rolling down a hillside.

My mouth went dry. I suddenly had no reasonable answer to that question. Who was I? My first urge was to define myself by my family, to answer "Rayseline Torquill" and let my father's reputation carry me through the conversation. On the occasions when the person I spoke to didn't know my father, they would generally know my uncle, and while that was a very different reputation to trade upon, he owed me.

But I had all but begged October to claim offense and take me from them. While that didn't sunder me from my family as a divorce would have done, it made the thought of trading upon them leave a sour taste in my mouth. It was time for me to start building my own reputation, since I couldn't rely on theirs.

"Raysel," I said, forcing myself to keep my eyes locked on his, refusing to look away. If he was going to stare at me, I was going to stare at him, and we'd see who blinked first. "Who are you?"

To my intense surprise, he threw back his head and laughed. "As if you don't know, little mouse! You walk my forest, you stand in the light of my fire, you must have encountered my Riders to have come here. You know me. All the bravery and bravado in the world won't change my answer to that question. I changed it once. Never again, little mouse. I am the man they made me, and shall be until the sky comes tumbling down and Oberon returns to let us into the deeper realms once more, where we can scatter and seek safety in the solitude we once made."

"I'm sorry," I said. "I never saw any Riders. I'm currently— My cousin, October? I upset her, badly, and she claimed offense against me. I'm spending a year in her service. I was in the room she set aside for me, and I must have fallen asleep. When I woke up, I was here. No Riders. Nothing but a nap gone really, really weird."

"Have they started reusing names in Faerie, then? I suppose it was inevitable."

I blinked. "What?"

"Oh, that Shakespeare fellow had the right of it. Our parents came into being with their names already singing in their hearts, and they named their children whatever they pleased, because there was no chance of confusion, not with so very few of us to choose between. Then we began to have children of our own, and we named them for the things around us. That was the era of Moths and Mustardseeds, Apples and Acacias. All the aspects of the natural world. But we ran out of those, over time, and by then, we had begun to steal the beginnings of culture and custom from the humans we lived alongside. We decided that to reuse names was an insult, and worse, a chance that someone who deserved it might be targeted with a spell that would then go awry, latching on to the wrong target when the names were unclear. We began stealing our names from the humans. They had so many, after all, and we reproduced so slowly. Surely we would never exhaust the supply. But they must have started to reuse them."

I frowned at him. "Why?"

"Because the only October I know is a changeling, and changelings can no more claim offense against purebloods than I can see the world through my own eyes." He smirked at me, leaning back in his seat. "I knew you for a liar as soon as you claimed not to have seen my Ride, and you've simply confirmed it, little mouse. 'Raysel,' you say. Another rose for my garden. My lady wife will be quite pleased. She likes roses well enough that when we came together, she birthed them."

I took a step backward. "You're not making sense."

The ravens croaked in the trees around me, softer this time, almost like they were laughing. The man smiled, slow and cruel. "Aren't I? If you're a fool as well as a liar, that's not something that can be held against you, but if you're simply refusing to see what's true because it frightens you, then I'm afraid I'll have to hold *everything* against you."

One of the ravens cried out—not a croak this time but a caw of fear and distress. The man's head whipped around, focusing on the bird as it fell out of its tree, landing next to a jagged, bloody rock.

"Who threw that?" he asked, voice low. "I will have your bones!"

"Run," hissed a voice from the shadows along the tree line. It was close enough that I flinched away, and more than half-familiar.

The man was starting to rise from his seat, rage all but radiating from his skin. Something about it was terribly familiar.

"Your bones *and* your skin," he roared. His head swung around again, white eyes focusing on me, as much as they ever focused on anything—he couldn't see me with his own eyes, I realized. He was watching me through the birds.

Which meant there was a gap in his sight where the bird had been knocked out of the tree. I turned and bolted for the opening, running as hard as I could, and his laughter followed me away from the fire-light, into the dark beneath the trees.

I've never been much of a runner. Terror was enough to put some speed into my legs, but terror doesn't last forever, and eventually I stumbled to a halt, heart pounding and lungs aching from the unfa-miliar exertion. I braced myself against one of the unnervingly person-shaped trees, waiting for my breathing to level out, or at least to calm enough that I could hear if any birds were nearby.

Eventually, I stopped wheezing. I forced myself upright, listening as hard as I could, and heard nothing but the wind rustling through the leafless branches around me. If someone had been looking for a landscape to use as the definition of "haunted forest," they could have done substantially worse than this one, which looked blighted in a way I didn't even have the words for. The branches weren't thick enough to block out this much of the sky, and yet they did, so com-pletely that when I looked upward, I couldn't see a scrap of starlight.

This place. I had never been here before, I knew that, but some-thing about it was familiar, like I had heard of it in a story. Maybe I was asleep, and this was a particularly vivid, frustrating dream. Or maybe I had been magically abducted from October's house despite the wards that should have protected me from anything of the sort.

I was putting a lot of faith in her wards, considering she was a changeling who had never shown much skill in anything outside of pure blood magic. But then, she shared her home with the King of Cats, his heir apparent, and a blind foster who was technically in trust to my father. Quentin might come from the least important noble family on the continent. He might also come from a family that car-ried a crown. Either way, Father would be held responsible if any-thing happened to him, and while my father can seem disorganized and distracted at times, he knows how to do his duty. He wouldn't let Quentin live with October if he didn't trust that she could keep the boy safe. So maybe putting my faith in her wards wasn't so foolish.

And that meant this *must* be a dream, because I couldn't have been taken from her house. I leaned my forehead against the tree, closing my eyes, and tried to focus on waking up. Nothing changed. I tried again, remembering the moment the elf-shot cure had filled my throat, and the dreams in which I'd been drifting had finally started to dissolve.

Nothing changed. I opened my eyes as I straightened, pulling one hand back to smack the tree, which hadn't done anything to deserve my anger. I felt bad about hitting it almost instantly, and not only because the impact stung my palm. Clutching my hand to my chest, I turned and leaned back against the tree, resting the crown of my head against the wood as I stared up into the starless sky.

Wherever I was, I was really there. I had been stolen again, snatched from a place of supposed safety and thrown into the dark. This iteration wasn't formless and black like the pit where Uncle Simon had thrown me and Mother, but it was dark and tangled and terrible and terrifying, and I didn't dare go back to the firelight or the man with the ravens for eyes.

And just like that, I knew who he was, and who he couldn't be, because Blind Michael was my grandfather, and he was dead, killed by October on one of her earlier hero's quests. I'd still been running wild and bitter when that happened, but I'd heard about it—everyone in the Kingdom had heard about it, the way she drove blades of iron and silver into his heart, after she risked herself to save the children he had stolen.

I'd been taken by a dead man, and "impossible" is a nonsense word that's more indicative of what people *want* to be true than what the actual truth is, almost always. This was really happening. That meant it wasn't impossible.

"Are you done having your little breakdown, or should I come back later?"

It was the voice from before, still only half-familiar. I jerked away from the tree, looking frantically around as I tried to find the speaker.

He sighed, heavily. "Try looking up."

I looked up. Not at the sky, this time, but at the nearby trees. And there, three trees over from where I stood, was a boy about my age, wearing simple, practical clothing—beige slacks and a loose white shirt with long sleeves and an undone collar. He was barefoot, which had probably helped with climbing the tree, and with sneaking up on me in the first place.

He nodded when he saw me looking, and dropped out of the tree to land in a crouch, which he straightened from slowly before he started walking toward me.

"Not who I'd have guessed I was going to see here, but hello," he said.

I blinked.

He was a little taller than I was, with tawny tan-brown skin several shades darker than my own, and dark hair inexplicably streaked in green. His eyes were a very deep blue, and his hands were webbed, although not as dramatically as a pure Merrow's would have been; the webbing only extended to the first knuckle.

And one of the fingers on his right hand was missing, cut off at the point where the webs connected. It gave his hand an asymmetry that was hard not to look at, even though I knew I shouldn't. It's beyond rude to stare, and would have been even if the missing finger hadn't been my fault.

"Dean," I said, shame washing through me like icy bleach. It left me cold and unsteady, stripping away what little calm I'd had remaining.

"Rayseline," he replied, sounding much calmer than I felt. "Any idea where we are?"

Speaking it wouldn't make it any more true than it already was, so I swallowed what I could stomach of my shame and said, "Blind Michael's lands."

"Your grandfather, the monster. The *dead* monster."

I nodded.

"And I'm supposed to think us both being here at the same time is a coincidence?"

"I don't know what you're *supposed* to think, or what either one of us is *supposed* to think," I said. "I don't know how I got here. I was at October's house, lying on the bed in the room where I'm supposed to be staying, and then I was in a tree."

"How did you get out of the tree?"

He sounded like he was actually interested, so I shrugged and said, "I fell."

He laughed.

I don't like being laughed at. I bristled, glaring at him. "It's not that funny!"

"It is, though. The kidnapper gets kidnapped, and the first thing they do is leave you up in a tree." He calmed, glaring at me. "I let them wake you up. That's the last bit of courtesy you get from me. I still know what you are."

"Lost, confused, and a little sore from falling out of a tree?" I ventured.

"Monster," he replied, almost calmly. "You're the person who kidnapped me and my baby brother, and nearly killed us both in the process. Elf-shot isn't a useful punishment. People don't learn from their mistakes because they sleep so long their lives pass them by, they don't get better, they don't *change*. October saved us, and if she wants to save you, too, I'll let her, because I'm not the one who gets to tell her who's worth saving. But that doesn't mean I'm going to forgive you, or that I'm going to forget what you did to us. I don't want you anywhere near me."

"So why did you save me from . . . ?"

"From Blind Michael? Because he may be your grandfather, but he's still a bigger monster than you ever were. I wouldn't shed any tears for you. That doesn't mean I want to make *him* any stronger than he already is. Stay away from him . . . and stay away from *me*."

Dean turned then, walking off into the forest, leaving me even more confused.

What the hell was going on?

One thing people don't consider much about elf-shot: while you're elf-shot, you're stopped. You sleep, and that's all you do. You don't starve or die of thirst, you don't wet yourself because you can't wake up to go to the bathroom, nothing. You just *exist*. I'd been just existing for so long that I flinched when my stomach growled, not fully recognizing the sound.

It growled again. I realized what it had to be and sighed, rubbing it with one hand.

"We've been hungry before," I informed it. "We'll be hungry again. You can deal with this."

My stomach kept growling, making it clear that it didn't believe me in the slightest. I sighed a second time, looking around the forest.

There was nothing obviously edible in sight, no berry bushes or possibly questionable mushrooms. Nothing. I turned in the direction Dean had gone. I was probably the last person he wanted to see, but he seemed to have a better grasp of this place than I did; maybe he could tell me where to find something I could eat. And if he couldn't, at least I wouldn't be hungry and alone.

I started walking after him, looking down to track his footprints in the leaves. Nothing had disturbed them since he passed; his trail was clear. I kept walking, stopping whenever I heard a sound, but as none of the sounds came from a raven, I felt relatively confident in continuing on my way.

I'd walked almost as far as I'd run when fleeing from my grandfather before a low rock wall appeared ahead of me, the individual stones stacked so that gravity held them together, each covered by a thick layer of moss that was the greenest, most living thing I'd seen since we arrived here. The trail led me to the base of the wall, and so I continued cautiously toward it, pausing when I got there to lean up onto my toes and look over the wall.

On the other side was a garden, in disrepair but still fruiting. Tomato plants and long vines covered in runner beans, half the fruit rotting where it hung, the other half looking perfectly safe to eat. Dean's footsteps continued through the wreckage.

My stomach growled again. I scrambled over the wall and tumbled down on the other side, landing once more on my poor, abused behind. I didn't wait for the aching to fade this time, just got to my feet and began filling my hands with tomatoes and beans, corn and blueberries. All the fruit had a dry, almost mealy taste to it, like half its moisture had been transformed into dust. I still chewed and swallowed every scrap I'd stolen. Theft was an insult. Pointless theft was an offense.

This garden, withered and wasted as it was, had nourished me, and I would remember that. I swallowed the last bite of bean, bowed respectfully to the plants, and resumed my pursuit of Dean.

His trail only went a short way before it bent toward another cluster of stone ruins, this one even more shattered than the ones around Blind Michael's bonfire. The walls were broken and crumbling, seemingly held together by patches of moss and clinging ivy. Nothing even resembling a roof or window remained. But I could smell smoke, not that far in the distance, and Dean's footsteps seemed to be heading in that direction. I continued onward.

There was a gap in one of the damaged walls. I ducked through it and found myself in a small clearing tightly ringed with trees, their branches twisted so tightly together overhead that a passing raven would have had little chance of spotting the occupants. There was a bonfire there, much smaller than Blind Michael's, and three figures sat around it. Dean, another boy whose near-skeletal frame and foam-white hair marked him as at least partially Sea Wight, and a girl in patchwork leather armor who looked as if she'd been cobbled together from half a dozen different types of fae.

Her ears were long and furred, like a rabbit's, which should have been an indication that she was at least part Pooka, but one of her legs ended in a horse's hoof, while the other was a more standard foot. Her face was a blend of Daoine Sidhe, Gwragen, and Baobhan Sith, while her eyes were an almost-luminous shade of yellow that would have been far more at home on one of the Cait Sidhe or Reynardine.

One ear twitched as I stepped through the wall, and she glanced in my direction. "I thought you said you'd shaken her off in the woods," she said, voice roving up and down octaves in an uneven sliding pattern, one word high and piping, the next low and sultry.

"I thought I had," said Dean, defensively. He turned to glare at me. "Did I ask you to follow me here?"

"Did I ask you to leave me alone in the woods?" I countered. "What the hell is going on? How the hell are we in Blind Michael's lands?"

"You've answered yourself in the asking: These are Blind Michael's lands, and here, all that matters is his will," said the girl, turning to focus on me. Her ears twitched as she did, rotating slightly, so that they were also pointed in my direction. Everything I said, she'd hear. Maybe everything I didn't say as well.

"How did we *get* here?"

"That, I don't know," she said. "Master seems to think there was a Ride to gather new children for his stable, but there wasn't. There hasn't been a Ride since he died. Mistress doesn't stand with the theft of children, says we have to be better than he was if we ever want to win our way out of this wood. Not all of us do. Some of us have been here so long there's nowhere else for going off to. Some of us know this is the best place for us to be. So we wouldn't care if there were a Ride, but there wasn't one. Don't know why everyone believes there was. Don't know why the Master's back, either. He's been dead a while. Dead people usually stay that way."

She sounded affronted by the fact that he hadn't. I blinked, very slowly, as I looked to Dean and the other boy.

The boy shrugged. "Don't ask me. I was at home, in my bedroom, trying to finish my book report, and then I was standing in a bog almost up to my knees. It took both my shoes while I was trying to get out of it. Not cool."

"Raysel, this is Scott," said Dean, with a heavy sigh. "He's a Sea Wight changeling."

"I prefer 'Sea Wight with extra bonus iron resistance and ability to

stay out of the water for more than six hours,'" said Scott. "I am
Aquaman."

"I thought that was a comic book character," I said, more bewildered than anything else.

Scott sputtered, then glowered at me. "Sense of humor. Get one."

"Scott, this is Rayseline Torquill. She's my . . . I have no idea what she is. She's my stepfather's niece, so I guess that would make her my step-cousin-in-law, or something like that. She's also the one who cut my finger off."

"I said I was sorry!" I protested.

Dean leveled a cold look on me. "No. You didn't."

"Well, I would have, if I hadn't been elf-shot all this time," I said. "I really am sorry. I wasn't thinking clearly back then."

"Because your mother was a rose bush and you weren't supposed to have been biologically possible."

"Yes!" I said, almost desperately. "I didn't understand what I was doing! I'm sorry I hurt you."

"Well, my mother was a fish, and I've never chopped anyone's fingers off."

"I—" I stopped, and sagged. "I can't say I didn't mean it, because I did it, it's done, and nothing I say makes it not have happened. And I can't make you accept that I'm sorry. It wouldn't be right of me to do it if I could."

Dean eyed me, apparently waiting for the catch. When it didn't come, he sighed, and said, "Scott's dad is one of my mom's subjects. It seems like everyone who just wound up here is like the two of us, part land and part sea. Everyone except for you."

"And me," said the patchwork girl, voice continuing its ridiculous slide up and down the octaves. "I've been here long and long and long again. This was my fire, before children started dropping out the sky and needing a place to sit and be warm where the Master wouldn't see them. I was took in one of the last Rides, but then a knight come out of the Summerlands and struck the Master down dead as dead in the dust, left us all with only our Mistress. She opened the stables and let us all out, who weren't proper Riders yet, and I've not changed further than I'd done before she freed us."

I frowned. "So why are you willing to help us?"

"Master's dead," she said. "Master's dead but Master's sitting there, bold as brass, and no one else seems to realize he's not supposed to be here. Sets me wrong, really. I don't like when things are other than they ought to be."

"How many of us are here?" I asked, glancing to Dean.

"Half a dozen that I've seen so far," he said. "That isn't counting you, or Medley."

"Medley" must have been the patchwork girl, because she nodded at the sound of her name, leaning back on her hands. "I don't count," she said. "This is my territory, and I can show where's safe to sleep and scavenge, and help with staying clear of the Riders, but only if you all allow that I'm in charge here. What I say's right is what's right, and argument's not my favorite game. Master doesn't like argument, either, but what he does if you argue him is a lot worse than I'll do. I might bite you, might snap my jaws and brandish my claws, but I won't do much beyond. He'll see you locked in the stables, and what's stabled . . ." She paused to shudder, then looked down at her hands. The fingers of one were much longer than the fingers of the other, making them look like they belonged to two entirely different people. "What's stabled changes," she finished.

"So we stay away from Blind Michael," said Dean.

"He's my grandfather," I said. "I never met him while he was alive, but—should I really stay away from him? If I can explain who I am, won't that make him want to help me?"

"He's still *Blind Michael*," said Dean, voice flat with disbelief. "He's not going to treat you kindly just because you're his daughter's kid."

"Which daughter?" asked Medley, cocking her head as she looked at me. "People say he had five of them with the Mistress, but they were all gone when first I came here, and there's only one who's returned since then. She came right as the Master returned, and the rest of you began appearing around my fire. I think it's all connected, although I can't say as how, and . . ." She leaned forward abruptly, clutching the sides of her head and grimacing. She stayed that way for a few seconds, rocking back and forth as if she were trying to soothe herself, then glanced back up at me. "And when I try too hard to think on it, my head hurts something awful. I don't think I'm meant for knowing that things aren't right as they are now. I think I'm meant for being like the rest of them, and believing the Master never died, and this is as things have always been. I'll guess it's some Firstborn nonsense. Master and the Mistress both are, you know, even if people don't speak of it so much as they used to do."

"If you're supposed to think like all the rest of them, why don't you?" I asked.

"Master's stables are terrible places," she said, shaking not just her head, but her entire body, a shoulder-down shudder that went on longer than seemed possible. "Stay in them for long enough, you start to change."

"Change how?" asked Scott.

"Change to all different sorts of fae at the same time. Your magic gets all mix-and-match first, and then your body follows, and last of all, your mind, until you think like all different things at the same time. Can't manage your magic until your thinking catches up, since half of magic is in the understanding, but can't change out the order. I was Hob and human when his people took me, ordinary as anything, and happy with my place in Faerie. Can't hardly clean a hearth now. But I can be a cat, or a fox, with the thinking of it, and cats and foxes both never much liked having people throw magic around when they were in the way. I think that whatever was done, whatever Firstborn nonsense this is, I'd spent too much time in the stables without going for a Ride, and so I'm not any one thing that the magic can hook all the way on to. Nobody else had spent as much time in the stables without Riding as I had. Once you Ride, you're all one thing, forever, and even sleeping in the stables won't change you more. Most of the Riders do, when they don't feel like going all the way back to their barracks."

"Okay, so we stay away from the stables," I said. "Which way is Blind Michael's bonfire from here?"

"You can't really intend to go and talk to the man," said Dean.

"He's my grandfather, and I have to do something," I countered. "I'm going to see if he can help us. I'm sure once he understands the situation, he'll be accommodating."

"That way," said Medley, pointing into the trees. "Close enough for a quick walking, far enough that he won't hear us as long as we're a little careful. Easier to steal supplies when you're close, easier to get caught when you're too close."

"I'll be right back," I said, and turned to go.

"Raysel!"

Dean sounded genuinely concerned. I stopped, looking back at him. "Yes?"

"Just . . ." He scowled. "Just be careful, okay? Toby will be *pissed* if a monster she already killed kills you when you're supposed to be serving her for a year."

"I will," I said, and started walking again.

This time, he didn't call me back, and I didn't pause.

Medley was telling the truth: her fire wasn't far from Blind Michael's. When I got back there, he was still seated in his tall chair, the trees around him dense with candles and ravens. The other chair was occupied now as well, by a yellow-skinned woman in a brown velvet dress with a scar along one side of her face. He was holding her hand, the two of them looking for all the world like a king and queen of the wood attending on their court. And in front of them . . .

I stopped, breath catching in my throat, and pressed a hand against my mouth like I could physically stop myself from gasping and giving my position away.

In front of them, on the other side of the fire from where I now stood, was my mother.

She was as she had been since her recovery from my attempt to assist Oleander in assassinating her: skin as white as polished bone, and long pink hair that changed shade between the root and the tips. She was taller than I was, and slimmer, two things I could easily attribute to the fact that no matter how much she looked like a mammal, she wasn't one. She was Blodynbryd, a Dryad of the Roses, and the yellow-skinned woman was her mother, Acacia, better known as the Mother of the Trees.

We call the children of Oberon, Maeve, and Titania "Firstborn," because all descendant lines of Faerie spring from them, but they're not the first of us, not really. Their children are the first of us, two steps removed from the Three and finally stabilizing into whatever Faerie needs them to be. According to the family history, Acacia bore the Dryads before she took Michael as her husband, and together they birthed the Blodynbryd.

If Acacia had taken another lover during the period Blind Michael spent dead—temporary as it had apparently been—she might have started a third descendant line, or simply borne slightly modified Dryads or Blodynbryd. It's always hard to guess, when the Firstborn are involved. Mother's children would always be at least partially Blodynbryd, if she had any more now that she didn't have me, and she wasn't going to be having them with Father. Their biology and their magic were too far removed from one another to make that possible. I should never have been born.

I remembered what it had been, to feel the sun nourishing me, to taste the soil beneath my feet, to sit among the roses and hear their slow, thoughtful whispers in a space that was not sound but was deeper than that, a communication buried in my bones. When my uncle had cast us down into darkness, he had been even crueler than I think he knew. He deprived two roses, both cloaked in flesh, of the sun.

Had either of us been purely Blodynbryd when he took us, I don't believe we would have survived long enough to find our freedom. I glanced at the dark sky above and wondered how Mother and her siblings had ever been able to survive here at all. There didn't seem sufficient sun for their thriving.

That was a question for another time. For now, the question before me was whether I could face my mother. I had fled Shadowed Hills more due to her than to my father, who would have been happy to begin training me in the ways of my newly modified magic, but who had always bowed before Mother's insistence that I was more her child than his. It was Mother who had always most wanted to control me, to shape me into a younger duplicate of herself.

In the darkness, she had been my only companion, my only company, and so I had clung to her as tightly as I could, unable to move more than a few feet away without the risk of losing her for hours or days—not that we'd had any reliable way of marking the time while we'd been trapped. Her voice had been the thin tether to reality keeping me sane through all those terrible, torturous hours. I'd believed she would always be my best friend in the world, my only friend . . .

And then we'd been freed, and suddenly she'd wanted nothing more than to open her eyes and find me exactly as I'd been on the day when we went gathering flowers and found ourselves thrust instead into a lightless hell. She wanted a sweet, malleable child, not a furious, broken young woman who didn't understand her own temper, who got quickly overwhelmed in crowds, who couldn't handle sudden noises or too many people. She'd been intending to raise me as a show dog. What she got instead was a half-feral creature kept too long in chains.

In a world where I'd never been imprisoned, where my magic could have been recognized and trained sooner, where they would have seen the signs of the war my body was waging against itself before that war turned unwinnable, I might have been happy to become her perfect daughter. I might have chosen a softer balance than all or nothing, willing to let October experiment with the warring factions in my bloodstream and seek a way to keep both sides of my genetic heritage intact. And—the greatest change between that world that never was and this one—if I had still needed to choose to make myself one thing or the other, I might well have chosen Blodynbryd. Father had a duchy to manage, after all. Mother had only ever had, well, me. Without the abduction changing everything, I would probably have remained her gleeful shadow, gathering flowers and fighting the growing rot within me as best I knew how.

Here, though . . . she wasn't supposed to *be* here. To be fair, I wasn't supposed to be here either; none of this made any sense, and I just wanted it to all be over.

Which began with speaking to the man who watched her as she spoke with my grandmother, a small, indulgent smile on his face. Careful to move slowly and avoid attracting too much attention, I started across the clearing, weaving between the haybales as I made for the trio.

More oddities presented themselves as I drew closer. Mother's feet were bare, exposing toes that darkened from the dead white of the rest of her skin, becoming brown and gnarled. Her dress, while it fit her well enough, clearly tailored to her form, was simple and largely shapeless, brown linen with green embroidery around the hems. It was the sort of dress worn by a daughter of the house when she wasn't meant to be attracting attention or commanding respect. A child's dress, in other words. Why would Mother, a married woman with a demesne and duties of her own, be wearing a child's dress?

Her hair had been pulled back and braided at the temples, forming a complicated knot at the back of her head, and that, combined with the dress, made her look younger than she ever had before.

It was strange enough that I almost turned and ran. I wanted to. I wanted to speak with Blind Michael even more, and I wanted this to end most of all.

I continued forward, until a raven croaked above me and I knew I had been seen. Still, Blind Michael didn't turn to face me until I had walked right up on the edge of their conversation, when he finally tilted his face in my direction and said, "*Bold* intruder. I have few uninvited guests. Fewer yet are willing to approach me so very openly. Why did you come back here?"

"I . . . I want . . ." It had seemed so easy from a distance. Walk up to Blind Michael. Tell him he was my grandfather and that I didn't know how I'd arrived here. Ask him to take me back to October's house, and to patch whatever hole in the wards had allowed for my abduction in the first place. But I hadn't anticipated the weight of his eyes, unseeing but still somehow focused as he looked at me through his ravens, and I hadn't known my mother would be there. She changed everything.

He chuckled, beginning to turn away.

I blurted: "I want to go home!"

"They all want to go home, in the beginning," said Acacia, joining her husband in watching me. "Even the ones who came voluntarily—and there are more of those than the stories admit, especially among the changelings, who have good reason to run—but even they cry for the familiar in the first days after they've been taken. Your wanting to go home is no special thing, child. You have my sympathies, but you cannot have my aid."

"I only wish I knew how you had come to be here," said Blind Michael. A raven fluttered down and landed on his shoulder, giving him a closer look at me. "There's been no Ride recent enough for you to be so untouched by this land. How are you here?"

"I . . ." I caught my breath, swallowing hard. Mother still hadn't acknowledged my presence. "I caused offense to a noble household. I was asleep in the room that will be mine while I serve them, and then I was here. Today. I don't remember a Ride, and if I seem untouched, it really is because I haven't been here very long. I'm not *supposed* to be here. Please. Help me go home."

"Why?" asked Mother, finally turning to look at me. She must have waited so long so she could school her face, because she looked at me like I was a stranger, like she had never seen me before. "If you were serving on a claim of offense, how is serving here any different? You'll be a Rider for my father's Hunt. You'll be powerful, strong, and strange, and there won't be anything like you in all of Faerie. And when it's done, you'll be free to Ride through the night on his business, and no one will touch or trouble you."

"Mother, I know you didn't want me to choose Daoine Sidhe, but this is more punishment than I deserve," I blurted, reaching for her.

She shied back, eyes going wide. "*Mother*?" she squeaked.

Blind Michael laughed. "Calm yourself, my moon. She's grasping

at whatever ropes she thinks might pull her from the pit of her pre-
dicament. They always do. She casts no aspersions on your character,
but it seems she doesn't know to whom she speaks."

"Our child—like all our children—is of a vegetable bloodline,"
said Acacia, voice icy cold. "You, from the looks of you, descend
from the garden of my sister, the Rose of Winter. You could no more
be my daughter's child than I could open the doors to deeper Faerie
with my own hand. Your pretense finds no traction here."

"But I—"

I stopped. Explaining the situation would take a long time, and
would probably confuse us all even more than we already were, especially as my mother truly seemed to have no idea who I was. It felt as
if I had been given my deepest wish in the worst way possible. I was
finally free of the weight of my mother's expectations and desires.
Because I was entirely free of my mother.

"Perhaps one of your Riders has slipped his leash and decided to
go collecting pretty pets for the empty stable stalls," said Acacia.
"Our Luna has named her a Rider, and so Rider she'll be; the next
we catch can be her steed."

I took a step backward, and then another, stopping when my shoulders hit against a solid wall of flesh. Tilting my head back, I looked
up at a hulking figure who seemed cut from the same patchwork cloth
as Medley. It wasn't the same blend of descendant lines, but it was
close enough to be clear as kin.

His hands closed on my shoulders, and I was trapped.

"To the stables with her," said Blind Michael. "Perhaps a night or
three will ease her tongue, and tell us what we need to know."

I was yanked off my feet then, and carried away from the three by
the fire, who should have been my family but were strangers as they
impassively watched me go.

The patchwork man threw me bodily into a low, dark space that
smelled of stale straw and too many bodies pressed close together. I
hit the ground and rolled, tumbling through the dark to land face-
down in a pile of rotting leaves.

Spitting bits of leaf and loam out of my mouth, I pushed myself up
onto my hands and looked around. As my eyes adjusted, I saw that
the space wasn't as dark as I had originally believed; sconces were set

into the walls, although they contained fat white candles in place of lanterns or torches. I was in the long central space of the stable, and stalls lined the walls, each one locked with tangled briars that looked like they would slice and tear the hands of anyone trying to open them.

Something moved in the dimness behind me. I turned.

"Who's there?"

The stable was long enough that even with my excellent night vision and the candles to lend their light, I couldn't see the far end. It sounded like something was shifting back there, hidden by the shadows. I pushed myself to my feet, dusting leaf litter and bits of straw from my palms as I peered into the dark.

"Whoever it is, come out," I called. "I'm not going to hurt you."

Of course, they might be planning to hurt me, but if that was the case, better to get it over with quickly.

There was a sniffling sound, and then a small boy, no more than six or seven, with waving sea anemone tentacles in place of hair, came shuffling out into the light. I couldn't name the bloodline he came from: as the daughter of a noble house, I should have been trained on such things from the time I was old enough to talk, and I had been, for the scant few years of my childhood in the light. But there had been no flashcards or etiquette lessons in our prison. What would have been the point?

October would know. Or Dean, if I saw him again. I could say "Hey Dean, what kind of person in the Undersea has hair like a sea anemone?" and he would just answer, and it would be a civil conversation with someone roughly my own age, and it would be amazing.

For the moment, though, there was a little boy creeping toward me, terror in his eyes and bands of soft white and blue pulsing through the waving tendrils of his hair.

"Hello," I said. "Are you alone in here?"

He shook his head, not saying a word.

"I'm Rayseline, but my friends call me Raysel, and a man put me here because Blind Michael didn't want me roaming free." I wished I could take my grandfather's name back as soon as I spoke it. The boy flinched away, looking more like a terrified animal than ever.

"He's not coming here," I said quickly. "He didn't want me free, and he didn't want me near his family, so he locked me up. Do you know how you got here?"

Again, the silent boy shook his head.

"He won't answer you," said a voice.

I turned. A girl had come out of the shadows near the main door. She was older than the boy and younger than me, perhaps twelve, with long, tangled blonde hair and fins running down the outside of her arms, translucent green with white edges that almost glowed in the dark. She was dressed in mortal-style clothes, blue jeans and a T-shirt with some boy-band idol printed on the front, and she was hugging herself defensively, which only put her fins into clearer view.

"Why not?" I asked.

"He can't," she said, with a shrug. "His father was a human, but his mum's a Tangie, and they can't talk when they're out of the water."

Well, there went my potential conversation with Dean. I sat down against the wall, hugging my knees against my chest. "You know him?"

"Not really," she said. "*My* mum pledges out of Roane Rathad, and he lives with his mum and brother all the way out at the edges of Saltmist. But sometimes she brings them inland, so they don't lose touch with the human side of their heritage. I think she hopes that if they spend enough time on land, they'll learn how to talk the way human people do, and have an easier time of it."

The boy scowled at her and made an emphatic gesture, using both hands. She rolled her eyes.

"I've told and told and told you, I can't read your hands," she said. "It's not that I don't want to, it's that I *can't*. I'm sorry."

The boy sighed heavily, lowering his hands and giving me a plaintive look. I shook my head.

"I'm sorry. I don't speak any kind of sign language," I said. "Some days, I feel like I barely speak English." I looked at the girl. "Do you know how you got here?"

"I was playing Call of Duty with some friends of mine, and then I—I don't know. It was like I blacked out or something. And then I was landing in this nasty little creek full of mud and crawdads. They pinched. I got out and went looking for a grownup, and what I found was a biker gang or something. They tossed me in here."

"How many of us *are* there?"

She shrugged. "About a dozen so far. And I'm not sure if it's an 'us.' You're the only pureblood I've seen. All the rest of us are either changelings, or we're a mix of at least two descendant lines. And we're all Undersea. That's the weirdest part. I don't see what you're doing in here with us, because you're not Undersea at all."

"Undersea?" I asked blankly.

She held up her arms, showing me her fins. "Siren," she said. She pointed to the boy. "Tangie. We've got Merrow and Fuath and Nixie and even a pair of Roane. We're all scooped out of the Undersea, and you're not. So why are *you* here?"

Dean was Undersea, with his Merrow mother. I worried a lock of hair between my fingers, trying to puzzle out the connection. "Do you know Dean Lorden?"

"Duchess of Saltmist's older boy, currently Count of Goldengreen in the Mists, so it's questionable whether he's my superior or not, since technically the Undersea and the land are distinct political entities," she recited, and I heard the echo of my own short-lived etiquette lessons in her carefully chosen words.

"He's here."

She perked up, losing her air of studied disinterest in an instant. "Here?"

"Not in this room here, but in this realm here. I saw him before they took me. If he's not in here, they haven't managed to catch him yet." Hopefully, Medley's presence meant he wouldn't be captured at all.

She nodded, looking toward one of the holes in the roof with sudden hope. "If he's loose, he might come and save us," she said. "My mother always says the Duchess of Saltmist is brave and stubborn and not very clever, and that her sons inherited all she is, so I'm sure he'll be fool enough to try and rescue us all if he knows we're here. Does he know we're here?"

"I think he knows there's more than just him and me and a boy named Scott, but I don't know how much more than that he knows." I also didn't know whether he would come to my rescue if he thought I was the only one who'd been captured. Even Medley's dire proclamations about the nature of the stable and its changes might not be enough to make him willing to save *me*.

Maybe it had been foolish to go to my grandparents expecting help. But how was I supposed to guess my mother would be there, or that she would somehow not know who I was?

I didn't think she'd been pretending, either. There had been no recognition in her face. I was a stranger to her, and my grandfather was alive, and something was very, very wrong.

I hugged my knees more tightly to my chest. "October will come for me," I said, voice low. "She's a hero. That's what she does. She comes, and she saves you."

"October Daye? The knight?" asked the girl with the finned arms.
I looked up at her and nodded.

"You know her?"

"I . . ." I didn't really know how to describe our relationship anymore. She'd been my father's knight when I was a child, and then she
was my uncle's child, by law if not by blood, and now she was my guardian, at least for the next year's time. So what were we to each other?
Finally, desperate to finish the sentence, I said, "She's my cousin."

"Whoa!"

The girl flounced over and sat next to me on the stable floor. "Tell
me *everything*."

I blinked. But she looked hopeful and fiercely brave, like she was
doing everything in her power to keep her terror hidden. If I could
help by telling her stories, what was the harm in that? I cleared my
throat.

"She eats *weird* stuff," I said. "Jam on meat sandwiches, and cheese
in soup, and I saw her put peanut butter on roast carrots once. She used
to be allergic to strawberries, but she's not anymore, because she's
given away too much of her humanity trying to keep Faerie safe. I
was . . . I was really rotten to her for a while, because I was hurting
after some bad stuff that wasn't her fault, but she still saved me when
I needed her to, because she saves everybody when they need her,
whether they deserve it or not."

More kids crept out of the shadows as I talked, including the Tangie
boy, who wedged himself right up next to me, so that his shoulder was
pressed into my arm. He still didn't say a word, just looked up at me
with wide, trusting eyes, and waited for me to continue.

So I did. I told them every pointless little thing I could, although I
stopped short of making things up. They began drifting off to sleep,
one after the other, lulled by the dark and the rhythmic sound of my
voice. Their breathing evened out, until I was the last one awake in
the great bulk of the stable.

And then I wasn't awake either.

I woke to the sound of footsteps impossibly, improbably overhead.
Opening my eyes, I looked up, and beheld Medley's mismatched face,
staring down at me from one of the holes in the ceiling.

"How long did you sleep?" she asked.

I looked around me. All the kids were still sleeping. None of them was going to tell me how long I'd been out. I looked up at her. "I don't know," I said.

"Best hope it wasn't long, or you don't get caught again," she said, direly. "What's given here is given for good, and what's taken is never seen again. You won't like what you'll lose."

That didn't sound good.

"Are you here to get me out?"

"I was originally just going to come and laugh at you for being silly enough to think you could argue with Blind Michael to begin with," she said. "You think like a princess, princess. You'll have to get over that."

"Okay," I said, meekly.

"But I was going to leave you locked up here and let you see what it feels like to be sliced into pieces while you sleep, until you don't know who's in your mirror anymore, and you'll never know her again, and then Dean said that wasn't nice, and you deserved a lot of things, but you didn't have to deserve that, not when there were better ways to punish you for everything you'd done, and so he said I should come and get you out, if I could do it without getting *me* caught in the process." She looked down at the stable floor, frowning. "That's a lot more than I thought. How many people are *in* there?"

I looked around, trying to count in the gloom, then glanced back up at Medley. "I think fourteen?"

"Fourteen," she said, glumly. "*And* you *and* Dean and Scott. That's so many!"

"Seventeen," I supplied, trying to be helpful.

She sighed heavily as she gave me a put-upon look. "I don't know if we can find food for *seventeen*," she said. "It's been mostly just me for the longest time. If I leave you down here, you won't need me to feed you. Michael feeds his Riders."

"Please don't leave us here," I said, voice dropping until it was barely above a whisper.

She sighed again, then began lowering a rope through the hole in the ceiling toward me. "Guess I have to get you out, then," she said. "Just be quick about it, before I go changing my mind like a person with sense left in her body."

The rope was thick and rough, spun from some sort of fiber I didn't recognize, not hemp or sisal. I stood, shaking the tingles out of my leg, and grabbed for it as soon as it was low enough. Medley continued to lower it until the bottom foot or so brushed against the floor, then gave it an experimental tug hard enough to lift my feet off the floor.

She nodded, face alight with satisfaction, lowering the rope back down. "You won't pull me down with the weight of you," she said. "Now, get them up."

It was clear from her tone that I would be going last. That was reasonable enough—I was the oldest person in here by a considerable margin, and thus probably the least likely to panic. That, and I had more to atone for than any of these children possibly could. I turned to the nearest children, beginning to shake them awake.

Some woke more easily than others, sniffling and swatting at my hands like they thought I was a part of the nightmare unfolding all around them. They weren't entirely wrong about that. I tried to make soothing noises as I helped them to their feet, then began lining them up in order of height. Age might have been more reasonable for what I was hoping to achieve, but that would have taken more time. I already had fourteen kids to wrangle. I didn't need to add precision to the mix.

When they were all awake, I looked up at Medley. "Do you want them to climb to you?" I asked.

She nodded, wiggling the rope so that it danced enticingly, like someone trying to charm a cat. "And be quick about it," she said. "I don't know how much time we'll have before someone sees us and realizes we're trying an escape."

I nodded, guiding the tallest child to the rope and pointing upward. "That's Medley," I said. "She's a friend. She has her own fire that's far enough away from the stable for us to be safe there, but you have to climb up and get to her. Can you do that?"

The child—a rangy changeling with both Roane and Daoine Sidhe blood who looked to be about thirteen—looked at me and nodded before grasping the rope and beginning to climb, hand over hand. It was agonizingly slow, and they were only about halfway up when Medley began reeling the rope in, pulling them along to the hole in the ceiling. Once she had the kid safely with her, she lowered the rope back down, and the process began again.

We got the first six up safely. Our trouble began with the seventh, who stepped up to the rope, sniffled, and looked to me before saying, in a meek voice, "I can't climb. Please, I can't."

I looked at her. She wasn't a changeling. Instead, based on the color of her eyes and the slight dusting of scales on her cheeks, she was a blend of Merrow and Tylwyth Teg. I blinked, then looked around the stable. "There's a lot of bracken on the floor in here," I said. "Has anyone tried looking for yarrow twigs?"

"It won't work," she said, voice small. "I broke my glasses trying to get away from the men who put me here. I ran right into a wall. I can't fly without my glasses."

That was an odd limitation, but for all I knew, that was normal for the Tylwyth: being able to identify a descendant line isn't the same thing as being able to recite their strengths and weaknesses, and maybe an inability to fly if you couldn't see clearly was one of theirs.

"All right," I said, and looked up at Medley. "I'm going to tie the rope around her waist, all right?"

"I should be able to pull her up," she said. "Are you confident in your knots?"

"Embroidery is one of the only things I'm any good at when it comes to my hands," I said. "That, and sewing in general. I do most of my own mending. I knit. Can't crochet, though. I just can't get the hang of the hooks."

The girl without her glasses giggled at that, and I smiled, feeling a little better about the situation even as I gathered up the rope and began to tie it around her waist. I paused then. When I wanted to use my yarn to support something, right around the middle would work, but it usually squeezed whatever it was tied around something awful. I undid my first loose knots and began winding the rope more carefully, forming a sort of seat around her legs, rump, and middle.

Medley watched with critical interest as I looped and tied, finally calling down, "What's taking so long?"

"I'm tying a harness so you don't crush her around the middle!" I gave the rope one last hard tug before tying off the final knot. "That should be good."

I stepped back. "Pull her up."

Medley began to pull, and the girl slowly rose off the ground and toward the roof. The other children, finally seeing me as a proper ally rather than a questionably trustworthy adult, clustered around me. I looked at the part-Siren girl, who was the apparently oldest of the children remaining.

"Can you sort yourselves into two groups?" I asked. "Ones who think they can climb on the right, ones who're going to need me to tie them on the left."

She nodded briskly and set to organizing the children.

The rope dropped back down. Of the seven children I had remaining, four had arranged themselves on the "can climb" side, while the other three thought they were going to need some help. I nudged the Siren girl.

"You first."

She blinked. "Me? Why?"

"I want to alternate tying knots and just sending people straight up the rope, to try and keep things moving as quickly as I can. You can climb. So climb."

We moved faster after that. The four who thought they'd be able to climb on their own were correct in their assessment of their own capabilities, and each harness I tied was a bit faster than the one before, although my hands were still chapped and aching by the last one. Rough rope is not the same as yarn.

Finally, I was the last person standing in the stable. I looked anxiously up, waiting for Medley to untie the Tangie boy and drop the rope back down for me. The pause stretched out, longer than any of those before. My chest started getting tight, concern flooding through me. Had they been spotted? Was Medley just going to leave me here? Was my punishment not just imprisonment in my grandfather's terrible, flesh-twisting stables but to suffer their magics entirely alone?

The rope dropped down in front of me. I looked up.

Medley looked down.

"You coming?"

I grabbed the rope, wrapping it around my waist and leg to anchor myself, then held fast. "I need you to pull me up," I said, managing not to sound ashamed of my own weakness. "I don't have the upper-body strength to make the climb, and even if I did, I chapped my hands tying all the kids."

She scoffed. "Excuses, excuses, princess," she said, beginning to reel in the rope, lifting me off the floor. I held on as tightly as I could, fighting the urge to close my eyes. After everything else that had happened, pretending what I couldn't see couldn't hurt me would be more than just silly.

Once I was on the roof, she took her rope back, looking around at the loose jumble of assorted children. "All right, kiddos," she said, in that up-and-down voice of hers. "Take a good look around you, because this is your last jaunt out into the open until we get you the hell out of here."

Obediently, the children started scanning our surroundings. Medley looked at me, lifting one mismatched eyebrow, and so I emulated them.

Seen from even the height of a rooftop, Blind Michael's land was as dark and crumbling as it had seemed from the ground, but there was slightly more logic to it. The forest surrounded most everything, branches providing convenient bases for candles and roosts for ravens. Clear paths snaked between clearings, ground beaten flat and smooth by hooves and feet. In addition to the central bonfire where Blind Michael's throne was placed, there were two smaller fires in similar clearings. Medley's fire, tucked as it was behind one of the more decrepit ruins, was obscured even from a height.

It seemed odd that the ravens hadn't seen it in one of their flights. The thought was followed by a wave of panic, and I spun to Medley, who smiled, just a little, as she nodded.

"There you are. You've asked the question. Now ask yourself why I'm standing so calm and easy if there's not an answer I can give?"

I forced myself to breath in as slowly as I could, then nodded. "The ravens. He sees whatever the ravens see."

"Yes."

"But you've been here a long time, and you don't want to be caught again. Yet you're not afraid right now. Why is that?"

"*My* ravens tell me you were taken trying to speak to his daughter. That right?"

I nodded.

"Well, when she comes out the garden to talk to her parents, it's usually because she's in a strop over something. Bit of bone too big for her liking in her morning fertilizer, not enough sun on her schedule for the week, that sort of thing. She's a demanding thing, and she's a great ally for me, even if she'd scream and turn me in as vermin in a heartbeat if she actually knew I existed." Medley smirked. "The rose comes out of her garden, and inside the hour, both the Lord and Lady of this place go into it. She forces the issue by refusing to be placated until they treat her like their special little doll. And when that happens any time close to the normal feeding for the ravens . . ."

"He has them fed while he's visiting his daughter?"

Medley nodded. "Keeps him from seeing too many things that might distract him from keeping her as calm as calm allows. You want to do something without him seeing you, you wait for Luna to break a fingernail or snag her dress, and you'll get what you need soon enough. Now come on, all of you."

"Where are we going?" asked the Siren girl.

Medley looked at her. "A little wariness will serve you well, but when I'm the only real hope you have, you listen to me and you don't question what I'm asking you to do, if you know what's good for you."

"I told you, we're going to her fire," I said, before the Siren could object to being effectively shushed. "It's very kind of her to show us a place we can be safe, especially since sharing her safe place with us makes it less safe for her. Everyone, get in a line behind Medley, right now."

Medley gave me an amused look as the exhausted, traumatized children obeyed. "You have a voice like my old kindergarten teacher."

"What's kindergarten?"

She blinked then, looking faintly wistful. "Something the mortals do. I got to go. Part of first grade, too, and then I was here, and everything was different, forever and for always."

That seemed to be all she had to say on the matter. She turned and walked toward the edge of the roof, the children following. I brought up the rear, where I could guide or gather any stragglers.

There was a heap of rocks and trash up against one wall of the stable, held stationary by tangles of briar. Medley began hopping nimbly down it, and the children followed, all save the Tangie boy, who froze, eyes wide, and stared at the descent in clear concern.

"I'll carry you," I said.

He turned immediately, stretching out his arms. I gathered him up and followed after the rest, more slowly than most of them, fighting not to slip and drop both myself and the boy—I needed to learn his name—into the waiting thorns. Soon enough, we were on the ground, and Medley was gesturing us all toward the cover of the trees.

We made it out of view just as I heard the first raven cry.

Dean had been tending Medley's fire while she went to get the rest of us out of the stable. He had been joined by half a dozen people closer to our age, including another boy with hair like a sea anemone's tangles. He jumped to his feet and rushed to snatch the smaller boy out of my arms, glaring at me.

I didn't fight, just let go and stepped back, raising my hands.

"I'm sorry," I said. "I didn't mean any offense. He just wouldn't let me put him down."

The older Tangie changeling looked to the younger, who nodded before starting to sign rapidly. The older relaxed somewhat and carried the younger one—who I assumed was his little brother—over to the logs around the fire, sitting and freeing his own hands in the process. They began signing back and forth, ignoring the rest of us.

I couldn't really blame them for that, given the language barrier. I turned my attention to Dean. He was watching me, a sarcastic expression on his face. "You have a nice chat with Granddad?" he asked. "He give you everything you wanted for your birthday?"

"No," I said, scowling a little. "Which you know, or Medley wouldn't have needed to come and save me."

"Take a look at it like this," said Medley. "I wasn't planning to go anywhere near the stables until we'd all had time to sleep and eat and sleep again. Means they"—she gestured to the children, many of whom had flopped down on the logs and were staring at the fire with empty, exhausted eyes—"would have been in the stables for hours on hours on hours. Some of them may have been already."

That was an alarming thought. I looked at the children again, trying to find any signs that they'd been transformed by the strange magic of Blind Michael's stables. They were an odd assortment—odder than I'd assumed, even, when seen by the firelight. Almost all of them were a blend of at least two types of fae, or fae and human, and their only commonality was that they all seemed to have had at least one parent from the Undersea. That still left me the odd one out: neither of my parents is from the Undersea, unless I missed a *lot* more genealogy lessons than I'd ever realized.

I wasn't as familiar as I probably should have been with the bloodlines of the Undersea, and I realized as I looked at the slumped, exhausted children that I wouldn't be able to tell if half of them had been transformed, as long as it was in a small way.

The alarming question of whether I'd be able to tell if *I* had been changed followed quickly on. I swallowed hard. Medley had said it began with the magic. My magic has changed before, when October rebalanced my blood; it used to smell of hot wax and mustard flowers, candles burning in a dark meadow. After the change, it still smelled of hot wax, but the flowers were gone, replaced by crushed blackthorn fruit. I reached down into myself, and was relieved when the answering surge of magic was precisely as I expected it to be.

I'd been awake less than a day. I couldn't handle another transformation, not yet. Maybe not ever.

Dean's face softened as the implications of Medley's words sank in, and he looked at me with slightly less scorn. "Well, then, your capture served a purpose. Still, it would probably be better if you'd try not to do it again."

"I'll get right on that." I sat down on the nearest log, and the smaller Tangie rose, moving over to claim my lap. I blinked at him in surprise.

His brother followed him, sitting beside me. Looking me full in the face, he mouthed "Thank you," exaggerating the motion of his lips until there could be no question of what he was saying. He touched his right hand to his chin and brought it down, palm-up.

Thanks are forbidden in Faerie, but it's possible that injunction only really applies to spoken thanks. We gesture gratitude all the time. "You're welcome?" I ventured.

He beamed at me.

"Can you—do you know how to write?" I asked. "If you do, I can read a little."

"A little?" interjected Dean.

"I was a child when my Uncle Simon abducted me," I said. "He locked me and my mother in an endless expanse of blackness, and we couldn't exactly practice my letters down there."

He blinked, looking stricken. "Simon *Torquill*?" he asked.

"Unless I have another uncle I don't know about," I said. "He was the one who grabbed us and—and broke me."

"He didn't do it to break you!"

"Is there a better reason to lock someone in a lightless prison and forget about them? Because I'd love to hear it."

Dean glared at me. "You don't know the whole story."

I gestured to the dark forest all around us with both hands. "Well, it looks like we're going to have time for you to tell it to me, now, doesn't it?"

Of course, that time couldn't be right away. We had fourteen confused children to deal with, children whose shocked malaise was quickly becoming restless whining as they grew hungry. What's more, the changelings our age were starting to get belligerent as their situation sank in. They'd been abducted from their homes and thrown into the hands of a monster. They were allowed to be a little irritable.

Eventually, Medley gathered up the older changelings, turning her attention on the children. "I know I don't have to tell you not to wander off, because you're all reasonably clever, and you know the monsters are real, and they're really here. If you're not by the fire when we come back, I'm going to assume it's because you don't want to be protected, and I won't come to fetch you from the stables a second time. Do you understand?"

I had never seen that many children that silent before. They nodded, none of them moving an inch or taking their eyes off of Medley's face.

"You all probably think I'm really mean," she said. "I'm fine with that, because if you're thinking I'm mean, it means you're still you enough to think at all. If Blind Michael's Riders take you, your magic goes first, and then your body, and finally your mind, and once that's happened, you won't think I'm mean at all. You'll think I'm *prey*. If you listen to me, maybe that doesn't happen. Stay *here*."

She turned to the older children. "You, though. You're coming with me, so we can find something to feed this whole mob. This is more people than I've ever had to look after, and I'm not doing it alone."

She glanced over her shoulder at me and Dean. "It sounds like you two have some things you need to work through. Go. Work them through. I'm not babysitting you, too. If you go that way"—she stabbed a finger at the trees—"you'll find an old garden that sometimes has things worth eating in it. Bring back what you can."

She turned then, herding her helpers off into the trees. I exchanged a glance with Dean.

"I don't think she's mean," I said. "I think she's practical. And *terrifying*."

"So terrifying," he agreed. "But she's also trying to keep us safe, and I can respect that. I don't want to be turned into something else."

"I don't either," I agreed. "I'm still getting used to being this version of me."

"You look different than you used to," he said.

I started walking for the trees, not wanting to have this conversation in front of the kids. "Yeah," I said, uncomfortably. "My blood was—bad."

"What do you mean? Blood can't be bad. Blood's just blood." His expression hardened as he followed me. "You better not be about to say that you're not responsible for what you did because your blood was bad and now it's not. I'm not listening to that bullshit."

We stepped into the shadows under the trees, moving away from the safety of the fire. I shivered, desperate to turn and run back before we got too far. It had been easy to be brave when I thought Blind Michael would listen to me, before I'd learned that my mother had no idea who I was. Something very strange was going on here, and I wasn't October, I wasn't a hero. I just wanted this to stop.

And going back wouldn't be what stopped it. I forced myself to keep walking.

"I wasn't going to," I said uncomfortably, even if I had been about to say something *like* that. "It's just . . . you know how your dad's Daoine Sidhe, like my dad? And your mom's a Merrow?"

"Yeah . . ."

"Merrow and Daoine Sidhe are both mammals."

"I know that. What's your point?"

"My mother *isn't* a mammal. She looked like one for a while, because she did some big magic I don't understand and stole the skin from a Kitsune girl who'd been taken by my grandfather. While she was wearing that stolen skin, her natural magic was almost entirely suppressed—and it seemed her vegetable nature was masked, to such an extent that she was able to get with child, and I was born. But I should never have been possible. I was mammal and vegetable at the same time, and my blood was literally poisoning me."

He stared at me. "This isn't some 'oh no oh woe I was impure' thing, is it? You mean that literally."

"I do." I shrugged. "If October hadn't been able to pull the Blodynbryd out of me, I think I would eventually have died from the fight that was happening inside my body. I hurt, pretty much all the time, and this is the first time ever that I can remember being awake and not having a fever." He looked mildly alarmed. I reviewed what I'd just said, finally settling on the part I thought was most likely to have upset him: "October changed me because I said she could. My parents asked her to do it, but I would have asked her myself if I'd known it was possible. I still don't know whether I picked the right bloodline. I think I did, but it's going to be a little while before I know for sure. I *hope* I did, because I can't try again."

"Oh." Dean was quieter now.

I looked at him as we walked. "And that's what I mean when I say my blood was bad. I mean I would have died, and not been able to make amends for any of the things I did. It was hard to think sometimes, when the fever was really high. Really bad ideas could seem like really good ones. When Dugan told me that I could be a Queen if I just listened to him . . ." I shuddered. "I don't even know why I would *want* to be a Queen. I didn't have a good reason then, except that I was mad at my mother, and wanted the power to make her and October both suffer. So I went along with it, and I stole you and your brother from your beds, and I hurt you. Nothing I say makes up for that, ever. I would never do something like that today. I'm not the same person I was."

"Literally," he said. Then, in a hesitant tone, he asked, "Does that mean you believe people can really, truly, all the way change?"

"I have to believe that, or I'm saying that I'm going to be a m-monster forever, and forever is a long, long time. People have to be able to change."

"Good. I'm glad you feel that way."

I glanced at him, bewildered.

"What do you mean?"

"Remember, you said it was your uncle who locked you in the dark?"

"Yeah. I think maybe we would have been able to realize my body was eating itself alive a long time before we did, if I hadn't spent so many years where no one could see me or notice what was happening to me. I did a lot of damage because no one had the chance to notice what a danger I was becoming, and that's because of Simon. I hate him."

"He didn't do it to hurt you."

I stopped to scowl at Dean. "You don't know anything about my family."

"But I do, when the family in question is Simon." He took a deep breath. "He's my stepfather."

"He's your *what*?!"

"My stepfather. He divorced Amandine—October and August both chose his side of the family—and he married my parents. He lives in Saltmist now, with them, and August, and my baby brother. I visit a lot, even though I don't live there anymore. So really, when it comes to Simon, I know a lot more than you think I do. I know he took you, and your mom, because E—because the woman he was working for told him to. She wanted you dead. He said all this during the trial to determine whether or not they'd let you wake up. It would've been better if you'd been able to hear it, I guess . . . but he took you because he was ordered to, and he bent his orders as hard as he could to avoid being forced to kill you. That was what she really wanted: for him to kill you and have to live with the consequences. Killing you would have cost him everything."

"So instead he cost *me* everything," I snapped.

"Can you really say that, when you're not dead, and your blood's not fighting itself anymore? You get to live. It's horrible what he did to you, and I know how sorry he is, and I know he'll apologize to you himself if he ever gets the chance, if you ever let him, and I know 'sorry' doesn't make anything better, just like you saying 'sorry' doesn't give me back my finger. But you're alive. You're here." He paused then, glancing at the dismal forest around us. "Which is maybe not the best illustration of my point, but you get what I'm trying to say. He didn't kill you, and that means things can get better. For both of you."

"I still don't like him," I said, and began walking again, pacing Dean through the trees. "You can't expect me to forgive him just because you tell me he had good reasons to do what he did, just like I don't expect *you* to just forgive *me* for what I did. I was hurt and confused and manipulated and not entirely in my right mind, but I still held your hand down and chopped off your finger, and like you said, 'sorry' doesn't grow it back."

Dean frowned at the ground. "Okay, we're both making sense, I guess. How about this: if I pretend not to hate you when we're around the kids, you try not to say anything nasty about my stepdad where they might hear."

"You want to trade treating me like a person for me not telling them that Simon's a monster? Done. My uncle isn't here, and we have enough monsters running around this place that we're going to have plenty of other things to worry about." The trees were getting thinner. I paused, cocking my head as I listened.

My hearing used to be keener, when it still held the echoes of Mother's stolen Kitsune skin. I don't know how that worked, how she was able to pass down traits she'd never possessed herself, but that sharpness of sound had been gone when I woke up, and I didn't think it was ever coming back. Maybe the version of me from before the elf-shot would have been able to hear the sound of wings passing overhead.

This one didn't.

"I think we're clear," I said, and started moving again.

We emerged from the trees into another of those deserted gardens. It wasn't the one I'd raided before; this one was larger, boundary defined by gnarled apple trees and the rickety remains of a rotting wooden fence.

Fat pumpkins and zucchini grew near the fence, while a scraggly patch of corn grew in one corner. Dean made a pleased sound and started for the fence, while I hung back. I had already been brave since getting here, and we'd all seen what that got me.

He looked back as he reached the fence, frowning at me. "Come on, Raysel. We already don't have a basket. I need you to help me carry things."

I nodded and started toward him.

And the sound of hoofbeats began in the distance.

I was close enough to the tree line to turn and run back before they got too close. Dean, on the other hand, was about fifteen feet away, open space stretching between us like a chasm that couldn't be bridged. He froze, one hand on a gnarled apple, seemingly unable to move as the pounding of the hooves drew closer.

"Dean!" I hissed, hoping it would snap him out of his fugue.

He looked over his shoulder at me and shook his head, resignation clear, and I realized what he was doing:

If we had somehow alerted Blind Michael's forces to our presence, they weren't going to stop until they apprehended an intruder. But we hadn't heard or seen any ravens, so odds were good that they didn't know they were searching for two people, or what those two people looked like. If we both ran, they'd follow, and we'd both be taken. If Dean, who was already exposed, stayed where he was, I could get away to tell Medley what had happened.

It was almost as brave as it was stupid. Being caught here wasn't a game, and I never wanted to see the inside of those stables again. It was that fear that kept me rooted where I was, unable to run either toward him or away from him. I was still standing frozen when the Riders came.

There were six of them, massive, towering constructs of flesh and armor. They were what Medley would look like when she was grown, and they were more than that at the same time: no simple puberty could explain the size or solidity of them, the thickness of their necks and arms, the seamless blend of their disparate pieces. They were what she would be when she was *finished*, when she had been returned to the stables to complete her transformation and then sent upon the Ride that would seal it forever.

They were what we would be if we let ourselves be taken and kept for long enough, and the thought was chilling, even as they rode to surround Dean.

Their horses were as large as they were, built to a greater-than-normal scale. They had to be, to support the weight of the figures that sat astride them. As they tossed their heads and snorted, their breath stirred Dean's hair, making him look like he'd been caught in a small, strange windstorm.

"Little boy," rumbled one of the figures, leaning closer to him, the way a child might lean in to study a bug.

"Little mouse in our master's garden," said another.

"Not meant to be here."

"Mice nibble at what isn't theirs to have. Nibble, nibble, nibble," said a third.

"Good thing we're here to play mousecatcher."

Dean made a small, terrified sound and took a step back, into the half-rotten fence. Not rotten enough; rather than breaking and giving him an exit, it stopped him before he could go any farther, keeping him in place.

The Riders laughed. Then, quick as a blink, one of them grabbed Dean and swept him up onto their saddle, lifting him easily as anything.

"Caught!" the Rider declared, to more laughter from the others.

They turned their horses then and went trotting back the way they had come. Not the direction of Blind Michael's fire.

I still waited for the hoofbeats to fade before I emerged and looked after them, and I retreated back into the trees, blocked from the eyes of ravens, before I started running in the direction they had gone.

In a land of tangled trees and narrow spaces, the size of the Riders made them easy to follow. They had to stick to the trails and rare patches of open ground, while I was free to move through their surroundings, traveling as fast and as silently as I could. I caught up to them several times, only for them to pull ahead again, until finally they reached their destination.

It was a low stone house, in style and construction like all the others I'd seen in this terrible place, but it was intact. There were glass panes in the windows, and what looked like a full roof on top of it. Strangest of all, it was sitting in a patch of daylight.

Night and day are malleable in the Summerlands, and this wasn't even the Summerlands: this was a Firstborn's private skerry, a realm created and tailored to his needs. That was why the trees were the way they were, why the convenient paths existed for the Riders, and it must have been why this single spot sat in flawless midsummer light. I glanced up at the sky. It was like someone had stitched a patch of cloudless blue into the gloom all around. There was no gradation between the island of daylight and the rest of the skerry, no gradual dawn; one moment, it was night, and the next, it wasn't.

A low stone wall cupped the house's yard, which was a riot of roses in shades of red ranging from champagne pink to carmine. After the general black and brown of the rest of my surroundings, the roses were like a slap across the face, a reminder that more existed than just this.

The Rider who had grabbed Dean handed him to another who had already dismounted, and then dismounted in turn. Together, the two of them dragged Dean to the doorway of the house and knocked, stepping back to wait at a respectful distance until the door was opened. I couldn't see who was on the other side, but then, I didn't need to.

Only Mother could grow roses like that in a place like this.

The Riders released Dean, pushing him through the doorway, and then they turned to go, joining their fellows on their horses before the whole company rode off down the way. Once more, I waited for the sound of hooves to fade before I left the shelter of the trees.

There were still no ravens. It must be very inconvenient, to externalize your eyes in creatures that had their own wants and desires. Blind Michael could see his whole land at once, but only if his ravens actually flew over it. Maybe he was limited enough that we didn't have to be afraid *all* the time.

And maybe that was bravado talking. So far, I'd left the safety of Medley's fire twice, and been taken or seen my companion taken both times. So maybe I wasn't the one who should be gauging how dangerous this place was or wasn't.

I crept out of the trees, scanning the sky for ravens before I ran for the little patch of daylight and through the gate into the rose-clogged garden. It appeared to wrap around the structure, and so, rather than turning toward the door, I began to weave my way between the rose bushes, heading for the back of the house.

The roses no longer recognized me as one of their own and bent their branches away from my skin, but I had a fair bit of experience at playing among them, and was only scratched a few times before I reached my destination. There were more roses behind the house, naturally, most planted along the wall, forming a second barrier to intrusion. There was also a large stretch of open green, surrounding a small greenhouse. Glass panes glimmered in the sunlight, held up by a polished silver frame. Every bit of it was spotless and perfect.

The greenhouse door was propped open with a large stone, and I could see people moving inside. I crept closer, for once grateful for the distinctive Torquill red of my hair: it helped me blend in with the roses, even if it was only a little. A little was better than nothing, at the moment.

"—is *very* upset with all these impossible people," Mother was saying, as I got close enough to make out words. "If you'll just tell me which of the Riders brought you here, this can all be over."

"And you'll let us go?" asked Dean.

"Why would I want to do that?" asked Mother, sounding utterly bewildered. "You're almost grown up, I can see it in your eyes, and that girl from before, the one who came to my father's fire, she's the same. This is where children *belong*."

"I don't think that's true," said Dean. "Not for all children. I have a little brother I love very much, and parents who will miss me. I have a boyfriend—his name's Quentin, and he's been here before. He can't lose another love to Blind Michael's lands, he won't take it well. Please, you have to let us go."

Quentin was dating *Dean*? I blinked. The last I'd heard, the foster who'd been foisted on Father during my absence had been grieving the loss of a human girl he'd gone and fallen desperately in love with. Most fae don't care much about the gender of their partners—Dean being male wasn't the surprise. Quentin recovering so quickly from a broken heart was. Maybe the boy was more resilient than I had assumed.

But then, he'd been squired to October since before I'd been elf-shot, and he was still alive. That implied a certain sturdiness I wouldn't necessarily have predicted from looking at him.

"Mmm, no," said Mother, sounding almost regretful. "You have to understand, it's not my choice whether you stay here or run free. But it *is* my choice whether you hide in my greenhouse, in pleasant plenty, or whether I call my father's guard back to take you to the stable where you belong. I named the last one we captured as a Rider. Would you prefer to be a steed? It seems you're already careless with your hands. A few more lost fingers won't change things for you."

I looked desperately around myself. There were no gardening tools. There were, however, more stones like the one she'd used to prop the greenhouse door. I grabbed the largest I thought I could lift and carried it with me as I moved toward the open greenhouse.

"Please," said Dean, sounding almost anguished. "You don't have to do this. I haven't done anything to hurt you."

"The Riders who brought you to me said they found you nibbling around the edges of my sister's garden," she said, voice losing its sweetness as it turned dangerous. "Ceres isn't here to defend what's hers, and so it falls to me to do it for her. I have to guard her garden, so that when she comes home again, it's waiting for her."

The gardens. I paused, suddenly understanding why abandoned gardens of half-dead produce would be scattered throughout Blind Michael's lands to begin with. I knew Mother wasn't an only child. I'd known that even before I knew she was a rosebush and not the fox she'd always pretended to be. She'd never been willing to talk about her siblings, only that there were more than one of them, and she had loved them very much, and they had each left home before she did, leaving her behind, which was why she'd never tried to find them.

Well, now, I was pretty sure the real reason she'd never tried to find them was that they would have blown her cover in an instant if she had, but the rest of what she'd told me in our long years in the dark still rang true. She had loved her brothers and sisters, and she had hated them for leaving her alone with their parents.

The gardens weren't accidental or planted by other escapees from Michael's stables. They were the homes of his other children, the ones who'd gotten away. He controlled the skerry, and so they had never completely rotted or been destroyed, but he didn't believe any of his lost children were ever coming home, so he didn't spend extra effort or attention on keeping those gardens healthy.

"I'm sorry," said Dean, with an air of desperation. "I didn't know!"

"You'll make a handsome horse," she said. "That green in your hair—why, I wager no one will be able to tell you from a kelpie."

She laughed then, a bright, tittering sound. I crept closer, rock in hand.

Hopefully, I'd be able to grab Dean and run without assaulting my own mother. Blind Michael wasn't actively hunting us right now—if he had been, there was no way I'd have been able to reach her house unchallenged, even if the ravens were still eating, or preening, or whatever it was they did after a meal. That would change if I hurt his daughter. There was no way he'd be able to forgive that.

Peeking through the greenhouse door, I saw all the fruits and vegetables she hadn't planted outside, ripe and bright and perfect in a way the discarded gardens weren't anymore—couldn't be, because the hands that planted them were gone. She was between me and Dean, but his eyes widened slightly as he saw me in the doorway, and she turned, eyebrows raising as she saw me there with the rock.

"Come to attack me, little liar?" she asked. "How did you get out of my father's stables? I doubt he gave you permission to leave."

"He didn't," I said, dropping my rock. Time for plan B, whatever that was. I didn't see a lot of options. "I let myself out. And it would be great if you could just let Dean go."

"Why would I want to do that?"

"Because we're asking nicely? Because we haven't done anything to you, and so there's no reason you need to do anything to us? Because your father's right when he says there hasn't been a Ride recently enough to bring us here; we don't know *how* we got here, just that there's been some sort of a mistake, and we're trying to stay alive long enough to get home. Because . . ." I paused, taking a deep breath. "Because if you let him go, and you let *us* go, then as soon as we make it back to our world, I'll find your sister and tell her that you miss her. You miss her, don't you? You wish she would come and visit you? I can tell her that."

She froze, expression going slowly blank. Then, with a small frown, she asked, "Which one?"

"What do you mean?"

"Which sister? I have several. Brothers, too. They all left me. They left me here with our parents, alone, and I don't *want* to leave, not like they did. The children who come here are better for it. None of my father's Riders regret."

Maybe not, but Medley had described the last change the stables made as the mind. Maybe they *couldn't* regret. "That's good," I said. "It would be awful to be turned into something you weren't, and feel bad about it after. But they cry when he puts them in the stables, don't they? They cry and they ask to go home."

"They're wrong."

"Why are they wrong? If this is your home, and you're happy here,

why can't they be happy in their homes? Why can't they want to go
back to the families who aren't here with them? Dean has a brother,
like he said. If you tell your father where we are, and we're taken,
he'll never see his brother again."

Mother's frown deepened. She had never told me what caused her
to finally run away from her parents and steal a child's skin in order
to flee the skerry. I couldn't remind her of something she had apparently never done—and I couldn't keep thinking of her as "Mother,"
either. She was a cutting, somehow taken from the woman I knew, a
rose who'd never grown in any other soil.

"Please," I said, trying to keep my voice gentle. "We just want to
go home. We haven't hurt you, we're not hurting anything, and we
were only near your sister's garden because we need to eat. We can
stay away if you want us to."

"The gardens are in disrepair with my siblings gone," she said,
slowly. "We could make a trade, if that was something you wanted
to do?"

"What kind of trade?" I asked.

"Weed," she said. "Weed, and hoe, and remove such stones as you
find. If you can rebuild a wall or patch a fence, do those things as
well, and whatever yet grows in the gardens is yours to have."

For a dizzying second, I thought Luna was asking me for weed.
Then I caught up with the rest of what she was saying, and realized
she was telling us what she wanted us to do. Carefully, I said, "To be
sure I'm understanding you correctly, you're saying that if we'll take
care of the gardens, we can have what we want from them?"

Luna nodded. "I won't shelter you—I can't shelter you—but I can't
maintain their gardens on my own, either. It angers Father to be reminded that they left us. I think he'd wipe their remnants away, if
Mother didn't insist he leave them as they are."

"We don't have any tools," I said. "We won't be able to do much.
But I'm willing to do what I can."

"You'll find tools in each of the gardens, if you search the structures yet standing," she said. "The collapse comes slowly and takes
what's oldest last of all. You'll be able to do more than you think you
can. Do we have an accord?"

I looked to Dean, then back to her. "I just want to be sure I understand exactly what I'm agreeing to," I said.

She frowned, clearly impatient.

"We find the gardens that belonged to your siblings, and we take care of them with the tools that should be somewhere nearby, and we can harvest whatever grows there. You won't give us shelter or help us, but you also won't tell your father where we are or what we're doing."

She nodded. "If you're caught, I'll send you to the stable without hesitation. But if you stay away from the Riders and the ravens, you'll be safe enough. Even the ravens can be bribed. They like a bit of fruit now and then, and Father can't watch through all of them at once. If they happen to find you in the open, you can toss them a piece of something sweet and hope for the best. You might even get it."

"Dean?" I leaned to see around her. "Is this all acceptable to you?"

He nodded, face pale and drawn. I looked back to Luna.

"We accept your bargain," I said. "We won't expect any more aid from you, and I hope that we won't need it."

"For your sakes, I'll hope the same," she said. She stepped fully clear of Dean, and I finally saw that his hands were bound with a loop of thorny briar. She waved her own hand airily; the briars dropped away, and he was free. "Both of you may go now. And don't come here again. Father is very protective of me, and he won't like it."

I didn't need to be told twice. Grabbing Dean's hand, I yanked him along with me as I ran for the front of the garden. He didn't have my gift for weaving between the rose briars; we had to slow down substantially while we pushed through them, and he had still been scratched several times before we emerged into open. I didn't let go of his hand. The webbing made his grip seem odd, but he held on as tightly as I did. I broke back into a run as soon as we were clear of the roses, pulling Dean through the gate and across the road to the shelter of the trees.

Once we were there, he jerked his hand out of mine. "I didn't need your help."

"Um, what?" I turned to blink at him. "What did you say?"

"I said, I didn't need your help. I could have talked my way out of that."

"But you didn't."

"But I could have."

"You know how to garden?"

He frowned at me, expression turning mulish. "No. But I was going to appeal to her better nature!"

"My mother is a rosebush who has to wear a bra, which seems like an unfair thing to do to a rosebush. That"—I gestured back toward the house—"is not my mother. It can't be. She doesn't know me, and while my mother may not like me very much, she loves me, and I have no doubt she would recognize me through any spell or enchantment. You can clone rosebushes by taking cuttings."

"Clone?" asked Dean, blankly.

"Clone," I repeated. "I think somehow, whatever brought Blind Michael back from the dead also let him get hold of a piece of my mother, and use it to grow himself a whole new daughter who doesn't remember ever leaving this place. That doesn't change who she essentially is, and please believe me when I tell you that you were never going to appeal to her better nature, because she doesn't have one. Not the way you're thinking. She has a core of self-interest as wide across as Kansas, but you were never going to convince her to let you go just because it was the right thing to do. Her mind doesn't work that way."

"Your family is fucked up," said Dean, after a horrified pause.

I shrugged. "Your parents married Simon Torquill. My mom's a plant, and my dad breaks things when he's forced to spend any real amount of time by himself. But then, your stepdad is my dad's brother, so that means my family *is* your family, and your family is also fucked up. We have some gardening to do, if we want to bring anything back to show Medley."

Dean scowled. "I don't like that you committed me to that."

"And I don't like your face. Come on. Let's weed someone else's tomato patch."

I started walking back toward what I now knew was Ceres's garden, listening for the sound of ravens. It never came.

The tools were in a long wooden box, remarkably unrotted, off to the side of the garden plot. I found us each a hoe and a pair of gloves, and we began taking care of the most superficial tasks. More detailed and demanding work would have to wait; for today, we were pulling the largest weeds, removing the most obvious debris, and hoeing up the biggest rocks. The garden seemed to appreciate our efforts. I never saw anything grow, but by the time we were finished, there were more tomatoes and beans ready for the harvest than there had been when we began, and when I bit into one of them, it was crisper and less mealy than the other vegetables I'd eaten here had been.

We stowed our tools carefully back in the box, filled our arms with produce, and started walking back toward Medley's fire.

We were going to survive.

* * *

Dean and I had managed to collect almost as much food, just the two of us, as Medley and her entire group of children. We brought it back to the fire, and I felt oddly satisfied, like I had done something worthwhile for once in my life. Even the youngest of them willingly ate the substandard vegetables, tired enough not to argue, as we all relaxed around the fire.

"You two work it out?" asked Medley, gesturing to me and then Dean with a half-chewed carrot.

"I think so," I said.

"I still don't like her," he said.

"But we can work together without fighting all the time, and I think we're going to have to if we want to survive and feed this whole gang."

Medley frowned. "Explain."

"A group of Riders caught Dean while we were scavenging," I said. "It wasn't his fault. He didn't do anything to attract their attention. We must have just missed a raven or something."

"When they were taking me to Luna, one of them mentioned her setting them to watch the gardens," he said. "If they'd been rounding up people all day, it makes sense that she'd have a watch posted. Blind Michael is very upset about what he assumes is one of his Riders making unsanctioned visits to the Summerlands and bringing back souvenirs. She wants him not to be upset, so she's trying to find the answer on her own."

"Unfortunately, there isn't one," I said dourly. "Which she's not keen to believe, because we can't be here if someone didn't bring us here."

"A Rider brought me here," said Medley.

"You're the only one," said Scott, voice sour. "I've been talking to all the other kids—we're all Undersea, we have a lot in common—and not one of us saw a Rider. We were all just here all of a sudden. Jia has her charger but not her phone, because she was holding it when she got dropped here. Half of us don't have any *shoes*. We didn't see any Riders."

"Okay, so something really weird is going on," I said. "That's nothing new. And we may have negotiated a way to keep us all fed."

"Negotiated?" asked Medley, sounding immediately and sensibly wary.

Quickly, I explained the conversation with the Luna who wasn't my mother, and what Dean and I had agreed to do for her. When I was done, I shrugged, and added, "There are at least two gardens, probably more. I assume you know where they are. If they all have gardening tools, she's not going to be upset that we're taking care of her siblings' plots. If anything, fixing up more than one of them may make her willing to help us out with something else in the future, if we think of something. If someone comes up with an idea for how we could all get out of here."

Medley nodded, slowly. "It's not something I would have done, I have to see and say that, but the gardens tend to be open spots in Blind Michael's nets. When the ravens go there, they're busy being birds—they're looking to feed, not spy."

"So we throw them little treats, and we keep them on our side," I said. "It won't stop them from reporting us if they're on duty, but it might keep them from doing whatever they do to get his attention. And we'll have something to keep us busy while we wait for a rescue, and food for our bellies, and a better shot at survival."

"This won't last that long," said Dean resolutely. "People will realize we're missing and come looking for us."

It must have been nice to have that much faith in people. But then, he didn't spend almost his entire childhood locked up in a lightless void. I shrugged. "Sure," I said wearily, not wanting to start another fight. "It's just that it may take a while, and we need to eat while we wait. This is a way we can try to do it safely."

"So we do it," said Dean.

We both looked to Medley. After a long pause, she nodded.

"Let's be gardeners," she said.

Days passed, turning seamlessly into weeks as we fell into a pattern of working and hiding—first the garden, to tend and harvest, then the forest and the fire, to evade Blind Michael and his Riders.

There were seven gardens, not counting Luna's explosion of roses: seven abandoned plots of land with crumbling structures around them and boxes of strangely untouched gardening tools hidden somewhere nearby. Like the first, each garden we approached responded with unbelievable quickness, fruit growing ripe and plentiful almost as we worked, like the gardens themselves were thanking us for taking care of them.

In the third garden, we found a well, and Medley replaced the rope on the bucket with her own, allowing us to pull up bucket after bucket of water. It came up green with pond slime in the beginning but began to clear and, by the fifth bucket, was as pristine as anything I'd ever seen. We filled the garden water barrels. The older Tangie changeling, whose name was Adam, lifted his little brother, Seb, into one of the barrels, sending water cascading in all directions, and Seb laughed—the first sound we'd heard from him—before submerging entirely. I peeked into the barrel. The anemone fronds of his hair were pulsing wildly with bands of color, and bubbles were rising from his nose, presumably as he breathed. I straightened and looked to his brother, who smiled encouragingly.

Okay. Well, most of us were some blend of Undersea bloodlines, and water was a precious thing. Medley was lowering others down into the well, two at a time so no one was alone, and I had never seen our motley little group so energized. Dean was pulling weeds nearby. I looked over at him.

"Do you want a turn in the well?"

"Merrow live in saltwater," he said, shaking his head. "And I do better without it than most of us do. The Daoine Sidhe is strong in me."

"You should still go down if it'll help you."

"I'm a Count on the land, and my mother is a Duchess in the sea. It doesn't matter if none of these people are my subjects, I still have a duty to place their welfare above my own."

"If you get sick because you avoid the water, will that help them?"

He glared at me and stood. "I think the apple tree could use some pruning," he said, and stalked off. I watched him go, swallowing a sigh.

Dean was under no obligation to forgive me, much as I was under no obligation to forgive my uncle, but he continued to insist that what Simon had done to me was somehow forgivable, while what I'd done to him wasn't. And he was allowed to feel that way, I knew that, but at the same time, it wasn't *fair*. Why did I have to be lost with only one person I knew, and have that person be someone with good reason to hate me?

A great spray of water radiated out from the barrel as the Tangie changeling inside grasped the lip and yanked himself up, declaring joyfully, "Words! I have water, and that means I have words again! Hello, hello!"

The Siren girl, whose name was Marlon, had told me Tangie could speak when they were in the water; apparently that applied to water barrels as well as ponds and the like. "It's nice to be able to talk to you finally," I said brightly. "Since you and your brother are the only siblings here, were you together when this happened?"

"Yeah," he said, glancing sadly downward. "I sleep in Adam's bed most mornings, because mine's too small, but we haven't got me a new one yet. So I go in with him, as long as he says he doesn't mind. We were both in bed and then I was in the stable by myself, already all locked up, and there wasn't any water anywhere."

"Which meant you couldn't talk to anyone," I said. "That must have been scary."

"Scarier than *anything,*" he agreed gravely. "We know how to talk with our hands, but it's not so easy that people can learn just from watching us a while, and we can both read and write, but that doesn't help much if you don't have paper or a tablet or something for writing on."

"How much water do you need? Would a bucket be enough?"

"I don't know," he said, sounding briefly downcast. "Can't we just stay here always?"

"There's no cover," I said, glancing anxiously up at the sky. "We can't bribe the ravens forever, and we're exposed here. I'm sorry, Seb. We can't stay here all the time."

He drooped, visibly disheartened.

"But between me and Medley, we can make sure you're always with the crew when we're doing this garden," I said. "Until we find a better source of water, that is. You deserve to be able to communicate."

He brightened again, making the gesture I had learned meant "thank you." I smiled.

"You're welcome."

Faerie forbids the act of saying thanks but not the reaction to it. Little things like that often make me think some of our rules weren't thought through very well before they were decided on.

"Now come on," I said. "We need to get a proper harvest to take back to the fire, or we won't be eating very well tonight, will we?"

"Before I get out of the water . . . Miss Raysel?"

"Yes?"

"Do you think we're going to get to go home?"

I hesitated, glancing around. Dean was watching me, very nearly glaring.

Looking back to Seb, I shook my head, and said, "I don't know. But the last time I was in a place I didn't want to be, I found that it was best to just let myself be there, and not focus on how much I wanted to be somewhere else. So for the sake of keeping myself as healthy and steady as I can, I have to think that no, we're not going to go home. Not for a long, long time."

Seb nodded, looking sad but understanding.

When I turned around again, Dean was gone.

Weeks tumbled into months. Dean and I fell into a routine of sorts; he did his best to avoid the fire when I was there, and only went with me on gardening trips if he absolutely had to. When we weren't tending the gardens and collecting food, he spent his time with the older changelings, while I spent mine with the younger kids, and with Medley.

She and I had a lot in common, in a way. We had both been taken when we were very young, and neither of us had been given the chance to grow up the way we would have if we'd been left where we were. We both enjoyed playing swordfight with sticks, and hide-and-seek when it seemed safe enough to do so—which it didn't very often, but the younger kids needed play or they got restless and irritable, and that would have put us in even more danger than a quick game through the trees.

If not for the fact that we slept on the ground and ate nothing but vegetables we'd picked ourselves, we might have been able to pretend this was a glorious adult-free vacation. And if not for the hunting horns that sometimes split the air and sent us scattering for cover, we might have been able to forget the monster whose den we were creeping around. Blind Michael didn't seem to remember that we existed, and certainly hadn't been sending anyone after us. I was grateful for that.

Whatever force had dropped us all here, it hadn't come again. There had been no additional waves of out-of-place children. I was grateful for that. While the group we had was perfectly fine, it was already straining the edges of what we could support.

But the best thing about spending time with Medley was the thing neither of us talked about, because there was no point in talking about it: she wasn't looking for a way out, and if one presented itself, she wouldn't be able to take it. This was where she belonged now, as much a part of the skerry as the twisted trees around us. Here, she was alone and frequently afraid, but no one looked at her like she was a monster, no one reacted to her with horror or confusion. Her own parents wouldn't recognize her if she went home like this, and she knew it. Choosing to stay in a place she understood was reasonable, and very much what I would have done in her position.

Maybe it was what I was already doing. Dean spent his free time trying to come up with elaborate plans for escape, while I spent mine figuring out new ways of serving zucchini to a group of increasingly less-picky changelings. I had given up. He hadn't.

And that was why it wasn't a surprise, not really, the day I woke to find Dean and the older children missing, the fire burnt down low, and horns splitting the night. I knew at once what had happened. I didn't want to know it, but I did. Sitting up, I stared at the open spaces where they should have been.

Medley sat up as well, heaving a great, weary sigh.

"I suppose it was time to move the fire," she said.

"What?"

"They've been caught," she said, and waved a hand in a wrap-it-up gesture, finger spiraling in the air. "That's what that horn means, when it sounds. Prey's been taken. Blind Michael will throw them to the stables, and then he'll question them, after they've had a day or two to soften up. They'll tell him everything he wants to know. They won't be able to stop themselves."

I went cold. "What?"

"Dean must have come up with some fool plan, decided that if they stole a horse they'd be able to Ride out of here or something of the like, and taken them off to try some heroic escape while the rest of us were sleeping." She shook her head. "There's always one who has to be a hero, any time kids get loose. It's too bad. I liked him."

I looked around at the younger kids. Seb was watching me with open despair. This couldn't happen. I couldn't let this happen.

"No," I said.

"No?" asked Medley.

"No, that isn't how this ends." I stood, watching her. "If the fire's already compromised, you don't need to worry about me being taken. Just move it. We'll find you."

"You can't intend to—"

But I did. I had already turned, and was stalking into the trees, heading not for Blind Michael's fire but for Luna's cozy little house with its patch of perpetual daylight and garden full of roses.

When I got there, I stormed right into the yard and banged my fist on the front door, stepping back to wait. Several minutes passed before the door swung open, revealing a small, spotless room in white and rosy pink. No one was there.

"Hello?" I called, stepping inside.

"I told you I wasn't going to help you," said Luna, as the door slammed shut behind me. I turned, and there she was, watching me. "Whatever you want, the answer is no."

To her, I was a stranger. To me, she was a copy of my mother, and I knew the subtleties of her expression. She was saying no, but she was saying it in the way that could sometimes be negotiated with, the way that was still willing to listen.

"We found seven gardens," I said. "We've restored them all. They're flowering now. We even cleaned out the well in one of them. We've been rebuilding fences, and I think the houses are starting to heal. I don't know how that can be possible, but it is."

"So? That was our deal."

"I don't think it'll last if we stop."

She stopped, expression going neutral. "Is that a threat?"

"No. Your father has taken half our number, most of our strongest workers among them. They were careless. It won't happen again."

"What does that have to do with me?"

"You can release them. Open the stable doors and let them out."

"I *told* you, I won't help you anymore!"

I looked at her, fighting the urge to flinch. "Then I suppose when your siblings' gardens wither and die again, you'll be comfortable knowing you could have stopped it."

She drew back, staring at me. "You'd starve yourselves rather than continue at your duties?"

"If it's starve or know we did nothing when our people were taken, then yes, we'll starve," I said. "There are fruits in the forest, if you look in the right places. We'll be fine." I wasn't so sure of that, but she was enough of a hothouse flower that I was willing to wager she'd never explored her father's lands to a degree that would reveal the lie.

"*If* I open the stables, this has to be the last time I help you," she said.

"It will be. They won't be that careless a second time."

She looked at me. I looked at her. Neither of us blinked.

Finally, she looked away.

"Father is hosting a bonfire tonight," she said. "I'll attend, and open the stable doors. You'll need to be nearby, to collect your people, because my aid to them ends with a lock. Do you understand?"

"I do," I said, quickly. "I'll be there."

"Good. Don't get caught."

Night and day were questionable concepts in Blind Michael's sunless lands. I wound up hiding in the trees nearby until a rickety phaeton pulled up outside the house, the horses pawing at the ground and snorting. The driver dismounted and went up to Luna's door, and I turned, beginning to move through the trees toward her father's bonfire.

She still beat me there, horses lending speed to her journey that I didn't have, but the door was locked when I arrived. I glanced through the trees. Luna was by the fire, smiling coyly at her father as he laughed. Playing the demure lady, then, father's pet and best beloved of the firelight. It was a role I knew, if not one I had any skill for playing.

I retreated to lurk near the stables, waiting until Luna broke free and hurried around the corner, a heavy keyring in her hands. I stepped out of the shadows. She didn't flinch or jump, just glared at me as she moved to unlock the door. "Last time," she hissed.

I nodded my understanding and, as she eased the door open, stepped up to fill the gap, half-expecting her to shove me inside. "All of you," I hissed into the darkness. "Come quickly. We don't have time to argue."

One by one, they emerged from the stable. If any of them had reached the point of cumulative time spent inside where the changes would begin, I couldn't see them yet.

Dean was the last one out. He frowned at me. I met his eyes, expression defiantly calm.

"Medley moved the fire, so I guess we're going on a scavenger hunt," I said, keeping my voice low.

"Guess so," he said, stepping past me.

I looked one last time into the depths of the stable, scanning for stragglers. There weren't any. We might all be trapped here, possibly forever, but at least we were still going to be together, and that was better than the alternative.

As I turned away, I shut the stable door. None of us were going back there. Ever, if I had anything to say about it.

We couldn't escape from Blind Michael's land, not on our own, anyway, but we could make the time we had to spend here something he didn't get to dictate. Terrifying as it was to contemplate, what happened next was up to us, and it was time to get moving. I was awake now. That meant taking responsibility for myself.

"Well?" called Dean. "You coming?"

"Yeah," I said. "Be right there."

It was time for us to go.